SENSATIONAL

ALSO BY JODIE LYNN ZDROK

Spectacle

SENSATIONAL

Jodie Lynn Zdrok

TOR
TEEN

A TOM DOHERTY ASSOCIATES BOOK
New York

SENSATIONAL

Copyright © 2020 by Jodie Lynn Zdrok

A Tor Teen Book
Published by Tom Doherty Associates
120 Broadway
New York, NY 10271

www.tor-forge.com

Tor® is a registered trademark of Macmillan Publishing Group, LLC.

Library of Congress Cataloging-in-Publication Data

Names: Zdrok, Jodie Lynn, author.
Title: Sensational / Jodie Lynn Zdrok.
Description: First edition. | New York : Tor Teen, 2020. |
Series: Nathalie Baudin; 2 | "A Tom Doherty Associates Book."
Identifiers: LCCN 2019045343 (print) | LCCN 2019045344 (ebook) |
ISBN 9780765399717 (hardcover) | ISBN 9780765399700 (ebook)
Subjects: CYAC: Murder—Fiction. | Supernatural—Fiction. | Ability—Fiction. |
Paris World's Fair (1889)—Fiction. | Paris (France)—History—1870–1940—Fiction. |
France—History—Third Republic, 1870–1940—Fiction. | Mystery and detective stories.
Classification: LCC PZ7.1.Z395 Sen 2020 (print) |
LCC PZ7.1.Z395 (ebook) | DDC [Fic]—dc23
LC record available at https://lccn.loc.gov/2019045343
LC ebook record available at https://lccn.loc.gov/2019045344

Our books may be purchased in bulk for promotional, educational, or business use. Please contact your local bookseller or the Macmillan Corporate and Premium Sales Department at 1-800-221-7945, extension 5442, or by email at MacmillanSpecialMarkets@macmillan.com.

First Edition: February 2020

Printed in the United States of America

0 9 8 7 6 5 4 3 2 1

To my brothers, in order of appearance:
Kenny, for the realm of ideas and culture.
David, for loyalty and imagination.
And to both of you for your pride
and for always bringing the funny.

1

June 4, 1889

Nathalie rushed along the Seine, passing an array of concerned faces. If the French she caught among the swathe of languages was any indication, everyone thought she was being chased.

No, she was the one doing the chasing, so to speak. Of time. She was simply in a hurry, trying to get around all the ambling tourists and avoid being late. So far, nothing had gone as planned this morning.

First of all, Christophe had sent word for her to come to the public morgue even earlier than usual, if possible. The courier had arrived as she was leaving the apartment. While Nathalie composed a pithy response, Maman reminded her to pick up bread, and Stanley made figure eights around her ankles with a meow. *Meeting S. and L. at the Palais des Beaux-Arts when it opens; will come immediately after. If J. is there, ask him to please wait— coffee.* Even that she had to start and stop twice, because Papa came over to give her a few sous for lunch. Second, the steam tram had been full—a frequent occurrence since the Exposition Universelle opened last month—and she'd had to wait for another.

Her eye caught the ivy-covered clock in front of the agriculture exhibit. She halted, heaving a sigh of relief and mopping her brow. Almost a quarter hour to spare. All that nimble darting through the crowds had bought her some time after all.

Good. Now she could enjoy a stroll the rest of the way. Jules often encouraged her, with her swift walking pace and propensity to plan too much in a day, to slow down. For the next few minutes, she would.

She went left onto the bridge, the old Palais du Trocadéro from the last Exposition at her back. It was the colossal iron skeleton in front of her, its Venetian red arches beckoning her to the grounds, that took her breath away. Again.

The Tour Eiffel had only been completed in March, but Nathalie could barely remember the Paris horizon without it. Somehow, the architect Gustave Eiffel and his builders made three hundred meters of iron lattice into something beautiful (so much for the smug critics who were convinced it would be ugly). She'd gone twice already to the first platform, marveling at the view and the feeling that came with being almost sixty meters up. Soon, the elevators would be operating, and she'd be able to ascend to the second platform and to the top. What would *that* be like?

As she crossed the bridge, stepping to the side to accommodate a carriage, the crowd grew even denser. The Tour Eiffel served as the grand entrance to the Exposition grounds. In the course of several months, ordinary land and city streets had been transformed into a wonderland of lush gardens and ornamental structures. From the Galerie des Machines at the opposite end to the cultural pavilions on either side of the tower and throughout the grounds, the landscape had become the epitome of both here and elsewhere. This extravagant international showcase wasn't the first world's fair of its kind, but Nathalie was certain it would be the best.

She walked under the Tour Eiffel and through the queue of people waiting to go up, narrowly dodging a spilled lemonade. Today marked her ninth visit to the Exposition. In her eighteen years, she'd never seen anything like it, this astounding display of culture and ingenuity. It was a celebration of the République, and despite never being prouder to be a Parisian, Nathalie found that the pavilions representing other lands intrigued her most.

Jules, after reading four world history books in the months leading up to the fair, called it *"Around the World in 80 Days* on Champ de Mars." She perused the Exposition's 288-page *Guide Bleu* frequently: She wanted to see everything, do everything (except maybe the agriculture exhibits, which sounded tedious), and observe everyone she could at the Exposition from now until October. A world map accompanied all her visits; whenever she visited a nation's pavilion, she circled the corresponding place on the map. She also made notes of her encounters—a conversation she'd had, food she'd sampled, a souvenir she'd bought. And then there were entries about the clothing styles, fascinating on any given day, as visitors from across the world weaved a tapestry of fabrics, cuts, and colors.

Nathalie stepped out of the Tour Eiffel's imposing shadow. Simone and Louis were easy to find, she in a white hat and fuchsia dress, he with well-coifed red hair and donning pale green. They were huddled over a grounds map at the designated meeting spot, the chairs in front of the Fontaine de Coutan. A powerful, ornate display of classical figures bearing torches, the fountain announced the cobalt blue Dôme Central with splendor. At night, the fountain was illuminated with streams of water in red, blue, green, and gold.

"I am so eager for this, I scarcely slept last night! And still I was delayed," Nathalie said, explaining why as she exchanged cheek kisses with both of them.

"The biggest culprit is Stanley, who tried to trip you, I'm sure of it." Simone winked as she folded up the map and put it in her dress pocket. The three of them walked toward the Palais des Beaux-Arts, opulent with arched windows and a lavish exterior, beside the Dôme Central. Flags projected from the top of the building; down below, palm trees and people lined the parterre. "Look at that crowd."

Nathalie squinted in the sunlight. "Much more than I expected at this hour."

"Like a busy day at the morgue," said Louis. "Which it sounds like it might be, if our favorite police liaison dispatched a courier to you so early. Mischief must be afoot. Mind if we go with you? We'd like to see what body or bodies have prompted a sense of urgency."

"What's this 'mischief afoot' talk?" Simone asked, tucking away an errant blond curl. "Is that another Shakespeare reference?"

"*Oui.*"

"Enough." Simone gave Louis an affectionate poke. He was in an acting troupe now, and they'd performed Voltaire's translation of *Julius Caesar* this spring. "That's the second one this morning already. It's too much for my unrefined cabaret sensibilities."

"*As You Like It,*" Louis whispered.

Simone tapped him on the shoulder. "Saying it quietly doesn't make it any less of a bad pun, Louis."

Nathalie laughed and assured them they could come along. Simone, once her neighbor, was more than a best friend. *Ma soeur,* they had taken to calling each other these days. Nathalie didn't have a sister, but if she could choose one, it would be Simone. Loyal, daring, and as colorful in spirit as she was in wardrobe.

Louis, Simone's beau of two years, had become akin to a favorite cousin. Full of puckish whimsy and daring appreciation for life's experiences, he was like no one Nathalie had ever met. He and Simone, both a year older than she, made for an entertaining, well-suited pair. ("Like brie and raspberry," as Simone often put it.)

The doors to the fine arts building opened right before they reached the portico, antiquity-inspired sculptures greeting them here as well. The exhibit devoted space to paintings and sculptures from France, England, and the United States, with the French art focused on creations from the Revolution of 1789 to the present. People disappeared through the statue-guarded archways as if the massive edifice inhaled them. Nathalie, Simone, and Louis filed in, pressed from behind by the ever-growing horde.

Once inside, they looked around in awe, as they did with nearly every structure at the Exposition. The expansive, airy dome proclaimed paintings and sculptures at every turn.

"Where shall we start?" asked Nathalie, admiring the winding wrought-iron staircases.

"Let's start down here and then go upstairs," said Simone. The three of them started walking toward a gallery of paintings, planning their route through the building.

The chatter of the crowd filled the dome like steam in a covered pot, taking up every meter of space that wasn't a display.

A woman's shriek ruptured it, a blade through the veil of banter.

The echo disoriented Nathalie; for half a blink, she didn't know where to turn. Then it became obvious.

"Over there," said Louis, pointing to the Galerie Rapp. "Where the sculptures are."

More beacons of distress.

A man's voice, moaning in horror, followed by a woman shouting, "*Garde!*" over and over again.

Screams swept the building like flames. The crowd spilled everywhere; most people bolted for the exit, some rushed toward the cries. Louis was closest to the commotion. He made eye contact with Nathalie and Simone as he evaded the people jostling past him. They nodded in silent agreement and followed him, wading through the rippling hysteria.

They were escorted through the gallery by crisply rendered statues capturing moments and essence. Women playing musical instruments. Gods in repose. Warriors bracing for battle. Infant angels reaching out.

Nathalie looked up to see a cluster of people at the second-floor railing along the perimeter, gawking at something below.

Their faces were frozen in alarm, as if they'd become sculptures, too. Nathalie followed their line of sight but still couldn't see the source of the mayhem.

Then finally she did.

As the tallest of the three, she saw it first. She stopped, five or six meters away, letting the mob buffet her.

Louis took another few steps and halted with a gasp.

"What is it?" asked Simone, standing on her toes.

Nathalie started to say, but before she could, Simone's face stiffened with shock.

The end of the center row. Pedestals as tall as people, plaster busts atop them. Heads of emperors and philosophers, white and neatly cast, led the way to the final base.

That one held a severed human head.

2

A guard shoved his way through the frenzy and reached the pedestal. Fright crossed his face, evident even from afar, before he regained his poise. "Stand back!"

A group of onlookers fell away, water through the cracks. The remaining people stepped closer, despite the guard's outstretched hands.

"I want to see," said Nathalie, taking a tentative step forward. Yes, she was an Insightful who had visions of murder scenes from the perspective of the killer. And it didn't matter that it was her job to report on dead bodies at the morgue for *Le Petit Journal* or that she'd watched the murderer Pranzini's execution by guillotine. This was unlike anything else, stirring up a novel ratio of revulsion and curiosity. She'd read about revolutionaries putting heads on pikes and had seen art depicting John the Baptist's head on a platter. And the day she'd learned about Marie Antoinette in school, she'd dreamed that the ill-fated queen's disembodied head followed her home.

This wasn't having a vision or reading a book. This wasn't attending an execution. This was seeing something appalling and uncomfortably compelling.

She wanted a closer look.

Or . . . maybe this *was* close enough. She didn't know what she felt. "Anyone else?"

"No."

"Yes."

Simone and Louis traded looks after talking over one another. "I'll stay here," said Simone, making her way to the wall. She leaned against it with a shiver, despite the heat. "You two go investigate. I don't need a better look."

Nathalie led the way past the sturdy busts, placid with vacant stares. She felt their collective gaze, half expecting them to blink.

They were in a river of people and panic, smells and sighs, drifting along and being pushed from every side. Floral perfumes and sweat and onions and candy all danced underneath Nathalie's nostrils before floating away to another. A couple elbowed past them to exit, the woman waving a Tour Eiffel fan, the man's eyes fraught with distress. A father picked up his child, who sobbed into his collar. She didn't have to understand all the languages around her to discern the fear in all of them.

Louis pulled her close. "Are you tempted to . . . you know . . ."

"Touch it? Not at all. I'll wait and do it at the morgue."

"Good," Louis said in a low tone. "I was hoping you'd say that."

Nathalie's visions of murder scenes—which began with the Dark Artist murders in 1887—came from placing her hand on the viewing pane at the morgue, in the room where the public viewed the bodies. For every vision, she lost a memory, however, ranging from a few minutes to several hours.

Except once, when she'd touched a dead body directly.

That body, of all corpses, had brought about the worst, most unexpected effect of all. The ensuing uncertainty and turmoil had endured much longer. She'd been caught in an interstice of great anguish, not knowing if she'd have her gift anymore while also being too afraid to use it. (Yes, she'd stood at Agnès's wake and promised her dear friend that she'd never again give up her gift. That was before. Surely Agnès understood?) In the months that followed, Nathalie's visits to the morgue had been solely as a reporter.

"Ouch!" yelped Louis, pulling back his stepped-on foot. People crammed the last few meters. Moving past everyone was like putting a hand into the candy jar when it was too full of berlingots to take one out.

The now-calm guard urged everyone to step away, but his firm tone fell into a soundless well of inquisition. The surrounding mob heaved like a bee's nest.

Finally Nathalie and Louis stood before the victim, three or four people in front of them.

Even though she'd spotted the man's head from across the room, even though she'd kept her eyes on it as she approached, Nathalie struggled to reconcile it with reality.

Two bunches of grapes, one red and one white, lay on either side of the head, draping over the side of the pedestal. A once-white scarf circled the base of the neck, resting in a pool of blood that oozed around the grapes. The blood dripped onto the floor and onto the bust of the emperor displaced by the head.

Drip. Drip drip drip. Red raindrops from a cloud of death, streaking down the bald head of the bust.

The man's features were strong, like the men who worked at the Mediterranean stalls at the market. Prominent nose, sharp chin, the next day's beard ready to grow. His skin, creased with the faintest signs of aging, was olive. A mop of dark curls nested on his head like a crown, cropped in an unusual fashion, short in the back and combed forward. It reminded her of—could it be? Her eyes studied the surrounding busts.

Yes. The cut of his hair resembled that of a Roman emperor.

Nathalie's stomach felt like it was being tugged from three sides.

And this head, this head connected to a person who was thinking and talking and laughing and eating and breathing not so very long ago, had become nothing but a flesh-and-blood pastiche.

A bearded gent in front of them turned around, pale and wan. "I need to leave," he said, motioning to cut through with one hand and covering his mouth with the other. In his haste, he stumbled and slipped on the blood, kicking the pedestal as he fell to the floor.

The pillar wobbled. Nathalie saw the head about to tumble off and put out her hands.

In a breath, she was there.

She stood in a cavernous room, dark except for a flickering candle, over a curly-haired man on his knees. Hands tied behind his back, white scarf tied around his throat, and a gag in his mouth, he was prostrate before a guillotine. Shriveled brown petals were strewn on the floor beneath him. No—not petals. Wisps of hair. Freshly cut hair.

Nathalie peered down through eyes that weren't hers at hands that weren't her own. Sinewy, a bit of hair near the knuckles. Not distinct, but clearly belonging to a man.

The killer bent over next to the man and kissed him on the cheek. The bound man recoiled and shook his head.

He wept.

Nathalie couldn't hear him. She could never hear them or any other sound. Only the voice of the killer.

Powerful hands secured the man's neck at the bottom of the guillotine, then the killer stood. "May the king live forever." The voice was falsetto, with a dramatic affect. He moved to the side of the contraption and pulled the rope.

The angled blade released and—

"Nathalie!"

Her mind hurtled to the present.

"Mademoiselle?" The wide-eyed guard reached for the bloody head in her hands. She passed it to him and stared at the crimson rivulets trickling across her fingers and wrists.

"*Non, non!*" She stared at the victim's head and back at her hands. *Hers* again. Not the killer's. "*Mon Dieu,* what have I done?"

Louis wiped her hands with a handkerchief. She watched as he grasped them to steady their trembling. His touch was comforting, reminding her that these really were her hands, belonging to her, not a murderer.

Covered in blood all the same.

Louis's normally ruddy cheeks were the color of chalk. "I tried to help you stop it. You—you spoke." He dropped his voice. "It's too late, isn't it?"

Nathalie gaped at him, unable to answer. Being unprepared for the vision took something out of her. She was accustomed to visions of murder scenes. And yet, could one ever truly get used to watching one human kill another? Only as a mask, the way her Insightful father was used to fevered sailors, the smell of illness and sweat, and getting sick after healing them. That was his gift and his curse.

She'd had to tell herself a lot of things in order to make sense of being an Insightful. Of what it was like to live in a world where most people didn't have magic in their blood from Dr. Henard's transfusion experiments. What it was like to have some singular ability that manifested because of who you were, how you thought, how you viewed the world. What it was like to be endowed with a gift that also demanded recompense and took something from you. How one tried to *get used to* seeing murder scenes through the eyes of a killer.

Some days, she was out of things to tell herself.

"I saw almost everything." She glanced at the guard, distracted and searching the crowd. Her eyes jumped to the pillar. The head rested on it again, as if it were just another sculpture. As if it didn't belong to the man she saw in her vision.

The guard was looking past them, waving. Before they could turn around, two policemen advanced through the chaos, ordering everyone to step away.

People scattered like ice cracks across a pond; the man who'd bumped the pedestal was nowhere in sight. Louis finished cleaning off her hands as best he could, and bunched up the handkerchief in his palm. He hooked his arm through Nathalie's. "The guard was preoccupied with ushering people away and making sure the gentleman who slipped wasn't hurt. I doubt he noticed anything other than you holding the head. I don't know about anyone else. How are you feeling?"

"Startled, but thinking clearly again," she said as they retreated from the pillar. Nathalie met the gaze of a woman whose brow would be a question mark if her muscles could make it so. *She* had noticed. "For now."

Simone rushed up to them, much to the scowling disapproval of people moving in the other direction. "In between shoulders and heads bobbing, I saw the fuss at the pedestal. I think I did, anyway. I couldn't tell for sure." Her eyes went to Nathalie's hands. "Did you . . . ?"

"Instinctively reach out and foolishly touch the head? Yes, because it's still part of a human, or was, and—I don't know. A reflex. I couldn't help it. And the vision . . ." A pair of girls close in age to her walked alongside her and ogled. She held her tongue, waiting until they were outside and the girls strolled away. One looked over her shoulder before quickly turning away again.

Nathalie looked around to make sure no one was eavesdropping and continued. "He used a *guillotine*. Like the one at La Roquette, but smaller. Maybe a couple of meters high."

Simone put her hand to her mouth and stifled a gasp.

"Who has a guillotine at their disposal?" Louis asked, stroking his own neck. "And who can carry a head into the Palais des Beaux-Arts unnoticed?"

Nathalie shuddered. "I wouldn't believe any of this if I didn't see it. I saw it and still don't fully believe it."

They walked back over to the Fontaine de Coutan, their moods so very different than when they'd left it not even ten minutes before. Somehow the surrounding architecture, striking and mighty, made her feel small. Not proud or inspired.

Nathalie gave them an abridged version of the vision, promising more details in a moment, and moved past the row of chairs to sit on the edge of the fountain.

She submerged her hands in the water and washed off the remaining blood. After thoroughly inspecting to make sure not one spot remained, she dried her hands on her beige linen dress, took a mint to mitigate the nausea that had overtaken her, and pulled out her journal. She wanted to capture the immediacy of this in case her memory interfered with it later.

Simone and Louis sat beside her and watched the frenzied activity outside the Palais des Beaux-Arts. "People are obviously telling other people what happened," said Simone, pointing toward the building. "As many are trying to get inside the building as there are escaping."

Simone glanced at Louis, who was neatly folding his bloodied handkerchief and placing it in a clean one. Simone jumped to her feet like she'd sat on a coal. "Uh, what are you doing? Whose blood is that?"

"The victim's," he said with the air of someone who handled bloody handkerchiefs every day instead of books at The Quill. "I cleaned off Nathalie's hands."

Simone put her hands to her mouth. "Why do you still have that?"

"Evidence."

"His *head* is evidence." She sat beside him again. "I've met you, Louis Carre. You want it as a revolting souvenir."

"Something to add to my morbidities and oddities collection? Perhaps that as well," Louis said, putting the bundle in his pocket. He rinsed his hands in the fountain as Nathalie had done.

Simone pointed to Nathalie's journal. "Make sure you write that down, too. That Louis has questionable taste when it comes to acquiring mementos."

"We knew that, but I'll note it anyway," she said, smirking. She kept her eyes on the journal and exhaled, serious once again. "Now, I'm going to write everything down as I describe it to you. I want—I need to record as much detail as I can. Please let me know if I've left anything out leading up to the vision. Even small details."

She read to them what she'd written up to that point. They talked it through, Simone and Louis asking questions ("Where's the body?") and speculating ("What if it's somewhere on the grounds of the Exposition? Or in the Seine?") as Nathalie wrote.

"Oh, it just occurred to me. *The hair!*" Louis tugged at his own ginger locks for emphasis. "He's a clever killer, making such a statement. Think about your history studies. Specifically the Revolution of 1789."

He searched their eyes, but neither Nathalie nor Simone grasped the point he was trying to make.

Louis ran his hands up the back of Simone's hair and made a snipping motion.

Nathalie gasped. "Of course. *La coiffure à la Titus!*"

The style of hair, named for the Roman emperor Titus, came from the Revolution a century ago; it was short in back and combed forward in a tousled manner. First worn by revolutionaries, then adopted by fashionable women of wealth, the style was a nod to the democratic ideals of the ancient world. And an homage to the guillotine victims, whose hair was shorn prior to execution.

"Loathsome," said Louis. "Isn't it?"

Simone's wide-set blue eyes seemed to grow bigger as she put a hand on his forearm. "Wait, the hair isn't the only tie to the Revolution. The scarf, too!" She clasped her neck. "Like the red chokers they used to wear as a tribute to guillotine victims."

"And now, white made red with blood." Nathalie regarded Simone and Louis. Each wore an expression of speechlessness that complemented her own bafflement. "Who would go to such effort? Be so ostentatious?"

With a deep exhale, she resumed writing. The previous day

was well-accounted for; she'd written in extensive detail about the abandoned shoemaker's shop in the 19th arrondissement the three of them had explored. She also reached further back, to two and three days ago, and wrote down everything she could remember.

How much time will I lose?

"Oh, Nathalie, my selfless friend, I hope it's nothing like last time." Simone patted her on the back, glancing at the journal.

Nathalie had only meant to write that, not say it out loud.

"I don't know what to expect this time." She closed the journal and returned it to her satchel. "The vision was horrifying; they always are. But at the morgue, I'm used to having some control. I know what I'm going to do. I know when it's going to happen. I can prepare."

Louis dragged his heel across the ground. "And I took you out of it. Was that a mistake?"

"Not at all. I appreciate how considerate you were, trying to help." Nathalie gave Louis a reassuring smile. "I think you also kept me from being a spectacle."

Simone put her hand to her mouth for a stage whisper. "He's best at making one of himself."

"One of us is considerate, and the other one makes jokes," said Louis, pretending to take offense. "Have you ever been taken out of a vision like that? I hope I didn't cause any harm . . ."

"I'm sure you didn't. People have bumped into me at the morgue a few times, and that's interrupted it." She stood, smoothing her dress. "I've never had any ill effects. I'm more concerned about what happens when I go to the morgue. I didn't have a problem last time, but even so."

After she'd lost three days of memory, Nathalie had taken a five-month hiatus from obtaining visions at the morgue. Then the murder of a young woman, a girl whose build and features reminded her of Agnès, had jarred her more than most. Death himself couldn't render the victim inelegant; even on a concrete slab, she somehow had a dignity that the morgue afforded very few.

The victim had been found in an alley wearing a silver scarf made of wool. A scarf that was also a murder weapon. Death by strangulation, according to Dr. Nicot, who performed autopsies at the morgue. Nathalie had been stirred to do more than write about it, and so she'd touched the glass, ready to embrace the consequences.

She'd had a vision, no different from those that preceded it, and lost a mere quarter hour of memory. Distinct warts on the murderer's hands helped solve the case of Marie-Noëlle Fabron, age seventeen. Nathalie then decided to resume using her gift and had since been compensated as an "Insightful adviser."

"You also took off months, not hours last time. Maybe it's too soon to acquire a vision," Simone offered.

Nathalie had thought that as well. Would she lose days again? Did the time away heal whatever the visions did to her mind, or did it have no effect at all? If she had a vision, would it be typical or deviate in some way? She had a decision to make. There was no logic, no path, no *Guide Bleu* for being an Insightful. It was experience, feel, and guesswork.

She much preferred reason.

"I'll decide when I get there. I'm inclined to take the risk." Nathalie searched her mind for a justification, because it was easier than thinking the worst. "Maybe it's close enough in succession that nothing will happen."

There you go, telling yourself things again.

A family with four children came beside them at the fountain. The youngest two reached over the edge. Nathalie watched as their hands plunged beneath the surface of the water. The same water in which she and Louis had washed blood from their hands. She winced when the children started splashing each other. She wished she could tell them to get away from this tainted fountain. Their mother gave them a sharp reprimand. The splashing halted.

The other two children threw in some coins, announcing they were making wishes.

Plop. Nathalie watched the coins hit the water.

Plop. The man's head dropping from the guillotine. The part she didn't see.

Simone and Louis rose, and as the three of them walked away, Simone spoke. "Perhaps you won't have to do it a second time."

"True. Christophe will worry, insist on my health. You know how he is. Jules as well. Maybe what he discovered was enough."

"Yes and yes, but that's not what I had in mind," said Simone, adjusting the brim of her white hat. "Think about everything we've discussed—Jules may not have been called in at all. Christophe has a body down at the morgue. What if it doesn't have a head?"

3

Nathalie had been so focused on the head of the victim at the Palais des Beaux-Arts that the notion of the body *already* being at the morgue hadn't come to mind. "How did that not occur to me? You're right, Simone. That could be what happened."

If so, Jules wouldn't have been called to the morgue. He was, like Nathalie, a natural Insightful—the descendant of someone who'd gotten one of Dr. Henard's blood transfusions. His gift was hearing thoughts through the touch of a head. For the living, he could read a thought for some duration leading up to the present. For the deceased, he was able to hear the final thoughts in the moments leading up to death. He assisted with suicides, too, tragedies to which Nathalie's power did not extend.

They strolled back toward the Seine, taking a route to the right of the busy Tour Eiffel. They passed the Monaco Pavilion, white with corners like miniature bell towers, and turned into a garden.

"I wonder," Louis began, "if they bring the severed head to the morgue, would Jules be able to get a thought reading?"

Simone threw her arm around his shoulder. "Shakespeare quotes, bloody souvenirs, and grotesque questions no one has the answer to. That's *mon ami.*"

"A perfectly natural question, *mon chou.*" Louis hesitated. "Natural given the circumstances."

They walked past the wooden Norwegian chalet with its pointy, sloping roof. Nathalie supposed that was to help snow fall off. They exited the garden and took the Decauville Railroad, the diminutive open-air slow train that took visitors from one section of the grounds to another.

While Simone and Louis counted aloud how many parasols they could see, Nathalie thought about Jules. Simone's joke aside, she did wonder if he'd be able to use his power with only a head. He'd been working alongside her at the morgue since late March of the previous year. Paris had gained some notoriety after the Dark Artist murders, and rumors had spread that a "young Insightful" had helped solve the case. A multitude of Insightfuls then stepped forward, eager to help the police—who wouldn't comment on getting any such assistance, from Nathalie or anyone else. "We prefer the realm of human reason," Prefect of Police Lozé had said in a newspaper article pondering whether the Insightfuls had been turned away.

That was for the public's benefit.

In truth, the Prefect of Police not only welcomed Insightfuls, but he'd also introduced compensation for them through a budgetary line item called "Miscellaneous Resources."

Nathalie was nevertheless surprised when, days after the article was published, Jules Lachance showed up at the morgue. Tall and lean, he had dark reddish-brown hair that sat whichever way it wanted to, along with a smile that was positively winsome. Christophe introduced him as a thought reader who might assist from time to time.

So Jules was added to the cadre of anonymous Insightfuls (Nathalie only knew of Jules and M. Patenaude, Papa's friend and the editor of *Le Petit Journal*) helping the city in some capacity, to the extent that the consequences of their powers allowed. Jules suffered temporary hearing loss for every thought reading he did and was only called upon for cases deemed important.

Jules Lachance. Her colleague, then her friend.

Now her beau.

"Nathalie, what do you think about going back to the Exposition afterward?" said Simone as they disembarked near Pont des

Invalides and walked toward an omnibus. "If you're feeling well, that is. We didn't actually *see* what we intended . . ."

"Maybe," said Nathalie, stepping on board the omnibus. "Otherwise, go without me."

Her mind was not on paintings at the moment. Simone tried, but neither she nor Louis truly understood what it meant to be an Insightful. They were casual about it at times, more prone to seeing the advantages over the drawbacks. Jules understood, needless to say, and it endeared him to her. His father was a German soldier his mother had taken up with during the Franco-Prussian War. ("I'm treasonous offspring," Jules often said in a tone that suggested he was both joking and not.) The soldier had gotten Henard's transfusions, one of the only Germans to do so, and passed it on to Jules.

He'd left long before Jules was born. Whether he'd ever manifested his power, or whether he'd even made it back to his homeland, was a mystery never to be solved.

"What was it like?" the man across from her on the omnibus said.

To whom? He appeared to be looking at her, but he was also facing her. He had a thick black mustache, oiled to points at the end.

"The head," he continued. "You caught the head that fell off the pillar in the gallery. I didn't get close enough to see it well. I recognize you, however."

Every set of eyes on the omnibus turned to her.

She flushed, then was annoyed that her cheeks betrayed her so. What did he expect her to say? "Why don't you go back and see for yourself? Maybe they'll let you hold it."

Louis unraveled his gruesome souvenir. "I still have the blood on my handkerchief," he said, waving it in the direction of the man. "Would you like to hold it?"

The eyes on board switched from Nathalie to the man, who glowered as he folded his arms.

Truly, though. If she'd seen someone catch a human head,

she'd want to know, too. The man had no way of knowing the consequences of that reflexive act.

Nor did she.

She sighed. Being an Insightful had been a blessing and a curse from the start. Nathalie remembered thinking that even when her ability presented itself, long before she knew the reason behind it. She'd asked Papa about it, if he regretted making the choice to get Dr. Henard's magic-imbuing blood transfusions. Regrets are like little slippery creatures, he'd said, that you have to hold more tightly or let go. Even if you set one free, it leaves a stain on your hand.

Yet it was Agnès's death that had put her ability, like so much else, in perspective. Nathalie both loved and hated her power to witness murders. Side by side those feelings existed, as if tethered by a rope; pull on one side and the other followed right behind, always equidistant.

The devastation of realizing Agnès's body was in the morgue, hearing Mme. Jalbert cry for her daughter, witnessing the knife plunge into her dear friend's throat . . . those were the worst minutes of Nathalie's life. She was able to reconcile her visions most of the time. Somewhere along the way she'd adapted and was able to file them away, probably tapping into the same mechanism of the mind that permitted doctors, nurses, policemen, and medical examiners to do what they needed to do.

Not with Agnès. Her death was never placed into a compartment under the guise of duty. Nor could Nathalie separate herself, or her ability, from it.

If it weren't for my power, I would never have been targeted and Agnès never would have been seen. Never would have been selected out of spite. Never would have fallen into the trap laid by my Insightful ability.

That sentiment was constant, water on the cusp of boiling.

The omnibus came to a stop. They stepped off into an already-thick crowd in front of Notre-Dame. "Shall I go right to

Christophe or go through the morgue first?" Nathalie asked as they walked across the square in front of the cathedral. Her eyes found St. Denis on the façade, holding his own head. She'd seen it so many times before and felt nothing. Today, her stomach rippled like the Seine after a storm.

Simone evaded a tourist with his eyes on a map rather than his path. "The body may not even be out, but we should look anyway."

"Have they ever done that?" Louis made a chopping gesture. "Put out a headless body?"

"Not that I've seen," said Nathalie.

Would the morgue display a headless body?

Or just a head?

"Ugh, everything about this makes me squeamish," Simone said, echoing Nathalie's very thoughts. "I still want to see it . . . I think."

The queue at the morgue was bulging with tourists like all the other queues at all the other venues in the city. The morgue, famous as much for identifying bodies (its official purpose) as for entertainment (the reason most people came), was in the guidebooks alongside the museums, the Catacombs, monuments, public gardens, and everything else that comprised Paris. After the Exposition ended in autumn, the crowds would still be here for the morgue. Nathalie couldn't imagine a time when they wouldn't be.

Mme. Valois was selling one bouquet of flowers after another, and the food vendors were all in the midst of transactions. When the lines weren't long, Nathalie often stood in them because watching people fascinated her. She had the option of entering whenever she chose, much to the dismay of others in the queue. ("What's this, morgue nobility?" was her favorite overheard comment.) She was no longer merely the anonymous morgue reporter. She was also Nathalie Baudin, Insightful adviser to the police. She'd come to know everyone who worked at the morgue, and, if not quite friends, they were comfortable familiars: the guards, fastidious M. Arnaud (with an equally fastidious mustache) and good-natured M. Soucy with a bulbous nose that somehow suited him; M. Cadoret, who stood watch from behind the morgue glass with placid cordiality; and stern Dr. Nicot, whose smile only made rare appearances.

Today the guard both inside and out was M. Arnaud, who waved in Simone and Louis with mild exasperation, as if letting in all three of them at once was a burden too great to bear.

They stepped inside amidst grumblings in several tongues. Nathalie let her eyes adjust to the dimness, then moved closer to the viewing pane. M. Cadoret stood beside the black velvet curtain in the display room, rubbing his eyes beneath round glasses that seemed too small for his broad face. He winked in acknowledgment when he spotted her.

Twelve corpses lay on the slabs, eight men and four women. A gray lace dress next to a woman missing a foot. A threadbare suit beside a man with jaundiced skin. A floral blouse and skirt for a young, emaciated woman covered with sores.

Not one of the bodies was without a head.

Other than the removal of a man's body that had smelled as if he'd bathed in wine before being found dead on a stoop, nothing had changed since the previous day.

"Same as yesterday, other than the removal of the drunkard," said Nathalie. "Must be in Autopsy."

Louis tapped the glass. "Or maybe they won't put it out until they've got the head."

A short woman in front of them whirled around. Even in the opaque darkness, her horror was evident. All three of them looked away.

"We'll meet you on the bridge," said Simone, hooking Louis through the elbow and accompanying him to the exit.

Nathalie went to the wooden door separating the display room from the rest of the morgue. The familiar, hideous Medusa on the door glared as she knocked.

Footsteps approached from the other side. The hinge grunted as the heavy door opened.

A slender young man with a single-dimpled smile greeted her. "Good morning, *ma colombe!*"

Jules? What was he doing here? Maybe Christophe *didn't* call them here for the headless body.

"You look bewildered. I know Monsieur Cadoret often answers the door, although not by calling you his dove. Or does he?" Jules said, stroking his chin.

Nathalie crossed the threshold and gave his hand an affectionate pat. "Not once," she said. She peeked around him, as if she expected to find a headless corpse in the corridor. "I didn't mean to be abrupt. I appreciate the humor, but I—I didn't anticipate seeing you here."

Jules's grin fell away as he raised a brow. "Why not?"

"Is Christophe in his office?"

"He is." Jules brushed aside the chestnut waves that tumbled across his forehead. "Something's happened. What?"

"Come, I'll explain it to both of you." Nathalie strode down the hall and into the office, Jules trailing her. Christophe was at his desk, affixing a corpse photograph into the documentation book.

"You're here sooner than I thought," he said, amiable as usual. "We have a most unusual case this morning. But first, how was the Palais des Beaux-Arts? I've not yet been."

Nathalie glanced from Christophe to Jules and back. "Horrid. And I thought that's why you called me here. I—I expected . . . *Mon Dieu,* I can't believe I'm saying this." She gathered her dress and sat in a chair. There were two now, ever since Jules had joined them. "I thought I'd see a headless body."

Behind her, Jules's breath caught, the quick trim of a wick. Christophe stared at her, unblinking.

"I apologize for sounding blunt. There's no elegant way to convey such news."

She straightened her arms and pushed her palms into her knees. After a lengthy exhale, she told them what had happened. Jules settled into the chair beside her, wringing his hands. Christophe put on his staid police liaison demeanor (except when she mentioned touching the head, whereupon he grew visibly concerned) and when Nathalie finished, he closed the documentation book. He and Jules made eye contact; suppressed disquiet passed between them.

"What is it? Clearly you're both thinking the same thing." Nathalie gestured to each of them.

"There's been a strange coincidence." Christophe reached for some paper and made some notes. "What you described would be upsetting in its own right, and your presumption that we had the rest of the body is a valid one. However, that's not why I called you here so early."

He and Jules shared another tacit look.

"It's not a body at all," Jules said, his voice quieter with each word. He rested his hand on the arm of her chair. "It's another head. A woman's. Neatly severed."

Nathalie's hand went to her throat, her fingers riding the smooth undulation of a swallow. "Like from a guillotine."

Christophe leaned back. "Dr. Nicot made that observation during the autopsy and was puzzled by it, as you might suppose. Yet your vision bears that out, not to mention the location. A pair of Exposition groundskeepers found the woman's head at daybreak."

"Where?"

"The Fontaine de Coutan. Affixed atop a bird's nest, which was floating on a sizeable plant—possibly something from outside the Pastellistes building." The pastel arts building, near the Monaco Pavilion they'd passed this morning, had showy, exotic greenery. "The head also had *la coiffure à la Titus*."

Jules bit his lip. "And . . . a white scarf."

The walls seemed to liquify ever so slightly in Nathalie's

periphery. The fountain she and Louis had used to rinse blood from their hands. Then the children. Those children submerging their hands in the same water that had swirled around a decapitated head and cleansed the stains of another.

Not one victim's blood. Two. Did those children get a trace of blood on their fingertips, wipe it on their clothes as they skipped away from the fountain?

How many other tourists would do the same today?

Nathalie balled her hands into fists. The head on the pedestal had seemed like a tragic joke, barbaric but . . . singular. Never, never did she imagine two.

Who could?

"We were there," she said, her voice small and faraway. "That's where I met Simone and Louis. Afterward, we went back there, and I wrote everything down, and we washed blood from our hands, and—and this family with children . . ."

She let go of the words, let them flow away. Like the blood dissipating in the fountain.

"My hands were in that water," she added. Tonight and every night the fountain would be illuminated. People would stand in awe, take in the sight, consider it a wonder of beauty and man's achievement. Not darkness. Not mankind at its diabolical worst.

Jules angled his chair closer to hers. She could tell he wanted to reach out but wouldn't, not in front of Christophe, whom he addressed as M. Gagnon. "I'll gladly take them in mine when we stroll."

She smiled and thanked him. Christophe's blue-eyed gaze strayed to her hands and then to his own.

For a moment none of them spoke.

Nathalie broke the silence. "Apart from me, apart from the family at Coutan and the crowd in the gallery . . . the whole city will plummet into fear. Again. Two years ago, it was the Dark Artist, London had Jack the Ripper last year, and now with the Exposition . . ."

"Monsieur Patenaude was going to keep this—well, the victim at the fountain—out of the newspaper for that reason," Christophe said, tenting his fingertips. "It would be disastrous for the Exposition. We hoped the groundskeepers, whom we've already asked to stay silent, were the only ones to have seen the head. Given the early hour and whatnot. My intent *was* to have the two of you use your abilities and otherwise keep the affair quiet, unless the body showed up publicly."

"And now?" asked Jules.

Christophe pressed his fingertips together harder. "I can't begin to say. I don't know what the plan will be for either newspaper coverage or morgue display."

Nathalie bit her lip and faced Jules. "You had a thought reading, then. *Oui?*"

Jules was fortunate in that many of his readings weren't dramatic. Natural deaths didn't trouble him as much—people's last thoughts were often of peace, poignant farewells, or relief at ending the pain. Or if they died suddenly, the random pieces of a day except for the last moment.

He hated hearing the final moments of a murder victim. Heartbreaking thoughts about loved ones, absent of goodbyes, the unjust suffering of the grief they were about to face. And then the bitter release of life itself: despair and terror, anguish and betrayal. The hearing loss was always more severe and longer lasting with murder victims.

"A cursory one," he said, almost as if it was an apology. "She thought about whatever was in her mouth—the rag, perhaps?— and told herself to be patient."

"Patient?"

Jules squeezed his shoulders together and dropped them. "That's all I perceived. Strong thoughts of Marie Antoinette, too. I wasn't confident that I heard or understood correctly, but your vision . . . the guillotine makes sense. She must have thought about how the queen was beheaded."

"Odd, but it could well be." Christophe rapped his knuckle on the desk. "Nathalie heard 'May the king live forever.' Coronation words."

Nathalie thought about the cropped hair. "Some gripe about the Revolution, a century later? Some sort of political motivation? And such an unusual affect with the voice." She stood. "Let me see the . . . the woman's head."

Christophe looked at her in that way; it was poetic and sensible and spoke of things neither of them could say, for he was betrothed to another. Nathalie had seen his fiancée once, and to her dismay, she came across as intelligent, witty, and sophisticated. And while it wasn't a formal engagement, as of February, Nathalie had been spoken for as well. "Are you sure? The last time you touched a body, there were . . . considerable complications."

Christophe, ever the kind protector.

"It's such a risk, Nathalie," Jules said, choosing his words carefully as he so often did. Rash speech was a rarity from him. "From what you've told me, that is. You don't know what to expect. It's one thing to take a chance when you know what might happen, and it's another when a swarm of questions surround it."

Jules, ever the gentle pragmatist.

Nathalie straightened up even taller. "Do you intend to touch the head from the Palais des Beaux-Arts? Two in one day, no matter how long you're robbed of hearing?"

He answered with a solemn nod.

"So do I, then. I'll, uh, I'll be fine." Yet she didn't know that. Couldn't know that. She did know she wasn't weak or going to adopt an air of fragility. Apprehension and dread coursed through her veins, but she didn't have to show it.

"Nathalie, please don't. Wait a day. Or two." Christophe pled with his eyes. She could almost see him looking into the past, remembering last time. The morning after her overnight with Simone, when she'd recognized the memory loss, he'd taken her to lunch. Talked to her about the days she'd lost, recounted what he knew. They talked about their childhoods and favorite foods and leisure pursuits (she never would have guessed that billiards and fishing were among his hobbies). When it was over, Christophe had told her she was brave and fearless and one of the most interesting people he'd ever met.

That, thankfully, she never forgot. It was preserved in her memory, her journal, and her heart.

Nathalie laced her fingers together. "That was almost two years ago and probably an anomaly. I had an intimate connection with the life that expired from that body. I don't know these . . ." Her voice trailed off.

People. It was hard to perceive a severed head or headless body as a person. Was she callous for thinking that? Hadn't she reached for the head at the Palais des Beaux-Arts precisely because of its humanity? Of course they were people. Had been people. She often mixed up tense when speaking of the recent dead, so close did she straddle the line separating life and death in her visions.

"These victims are strangers," she continued, her voice shaky. "The man was, and I'm assuming the woman was as well."

Saying it out loud, weaving that unsteady tale of justification she herself didn't fully believe, gave her bravado. Although she appreciated their concern, the more they insisted she "rest," the more she wanted to invoke a vision. Jules picked some invisible lint off his cuffs, and Christophe rapped his knuckles on the desk yet again.

Nathalie moved toward the door, chin up. "Let me do what you called me here to do."

With an expression somewhere between reluctance and resignation, Christophe stood from his desk. "Over to refrigeration, then."

Suspended death.

Every corpse that arrived at the morgue ended up in refrigeration. Chilling the bodies, a process that took hours, arrested the relentless march toward decomposition. The air in the access room was cold and crisp, like an early November day of brown shrubs and dead trees.

Most of Nathalie's visions happened in the morgue viewing room, as discreetly as she could manage. Not every murder victim was put on display; some were known or quickly identified but nonetheless brought to Dr. Nicot for autopsy. When that happened, she'd have a makeshift "display"—someone would hold a pane of glass over the body for her to touch. Whether the protective barrier of glass was a necessity to lessen the effects of memory loss, an emblem of superstition, or some combination thereof, she didn't care. Every Insightful had to moderate the consequence of his or her gift to keep from being eroded by its power.

Jules's ability worked the opposite way. The viewing pane made fainter the thoughts of the dead, like listening through a thick wall. He did his thought readings either in Autopsy or in the display room, where M. Cadoret would draw the curtain while Jules touched the heads of the deceased.

Never had Nathalie gone straight to refrigeration. And yet with no body, how much of an autopsy could be done?

The three of them stood beside a refrigeration compartment,

Christophe wearing gloves and Jules holding a pane of glass. A portable shield for her vision, as she liked to think of it. Part of her armor.

Christophe pulled a lever. The automated belt rumbled before coming to a creaky stop, and he opened the compartment door.

Nathalie quivered, crossing her arms and pretending it was the cold air. It wasn't.

Despite preparing for it and having seen and *held* a human head that very morning, she gagged in disgust.

"That was my response as well. I think it's a natural reaction to something so . . . unnatural." Jules tightened his grip on the glass, eyes locked on the head. "It—she—reminded me of the Medusa carving on the door, only with feathers."

Two long, purple feathers were twisted into a circle and lodged into the woman's short tresses. Her eyes, framed with long lashes, were shut and her skin, the white-gray of plaster. She looked more like a statue than the head at the Palais des Beaux-Arts. Her hair was coated in frost, making it look sepia.

Nathalie conjured up an image of the two heads side by side in the display room. She hoped they didn't end up in public view, at least not together like some sick exhibition resembling dummies at the hat shop where Jules worked.

"Where do you want to do it?" Christophe cradled the head by the ears and tilted it back, as if the rest of the body were laid out on a slab. She looked more human this way. Less like a vase. Or a Medusa.

"Right here is good."

Jules stepped forward and extended the pane over the head.

"What a painting we'd make right now," Nathalie said with a nervous titter. "Look at us. This is so absurd."

And tragic.

And reminiscent of the last time a murderer ushered in a period of violence and duress.

Was that what was happening? Because that was Nathalie's

true worry. Not the grisly head, not even the unknown memory loss that would visit her like an unwanted guest. The daunting, sustained panic of another Dark Artist. Or Jack the Ripper, who petrified London last fall and who, unlike the Dark Artist, had never been found.

She couldn't endure that. Not another descent into a labyrinth of curated fear.

Jules lowered the glass. "Something's wrong, isn't it?"

"Too much thinking, that's all." Her eyes flitted between Jules and Christophe before settling on the head. She gestured for Jules to lift the pane once again. Once he positioned it several centimeters above the head, she placed her fingertips on it.

She stood in a room, hollow and dim. A candelabra sat on a table to the left, throwing light on a chessboard.

The woman knelt, whimpering silently, for Nathalie couldn't hear it. She wore a long purple dress and a small, light gray hat embellished with purple feathers and silver beads. Rag in her mouth, hands tied behind her back, she glared at Nathalie. At the killer.

He crouched down and put his face near hers, close enough to feel the breath from her nostrils. Close enough to see the rouge on the woman's cheek.

Fierce as a rabid dog, the woman jerked her head toward him, thrashing. Nathalie saw a glimpse of something in her teeth, then the pressure of a strike. The murderer staggered back, hand to his face.

Nathalie could only see through one eye.

The woman spit something out, the corner of her mouth lifting into a smirk.

The killer searched the floor for the weapon. Where was it? And what was it? There, a gleam in a shadow. Something ivory, a few centimeters long.

A rook. From a chess set. The killer kicked it away. He grabbed the woman and shoved the rag farther down her throat.

Nathalie gasped when she returned to the present. Her hand went to her eye, but she felt no pain. She felt nothing at all in visions; indeed, touch itself was a curious sensation, belonging to her and not, as with sight. She never experienced taste or scent, never heard anything save the killer, if he or she spoke, and had no voice of her own to speak or scream or cry.

At her nod, Christophe placed the victim's head back into the refrigeration unit. Nathalie watched, a gesture of respect for the woman's rebellion, and waited until he was done before speaking.

"Your reading about patience and something in her mouth," she began, facing Jules. "It wasn't just the rag. She attacked him with a chess piece."

Jules cocked his head. "Before he tied her up?"

"After. I don't know how she managed it—I didn't see that part. She was bound and in a prone position, like the other victim. She whipped her head when he neared her face, like this." Nathalie demonstrated the movement, feeling a rush of gratification. She hoped the victim had felt that, too, if only for a moment. "I didn't feel the pain of the strike, but I could only see out of one eye after that."

"I admire her spirit," said Jules as he tucked the pane under his arm. "Valiant."

Christophe led the way out of the room and raised a finger. "If the killer murdered them in the order we found them, then the attack didn't blind him. You saw clearly in your other vision?"

"I did." She shared the rest of the details, finishing as they turned into the Autopsy room. It smelled of neither the living nor the dead; the permanent odor was some exaggerated, medicinal in-between, the cloying stink of chemicals layered upon death.

The room was free of other bodies, dead and living, at the moment. It was a space of scalpels and other precision instruments, fluids, and anatomy posters on the wall. Nathalie studied the items on a side table; the indelicate postmortem saw was by far the most interesting (though she had no desire to see it in use). Dr. Nicot kept everything exceptionally neat and organized. The room was used daily to dissect and examine bodies, yet it looked untouched.

Christophe collected the glass pane from Jules and put away the gloves.

"Chess," said Jules, who'd wandered over to an anatomy map. "A rook in this vision. And a line about a king for the other victim. Maybe emperor is synonymous with king, if only because it suited the, uh, display in the gallery."

Nathalie thought about the woman's hat in the vision. "The feathers from the hat were placed in her hair after her death. Her hair hadn't yet been cropped. The scarf hadn't been tied around her neck yet, either." She swallowed. "Might the positioning of the feathers signify . . . a crown?"

"As in, the most important piece in chess," said Christophe, bobbing his head in affirmation.

Nathalie looked up from the jar of blue liquid she'd been inspecting and turned to Christophe. "Why get rid of the queen first, then? If that's the pattern of death, then he's made his statement. And we have nothing else to go on. How does a chess connection help us now?"

"It doesn't. Not yet." His voice had the optimism of a discovery. "But if we're right, then this may be the start of a game—chess or otherwise—with a killer."

Jules leaned against the autopsy table. "And the next move is his."

5

Nathalie craved friendship at the moment, anything to stay away from her own thoughts. Left alone with them, she might worry too much about the consequences of her visions or grow nauseated recalling what it felt like to hold a bleeding human head in her hands.

She and Jules left the morgue, with Christophe promising to send for Jules should the head from the Palais des Beaux-Arts arrive.

"I'm afraid," Jules said, as they wound their way through the crowd outside, "I didn't have a sweet to bring you today."

Nathalie smiled. Jules did a twice-weekly apprenticeship with a chocolatier and often brought her a confection from the shop, inspiring both her gratitude and a nickname. "I don't have much of an appetite, *mon bonbon*, but that's most thoughtful of you." She kissed him on the cheek as they approached Simone and Louis on the bridge from Île de la Cité to Quai Saint-Michel.

"Well?" asked Louis, as expectant as a child on Christmas morning.

Nathalie and Jules told the story together, each chiming in with details. Vision and thought-reading details never ceased to fascinate their friends.

"*Two* heads?" said Simone, for about the fifth time. "I can't believe we were at both sites."

Louis patted the pocket that held the grim souvenir. "It's rather thrilling."

"Yes, it is. But it's also disgusting." Simone flattened her palms on the railing. "How does one smuggle not one, but two heads onto the grounds of the Exposition?"

Louis peered over the side of the bridge into the Seine. "What does one do with . . . the rest of the body? Will some unlucky bridge crossers see a headless body or two float down the river? Maybe they wouldn't float, actually. I suppose it depends how long they've been dead, or where they'd float from."

Simone elbowed him. She did that so frequently, Nathalie often wondered if Louis had perpetually bruised ribs. "What's next, you'll suggest throwing a *bal des victimes*?"

The anecdotal dancing balls thrown in honor of French Revolution guillotine victims involved wearing mourning clothes. Gentlemen bowed to their dance partners with a jerky head bob indicative of execution rather than the customary gesture.

"Oh, Simone, do you think that ill of me? That would be in poor taste," said Louis, affecting a pout. "Besides, I think you have to be related to a victim to partake."

"You are many, many kinds of terrible," Simone told him, crossing her arms.

Nathalie was amused by Louis's gallows humor, most of the time. At the moment she wished Simone would throw him another elbow.

Jules joined Louis in looking over the side of the bridge. "Maybe we'll be the ones to find the body, given the talent the three of you have for being in proximity to where heads end up."

"It's your turn to find something," Louis quipped.

Nathalie shook her head. "You're both many kinds of terrible."

Jules blew her a kiss before staring at the water again. "Imagine if we could see the ghosts of *every* body that's ever floated down the Seine?"

Nathalie didn't think about bodies in the Seine when she stood on this bridge. She had a mild aversion for this bridge, in fact. It was here that she'd stood side by side with Christophe, the two of them looking at the river, when she learned he was betrothed. That was almost two years ago, and Christophe still wasn't married, but she still held it against the bridge. And avoided crossing it whenever possible.

"What about the Loire," said Louis, "with all the mass drownings in Nantes during the Revolution?"

Four months of executions during which people who didn't support the Revolution were sent to watery graves in "the national bathtub." Nathalie was glad she wasn't alive during that dark period of French history.

Simone inserted herself between the young men. "Instead of pondering ghosts and bodies, headless and otherwise, why don't we do something more palatable, like go to Café Maxime's? And then maybe back to the Palais des Beaux-Arts?"

Nathalie lifted her satchel. "I have to write my article, but I can do it in between sips of coffee and exchanging theories about the murders. I need the company. Jules, I know you have to go to work soon, but can you come with us for a while?"

"I'm afraid I can't," he said, putting his hands in his pockets. "Monsieur Lyons has hats that need to be counted, sorted, and 'sold with as much charm as is suitable,' and if I don't leave now, I'll be tardy."

Simone turned around, pressing her back against the railing. "Before you go . . . would the two of you like to be my guests at the club tomorrow night at eight o'clock?" She clasped her hands, her tone full of expectant glee. "It's for that new show I've been talking about, the one we're debuting next week. They want to put on a few advance performances before the paying public arrives, invited guests only."

Nathalie and Jules thanked her, assuring her they'd be there. Jules stepped away from the railing and came to Nathalie's side. "I'll come by around seven, yes?"

"I'll be wearing my 'I'm Proud of My Best Friend the Entertainer' dress," said Nathalie. Jules kissed her on the hand and bid them all farewell.

After an hour at the café discussing the possibilities, both about the murderer and what sort of reading Jules might have, the three of them returned to the Exposition. Nathalie was doing her best to put everything out of her mind, and no one was better company at such a time than Simone and Louis.

The grounds were as busy as ever, horse-drawn carriages trotting across the pavement and ladies with hats and fans in every direction. The daily noontime cannon shots went off, spooking Nathalie (she really did not think such pomp was necessary to announce a midday repast). The Palais des Beaux-Arts was open, but the section with the sculptures was closed off. The second floor was roped off as well, and with no guard in place, they slipped past the closure and stole along the walls of the painting gallery. Two policemen stood near the infamous pedestal along with the unfortunate guard to whom Nathalie had handed a human head not so long ago. The blood had been cleaned up, and one of the men was taking notes. The victim wasn't there; no doubt the head was en route to the morgue.

"What are you doing up there?" one of the policemen shouted at them. "That gallery is closed!"

Louis feigned innocence on their behalf, and they exited in haste.

From there, they went through the galleries that *were* open, leisurely taking in the American and French paintings. (Simone's favorite was *The Morning After the Ball*, which showed a young woman reading the society pages in bed, whereas the garden scene of *Joan of Arc* captivated Nathalie most.) As they passed by the Café des Beaux-Arts, Nathalie saw a blue booklet at an empty table.

"Ah, look what someone left behind," she said. "I already have one. Would either of you like a *Guide Bleu du Petit Journal et du Figaro?*"

Simone held out her hand, and Nathalie gave her the book. "It's *du Figaro et du Petit Journal.*"

"I know," said Nathalie. "But *Le Figaro* is the competition. And while we're talking about newspapers, I must be going. Time to turn in my article."

She said goodbye to them and wished Simone *bonne chance* in the show tomorrow night.

Nathalie stepped back outside, circumventing the fountain— she really couldn't bring herself to look at it right now—as she left the grounds to make her way to *Le Petit Journal.*

Now she was alone with her thoughts again.

The Exposition had increased the pace of life all over the city, including in the newsroom. Even in the days of the Dark Artist, she'd never seen it so hectic. The hum of activity today told her that word had already gotten out about the victim in Galerie Rapp. Christophe said the death of the fountain victim would be kept out of the newspaper. Was it a secret they were all keeping, or did only M. Patenaude know?

Several colleagues greeted her—fortunately her days of having to adopt the disguise of an errand boy were long gone—as she made her way upstairs to M. Patenaude's office. She waved to an intently focused Arianne, M. Patenaude's clerk and the only other woman employed by the newspaper, before knocking on the slightly open door.

She peeked in and saw him scrutinizing a paper, glasses at the tip of his nose. His Insightful gift was the ability to discern truth in speech and writing; in exchange, his eyesight suffered temporarily, and he had glasses with a variety of thicknesses to accommodate this drawback. Today, they were something just beyond moderate.

When he gave no sign of acknowledgment, she knocked louder.

He looked up with a start. "Oh! Good morning, Nathalie." M. Patenaude's initial smile faltered with realization. "You're early with the morgue report. I suppose that means you've already . . . observed what's there?"

"Unfortunately, yes," she said. Everything she'd seen so far today raced through her brain. How could this be real? "And I was also at the Palais des Beaux-Arts this morning."

M. Patenaude put his elbows on the desk. "Were you there when—"

"Yes, and I unexpectedly got a very good look." She sat in the chair across from him, knuckles tapping the polished wooden arms as she paused to gather her thoughts. The further away she got from the beheadings, the less tangible they felt. More absurd. More shocking. Like something on stage rather than the Exposition grounds.

As she found the words to communicate her gruesome visions, M. Patenaude settled into his chair. His gift had waned considerably in recent months, and she felt sorry for him. Although he could still distinguish between honesty and dishonesty, his ability was beginning to fade. It was something that happened to some but not all Insightfuls, much the way some people developed conditions of the skin or eyes or teeth and others did not. No warning, no apparent incident to cause the shift. His power simply wasn't there when he reached for it as reliably as it once had been. M. Patenaude was in his late forties and posited that age contributed to the change, because that had been known to happen. His wife, whom Nathalie had never met, was also an Insightful. Her gift was a superior sense of direction, such that she could examine a map once and know how to get around, unable to get lost. As far as Nathalie knew, Mme. Patenaude's ability remained intact.

When Nathalie had discovered her own gift, he'd shared his

experiences as an Insightful (albeit, like Papa and Aunt Brigitte and most Insightfuls older than her, he was one by choice). Few knew of his power—several friends, a handful of city officials, and *Le Petit Journal*'s publisher. He'd once described the ability to hear and read truth as akin to musical, with untruth being off-key. "Silence more and more," he'd said with moist eyes, when he'd shared the news with her and Papa over lunch one day.

She wondered if Papa's gift would ever fade. Or Aunt Brigitte's, as distorted and harrowing as it had become. Or her own. This ability she'd both loved and loathed at times but had ultimately treasured because it was an essential piece of her identity, inseparable from her and how she saw the world. It was good to be young and not have to worry about that for some time. Her forties were a long time off.

M. Patenaude, fidgety as always, chewed his lip as Nathalie concluded her recollection of the day's events. "This is an unspeakable tragedy for the families of the victims. My guess is that both of these victims were tourists, if only because they'd be less likely to be missed, particularly if they were alone."

"Which means this is a predicament for the Exposition," Nathalie concluded.

"That it is." M. Patenaude reached into the pocket of his coat, draped over the back of his chair, and removed a cigarette case. He offered Nathalie one—something he'd done since her eighteenth birthday earlier this year, as if turning eighteen would suddenly inspire her to smoke—and struck a match for his own. "There's no choice but to run the Palais des Beaux-Arts story, but we'll hold on to the Fontaine de Coutan one for now."

"Unless the body shows up in public."

M. Patenaude drew in some smoke, then slowly released it. "Calamitous. Weeks into the Exposition. Let's hope this was a pair of bizarre, isolated incidents that can be dismissed as such. Otherwise, we'll have the whole world wondering if Jack the Ripper has crossed the Channel and altered his methods."

The thought twisted her insides like a pair of wringing hands. "What if he did?"

M. Patenaude waved his hand, leaving behind a worm-shaped trail of smoke. "Let's not take that path for the moment. Right now, I want to make sure people aren't scared away from the city. I'll be interested to see how Monsieur Barr has his reporters at *Le Figaro de la Tour* handle it."

Nathalie envied the rival newspaper, with its temporary office on the second platform of the Tour Eiffel. It was set up for Exposition coverage, and even though M. Patenaude had promised she could do some reports about the fair, turning her article in at Rue Lafayette was not nearly as exciting.

M. Patenaude tapped some ash into his tray. "Anyway, how these murders are handled is a separate matter. I'll take a look at your article."

She handed it to him, eyes roaming around the room as he read. Every surface was covered with newspapers, documents, and illustrations. The framed pages on the wall surrounded a window with a stellar view of Paris.

Upon getting approval with two minor revisions, Nathalie handed in her article to Arianne. The two of them, separated by a decade or so, spoke for a few minutes about the Exposition, with Arianne proudly presenting the green silk pouch she'd bought at the Japan Pavilion. As Nathalie exited the building afterward, she saw Roger Jalbert, Agnès's brother, from afar. She was fond of him, even if seeing him both lifted her spirits and crumpled them; she couldn't look at him without being reminded of Agnès. He was almost twelve now, and despite the fact that his family was well off enough that he needn't work yet, he was captivated by the newspaper business. He wanted to work the presses someday. He was too young for that, but Nathalie had been able to get him a job in the mailroom.

It was, she maintained, the least she could do. She was the reason his sister was dead.

6

When Nathalie—after somehow remembering to pick up bread—got home, her parents were getting ready to visit Aunt Brigitte at the asylum. Maman had the day off from the tailor shop; Papa, a member of *La Royale*, wasn't due to go back to sea for another month or so.

"*Ma bichette*, would you like to come with us to see Tante?" Maman asked as she patted her ever-neat chignon.

Her parents still referred to her as their "little doe," and despite being taller than Maman and nearly as tall as Papa (if she stood on her toes), she welcomed it. One of the few elements of childhood that hadn't slipped away just yet.

Stanley sauntered out from underneath a dress form that held one of Maman's creations in lavender muslin. Nathalie picked him up (and asked him how much white fur he'd left in his wake).

"I would, Maman." She didn't want to wait until her parents returned to talk to them. "It's been a wretched morning. I have a lot to share with you on the way there."

Not to mention, she was curious to see what Aunt Brigitte's recent dreams might entail, and if she'd be sound enough to convey them.

Saint-Mathurin Asylum wasn't that old, hadn't been built 700 years ago like Notre-Dame, but it seemed eternal. Grime-covered stone on the outside, stark and dreary on the inside, its walls were held together by the cries of a thousand troubled souls.

It hadn't taken any longer than usual to arrive, not as far as measured time would show. The duration of the trip was another matter. The news of the murders and Nathalie's episode at the Exposition had shaken both Maman and typically steadfast Papa. The worry over what might happen to Nathalie hampered their pace; it waltzed between her parents like a maliciously gleeful imp, making every step seem slower.

They made their way to Aunt Brigitte's floor without a sound, save for their footsteps and the occasional whine of a door hinge. The quiet dispelled when they opened the door, the smell of urine and juniper assaulting them, and proceeded down the hall. A patient muttered to herself, another hummed loudly while staring at an empty wall. Somewhere, someone yelled at a nurse for stealing her pillow.

They found Aunt Brigitte in a common room, looking out a window into the courtyard. She was elated to see them, wrapping her thin frame around Papa as if it had been months and not six days since she last saw him. She complimented Nathalie on the perfume she was wearing—bergamot, a birthday gift from Jules in February—and responded with delight when Maman presented the tasty madeleines she'd brought.

"Did you make them? Or are they from the fair?"

"Neither," Maman replied. "A street vendor on our way here."

Aunt Brigitte scrutinized the madeleines and put her ear to them, like they had a story to tell.

"Speaking of the Exposition, Tante," Nathalie began, "we, uh, we have each been there several times."

"It's still happening?"

Papa took a seat on the tattered sofa, Nathalie and her mother flanking him. "For many months yet," he said.

Nathalie and her parents took turns describing some of the attractions at the Exposition while Aunt Brigitte nibbled a madeleine. After her own reminiscing about the 1867 World's Fair, including her fascination with an Egyptian temple and the sight of a mummy, Aunt Brigitte very abruptly ceased talking, as she sometimes did.

She put her hand on the window, and Nathalie's eyes fell on the pinkish-white, jagged scar on Aunt Brigitte's wrist. The physical remnants of a suicide attempt several years ago, where she'd gnawed at herself during the night. The doctor and nurses had told the Baudins not to discuss it with Aunt Brigitte, so they never did. Nathalie disliked that decision, even if it hadn't been hers to make.

Across the room a woman who couldn't have been more than a decade older than Nathalie reclined in a chair staring straight ahead. Suddenly she laughed and bent over to take something off the bottom of her shoe. Then she ate it.

Nathalie's eyes swung to Aunt Brigitte once again. She'd been mostly coherent on recent visits, a tragic variation of almost-well, if such a state existed for a shattered woman doomed to an asylum. Tree leaves brushed against the glass, pleading to come in. "I had a dream about you, Nathalie."

The words she'd both dreaded and hoped to hear.

Aunt Brigitte's predictive dreams, the effect of the Henard experiments and the cause of her madness, always had an element of truth. Sometimes many elements of truth.

Nathalie focused on the laces of her boots. "You did, Tante?"

"You were younger, maybe nine or ten, and sitting in a cold, damp room. A man was looking over your shoulder, but you never noticed. You were playing with dolls." Aunt Brigitte traced the outline of a leaf on the window. "And you took the heads off, one by one, and lined them up."

Nathalie kept staring at her shoes and pressed her heels into the floor. Out of the corner of her eyes, she saw the muscles in Papa's strong forearm tense. Maman gathered the fabric of her dress into a fist.

"I never did like dolls," Nathalie said, forcing a chuckle. "That's why Maman and Papa let me keep Stanley. I much prefer cats."

"What an unsettling dream." Maman spoke so quickly, she nearly interrupted Nathalie. She was skilled in acknowledging Aunt Brigitte's dreams without dwelling on them. If Maman sensed Aunt Brigitte might get upset ruminating aloud, she'd try to reroute the conversation. ("It's better that Tante doesn't know the significance of her dreams," Papa had said more than once.)

Why Aunt Brigitte occasionally had prophetic dreams about Nathalie, beginning with the one that had saved her life, was a mystery. Whether the change was in Aunt Brigitte or Nathalie didn't matter; something bound them together now. Nathalie loved her aunt but was uneasy with this new tether, because she still couldn't dismiss the worry that perhaps she, too, would end up in an asylum. What if she woke up one day and could only relive every vision she'd ever had over and over and over again?

"Dolls, dolls, dolls. I never did like dolls." Estelle, restless Estelle, passed them. She always seemed to be in motion, despite her aged and frail appearance, and repeated much of what she heard. Sometimes, she was peaceful. At other times, Estelle was strikingly vehement, having once gripped Nathalie's arm so hard a bruise appeared the next day. "I never did like dolls."

Tante watched Estelle go by, then took her hand off the window. She faced Nathalie, the corners of her mouth sunken with solemnity. "Do you want to know how the dream ended?"

"Yes."

"Me too. Except *she*," Tante said, pointing a bony finger at a woman across the room, "woke me up. Pulled the sheet off me."

Papa stroked his mustache. "Who is she?" He peered at the woman, who was asleep with her mouth open on an uncomfortable-looking chair.

"Véronique. New roommate. The other one is in the infirmary, so it's only us. She never stops babbling. Thank God she sleeps so much." Aunt Brigitte scrunched up her face and lowered her voice. "I don't like her. She boasts about killing her neighbor and changes the story every time she tells it."

Nathalie couldn't tell from her aunt's tone if it was the murder or the variations of the story that she found so distasteful. She followed Papa's gaze as the woman roused.

Her hair was brown with streaks of gray, like Aunt Brigitte's, except a tangled mess of curls. She had a lean face but carried weight on her bottom, with thick ankles. When she sat up and faced them, Nathalie recognized her immediately.

That woman had indeed killed her neighbor.

Nathalie had seen it once in a vision.

"She poisoned him," Nathalie told her parents as she opened the door to leave the asylum.

"Who?" Maman asked, picking up her skirt as she made her way down the steps. "The new roommate?"

"Yes. The widow Véronique Didion. Remember the case I helped with, maybe eight or nine months ago?"

Papa took his pipe out of his pocket. "Ah, I think you wrote to me about it, Caroline. The soup?"

Maman's hazel eyes widened. "Oh. *That* one."

The one that Dr. Nicot, after his initial inspection of the corpse, had deemed a possible poisoning.

Nathalie leafed through her journals later that evening to see what she'd written about it months ago. The victim ended up on display because he'd taken a walk after dinner and died in a park.

No bloodshed, no violence. A subtle murder.

A woman's hand, wearing a pewter ring with a light blue gem on her third finger, poured soup into a bowl. The killer then left her apartment and went upstairs to another. She knocked on the door and was promptly let in, warmly at that. "Mushroom soup," she said. While Nathalie couldn't be certain of facial expressions, it felt as if the woman may have been smiling.

Poisonous death cap mushrooms.

She might have gotten away with it if it hadn't been for Nathalie. She'd evidently stayed with him and taken back her bowl, because nothing had been found. His body hadn't been discovered for two days.

Nathalie had followed the newspaper coverage closely, so closely that she felt as if she knew Véronique, in a strange way. (Was knowing someone and knowing of someone the same thing? No, she knew better than to think that.) The woman's reason for killing her neighbor, a man half her age? She claimed he was not a man at all, but a fallen angel taking on the guise of a human, as evidenced by the "wicked harlot" with whom he kept company.

Jealousy without adequate basis, the newspapers wrote.

Madness, the court declared.

And now, there she was, a troubled and broken woman who'd be sleeping in the bed across from Aunt Brigitte. Never to know that the young woman who came to visit, who tended to her tante with such patience and empathy, had witnessed the disturbing truth that condemned her to that place.

7

The next morning, Nathalie went to the morgue shortly after it opened. There were no new displays. M. Arnaud was again on guard duty, smoothing out his mustache when he told her in a pressed whisper that Christophe wanted to speak with her. She was certain that meant there was news about the murders or victims.

"I'm afraid not," Christophe said, closing the office door behind her. "I do have some news about what Jules heard. The details imply the man was Italian."

Jules's gift was independent of and thus transcended language, something Nathalie considered elegant (and envied more than a little). It didn't matter what someone's words aloud were or even if they could speak at all, Jules could still understand the thoughts. So much more magical than her own gift.

"Two thoughts stood out." Christophe held up one finger. "The first was of the man's wife and young daughter. A picnic, under a tree and beside a stream, a vineyard in the distance. Reading a book in Italian. The three of them smiling, talking, eating, playing. Being a family."

Nathalie winced. Jules said the final thoughts of murder victims, when they weren't pure emotions and instinct, were often of loved ones. It pained him to hear those thoughts the way it pained Nathalie to see that moment when victims realized Death was about to place his hand on their shoulder. "A blessing for the man to have had that memory among his final thoughts, a tragedy that his loved ones will find that same memory to be bittersweet."

Christophe's voice softened. "I'll omit the rest of the details because you can imagine . . . love, fear, resignation, and sadness." He paused, perhaps thinking of the very details he'd spared her, and slowly raised the next finger. "The second thought was drowsy confusion, waking up as you'd seen him—on his knees, pieces of his hair on the floor. He remembered a stranger asking him if he needed help, nothing else."

"So he does something to impair them?"

"Or finds them that way," Christophe said. "There's no evidence of a blow to the head."

"Then he . . . dresses them up somehow? The feathers on the woman reminded me of a costume." Why would someone do that? Do any of this?

"That's what we have so far." Christophe folded his hands over the death register. "The most bizarre pair of murders I've ever encountered. None of it makes sense yet."

They spoke some more, then Nathalie could see him twitching, something he did when he wanted to resume work but was too polite to ask her to leave. She stood, excused herself, and paused. Something was different about the office. There was no window in here, so it wasn't the light. The usual smell, a wisp of the morgue's general scent of autopsy chemicals combined with documents and Christophe's woodsy-orange cologne. She looked at the walls.

Ah, that's the reason.

"The autopsy print has a companion," she said, gesturing to the picture of men—one of them smoking—preparing to dissect a body. She'd studied it during her initial visit to this office after her first vision. The second print was a blue lake amidst the mountains.

"Oh, Marianne sent that," he said, blushing upon mention of his fiancée's name. "It's the Interlaken in the Swiss Alps."

"Ah. It's idyllic. Very serene." She nevertheless wished he'd hung it in his apartment. It did not suit the office at the morgue.

Also, she had no desire to see it every day.

"Right now she and her family are there. I'm joining them. Did I tell you? On holiday. Next month, for three weeks."

"In the middle of the Exposition?"

"The Exposition goes until October. Why should that matter?"

Because I don't want you to go.

"No reason," she said, her feeble voice not, she realized upon hearing it, very convincing. "I mean, the murders and whatnot. Although I'm sure you need a holiday."

"I haven't traveled in some time. Lorraine with friends five years ago. Then Nice with my cousin about three years ago. I think I told you about that vacation?"

She nodded. Beaches and fishing and restaurants and ruins. Everything a vacation should be (except fishing, which did not appeal to her).

"I hope you get to see the Mediterranean someday, Nathalie." His eyes reflected a fond memory. "Switzerland should be something to see. And that lake looks like paradise for fishing."

Nathalie tried to smile, but her muscles didn't cooperate much. Or was it her heart? She knew he wasn't hers to have, nor was she his. She'd followed this path of thinking many times before, and the wayfinding remained the same. Circular.

"Do send me a postcard," she said, opening the door. The last time she'd gotten a postcard was from Agnès in Bayeux, where they were supposed to spend the summer together. She'd later tucked that postcard into the journal where she'd written about Agnès's death.

"Certainly," he said, but it was an awkward response, one that made her regret asking.

Decapitated Head Jolts Palais des Beaux-Arts

Nathalie saw the newspaper story, shouted by *Le Figaro*, on her way to *Le Petit Journal*. As she stood waiting to cross the street, she read over the shoulder of a man sitting on a bench.

MURDER at the Exposition!
A white scarf, a bunch of grapes, *la coiffure à la Titus*, and a nauseating amount of blood.

Yesterday morning's Palais des Beaux-Arts visitors sought aesthetic pleasure but found a hideous reminder of mortality instead: a human head placed on a pillar in the Galerie Rapp, the room of sculptures.

"I didn't think it was real," said Mademoiselle Catherine Grasson, who was among the first to see the murder victim. "I thought it was some artist's attempt to confound us, until I got closer."

Who the victim was or how—

Then the man turned the page. He folded the paper and read some article about politics. Nathalie wanted to see not only what was said, but also if the Fontaine de Coutan victim was mentioned. She accidentally let out a *hmmph*.

"*Pardonnez-moi?*" The man turned to her, frowning. "Mademoiselle can get her own newspaper."

She slinked away. From there she went to *Le Petit Journal* to write her morgue article in the newsroom. Now that she was no longer masking as an errand boy, she could use a desk to pen her article without causing a stir. As much as she enjoyed being out and about in Paris, sometimes she preferred the chaotic tempo of the newsroom, especially now. At least she wouldn't have to share a bench or be distracted by café customers or have tourists interrupt her to ask for directions.

While she was there, she saw the day's paper. In contrast to *Le Figaro*, it was understated (*Exposition Has an Unexpected Exhibit*). Two witness quotes were provided, as were three quotes from other visitors about the Palais des Beaux-Arts or the Exposition as a whole. She knew what M. Patenaude's editorial direction had been and applauded him for it through Arianne when she turned in her article.

On the way home from *Le Petit Journal*, she pressed herself up against the window of an omnibus and sighed. The jasmine-scented woman next to her was constantly reaching in her red satchel for something, like a magician preparing for his next trick. All it achieved was the throwing about of elbows and hips that landed in Nathalie's side. With every inadvertent poke (followed by an absent-minded apology), Nathalie made herself smaller. Any more and she'd be part of the interior. Not to mention, jasmine was a most unpleasant scent.

Then, as if she weren't in enough discomfort, Nathalie was sweating far, far more than the climate in the omnibus warranted.

She watched through the shoulders opposite a carriage go by, something ostentatious with a heavily made-up woman inside, probably a duchess or baroness or some other -ess; she couldn't remember which frivolous relic of nobility was which. The carriage itself captivated her nonetheless, with its two pristine white horses and the gold trim framing the mural painted along the doors.

The opposite of the omnibus, noisy and rattling and drawn by tired, overworked horses.

The omnibus. Nathalie looked around, and as she did, her fingers and toes tingled. The sensation crawled up her arms and legs like a quartet of vines, wrapping itself around her neck and torso. She wiped sweat off her forehead and jerked her hand away as if stung. Her skin was cold. Shouldn't it be *hot* if she were sweating?

Nathalie looked around again. This was not possible. Was she dreaming?

She'd boarded a steam tram going to Passage des Panoramas to browse the shops and watch people. It had been pouring, and she almost slipped as she got on, nicking her shin.

Nathalie turned around to stare out the window. Bright and

sunny. She then noticed her clothes, dry without a hint of moisture. Her dress was the light blue linen one, though she was certain she'd chosen the daffodil-colored cotton one that morning.

The buildings, the street signs . . . they were all wrong. Her heart sped up. How could she think she boarded a steam tram and end up on an omnibus in another part of the city? Not just any route, but the one—

No. That didn't make sense, either.

Swallowing hard, she lifted her dress up a few centimeters to inspect her shin. A healed-over laceration.

What is happening?

A woman with a needlessly bulky red satchel was seated next to her.

"*Pardonnez-moi, Madame.* Do you speak French?"

"*Oui.*"

"I was daydreaming." Nathalie touched her temple. Her skin seemed even colder than before. "What is our next stop?"

"Boulevard Voltaire."

Nathalie's initial thought was accurate, the improbability of it notwithstanding; this *didn't* make sense. But here she was, on the omnibus route home from *Le Petit Journal*. She must have turned in an article—for a trip to the morgue she didn't remember.

She shivered. Why was it so cold on a sunny day?

Other passengers stole glances at her. She recognized the stealthy, fleeting "what is wrong with her?" looks; she'd received them often enough at the morgue.

Nathalie pulled her journal out of her bag and opened it to the last page of writing. Tuesday, 4 June, 9:30 p.m.

The date did not make sense.

Today was the third. It had to be.

8

Nathalie turned to the woman beside her again. "Madame?" There was no way to ask this without sounding foolish, but she had no choice. She attempted a modest laugh that ended up sounding more like something had caught in her throat. "My days are all amiss. What's today's date?"

The woman, who emitted an off-putting plume of jasmine, replied to her without looking. "Wednesday. The fifth of June."

Yet in her mind it was June third. A Monday. In several hours, she, Simone, and Louis were supposed to undertake one of their favorite excursions of late, investigating abandoned shops and buildings. Inspired by a trip to the Thermes de Cluny, the ruins of Roman baths in the 5th arrondissement that were now part of a museum, they'd begun their own adventures. (Both those open to the public and those that required something of a hunt, usually initiated by Louis.) Today, they were to explore an abandoned shoemaker's shop; Jules was at Rue du Chocolat and couldn't join them.

She skimmed the journal and found her account of the exploration.

Which she couldn't recollect. At all.

Nathalie could remember nothing, not one thing at all, of the past two days. It was as if she'd gone to sleep on the tram and woke up on the omnibus.

What else had happened?

She continued reading and felt her jaw go slack when she got to the yesterday she didn't remember, this gruesome yesterday full of shock and blood. Her own written words horrified her. For a moment, she wondered if this was fiction, a short story in the vein of Poe.

She'd touched a severed head in the Palais des Beaux-Arts, then another at the morgue, with visions unlike any she'd had before. A *guillotine?*

Such irony, to use it as a weapon. Poor Dr. Guillotin, who'd suggested a hundred years ago that a quicker, less painful means of execution be devised. Opposed to punishment by death, and yet his name came to represent it. He had to be shaking his fist from his coffin at Père Lachaise Cemetery right now.

Her mouth went dry as she read and reread her notes. In addition to the abhorrent murders, there was an entry about another murderer, who happened to now be Aunt Brigitte's roommate. Véronique Didion. Murder and murderers were everywhere, it seemed.

And this, here. The memory loss she'd feared.

I sit here at the Fontaine de Coutan, not knowing if I'll recall sitting here. That's always true to some extent following a vision, but this? I don't know what to expect. I hope the consequences aren't as dire as the last incident of this sort, yet hope can only get me so far. I'm going to <u>try</u> not to think about it. Is that foolish? Probably. I shall make an attempt, anyway. Perhaps I will only lose minutes or hours.

What did it matter that she'd anticipated it if she didn't even recall having the expectation? It was a waste of worry. She could not say if she'd held true to her own proposed plan. Was she fixated on it right up until the moment it happened? Or had she succeeded in pushing it to the side somewhat, like a heavy piece of furniture that could be moved just enough to reach behind?

Then she felt something else. Guilt, because a part of her

found solace in the memory gap. She'd forgotten horrible events and was relieved to have forgotten them. She was distressed about the memory loss, about holes in her mind like a moth-eaten skirt. Yet she was grateful for a sliver of it, that sometimes losing something saved her.

Nathalie didn't know what to do with dissonant epiphanies of that sort.

She disembarked, rubbing her arms to stay warm despite the early June sun beating down. Last time she'd touched a corpse, August 1887, the sensation of cold had been overwhelming. She'd worn winter clothes for days.

"Oh!" she exclaimed aloud, startling the woman with the red bag, who'd been in front of her.

The woman pursed her lips and shook her head before disappearing into the crowd. Nathalie took a few steps to the side and reached into her own satchel.

Voilà!

If a hand could express joy, hers would have done so as it grabbed a sweater.

Bravo, Nathalie of yesterday. You packed a sweater to go along with that anticipation.

Putting on the sweater didn't alleviate the chill entirely, but it made the feeling tolerable. She continued home, buying a newspaper along the way. Indeed, *Le Petit Journal* had refrained from publishing a salacious account.

It didn't stop the rumors. While waiting to cross the street, she heard a couple talking, with the man claiming the disembodied head at the Palais had sighed while the guard was fending off the crowd. Then for most of the walk home, Nathalie followed a group of friends—who reminded her so much of herself, Jules, Simone, and Louis—discussing all the places they'd heard the headless body might be.

"Hidden in Notre-Dame."

"Sprawled out in the Catacombs."

"In the sculpture gallery at the Louvre."

"On a stairwell in the rare book section of Bibliothèque Sainte-Geneviève."

Their conjecture reminded Nathalie just how big the city was, just how many places there were to hide the dead.

And a murderer.

Stanley was in the window as she approached the apartment building, and then waiting for her at the door. The last time she saw him, he had been catching a mouse that Papa said to let him eat. (Nathalie did not; she ushered the unfortunate creature back to its hole and plugged up the opening with a rag.) Maman had been making jam and Papa was tending to bills and paperwork. No one was home now except Stanley, who must have registered her cold skin, judging by his uncharacteristic squirm when she picked him up.

She examined her shelf of keepsakes to see if she'd deposited anything there in the last few days, something to anchor her memory. But no. Nothing new. The bird skeleton (one of Stanley's catches) and the porcelain cup from Aunt Brigitte filled with a few of Nathalie's baby teeth and Stanley's shed claws. The mourning brooch with her grandmother's hair and Silvain, her stuffed rabbit from childhood, along with the more recent additions of a gargoyle coin, an Egyptian pyramid figurine from the Rue du Caire last week at the Exposition, and a tiny metal Tour Eiffel.

Her eyes lingered, as they so often did, on another possession. The sand and shells from Agnès. Nathalie had been delighted by the gift that day Agnès gave it to her in Le Canard Curieux and made her promise to bring it back to the ocean when they'd go together. Since Agnès's death, the sand had become so much more. Her last gift. A symbol of the summer together they never had, but might have had the following year, if things had been different.

Her grief over Agnès's death hadn't taken a straight path. It started out that way, acute and shattering and filling her nights with restlessness and torment. Then Nathalie was consumed by, or perhaps channeled her grief into, the focused pursuit of the Dark Artist and his vile companion, whose name she'd stopped saying long ago.

Since then, the grief had meandered, a trail with branches in lost woods where everything blended together indistinguishably. And from which there was seemingly no exit. Almost two years had passed, and still the sights of a knife tearing Agnès's throat and then Agnès on a slab at the morgue stamped themselves onto the backs of her eyelids, like a press printing out a newspaper again and again.

She'd even trade that imagery for the events she witnessed yesterday, as atrocious as they must have been. Anything to get rid of Agnès's death. She couldn't undo the murder, but she'd settle for undoing the sight of it.

Outside, someone screamed. A boy. She ran to the window, only to see him laughing. He was with some other children in front of the apartment across the way, playing a game.

Nathalie shut the window, annoyed at herself for being skittish. Couldn't she tell the difference between screams of joy and screams of terror?

9

No, she couldn't. Not anymore.

Nathalie took some winter dresses out of her wardrobe, deciding on a brown velvet one. She slipped it on, grateful for the warmth.

Her life had changed since Agnès's death. She wasn't a novice Insightful anymore; she understood her unusual gift. It was so deeply embedded in her that if it weren't for the record of her journal entries from years ago, she'd hardly remember what her perspective had been before the discovery of her power. She was a more experienced morgue reporter, too. She'd learned, she'd grown some, and she'd found affection in her relationship with Jules.

But Agnès hadn't grown in that time. She remained and would always remain sixteen years old, never again able to enjoy a trip to the pâtisserie or the sound of a violin or the flirtatious grin of a suitor. Agnès wouldn't be a wife or a mother as she'd hoped. And Nathalie grieved this as well. Not just for Agnès but also herself, for how connected would she feel to Agnès at age thirty-two, when a lifetime separated them? Would she miss Agnès as much, or would her childhood friend seem too much like a child to properly miss and relate to any longer?

In a strange sense, Nathalie mourned what might be the eventual loss of loss itself.

She worried about Agnès fading from memory as other memories filled her head. She also wondered if her Insightful ability might interfere. Until now, it had stolen her immediate memory, with random onset and relatively random duration, except when she touched a corpse. What if the arms reached further back into her past? What if that last day she'd spent with Agnès, something she visited in her mind a thousand times over, was one day erased? She had no reason to think it would happen, but there was no governance to Insightful power, no rules or laws or anything resembling permanence or certainty. So Nathalie had written it all down. An entire notebook was dedicated to Agnès, full of everything Nathalie could remember as well as her meditations on grief and loss.

Even then, her memories were confined to words, fixed in whatever prose Nathalie used to describe those memories. This was true for Agnès and for all of Nathalie's memories committed to paper for fear of being lost (and particularly so for those that were).

Her thoughts were interrupted by the squeak of the apartment door. She hadn't locked it behind her.

"Nathalie?" called Papa, his footsteps crossing the parlor.

"Yes, I'm home."

She waited. Would he want to talk, expect her to come out? She didn't want to speak to anyone just yet and hoped she'd be afforded some privacy.

When she heard the sound of his chair settling, she knew he was likely preparing his pipe and getting ready to read.

Good. She'd talk later. Not yet.

Nathalie wiggled her toes; her feet were still cold. She opened a drawer and found some wool socks, making sure not to glimpse at the small, somewhat distorted mirror Papa had brought back once from Venice (he claimed to have won it in a card game). "I must look preposterous," she said to the reflection she refused to see.

She fingered the spines of her notebooks. How many more would she fill up in her lifetime? Papa's goodbye when he went to sea last April. Maman's fortieth birthday last September 28. Her second kiss with Jules. They'd been struck from her memory, as if someone had gone into her mind and crossed out lines from her inner narrative. All she had to go by was whatever she'd written down or what others could tell her. Still, it didn't feel like her own. No matter how many times she read the words or her description, she couldn't bring back the memory. It was like reading an autobiography written by another self.

Stanley moseyed in, tail in a question mark, and leapt onto the bed. "Good idea," Nathalie said, taking a notebook off the shelf at random. She took an extra blanket out of her wardrobe and got under the covers as Stanley curled up at her ankles.

She opened the notebook, part of which included this past February and the first time she'd gone out with Jules as more than friends. They'd walked through several galleries of the Louvre.

We stopped to admire the Winged Victory of Samothrace, and when it was time to move on, I took a step. "Wait," said Jules. "I have something for you." He reached into his coat pocket and produced a small bundle. I took it from him with a smile and opened it—a delicate chocolate, shaped like a dove. "I started an apprenticeship with a chocolatier this week, and this was from my first batch."

I'm certain I blushed. I thanked him and asked if he'd like me to enjoy it now or later. He insisted it was up to me, so I took a bite. It was luscious and melted just perfectly. "Délicieux! Shall I call you mon bonbon?" I said with a laugh. I did, for the rest of the day, and Jules seemed rather to enjoy the sobriquet. Perhaps I will continue to refer to him as such from time to time.

After we'd taken in two hours' worth of art, we went outside to the Jardin des Tuileries. The plants, shrubs, and flowers all had their brown winter coats on, dusted with snow. Our two pairs of footsteps were all the life the garden needed.

Sleepiness overtook her, and the next thing she heard was Papa's voice.

"*Ma bichette?*"

Nathalie's eyes fluttered open. She was surprised to find herself chilly and in bed in the middle of the day. After a moment, she shook off the mantle of slumber, awareness trickling back.

He stepped into the room, smelling of sandalwood and smoke. "Are you not feeling well?"

"It's happened." She hugged the blankets, inviting their warmth. "Two days this time, not three. I can't remember anything between being on a steam tram on Monday and sitting on an omnibus this afternoon."

Although Papa's face was never as readable as Maman's, Nathalie knew there was a mélange of feelings behind that docile canvas. "I am sorry this happened, *ma bichette*. I hoped . . . I don't know," he said, his hand gripping the doorframe. "I hoped last time was an accident of circumstance, something that wouldn't ever be repeated."

"Me too." She rolled onto her back. "I'm cold and exhausted. And sad." *And weak. Like this ability is ultimately too strong for me.*

Papa kissed her on the forehead. "I know."

"Do you feel tired sometimes? From being an Insightful?"

He paused before replying. "Most of the time."

Nathalie stared at the ceiling. A cobweb drifted back and forth like a miniature noose. "If there's anything good I can say about this, it's that I'm relieved I don't remember seeing the heads, either in person or in my vision. For all the duress this ability has given me, at least it protected me this time."

Papa nodded. "Once we had a fever outbreak on the ship, and in healing, I took it on. This time it wasn't diminished, and I was sicker than some of the men I healed." He halted, overtaken by the memory. "We were in port at Shanghai and a skirmish broke out in the city; knives were drawn and one of my friends was stabbed. He died then and there."

"It could have been you," Nathalie said. She hadn't been aware of Papa's brush with death. How many others had he encountered, both at sea and on land? She didn't want to know.

"Yes. It could have been me."

A knock on the apartment door interrupted them. Papa disappeared into the parlor. Then, she heard the timid creak of the hinge, followed by prolonged murmuring.

The hinge signaled a proper hello, and footsteps came through.

"I'll let her know. Please do sit," Papa said, his voice loud as it drew near. He poked his head into her room. "Jules is here."

"Is he?" She slipped out of bed. "Why?"

Stanley hopped off the bed and scooted out the door Papa held open. "He said you were going to see Simone in a show. Do you remember?"

She sighed. Despite anticipating a memory loss, she obviously hadn't prepared for everything. "I didn't write that down. So no. I don't."

"I—I told him that might be the case. Shall I send him away?"

For weeks Simone had talked about the show, and while Nathalie didn't recall making plans to attend tonight specifically, she certainly didn't want to let down her dearest friend.

"I'll go. It will take me some time to get ready. This is important to Simone, and . . . I don't mind the distraction." She tossed off her covers, took off her wool socks, and sat up. "Is Jules able to hear well?"

Papa made a gesture indicative of "somewhat."

From what she'd written, he'd done two thought readings yesterday—and others, if Christophe needed them. Thought readings for murders took more out of him because they were so intense.

"I hope he's able to enjoy the show," she said, as her father left the room.

What a strange sense of normal it was, she thought, to share not only their Insightful gifts together, but also the consequences of them.

Papa relayed everything to Jules and then excused himself to tend to elderly Madame Bisset downstairs, who needed him to hang a picture for her.

Choosing what to wear was a challenge, even with an ample variety of clothes in her wardrobe. Maman made exquisite dresses, skirts, and blouses for her, using materials far above what they could otherwise afford that she acquired from the shop, either through discount or excess merchandise. Jules didn't have the benefit of refined clothes. For his sake, she was careful not to wear anything that would draw attention to the contrast when they were out together. She sensed the disparity troubled him at times and didn't want to exacerbate those feelings. Were it not for her mother's profession, she wouldn't be so fortunate herself, and she never forgot that.

No, the reason Nathalie had difficulty now was because she was exceedingly cold and inclined to dress as if it were January. She couldn't keep on this velvet dress, despite how it and her thickest wool skirts beckoned her. Last time, her memory loss was three days and so was the coldness, so it stood to reason that losing two days might result in two days of struggling to stay warm.

Who knew? No two Insightfuls had the same experience. Her ability was born of science but had the untamed spirit of art.

Nathalie opted for a red-and-gray striped taffeta dress, the silver bracelet with smooth red glass Jules had given her, and a deep gray shawl she'd bought in the Cambodia Pavilion. She brushed her hair and pinned it up. Deciding her neck would be cold, she selected a red velvet scarf to wear with her overcoat.

As soon as she held it, her mind went to the words in her journal.

They each had a white scarf around their necks, covered in blood.

With a shake of the head, she returned the red scarf to the drawer and picked out a black-and-gray checked wool one instead. Even if she couldn't remember, it just didn't feel right to wear anything red around her neck today.

She put on a hat and evening gloves, draped the scarf and coat over her arm, and entered the parlor. Jules stood, dapper in light gray pants and pale blue shirt, holding his dark gray hat. "Apologies for making you wait. I had to find clothing layers to account for winter on a late spring night."

"You look stunning," he said, taking her hands in his and kissing her on the cheek. "How are you feeling?"

"Before or after *mon bonbon*'s arrival?"

"Ah, speaking of which . . ." He picked up a small bundle he'd placed on the table and handed it to her. "Chocolate with a raspberry filling."

Nathalie opened it with a grin and inhaled the scent. She tossed it in her mouth, giving him a muffled "*Merci!*" as she joined him on the sofa. She shared with him a version of her feelings that was more appealing than what was underneath, like the dresses that covered Maman's mannequins. No need to talk about how embarrassed or weak she felt, not yet. Maybe not at all, not even to Jules. As she spoke, she noticed how intently he focused on her mouth.

"How's your hearing today, Jules?"

He smiled in a way that told her he, too, was trying to hide the extent of his magic-engendered affliction. "Much better than it was earlier. I was isolated this morning, couldn't hear very much at all. My mother and Faux Papa quarreled, so just as well. I took Suzanne for a walk." He touched his earlobes, his eyes on a distant something else inside him. "Faux Papa" was his mother's husband, a gambler Jules was compelled to call father at home but gave the added designation otherwise. Suzanne was his six-year-old sister, an apple-cheeked delight. "It's still dulled, but steadily improving. I'm hopeful I'll be back to normal by the end of the evening. Don't whisper anything playfully untoward to me, lest I ask you to repeat it more loudly."

Invoking Simone, she nudged him with her elbow. "Warning noted."

Just then there was a rustling at the door, followed by Maman coming through it with a bag of provisions. Jules immediately stood and offered to help. Nathalie rose, too. Together they put the food on shelves and in cupboards while Nathalie told her mother what had happened.

When they left for Le Chat Noir, she took Jules by the hand.

"Thank you for being so good to me," she said. "I'm grateful for your multitude of kindnesses and how willing you are to talk to me. And to let me talk to you."

Then she told him a truer version of her feelings, and he did what was most important to her—he understood.

10

Gaudy Venus with a splayed-out palm tree, glittering with electric lights, hailed them to Le Chat Noir.

Nathalie slipped off her coat and gloves as she and Jules stepped inside. A hulking man with an unkempt beard and an ill-fitting evening coat checked their names off a list, his eyes staying on Nathalie longer than she considered appropriate. He remarked to Jules about his good fortune in accompanying this "fetching lady" and gestured for them to proceed.

The club had two floors: food, drink, and performances on the first floor and the shadow theater with its moving silhouettes on the second. Paintings of black cats under the moon and twirling ballet dancers reminded patrons that the heartbeat of this cabaret was art.

Louis, easy to spot with his deep red pompadour hair, waved to them from a center table near the stage. He had a small bouquet of roses on the table, no doubt for Simone, and three glasses of wine.

The club pulsated with unbridled exuberance. Nathalie had been here several times in the last couple of years, and while it wasn't something she could do nightly like Simone, she understood the appeal. Everyone was in high spirits; there was a smile in every direction. Lovers shared gazes hinting at secrets when they weren't sharing kisses; impromptu dancers heard the music before it even began. Someone was doing a tarot card reading at one table; at another, dice rolls were followed with back slaps and guffaws. Every man and woman in the room was so alive.

Quite a contrast to where Nathalie spent her days.

Jules pulled back Nathalie's chair and then, after almost getting a drink spilled on him by a rushing waiter, settled into his own. After a round of greetings and proffered wine, Louis's eyes took on a devilish glint.

"So," he said, flattening his palms on the table, "have you heard the rumor?"

Nathalie and Jules shrugged in unison. "I haven't heard much of anything today," Jules added, poking him.

Louis leaned closer, oblivious to the dark humor, with a conspiratorial look in his eyes. He loved being the bearer of news. "It's being said they found one of the bodies."

Jules darted a glance at Nathalie. "Louis, I don't know if—"

"Where?" Nathalie appreciated Jules's chivalric concern, given what they'd discussed on the way there. Yet she didn't want to be depicted as *delicate*. She'd lost two days, not the ability to hear about a killer. This was about the crimes, not her.

She hoped.

Louis wrinkled his longish nose. "The sewer, of all places."

The Paris sewers, an engineering feat so impressive that it was a tourist attraction, were watery avenues mirroring the city above. Hundreds of meters of tunnels wormed their way underneath the city, carrying filth and waste and secrets.

"Who told you?" Whereas Louis indulged in gossip here and there, Jules was more discriminating. He aimed for facts, wanted to know the *whys* and *hows*. Maybe it stemmed from his Insightful gift or his time spent helping with cases; whatever it was, Nathalie valued his discretion.

Louis sat back and nodded toward the bar. "Up there. Overheard two men talking. I didn't hear much because they walked to their table shortly thereafter."

"So what?" Jules smirked. "You should have followed them. Tell them your inquisitive friend Jules wants to know how they found out. Sit at their table until they explain themselves. Threaten to read your poetry to them."

Louis chuckled. "Let me go ask them now," he said, pretending to get up.

"I'll do it. Where are they?" Nathalie eyed the room and pointed to a pair of very old, very drunk men. "Is that them? Quickly, give me a poem." She laughed, but instantly her mouth went sour, as if the laugh were spoiled food.

Why were they joking? Why was *she* being so lighthearted? Nothing about this was funny, not the murders, not the rumor, not the idea of a body in the sewer. And certainly not what it had done to her.

Louis rested his elbows on the table, expression somber once again. "If it's true, I wonder if the other body is in the sewer."

Jules, ever the studious one, reeled off some facts about the design of the sewers and how many kilometers they were. As Jules spoke, Louis's eyes flickered to Nathalie. Suddenly he stared at her as if seeing her for the first time tonight.

"Nathalie, you're shivering!"

"Am I?" Whatever coldness she felt was replaced by heat rushing to her face.

Louis put his hands to his cheeks. "Oh, no. I can't believe I didn't think to ask how you were doing. Especially after Jules's remark about hearing—"

"I didn't think you were listening."

"I was, Jules. But I had to get the story out first." He winked at Jules then turned to Nathalie. "Last time I remember how you— when you—" He stopped himself and flattened his palms on the table once again. "Did you lose . . . days?"

Jules put his arm around Nathalie. His warmth felt delightful, and she pressed into him lightly.

"I lost days."

"Yesterday, I assume." Louis winced. "And . . . our adventure at the empty shoemaker's shop?"

"You knocked over a rack and Simone found a love letter under an old ledger."

Louis's face had a tint of hope. "So you do remember?"

She frowned. "*Non*. Only through notes, from Monday afternoon until my ride home on the omnibus today," she said, drawing her shawl closer. She described to him the feeling as she realized it, and was answering his questions (Louis always had questions) when the club's founder, M. Salis, took the stage.

"You, sir," said M. Salis, pointing to a gent on their left in perfectly ordinary garb. "Has anyone told you tonight how hideous that shirt is? Please do your fellow man a visual courtesy and dispose of it when you leave here tonight."

The crowd laughed, well-acquainted with the sharp tongue of the sardonic master of ceremonies toward his audience.

"Ladies, gentlemen, and the rest of you too uncouth to be either, welcome to the show." M. Salis smoothed out his jacket in exaggerated fashion. "May I present my cohort Aristide Burant and a cast of lovely ladies who will distract you from the mediocre humor in his act."

Simone and nine other girls took the stage in bold black-and-white costumes covered with ribbons and beads. They posed and danced as the cabaret singer, wearing a black velvet jacket, red shirt and scarf, and tall boots, sauntered on stage. For the next hour, he sang satirical songs about the minutiae of Parisian life, with political commentary and bawdy humor that made Nathalie blush.

The show was entertaining (if unrefined), and Nathalie was more than proud of Simone, who radiated joy, beauty, and confidence. Just a few summers ago, Simone had sat with her on the Rooftop Salon, their name for the open-air space atop their apartment building. They'd stared at the stars and spoken of their dreams: Nathalie to work for the newspaper and Simone to be a performer. And here they were, each doing exactly that.

"Well, did you love it?" asked Simone, bouncing over to their table about five minutes after the show concluded. She sat on Louis's lap, hugging him and the roses. She still wore the bright lip color and rouge she'd had on during the performance but had changed into her own dress, which somehow didn't look out of place at the cabaret. "Or did you *love it?*"

"I found it to be moderately entertaining," said Jules, faking seriousness.

Nathalie joined in. "And I considered it to be somewhat amusing."

Then they both broke into grins, praising her and the show.

It wasn't the time or place for Nathalie to tell Simone what had happened, so she trusted Louis would.

As they were talking, Simone bubbling with joy throughout, Nathalie took in her surroundings. People were talking, laughing, imbibing, smoking, trading stories. Life all around her. And try as she might to lose herself and simply enjoy her time among friends, all she could think of was how there might have been a body in the sewer and how she had lost two days of her life.

The walk home was leisurely, the night air a refreshing change from the smoke-filled hall. Nathalie and Jules walked hand in hand. Or rather, hand in gloves. Nathalie had been too embarrassed to wear them at Le Chat Noir and couldn't wait to put them on again.

They passed by *Le Petit Journal*, humming away with news and events as it always was.

"I have an idea," Nathalie said, halting a few meters beyond the entrance. "Two, in fact. Stay here—I'll be just a moment."

With that, she dashed into the newspaper building.

11

The sewers were a vast subterranean city of their own, akin to the Catacombs, but housing ever-moving rainwater and waste rather than bones eternally at rest. Paris above and below, light and dark, all both hiding and revealing various facets of human existence.

Nathalie had been only once before. She, Jules, Simone, and Louis, finding the newly offered official sewer tours too expensive, had devised their own very unofficial one of short duration. (A tourist noticed them slithering down a side tunnel and screamed, creating a fuss they knew wouldn't end well, so they'd fled in haste a mere quarter hour after entering.)

The most distinct feature of that incident had been the foul odor. She could not imagine the lot of the night soil collectors, the men tasked with obtaining waste used for fields in the provinces.

Yet somehow she'd forgotten just how overwhelming the smell was, even with the aid of a patchouli-scented handkerchief through which to breathe.

Last night after the show, Nathalie confirmed with a newsroom colleague (her first idea) that a body had been found in the sewer. She proposed to Jules that in the morning they go on one of the tours, sort of (her second idea).

They waited for a distraction at the entrance—sometimes it was nice to live in a city of distractions, and confused tourists inadvertently helped in this regard—and joined the group.

Now, here they were in the sewers, trailing a group of tourists in order to . . . to what?

Look for clues?

Seek the murderer?

Find the other body?

Yes to all, to some extent. They agreed to pick up any objects that might, possibly, in some way, be of interest to the police.

Yet none of those were plausible questions, really. Instinctive curiosity drew her here, not a logical, seamless plan. Or at least, if she'd had a plan or had thought through something later in the evening, it must have been swallowed by her ability last night. She'd been so caught up in the memory loss of touching the first victim's head that it didn't occur to her that a second would follow—the gap she'd suffer from the victim in the refrigeration room. As it were, the end of the night escaped her. She recalled saying good night to Jules and planning to meet; after that, she didn't remember anything until waking up this morning.

"I'm going to be disappointed if we don't run into Jean Valjean," said Jules, who had a fondness for *Les Misérables*.

Nathalie stroked her coat-covered arms. Even though she was much less cold today, the humidity in the sewer exacerbated whatever remained. "I'd rather meet Fantine, but I'd greet Jean with enthusiasm, too."

Before she could comment on the renovated sewers being much more hospitable than they would have been in the 1820s of *Les Misérables*, a wave of chatter overtook them.

They were following a lively group from Canada. So she gathered, anyway, based on their archaic French phrasing and pronunciation of certain words (she thought the boy in front of her had a problem articulating "dz" for "d," until she heard them all speak that way). Several men ushered them along, answering questions and expounding on the history of the sewers.

Jules put his chin over her shoulder. "'Monsieur, is it true a headless corpse was found in here not so very long ago? My guidebook didn't say anything about that.'"

She wagged a playful finger at him. "You're being influenced by Louis's gallows humor. I shouldn't encourage it."

"No, no. *Tourist* humor."

"That I can comfortably encourage."

When they reached the carts that would bring them to boats, Nathalie feigned light-headedness. They turned to leave; the nattering tourists didn't notice. One of the men moving the carts asked if they needed an escort out.

"No," said Jules. "We see the street markings along the walls. We'll find our way out. *Merci!*"

The man eyed them, suspicion crackling through his gaze. After an extended pause, he nodded, providing them with directions "just in case."

Once the group was out of sight, Nathalie and Jules doubled back and went down a side passage that was much more dimly lit. The edge along the water was wide enough for one of them at a time.

Jules stooped to pick something up. A man's hat, gray felt with a hole in it. "Keep?"

"Keep everything. We can sort it out later," said Nathalie. "And it looks like yours, so maybe you can have a second if the police don't want it."

"Or maybe you can have it, so we'll have matching hats." Jules winked as he put it in Nathalie's satchel.

"I think we're under Rue Fabert right now, or close to it." She held her handkerchief up to her nose and inhaled. "There's a pneumatic tube here, see it along the wall? I know there's a depository on Rue Fabert."

They approached the end of the smooth, vaulted tunnel, and saw the sign marking; Nathalie was correct.

"Left is toward the river," said Jules. "Let's go that way."

She kicked something small but solid. "Ouch! My toe!" She picked up the object and held it to the light. Half the length of her forearm, dull on one end and sharp on the other. "Some sort of rusty tool," she said, throwing it in her bag.

They edged along, about to reach another turn. Her skin was clammy, from the sewer, her strange bodily reaction, nerves, or all three.

"Who's there?" A man's voice, reverberating through the darkness, followed by a footstep.

Just one.

Jules withdrew into a shadow, tugging Nathalie along. She glanced toward the main tunnel. A rugged man stood in silhouette, his stance aggressive and poised for attack.

"You shouldn't be here." A gruff, agitated voice.

They pressed their backs against the tunnel wall.

As she slipped the patchouli handkerchief into her pocket, she ventured a peek.

He was gone.

She couldn't hear her own breathing. The noise of rushing water filled her ears, suspending her ability to detect any but the brashest of sounds. If the man approached them softly, she wouldn't know it until he was on top of them.

That might have been his intent. The folly of a single footstep, then unnerving quiet. Perhaps silence was the sound of caution.

She moved closer to Jules, taking his hand. "Did he leave? Or is he in shadow, like us?"

"I don't know. We should go the other way, just to be sure."

"Away from the main tunnel?"

Jules looked past her, searching the darkness. His grasp suddenly tensed and he pulled her. "Let's go!"

They burst down the tunnel, opposite from where they came, into the unknown.

Jules reeled into an opening on the left and halted, Nathalie almost slamming into him. The passage was blocked. A barrier separated them from a section of the sewer system, thick with pipes and valves and levers.

Thunk. Something on the other side of the system. Banging on a pipe.

Thunk, thunk.

"This unknown or that unknown?" Nathalie pointed to the pipes. "Try crossing that or turn around and run into whoever is chasing us? I say pipes."

Jules gave one quick nod and stole across the walkway to the pipes. He stepped over a rail, found his footing on a platform, and helped Nathalie over. Five large pipes stood between them and a clear path. They maneuvered their way around one, then another. They were approaching the third when a rapid series of clangs erupted from the pipes, followed by a loud hum.

Nathalie flinched. The sound intensified, and she motioned for Jules to hurry.

He resumed crawling around the third pipe with Nathalie right behind him. She turned around. A shadow moved. A man? The reflection of the water?

She didn't want to find out.

A deafening release of water pushed through the pipes. If they screamed right now, no one would hear them. Nathalie pressed her hand to Jules's back to hurry him along.

They stepped over and around the last two pipes. The tunnel ahead was clear but split sharp left or sharp right. Jules hooked right and halted. "Other way!"

He wheeled around and ran down the opposite tunnel. Nathalie dashed after him, peeking over her shoulder long enough to see that same silhouette. The hulking man lumbered after them. Her heart pounded three times faster.

He'd disappeared from the original tunnel.

To ambush us on another route.

He wasn't content to let them go.

He wants to trap us.

They scurried along, taking the first opening on the right, then darting left. Very dark, very empty, and very narrow. No street signs in sight.

They eased along the tunnel, hearing nothing.

"Two more lefts and we should end up back where we came from," whispered Nathalie. Exploring places had made her attentive to details and directions in spaces great and small. "I think."

"Agreed." Jules peered around her. "Clear for now."

They hurried along until they reached one left, then the second. Nathalie was about to turn the corner when her foot slipped. "Jules!" She fell, catching the ground with one hand and water with the other. And something else. She had gloves on, so she couldn't tell what it was. Thin and hard but some softness.

A bone?

With clothes over it?

No. Not that.

A dead bird?

No.

Leaves, branches. Something natural. Not a head. Not a body.

She tried to regain her balance but almost tumbled into the water, falling hard on the edge of the walkway. Her lungs squeezed out all the air she'd been holding in them. She gasped and gasped and still couldn't get in enough air.

Jules grabbed her wet, gloved hand, stuck his foot against hers for leverage, and hauled her up.

"I'm not hurt. I just need to breathe."

Where was the man now?

Jules put his arm around her shoulder, eyes moving in every direction, as she drew in some air. *Breathe.*

After a few deep breaths, she was back to normal. She signaled Jules and began making her way along the wall, leading the way. Water flowed on their right, quieter now. The tunnel angled up as they passed a footbridge. She recognized where they were, back in the original tunnel where they'd seen the man. The main sewer lay several dozen meters ahead of them. At last.

Nathalie yanked Jules's sleeve and gestured toward the tunnel. They took a few steps. Jules stopped, and something splashed behind them. Nathalie jumped.

"I threw in a centime," Jules whispered. "Distraction. If he's around."

Something scampered across Nathalie's foot. A *rat*. She put a soggy-gloved hand over her mouth to mute a squeal.

It was too late.

Footsteps crossed the bridge behind them.

They broke into a run.

Light shone from behind, dancing along the walls and the water as they ran toward the main tunnel. Nathalie was several steps ahead and veered left.

She was disoriented. Left or right? She waited for Jules. "Which way?"

His eyes were wide. "I don't know!"

"Neither do I. Pick one!"

He looked up and down the sewer tunnel. "There!" he pointed.

She raced ahead, hoping he was correct. Otherwise they'd be lost.

Trapped.

"This isn't it!" she cried. She'd been running too long; it hadn't been this far. There was no choice now other than to keep going.

But it *was* the way. A beam of brighter light lay ahead, and she caught the sign on the wall. This was it.

She charged toward the entrance, Jules close behind. Then a third pair of footsteps.

"*Arrêtez!*"

They did not.

Nathalie ran ahead, her nose and lungs rebelling against the rank air, until they reached the stairs.

The man caught up to them. "What are you doing here?" he demanded. Bearded and sweaty, he slapped a hand on the railing.

He was dressed in a blue uniform. A sewerman.

A *what?*

The routine harmlessness of it all was nearly comical. Her heart resumed its normal rate, and she let out a sigh.

Who did she think was chasing them, anyway? The killer?

One encounter underground with a murderer more than sufficed.

Jules put his hand to his mouth, trying not to laugh.

The sewerman, for one, was not amused. "I said, what are you doing here?"

Nathalie stifled a grin. "Looking for Jean Valjean," she said, then bolted up the stairs with Jules at her heels.

As they neared the top, a slew of police officers ran past them, practically shoving them out of the way, and into the sewers.

12

Nathalie watched the men go down, staring at the dark space below long after they disappeared from sight.

"I know what you're thinking," said Jules, wagging his finger.

"Because you're thinking the same?" Nathalie lifted her head with a sly grin. "We could at least *see*. There's only one reason I can think of as to why they'd all go charging into the sewers like that."

"To retrieve the mischievous pair of young people running about in dark passages?"

"Two reasons, then."

"I can think of a few more." Jules straightened out a frayed collar. "We should be prudent. We can laugh now, but we weren't laughing five minutes ago. We *did* get chased away."

"True, but now that it's over—oh!" She gripped Jules's wrist. "What if the sewerman *is* the killer? We could see it all unfold!"

Jules paused, almost as if he were considering it. "Whatever the police are doing, I don't think they'd want us to watch over their shoulders."

"Such focus on the details, you."

"We still have to go to the morgue, too," said Jules as they climbed the final steps onto the street.

"More details."

If she'd recognized one of the policemen, she might have resisted more. Jules was right, however. In all likelihood they had a headless body to tend to, though neither expected to have the aid of their gifts. Nathalie only had one vision for each murder victim. Of all the malleability her Insightful power had displayed, that never varied; she had one chance to gather all the details she could. As for Jules, he'd never encountered a headless body. Given that his very ability was contingent upon placing his hands on a head, a thought reading seemed unlikely.

In any case, she was eager to tell Christophe what they saw upon leaving the sewer.

Nathalie tucked her handkerchief in her dress pocket and greedily took the above-ground air into her lungs. For whatever disagreeable smells Paris carried to her nostrils on any given day, they were far preferable to the sewers.

"Here," Jules said, reaching into his pocket. He produced a sodden piece of parchment paper with a coin-sized hole in it. "I saw this when I crawled over the equipment. It was stuck to the side of a pipe and I shoved it in my pocket."

Nathalie's eyes widened. "I'm impressed you had the presence of mind to do that as we were being chased," she said, taking it from him. There was handwriting on it in neat rows, with block lettering at the start of almost each line. The ink had run, rendering the words illegible. "Hat, tool, paper. Hmmm . . . should I have taken the leaves?"

"I think we can describe leaves well enough." He kissed her on the cheek. "I do admire your diligence, though."

From there, they took a steam tram to the morgue. The queue was like a snake in the sun, elongated and winding. Persnickety M. Arnaud waved them through (with pursed lips) and his more jovial counterpart, M. Soucy, was stationed inside. He whispered a cheerful *"Bonjour!"* when they crossed the threshold. She thought she picked up a faint trace of alcohol from him.

The headless corpse wasn't on display.

Two new bodies were. A stocky man with greasy, dark hair and a woman with boils on her arms and sunken eyes.

"Let me see if there's anything here," she murmured to Jules, stepping to the side. She removed her right glove, since dried from the sewer, and placed her fingertips on the glass.

Now she was in an alley. A circle of men shouted soundlessly as an enraged bald man came at her. He swung hard and landed a punch. The killer launched one in return, straight to the man's throat. The man clutched his neck, eyes wide with the panic that the recognition of finality brings, and collapsed.

Nathalie came to, needing to catch her own breath. Jules was holding her by the elbow.

"You mumbled, 'No, no!'" Jules said, letting go of her arm. "Which one was killed?"

She put on her glove. As they approached the Medusa door, she told Jules what she had seen.

M. Cadoret answered, graver than his usual demeanor. Tall and brawny, he was completely without hair—not just his head, but also his eyelashes and eyebrows. He always wore a hat, even though most men removed their hats in the morgue. "Monsieur Gagnon isn't available at the moment, but he did say to bring you into Autopsy if you came by. And Jules, I have one for you to read, as you saw."

Only one? There were two new bodies.

Nathalie waited in the corridor while Jules accompanied M. Cadoret to the display room. When they returned, M. Cadoret pinched the frame of his tiny glasses and licked his lips. "I must tell you," he said as they walked toward Autopsy. "It's an, uh, especially disconcerting sight."

Nathalie was about to ask why—murder victims were always unsettling to see—when the body on the table explained it to her.

M. Cadoret left them, and Dr. Nicot, brows almost perpetually knit in concentration, muttered a hello to them.

The headless corpse had a sheet up to the chest.

She gasped.

"It doesn't seem real," she blurted. "I'm sorry. That was unkind."

Dr. Nicot stroked his gray beard. "Even in this line of work, we don't often see a body without a head. So much of what we understand as human is connected with a face or a voice that the absence of it . . ." He scratched his jowls. "Your response is not unexpected, let's phrase it as such."

Jules hadn't taken his eyes off the cadaver.

"I realize neither of you may be able to do your work here, but you may try if you wish," said Dr. Nicot. "There is something of note here."

He gestured for them to come forward. As they flanked him, he pulled back the sheet. The swollen, bloated body had a small hole, above the stomach and to the right.

"Postmortem." He drew the sheet up once again. "How, we don't know. It could have been a stab wound, an object inserted there, or something that happened in the sewer."

"There's no reason for me to see anything, but I'll try," said Nathalie.

Dr. Nicot reached for the pane of glass and held it over the body. Nathalie removed her glove once again, placed her hand on the glass and . . . nothing. As expected.

Jules placed his hand on the chest of the corpse as Dr. Nicot returned the glass. "Nothing."

The man's clothes, stinking and discolored from blood and sewage, hung in the corner. A once-white shirt and dark brown pants with an elegantly cut evening coat.

Dr. Nicot took some instruments out of a drawer. "Unless you want to be here for this, it's best to step out now."

Nathalie had never been present for an autopsy and didn't care to be now. Although her penchant for learning was vast and undoubtedly morbid, she was nevertheless put off by dissection and organ-handling. "No, thank you," she said with a timid smile as she and Jules left the room.

Colder in the morgue than outside in the sun, she buttoned

her coat and put her glove back on. "Did Monsieur Cadoret have you do one thought reading or two?"

"Only for the woman," he said. "Lots of coughing and problems breathing. A tuberculosis patient who disappeared from a hospital days ago. The hospital made an inquiry to ascertain whether it was of her own volition, and it was. She died under a bridge."

"Oh." Nathalie was focused on murder victims and forgot, from time to time, how tragic lonely, sickly deaths could be. "Why no reading for the man who died in the fight?"

"He said it wasn't necessary and that Monsieur Gagnon would elaborate."

When they went to Christophe's office, his door was closed. Nathalie could hear him talking inside; the cadence of his voice suggested he was carrying on a conversation. Although she didn't catch the words of the other speaker, she could tell it was a woman.

Nathalie and Jules passed the time talking about their adventure in the sewers. What had been frightening to experience became titillating to recount.

"It's all in how it ends, isn't it?" remarked Nathalie. She meant today, the sewers. Yet wasn't that always so? Beginnings and middles danced around memories, changing partners here and there, but endings stayed on the floor long after the music stopped. Even she with her occasionally stolen recollections knew that.

Jules unwittingly reined in her drifting thoughts. "Say it again?"

"Oh. Is your hearing starting to waver?"

"Unfortunately, yes." He took out his pocket watch, a bequest from his uncle, a watchmaker who'd died of tuberculosis when Jules was thirteen. "Perhaps that will serve me well at *la chapellerie* if Monsieur Lyons reprimands Jacques for spending more time talking to customers and neighboring shopworkers than working."

Nathalie smirked. Jacques was the gregarious son of the far-less-gregarious M. Lyons. "Doesn't that happen nearly every day?"

"Other than when Jacques had a sore throat over the winter, yes." He touched his ear lightly, a movement he often did when his hearing loss began, as if he could soothe it away. It was a boyish gesture, something Nathalie pictured him doing as a child when he first discovered his power. "Speaking of Monsieur Lyons, I'm confident he's cursing me at the moment. I'm late for work."

"You have to leave *now*?"

"As it is, I'm trying his patience by always asking him to accommodate my time here and at Rue du Chocolat."

Nathalie admired his work ethic. Three jobs, yet he never seemed overwhelmed by all the responsibilities heaped on him by his family. She didn't like that he had so much less leisure time than she; she was not only ashamed of that sentiment but also that she'd once admitted as much to Simone. ("He has to do what he has to do," Simone had said with a shrug.)

"I'll see you on Friday," she said, making sure he was watching her when she spoke. "You'll come by at six o'clock?"

He confirmed. They were going to Simone's for a while, then to the Exposition. After the nightly fireworks, they planned to go up the Tour Eiffel.

"It's windy on the tower, so you might wish to bring a coat," Nathalie said.

"And maybe a *bonbon*." He kissed her on the cheek. "But . . . probably not."

"Has anyone told you lately how unbearable you are?" She pretended to shoo him out the door, and Jules made a comical face as he waved goodbye.

After he left, she leaned against the wall and waited. And waited. And waited some more.

She folded her arms, uncomfortable from standing and increasingly impatient. Who was this important guest? Twice she'd tried listening at the door, but some street musician outside hampered her ability to hear anything besides his mediocre renditions of patriotic songs (on a violin no less. Who played "Coming Back From the Parade" on a string instrument?). She was about to write her statement down to leave with Dr. Nicot when Christophe's door opened, startling her.

A young woman several years older than Nathalie stepped out. She made eye contact with a demure half grin. Her clothes were plain; her sapphire eyes were deeply set and her mahogany hair was pinned up in braids.

"Oh!" said Christophe, several paces behind the young woman. "Chance smiles upon us. Mademoiselle Thayer, this is Nathalie Baudin."

"Please call me Gabrielle, both of you."

Christophe invited her to call him by his first name as well.

Who is this Gabrielle and why was Christophe talking to her about me? And even Jules calls him Monsieur Gagnon. So familiar, so soon?

"Gabrielle will be working with us," he continued, "until we make some progress with the decapitation cases." Christophe spread his arms out, as if they were a family about to gather for an embrace.

"Ah, I see," said Nathalie, although she didn't, really. Perhaps Gabrielle was here to assist Dr. Nicot in Autopsy; she'd heard he might be getting an assistant. "In what manner?"

Gabrielle offered an almost apologetic smile. "I'm an Insightful."

13

Nathalie glanced at Christophe, who was wearing his taut but gracious police liaison smile, and back at Gabrielle.

Then she remembered to smile herself. "Is that so?"

"We were about to go to Maxime's," Christophe said, waving his hand toward the exit. His eyes landed on her gloves, then her coat. "If you'd like to join us, please do. How are you feeling?"

She didn't want to answer that, not yet. And maybe not at all in front of Gabrielle. Nathalie needed to find out who she was first. That she was a fellow Insightful wasn't enough.

"Better than yesterday. We can talk about that *à un autre moment.*" She peeked inside the empty office. "I had a vision. Shouldn't we tend to that?"

Gabrielle shifted her feet and looked away.

"In Autopsy?"

"No, the morgue room. Exceedingly brief. There was a man, stout and bald. No exterior wounds, so—"

"*Oui,*" said Christophe. "Killed by a single punch to the throat."

Nathalie flushed. "As a matter of fact, yes."

"Very good. Thank you." Christophe went back into the office and opened the death register where he took notes. Nathalie followed him, handed him Jules's written thought reading for the woman's death, and made to take a seat.

"Let me note these, and we'll go," he said, taking the pen from his inkwell. He scratched out something, read it back to himself, and closed the register. "It was a fight after a Freemasons meeting. The victim disrupted it, a stranger who went on a political tirade. Two men followed him out, then cornered him in an alley. An altercation ensued, and one of the men punched him in the throat. When he dropped, they thought he'd merely fainted."

"Did the man who landed the fatal blow confess?"

"This morning, yes."

That's why M. Cadoret didn't have Jules do a thought reading. So Nathalie had endured a vision—and invited more memory loss, so soon after the others—for something they already knew? "In the past when I've come, one of the guards has always intercepted me to let me know if there's a murder victim whose assailant is already known. Such that I don't invoke a vision for no purpose."

Nathalie took her hand off the chair. Her eyes darted around the room and landed on the Switzerland print, which only exacerbated her annoyance. Although she didn't remember her visit to Christophe yesterday, she'd made a cursory note about it. (C. *going to Switzerland next month; she sent a print and unfortunately it is now in his office.*)

"And someone should have today." Christophe held up his palms. "I apologize for the poor communication. Between the body of the first victim and Gabrielle's arrival, and on top of that a disagreement among whether or not to display the headless victim . . . I neglected to inform either Monsieur Arnaud or Monsieur Soucy."

That was unlike Christophe, to have an oversight of that sort. She tried to hide her disappointment but presumably failed, given the shimmer of guilt that passed over Christophe's face. "Nathalie, I'm so very embarrassed. I apologize. Especially after . . ."

"Mistakes happen." Nathalie forced something resembling a smile. She watched as Gabrielle hovered near the doorway, blinking much too frequently. "We should make our way to Maxime's before it gets too crowded."

They left the morgue, encompassed by the melodies of the street musician, now joined by two others to form an enthusiastic French trio, and a group of forty or so tourists following a guide. Nathalie removed her gloves and coat (no need to call attention to her coldness over lunch) and caught up to Christophe and Gabrielle as they made their way through the crowd.

While approaching them, Nathalie noticed that Gabrielle had a mild hitch in her gait. Her feet moved lightly but uncertainly, as though they couldn't trust the cobblestone below despite keeping pace.

"The limp is from using my gift," said Gabrielle without turning to her.

Nathalie knew her cheeks matched the pink of her dress at the moment. "That was rude of me. I didn't mean to stare. I don't like it when people do—" She halted, her embarrassment stepping aside when Gabrielle's words belatedly reached her brain. "Oh! What . . . what's the nature of your ability?"

She threw a glance at Christophe, who opened his mouth to say something, but Gabrielle spoke first.

"If I place my hand on the feet of someone who is ambulatory—or was, because it works on the dead as well—I can determine the route they've walked recently. Path tracing, I call it." Her tone was unaffected, no different than if she were providing the time of day. She still didn't make eye contact with Nathalie but stared ahead at the bridge in front of them. "It's more intuitive than visual. If I were to place my hands on your feet once we got to the café, I'd know we left a building. Maybe the morgue, if it had a distinct walking pattern, like pausing in the viewing room if we were visitors. And I'd perceive that we crossed a bridge because of the angle and the feel underfoot, then another street.

And I'd sense the proximity of other pairs of feet, so I could tell if you're in public or in a queue or home."

How unusual. "How interesting!" Nathalie said, trying to show the enthusiasm Gabrielle herself did not.

Gabrielle drew a square with her hands. "I'd see it like a map, the way a person thinks through it: I started at the morgue, I went here and there, and I ended up at the café. I can't tell specific addresses but more general areas; I think it has to do with places I myself have been. The better I know a route, the stronger I sense it."

"And it hurts your own feet?" Nathalie asked.

"Not so much pain as numbness to varying degrees. Sometimes it sets in immediately, sometimes later. It . . . impedes my ability to walk. At times, not always."

As with all Insightfuls. Unpredictable consequences of unpredictable duration. The magic decided, not the person whose blood flowed with it.

"I hope having three of you on the case will lessen the burden," Christophe said. "Of consequences, that is. And you, Nathalie. Are you feeling well enough?"

They were crossing the bridge, the bridge Nathalie resented. Before she could respond, the Notre-Dame bells tolled. She loved their deep sonorous bellow; she was particularly grateful for it, and how it prevented her from answering at the moment. She'd walked across the bridge with Christophe since that disappointing conversation two summers ago and always felt awkward doing so, unable to be articulate. Not that he'd ever know, or even guess. He'd care if he knew, of that she was certain. That was precisely why she did not want him to.

They were well past the bridge and almost at Maxime's by the time the bells finished. Nathalie turned to reply to Christophe just as a beggar clutched onto his sleeve, asking for a centime and getting distracted when someone else threw one in his cup.

Maxime's was lively, as always. Nathalie's favorite waiter, Jean, walked them to the back of the café. She was too preoccupied with spying on the patrons, clothing styles and compelling faces from all over the world, to notice the route they'd taken. When they arrived at their table and Jean held out the chair, Nathalie's breath caught in her throat.

"Is there . . . anything else?"

"Exposition crowd," said Jean with an apologetic lift of his shoulders.

Christophe gestured toward the exit. "Would you rather go to another restaurant?"

He knew. He understood. So did Jules, Simone, and Louis.

She didn't want to create an inconvenience for anyone. "No, this—this will do."

Nathalie sat in the chair and became like one of Rodin's bronze sculptures, fixed and hefty and softly undefined at the edges. This was where she'd had her last moments with Agnès over a shared pain au chocolat. This table, this chair. For almost two years she had avoided it, just as she never returned to Le Canard Curieux where they'd had what became their final lunch. They'd planned to meet again for lunch a week later. Instead, Agnès was a corpse in a matter of days, and on the day they were to have lunch, her body was en route to her grandmother's property in Bayeux on the Normandy coast.

Nathalie had never since sung the melodies Agnès roused the café into singing that day. She hadn't touched another pain au chocolat since that day, either.

"Christophe tells me you've known of your ability for about two years. How did you discover it?" Gabrielle interrupted her thoughts, in a well-mannered tone and with a courteous smile, as if she weren't sitting in Agnès's seat.

"Dramatically." Nathalie's eyes fell on the large, oval amethyst ring Gabrielle wore on her right hand. She'd noticed it on the walk over, how garish it seemed compared to the rest of Gabrielle's unfussy appearance, including a modest gold crucifix ring on her left hand. "And by accident."

Christophe clasped his hands, perhaps a bit too firmly.

Gabrielle raised her eyebrows in anticipation. "I'm aware of your contributions in the Dark Artist case. My father makes it his business to stay apprised of Insightful happenings and rumors, through some channel or another. It's a pastime for him, truly. He was so inspired after the news of the beheadings spread that he gave my name to the Prefect of Police, certain I could help." She clenched her jaw and then plastered on a rigid smile. "Congratulations on doing such good work. How did it, uh, all come to be?"

"*Merci*." The same question, asked differently. With a sigh on the inside, because she didn't see any gracious way out of this conversation, Nathalie recounted her circuitous path to comprehending her identity as an Insightful. Gabrielle nodded along in apparent empathy, and Christophe's clasping loosened up as the conversation progressed. They ordered lunch and were served quickly, despite the crowd.

Nathalie didn't disclose anything about Agnès—or any more detail than necessary, frankly. Gabrielle was a stranger with a mostly unreadable affect thus far, and Nathalie had too much to protect to open up just yet. And how much had Gabrielle shared? Not enough. That they were about to become colleagues meant cordiality, but time would tell if it would, or should, be anything more.

"Scotland Yard nearly brought her in for the Jack the Ripper killings," said Christophe, in between bites of artichoke, "but the Chief Constable objected strongly to the use of Insightfuls."

Gabrielle beamed at Christophe, as she did each time he spoke. Even when, like this, there was nothing about which to beam. That affect was decidedly *not* unreadable.

"I named my cat Stanley because he strikes me as British, even though I found him on the carousel at Luxembourg Gardens," Nathalie said, swatting an invisible fly to get Gabrielle's attention again. "And while I'd love to travel to London, I'm glad I didn't have to witness the Whitechapel murders."

Christophe leaned forward. "How are you doing after the other day?"

She poked the teaspoon on her saucer. Gabrielle had asked two versions of the same question, and Christophe had asked three times. Either they were both persistent or the fragility of her coyness was obvious.

Nathalie wanted to tell Christophe how she was doing, sincerely and without all the trappings of superficial banter. That two days of her life had fallen into a chasm of time, that she'd been excessively cold, though much less so today. She wanted to tell him about her trip to the sewers with Jules. But that was a moment for the two of them, not the three of them.

She responded with a look she hoped conveyed all of that. Or at least, the notion that she'd provide the details later. "As expected," she said. He gave her the faintest of nods.

He understood.

Silently thanking him, she turned to Gabrielle. "I was late to discover my ability. Might never have known it existed at all if I didn't happen to touch the morgue viewing pane by accident one day." Nathalie thought of that first encounter, the little girl behind her crying out suddenly and startling her. Her hand grazed the glass and the rest . . . well, here she was, sitting in a café discussing everything that constituted *the rest*. "How did you come to know yours?"

Gabrielle pressed her lips together. She, too, was weighing how much to say; Nathalie could tell.

"My parents brought me to Dr. Henard for a transfusion when I was a baby. I'd just learned to walk. They didn't get transfusions for themselves, but they wanted it for me. They thought it was the greatest gift they could give me."

Nathalie absorbed the significance of that. It was one thing to inherit Insightful blood, and it was another to choose the transfusions. To have the choice made for you was yet another, and perhaps the most complicated of all. Gabrielle didn't say that. The way she spun her crucifix ring as the words came out did.

Then Nathalie came to another conclusion. "Is that why your ability is connected to locomotion? Because you were learning to walk?"

"That's the belief, yes. I don't even remember my first episode. According to my parents, I was four years old and woke my father up from a nap by touching his feet. I babbled on and on about where he'd been that day in great detail." Gabrielle twirled the crucifix ring some more. "Not until a few more incidents along those lines did my parents comprehend what was happening."

Nathalie took a sip of coffee and collected her thoughts. She had many questions for Gabrielle but wanted to restrict them to a few; to ask too many questions was also to invite them, so she had to balance her desire to know with her own wish for distance. "Dr. Henard must have died before they had a chance to ask."

"Yes," Gabrielle said, mouth twitching. "They thought I was a failure. So much so that they didn't bring my two younger siblings for a treatment. You can imagine how pleased they were to find out that I'd manifested an Insightful power after all."

"Gabrielle might be able to help us given the . . . unusual nature of the crimes," Christophe said, tapping his fingers. "One of the victims is likely a tourist, if not both. We might be better able to identify them and how they encountered the murderer if we can trace their paths. Anything we can learn is beneficial."

"That's . . . good of you to share your gift with us," said Nathalie as she drummed the side of the cup.

"I don't know if *good* is the word. I'm a reluctant Insightful," said Gabrielle with a bitter frown. She pushed her plate away. "I think it's unnatural. We have no right to endow ourselves with magic, regardless of the 'cost.' I'd end every ability today if I could, beginning with my own. I despise it."

Nathalie's skin prickled. Her cautious interest in Gabrielle retreated a step. Although she didn't know that many Insightfuls, those she knew or knew of had conflicting feelings about their power. Few grew outright enamored with it, and few detested it. Regret or resignation, perhaps, but not ardent disdain. She didn't expect such sharp words from an unassuming young woman whose demeanor until now had seemed subdued, if not timid. A glance at Christophe suggested he thought the same.

Jules had heard from someone once that there was an Insightful who helped other Insightfuls obtain new identities and brewed concoctions to remove their powers. Or was it a potion that changed the negative effects of the ability? It was so wrapped up in mythology that Jules was skeptical. When she'd asked M. Patenaude about it, he'd said he'd heard the stories as well. The alleged Insightful was either a secret apprentice to Dr. Henard, chosen to protect his secrets, or a mind reader who stole Henard's knowledge of blood transfusions and magic. Such were the rumors.

Nathalie wished she knew for sure that this Insightful apprentice or mind reader existed, because she'd send Gabrielle right to him. If anyone desired to be rid of her power, it was the young woman before her.

"Why use your ability at all, then? Or admit to still having it?" Nathalie asked with trepidation. "If you don't make an effort to use it, it will be like you don't have it at all."

"Latent power is power all the same. As to why I'm using it, why I agreed to the summons when the Prefect of Police inquired and my father insisted?" Gabrielle's thumb pressed firmly into the crucifix ring. "Redemption."

Nathalie furrowed her brow. This was a much weightier conversation than she expected today. "For what?"

"The sins of my parents. And my own guilt." She shook her head. "I already told my father I'm not going to do this continuously, like you."

Was that an insult? Or simply a declaration of her own limits?

"Nathalie has other responsibilities that bring her to the

morgue frequently," said Christophe, tactful enough not to mention the newspaper. "She's an invaluable adviser to us."

Modesty might have been her response under other conditions, but at the moment, Nathalie found herself sitting up straighter.

"Oh, well that's understandable," said Gabrielle, as if Nathalie needed her approval. Her expression softened. "It's not something I could do in a sustained fashion. I've agreed to aid on this case, as best as I'm able. If I have to be cursed, I'd rather use my ability, obscure and otherwise useless as it is, for good."

"Most Insightfuls do, thankfully." She couldn't bring herself to say *us* with Gabrielle, not with the discussion going this way. "My father is a healer."

Gabrielle started to say something and then stopped herself. She turned to Christophe. "I have another engagement, as I mentioned before, before going to work at the library. I'm sorry I wasn't able to perceive anything of great importance today. It's been a while, so perhaps my power has weakened. You'll send for me if there are . . . others?"

He assured Gabrielle he would, adding that he was grateful for her help. She left money for her portion and bid them farewell, cordially to Nathalie and (in Nathalie's opinion) more warmly to Christophe.

She was barely out of earshot when Nathalie spoke. "What did she see? With her tracing?"

Christophe dabbed his mouth with a napkin. "The victim leaving an establishment—restaurant, café, tavern—and crossing a street. Possibly Quai d'Orsay. Then a bridge that could be either Invalides or l'Alma. No clues to the murder, but at least we can make inquiries at the local hotels, see if a guest matching this description disappeared without paying."

"Good. I'm happy she could help." Nathalie spied the empty chair—Agnès's seat. "But I dislike her."

14

Jean came from behind Nathalie to clear their plates, startling her. For a moment she thought it was Gabrielle returning to the table just in time to overhear what she'd so candidly uttered.

Christophe waited for Jean to leave before continuing. "I knew she wasn't enthusiastic about the prospect of advising at the morgue. Even so, I wasn't prepared for her to convey her feelings so strongly. Her father insists she do this, and as you can see, she's not comfortable. I don't think she meant to offend with her cynicism."

Nathalie wasn't sure if she did or didn't, and she wasn't in the mood to offer a magnanimous take on Gabrielle's attitude.

"Now," Christophe said, his eyes earnest, "I've been thinking of you a lot since yesterday. You wouldn't answer me properly in front of Gabrielle, and now I understand why. Please tell me how you are. I see you're dressed for something other than a hot, sunny day. How much are you suffering? Is it as debilitating as last time?"

Her heart flooded with affection for him, as it so often did. For two years he'd shown a tenderness toward her that never wavered. While he might be busy or consumed with work at times, or make a mistake like today's misunderstanding, Christophe was nevertheless a constant.

He patted her forearm and jerked back his hand. She knew it was not only the coolness of her skin but also what it signaled. "Oh, Nathalie."

"Not as cold as a new arrival at the morgue." She placed her hand where he'd had his, the ghost of his brief contact lingering long past the touch itself. "Far from normal, nevertheless. And yet, much improved since yesterday. It started on the omnibus."

He sat, hands gripping the arms of his chair, as Nathalie gave him a modified version of how she felt. As with Jules the previous day, she presented a braver Nathalie than the one that truly existed. She mentioned last night's time at Le Chat Noir and how Louis's news had resulted in a trip to the sewers.

"You did *what?*"

"I've only been once before, and I was curious . . ."

"To see if you could find a corpse? You don't see enough at the morgue?" Christophe crossed his arms with a raised brow.

"I don't know. The architecture of it all. Clues." She intertwined her fingers.

He stared at her expectantly.

"It's not much but we did find a *few* items," she said, feeling around in her satchel. She presented him with the hat, tool, and parchment.

His arms were still folded. "The hat of a tourist, a sewerman's tool, and some university student's glossary or some such."

"You don't want them?"

"I don't have a bag with me, but when we leave, follow me to the office. I'll put them there for now," he said, reluctance shading his tone.

Well, now she certainly would not be telling him they got chased away by a sewerman. "We saw a group of police officers run by on our way out."

"I'm amazed you didn't go right back in."

"I wanted to, but Jules—"

"Was there to talk you out of it, fortunately. I'm not aware of another body yet, but my goodness, Nathalie." He pinched the bridge of his nose and blinked slowly. "I like your spirit of adventure. I really do. I admire it, even. What I don't admire are the risks you and your friends take sometimes. Just . . . be careful, would you?"

This wasn't the first time Christophe had scolded her for indulging her investigative side, and that was without even knowing about the excursions they'd taken to abandoned *châteaux*, forgotten salons, and hidden ruins. It was a familiar patter by now—he gently voicing his concern, she promising to practice vigilance. Nathalie wasn't about to suppress her inquisitive nature, as it were, and his protective side wasn't going to abate. And so they continued this dance, and on Nathalie's side anyway, it wasn't entirely unwelcome.

"I won't do anything reckless," she said, acknowledging they might have different interpretations of that term. Besides, if that was the second body the police were running after, she had an inkling about it even before he did. Which, she would never admit to Christophe, was the very thrill that justified these little quests.

She exited the morgue and, seeking shade, made her way to some benches under a linden tree. Despite the proximity of some (needlessly boisterous) young men, Nathalie settled in to write her morgue report. Describing the stocky man who'd been killed in the fight unsettled her, as it always did when she had to report on a victim whose death she witnessed. The sickly woman cultivated her sympathy as well, because it wasn't right to die in the public domain.

That's how it was, doing the morgue report. Two years of writing about bodies, and still she wondered, from time to time, about the lives behind the corpses everyone came to see with such morbid curiosity. But she didn't always think about them that way, as people who'd had a life and loved ones. She wasn't sure if that was good, bad, or something to which facile labels like good and bad simply didn't apply.

By the time she was done, the boisterous young men had left. A man around Christophe's age, freckled and with whitish-blond hair right down to his eyelashes, sat beside her. Lanky with very upright posture, he was reading a book—something on the Revolution of 1789, if the conclusion from her peeks was accurate—and turned the pages far more noisily than pages should be turned.

Was everyone annoying today, or was she just irritable?

Before too long the blond page-turner left. He went to the morgue queue, still reading his book. The woman in front of him had a parasol in one hand and a *Guide Bleu* in the other.

That reminded her. She'd wanted to count.

Nathalie took her world map out of her bag. Her map of wishes, as she'd thought of it: wishes for travel, wishes for experiences, stemming from her discoveries at the Exposition. She'd made brief notes on the map and then, in a journal devoted solely to the fair, more extensive entries. Her intent was to visit each of the nations represented (more than thirty of them), then revisit them until the fair concluded, with the aim of learning something new each time.

Seven nations circled so far. She placed a finger on the two most recent, both so very far from France.

China: A woman with black hair pinned up in sticks, in alluring fashion, painted a dragon figurine with the most incredible precision.

Argentina: Here I sampled a sauce so delicious that I would travel there just to enjoy it more. Dulce de leche, it is called. Heated milk and sugar, similar to caramel.

Thankfully she hadn't lost them to memory. How much of her time at the Exposition would suffer the consequences of her Insightful power?

The Palais des Beaux-Arts had, twice already.

And so, now that her article was written, she aimed to see it again.

15

Maybe this time I'll remember it.

She strolled in solitude amidst the crowds, in the way one could in a city, being part of everyone or no one. Sketches, drawings, paintings, the Galerie Rapp where the victim had been. And now, she wasn't even sure which pedestal had held the head.

It was a strange thing, not only to lose memories but to be cognizant that you might. Long ago, Nathalie had given up trying to guess what would be taken from her and what wouldn't, trying not to live her life around the unexpected placement of a gap. So she'd always proceeded as if she would never have a lapse. It was either that or sit on her bed and do nothing except wait. Might that have been more pragmatic? Arguably. But this ability had enough power over her, and she exerted what control she could by living no matter what.

She stepped outside the Palais onto Champ de Mars, deciding where to go next. The Dôme Central called to her. She'd been to the Galerie des Industries Diverses and would be going again to part of it with Jules, Simone, and Louis soon, but there was a clock exhibit she wanted to see.

As she turned left toward the Dôme Central, a shadow came near her own.

"So you *do* go somewhere other than the morgue, the newspaper, the café, and the sewers."

She turned to see Christophe, who tipped his hat to her.

"Well, you know for certain I've been to the Exposition before. So that's five places," she said with a chuckle. "You didn't say you were coming here!"

He shrugged. "Ah, well. You mentioned it in passing as you left, and it's a beautiful day. I decided to step away for a while and come myself."

"I'm glad I could be a favorable influence," she said, almost certain she was blushing.

He looked around them at the palaces and pavilions. "What are you going to visit?"

"Industries Diverses." She pointed to the opulent Dôme Central. A breeze carried over the scent of his orange blossom cologne, tinged with a pleasing woodsiness. "And you?"

"I was just going to wander, really."

She wanted to ask him if he would like to stroll with her. What if he said no? He was betrothed, after all. Other than Jules, she never went out alone with a gentleman, not even Louis.

Then again, one only passes through this garden of life once, as Simone often said.

"Would you . . . like to accompany me?" Her mouth suddenly went dry. She wanted to say something else, to make a joke or self-deprecating remark, but her tongue refused to form anything.

"That would be delightful," he said, his blue eyes twinkling (either that, she thought, or the perceived twinkle was a trick of the sun).

As they walked along the parterre, her stomach leapt out of her body, trotting along on the ground ahead of her a few steps until she caught up with it.

They stepped inside the building's vestibule, the grand gallery a marvel of iron and glass, with scarcely a pillar, wall, or alcove untouched by elaborate scrollwork.

The entrance to the horological exhibit was twin pillars capped with clocks. Timepieces of every size, handmade and machine-made from all over the world, were laid out row after row.

They stopped before an enormous grandfather clock, and Christophe snickered.

"When I was young—*very* young, maybe even before school—I thought that if I moved the hands of a clock in the opposite direction, I could reverse time." He rolled his eyes with a grin. "One afternoon, I'd gotten in some trouble. Knocked over my father's inkwell after climbing atop his desk and ruined some of his papers. As punishment, I wasn't allowed to go outside and play. To my young mind on a summer day, that was the equivalent of being confined to a dungeon. So I thought if I could change the time, I might be able to go back to earlier in the day before it had happened."

Nathalie laughed. "Clever, even then."

"Maybe not that clever," he said, shrugging. "It didn't work, that's for certain."

They looked at a few more glass-encased exhibits, many of them involving complicated temperature and pressure readings that she didn't understand. She sensed Christophe didn't, either, so she didn't feel too badly.

A question danced its way into her mind, and even though she wasn't sure it was a suitable one to ask, she did. She had a feeling that if she didn't, the query might dance and dance until she gave it words. "If you *could* go back in time, what would you change?"

He kept his eyes on what was apparently a very interesting timepiece, all of a sudden. "My sister died tragically, as you know. I wish I could have prevented that somehow. And so many other crimes, wishing I'd been able to contribute something to catch a criminal or catch him sooner. You?"

"Agnès, for sure. I wish I could have done something to save her. And like you, I wish I could have helped sooner. My gift has been useful at times, and not as effective as I wish at others."

And I wish I'd met you before you were betrothed to another. Now Nathalie found that same timepiece suddenly very interesting.

"How professional and noble of us," he said, turning to her with a modest smile. "Wishing we could change time for other people. What about ourselves?"

It had gotten very, very warm in the horological exhibit. Nathalie proceeded to the next glass case, willing her flushed cheeks to unflush.

"I wish I had . . . met certain people at other times in my life, made certain choices. The usual." *Did I just say that out loud?* Her cheeks had to be scarlet by now. "In general, you know. We're on the path we're on, so it all works out well enough. As long as we're happy with the path."

"True," said Christophe, whose cheeks were also tinged with pink. "Any other path, any other change in time, and we wouldn't be here, at this moment, in this conversation."

Nathalie was tempted to make a joke, add some levity to the moment or dismiss it somehow, but she decided against it. She let his words linger, surrounded by markers of time, hoping this memory was never taken from her and never faded.

When they saw everything there was to see in L'Horlogerie, they left the building, and Nathalie wasn't sure what to do next. Part ways? Ask him if he wanted to see something else? Say nothing and see what he proposed, if anything?

Nathalie chose the latter. They walked along the Champ de Mars again as they spoke of the clocks, passing the Fontaine de Coutan and making their way under the Tour Eiffel. As they returned to the entrance of the fair, near the Histoire de l'Habitation Humaine, he paused.

"There are forty-four buildings here," he said. "I don't propose we visit all forty-four, but perhaps we can try some Russian tea from a samovar? I hear it's very good."

The spicy black tea with a hint of strawberry *was* very good. She'd never had tea from something that resembled a silver vase and certainly never with jam spooned into it. And the sweet, buttery cookies served alongside it were delightful.

They meandered for a few minutes among the architectural dwellings designed to tell the story of how humans lived, from the earliest times until the Renaissance, all over the world. They walked through the Japan, Persia, Africa, and Greco-Roman exhibits before she saw someone reading a newspaper.

She *did* have a morgue report to submit. And, given that she was so inspired, she wanted to write a short piece about the horological exhibit. Maybe M. Patenaude would consider running it.

Reluctantly, Nathalie suggested they part ways, and soon after, they did. Christophe apologized for having taken up so much of her time, a sentiment she quickly refuted.

"It's I who have taken up too much of yours," she said. "That's what you get for strolling the grounds with someone ever-so-curious about ever-so-everything."

Later that night, as she wrote about the day's events in her journal, she wondered if it had been a coincidence. Or had he merely portrayed it that way? Perhaps he wanted to make sure she was well, or perhaps he felt sorry about her memory loss.

Or maybe he just wanted to see some of the Exposition on a splendid June day.

It didn't matter, she decided. And she didn't really want to know. She was just happy the afternoon was what it was, and for once, chose not to think too, *too* much about why.

The policemen rushing past Nathalie and Jules in the sewer were indeed investigating a report of another headless body. It was a false lead; the next morning as she entered the morgue, she learned from an unusually solemn M. Soucy that the body of the female victim had been found in a trunk outside a hotel in the 7th arrondissement.

The woman's body was not on display. Yet Nathalie was astounded to see the body of the first victim, and several centimeters above it, his severed head. She had no recollection of having seen his face before, but it was consistent with the notes she'd taken and she recognized the clothes from Autopsy—except for the bloody white scarf that had been wrapped around the base of his neck. Now it hung, along with the rest of his garb, behind him.

Two years of writing the morgue report and assisting with murder cases, and still she couldn't take her eyes off this corpse, body and head reunited.

I touched that head. That poor man's bloody head fell off a pedestal in the Palais des Beaux-Arts and I caught it. Lost two days of my life because of it.

Nathalie looked down at her hands, no longer cold and feeling normal once again; the chill had left her, at last. She couldn't reconcile those hands and that head, the one over there on the other side of the glass, held by them. These same hands that gave her visions and wrote morgue reports and helped Papa knead bread at times.

Visions. Would she have one now? No, certainly not, and a swift touch of the viewing pane confirmed as much.

She observed the other visitors. They, too, were riveted, unable or unwilling to move along until prompted by M. Soucy. Many of them were tourists, from what she could overhear.

Welcome to Paris. Never mind the Exposition. The real show was here, among the dead.

Christophe had maintained that they weren't going to display either of these victims, though, so as not to prolong fixation on the deaths. What had changed?

"The mind of Prefect of Police Lozé," Christophe explained several minutes later when she was in his office. "Thanks in part to Monsieur Patenaude's dear friend, Monsieur Bennett."

"Oh," said Nathalie with a frown. Christophe's use of "friend" was facetious, for the American M. Bennett was no friend to

M. Patenaude. He wasn't an enemy—M. Patenaude was too savvy to get in public feuds—but the relationship was distant at best. Joseph Gordon Bennett, eccentric editor of the Paris edition of the *New York Herald,* lived an extravagant life and, as Papa might say, "was very pleased with his mother's son." As an American, Bennett was, M. Patenaude had said, "utterly indifferent to the perception of France by the rest of the world."

"Lozé was recently seen at one of Bennett's aristocratic soirées on his Versailles estate, conversing with the editor at length." Christophe held up his hands, a gesture that so often reflected his status as a liaison. Although he was by nature very diplomatic, Nathalie could tell when being an intermediary exasperated him. "Several privy to that conversation say it's not unrelated to the fact that the Prefect of Police now believes 'the morgue should enhance what's been reported.' And that 'Paris would look weak' if it tried to hide this for the sake of the Exposition."

Nathalie folded her arms. Meddling American and his fancy parties (although truthfully she would quite like to attend one, just to see what the nobility *did* at parties). "What about the woman, this monster's 'queen'?"

"We *may* have an identification," Christophe said, holding up a finger. "Someone is coming by today. Somehow we've managed to keep this one out of the papers; so as far as people know, there's only one victim."

Nathalie wanted to ask, but also didn't, her next question. "Has Gabrielle returned?"

"Only to tell me that she needs more time to think about getting involved." Christophe shifted in his seat. "She suffered significant numbness in her feet after the first vision—it worsened as the day went on—and she declined to help with the second."

"I dislike her."

"Yes, I know. You've mentioned that."

Didn't he realize that Gabrielle was perhaps not all that necessary? Maybe even more trouble than she was worth?

Nathalie had a small memory gap of yesterday, owing to the wasted vision of the man killed in a fight. She lost some time in the early evening when she'd reclined to read the French translation of *The Woman in White*. At some point while reading, she didn't recall opening the book, much less being on page sixteen. She would much rather have forgotten her rendezvous with Gabrielle.

Christophe stood and took a volume of photographs from the shelf.

"I want to show you something," he said, opening the book to the most recent page. "Look here."

He pointed to the naked torsos of the victims, above the stomachs to the left. Both had a small hole in nearly the same place.

"We saw that yesterday on the man," she said, shaking her head. "Dr. Nicot said it was postmortem but didn't know what caused it."

"Now we do: a nail. We found one in the trunk with the woman's body, and it fits. Undoubtedly it fell out. It's possible that the man's also did and that it's sitting at the bottom of the Paris sewer."

Nathalie stared at the photos. "Nails. Why?"

"That's the mystery," said Christophe. "Or rather, one of them."

16

The female victim, Camille Bertrand, was identified that day, as Christophe had supposed. She was thirty-nine years old and from a well-to-do Paris family, a widowed socialite known to dwell in the opium dens for days at a time, a secret her wealthy family spent a good deal of time hiding. When she didn't turn up after a few days, they began to worry and checked with the police, who directed them to the morgue. The family made a donation to the Daughters of Charity of Saint Vincent de Paul in the name of discretion, and it was agreed upon that no connection to the other guillotine victim would be made.

The male victim was, as suspected, a tourist from Italy. Enzo Farini was forty-three and here visiting the Exposition with a group, and he'd been displeased with the hotel and moved to another. He was to rejoin the group on the return trip by train, and when he didn't report to the station, inquiries were made that eventually led to the police. Farini's wife had been sent a telegram and came to Paris the next day.

Newspaper coverage varied in salaciousness. *Le Petit Journal* adopted a tone of grave concern but reiterated the wonders of the Exposition, as before. *Le Figaro de la Tour* took advantage of its vantage point and relative proximity to the murder and focused on profiling the Palais des Beaux-Arts overall, complete with a map indicating which pedestal Farini's head was on. Bennett's Paris edition of the *New York Herald*, in a somewhat superior tone, postulated as to the who, how, and why of both the murder and the rumored use of a guillotine. ("A leak from the police, apparently," Christophe conjectured.)

"The Exposition will survive," said Simone, several days later. "People came to see the Tour Eiffel, among other wonders. They aren't going to scatter because of a murder."

"And they don't know there's been two," Louis added. "If they're frightened away, there's that much more room for us."

Nathalie and Jules had arrived at Simone's apartment a few minutes before, Louis handing them a glass of wine almost as soon as they came in. The four of them settled into the modest and not-all-that-tidy parlor, discussing their Exposition plans for the evening. The Galerie des Machines, some food, the fireworks, and finally, a trip up the illuminated Tour Eiffel after dark.

"How lost do you think we can get?" asked Louis.

Jules tapped the stem of his glass. "Is that a rhetorical question or an invitation to go where we shouldn't be?"

"Both." Louis winked.

"*Nous verrons cela*," said Jules.

"Yes, we will see about that," said Simone. Then she clapped eagerly and stood. "Now, I have a surprise for you."

"Three surprises, in fact," added Louis, rising as well. "Close your eyes."

Jules threw him a suspicious look. "Are we going to like these surprises?"

"Two for sure," Simone said with a giggle. "We'll see about the third."

Nathalie and Jules reclined on the (always dusty) sofa, eyes shut. Two pairs of footsteps left the room.

"The wine relaxed me," she whispered to Jules. "If they're gone too long, I might fall asleep."

Jules responded by pretending to snore, and they laughed before slipping into patient silence. Then Nathalie heard a squeak, a peep of a sound she couldn't place. Or was the wine getting to her? The footfall returned once again.

"Ready?" asked Louis. "Put out your hands."

Nathalie obeyed, and something very soft, tiny, and warm was placed in her palms.

Mew!

She opened her eyes and grinned. Both she and Jules were holding adorable black-and-white kittens.

"Say hello to Max," said Simone, bursting with joy. "Named after our favorite café."

Louis patted the kitten trying to crawl out of Jules's hands. "And that's Lucy. She's named after a character in my poem, the one published in *Le Chat Noir*'s journal last month about a beguiling girl with freckles on her nose. That cute ink spot"—he pointed to the kitten's nose—"reminded me of that."

Jules endured a swat on the cheek and gave the kitten a hug.

Nathalie kissed Max on the head. "*Merci!* Stanley could use a playmate. I can keep him, right?"

"Of course you can't." Simone playfully stepped on her shoe. "But you can visit them anytime!"

All four of them cooed over the kittens, which Simone had gotten from a neighbor, until the baby cats mewed to be put down. Simone collected them with hugs and kisses and returned them to the bedroom.

"Is that surprise number one or number one and number two?" Jules held up one finger on one hand and two on the other.

"One and two," Louis said as Simone came back into the room. "The third is pending."

He poured the rest of the wine into their glasses. Nathalie sipped, indulging in the way it subtly slowed down her often-busy mind. A short while later, when all four glasses were empty, Louis got up and took another bottle from the wine rack. (Simone didn't have much furniture; she did have a wine rack, though.)

"Thank you, but I don't need any more," said Nathalie, sliding her glass away. "I've had enough for now."

"As have I." Jules put his glass beside Nathalie's.

Louis stood at the table, back to them as he opened the bottle. "Oh, this is different, my friends," he said, calling over his shoulder.

Nathalie glanced at Simone. She and Louis were nineteen, and they frequented clubs and were generally more attuned to fashionable food and drink. "What kind is it?"

"That's surprise number three," she purred.

Mild annoyance brushed over Nathalie. If it was such a surprise, why didn't they serve it first?

Louis came over, poured generously into the four glasses, and returned the bottle to the dining table. Simone picked up her glass and drank, then smacked her lips.

Jules reached for his glass. "Is it very expensive?" He sniffed the wine. "Some extraordinary vintage?"

"Try it," said Louis as he took a sip of his own.

Relenting with a shrug, Jules put the glass to his lips. He took a hesitant taste. "Doesn't taste much different from the other."

Louis and Simone shared a sly smile.

Now all eyes were on Nathalie. Simone nudged the glass toward her. "Well?"

Nathalie shook her head. "Well, I don't *want* any. Especially if you're keeping it a secret as to why it's so special."

"I promise I'll tell you. Please try it. You don't have to finish it—Louis may have poured too much. Have just a taste. For me?" Simone did the puppy look she'd perfected over the years.

Where was that stillness Nathalie had been enjoying a few minutes ago?

Maybe another few sips would bring it back. And she didn't want to cause a fuss and change the mood of an evening out just because she resisted some wine.

That pout of Simone's. It worked on her like a magic trick every time.

How could it hurt to have another two or three sips?

"If it's that important to you for me to have a sip of mysterious wine, then so be it." With an exaggerated sigh, she picked up her glass. "Never let it be said that Simone Marchand is not persuasive."

"*Santé!*" Simone raised her glass and they all repeated the toast.

It was good enough wine, Nathalie thought after her first sip, nothing exceptional. Not wanting to offend, she complimented the taste. Jules followed suit, remarking on the finish.

"So, what's the surprise?" asked Nathalie.

Louis retrieved the bottle from the table and came back displaying the label for them. Nathalie inspected it. *Vin de coca.* She'd never had it, but she knew the combination of wine and coca leaves made for a powerful concoction. "Like Vin Tonique Mariani?"

"Stronger, apparently. Someone brought it into the club last week, made at home or something along those lines," said Simone, swirling the wine in her glass. "We tried this side by side with Mariani, and the claim was valid."

Nathalie peeked inside her glass, as if the wine would have visual indicators of its effects. "What makes it different from other wine?"

"Don't you want to find out?" Louis arched a brow.

She didn't. And she did.

It might have been the temptation of friends, or it might have been the groundwork laid by the preceding glass of wine. But Nathalie was intrigued and decided she would take three sips, no more.

17

They continued drinking and talked about the Exposition, with Louis sharing what he'd seen the previous day at the Forestry Pavilion. After she reached three sips, Nathalie opted to make it five. Relaxation had overtaken her once again. So had something else.

At the start, it was imperceptible. Nathalie thought everyone was speaking more loudly. Jules sneezed twice in a row, and she was suddenly enamored with his left ear. It really was perfectly formed, like the golden mean applied to an ear.

Simone was chuckling and weeping at the same time; she'd nearly finished her glass. Nathalie took a few more sips (she'd stopped counting) and listened as Louis spoke very quickly (was he even speaking French?) about some count named Montesquiou-Something who had a jewel-encrusted pet turtle. But she was still thinking about Jules's ear and how after Louis was done talking and Simone was done laugh-crying, she was going to mention something about his ear. And then maybe after that, she'd suggest they conduct a séance, because why not?

Nathalie took the final gulp of her wine and put down the glass. Or tried to, because someone had moved the table since she last picked up the wine glass and her aim was off. She caught it, barely, and shook her head. When she did, the room spun, and the fleur-de-lis pattern on Simone's chair danced in circles. She steadied herself on Jules's arm, even though she was sitting. Probably a séance wasn't a good idea after all.

"Is something the matter?" Jules turned to her, then squinted.

"I think I can hear you breathing. Is that you breathing?" He looked at Louis. "Or is that you?"

"I certainly am breathing, Jules. We all are. Otherwise we would be in the morgue and not Simone's apartment." Nathalie laughed as she finished the sentence.

"Wait," said Louis, standing, "only if we didn't know who you were. We do, and we're right here, so there's nothing to worry about. And before too long we're going to be at the Exposition and not in Simone's apartment."

Simone guffawed. "Louis! You are so *cheeky*!" Then she pinched his behind.

They all doubled over in laughter.

Just then, the two kittens tumbled over one another into the room.

Two kittens or four?

Two. Indisputably two.

Jules finished his wine and called to the cats. "Maximus and Lucille!"

"It's Max and Lucy," said Simone, purposely loud (Nathalie assumed).

Louis walked over to the wine bottle and brought it over, adding a splash to each glass until the bottle was empty. "*Au revoir, vin de coca.*"

"Did you like it?" Simone's eyes were glassy.

Nathalie was not interested in shaking her head again, the last instance not having gone very well. "No and yes. I don't know. Ask me tomorrow."

"We thought it might make for an interesting trip to the Exposition," added Louis.

And it did.

Nathalie couldn't remember how they got there. Not because of a memory loss, but because things were . . . hazy. There was a crowd, then there was an omnibus and some more laugh-crying by Simone, and then somehow they were at the Exposition Universelle.

The exterior of the Galerie des Machines was a towering mass of mosaics and colored glass, and the overwhelming iron-and-glass expansiveness of the interior had the four of them gaping for half a minute before proceeding. With many diversions and a not-very-logical path, they explored the technological exhibits. The building covered over eighty thousand square meters, according to Jules. (He was a repository of such facts, although Nathalie wondered if the *vin de coca* had him spouting the wrong number.) In any event, it was enormous with lots of iron and whirring machines and engineering devices she didn't understand—even without the *vin de coca*—but appreciated nevertheless. Her favorite were the phonographs, a name she thought most amusing, which spouted "Vive la France!" and some patriotic music. This Thomas Edison inventor the newspapers lauded was most clever.

They tried several doors for personnel only; all were locked. They did come across one unattended door slightly ajar and, alas, there was nothing of interest there but storage.

Louis shut the door with a disappointed sigh. "You would think, with sixteen thousand machines, there'd be something of interest in an open door."

"It's all out on the floor," said Jules.

"These machines are making me dizzy," said Simone, rubbing her temples. "Can we go see something else?"

For a short time between the Galerie des Machines and the Galerie de la Bijouterie et la Joaillerie, where Simone told Louis to get her a necklace like the one with a hand-sized gem she saw on display, Jules lingered too long at the all-chocolate Venus de Milo exhibit and lost them. When he caught up with them, he said he'd run into someone he knew. Nathalie forgot who almost as soon as he said it; she and Simone were much more interested in discussing the Imperial Diamond (thirty carats was too big, they decided).

From there, they went to the Galerie de la Chasse, Pêche, and Cueillette, where each of them did impersonations of the animals attacking hunters, instead of the other way around. Afterward, they went outside and sat on the steps to take in the fireworks, with Louis receiving no shortage of Simone elbows for asking "What cracker is this same that deafs our ears?" too many times. Louis insisted that it was a Shakespeare quote, and Simone insisted that she didn't care.

By the time they made it past the illuminated Fontaine de Coutan—which was more magical than Nathalie had envisioned—to the base of the Tour Eiffel, the effects of the wine had begun to wear off. Riding the elevator to the second platform proved to be a moderately terrifying experience that had Simone squealing not once but twice (to the dismay of her fellow passengers, including Nathalie), though once Nathalie got off, she realized it wasn't so scary. As they took another elevator to the top, the lights of the tower came on, dotting the outline of the structure.

"How far do you think we'll be able to see?" asked Nathalie as they stepped off.

Before Jules could answer, she saw for herself.

The moonlit city gleamed in every direction, speckled with gaslamps. The Seine made a dark, swirling path through it all, overseen by silhouetted trees and stately buildings. Simone and Louis took in the sight, shoulders touching. Nathalie got closer to Jules, and he put his arm around her waist, hugging her close. A cocoon of wind surrounded them, somehow comforting.

"My goodness," she said, turning to him, "it's—"

"Beautiful?" he said, ending the sentiment with a tender kiss. It wasn't their first, but it warmed her heart in a new way. Here, above Paris, how could it not?

When they left the Exposition, reluctantly conceding defeat to fatigue, they took the ferry across the Seine.

"Look at that," said Simone, leaning against the rail. She pointed to the right of the Tour Eiffel. "A lot of commotion over there, off in the distance."

Louis rested his chin on her shoulder. "Hmmm. People are shouting something. Can you make it out?"

The ferry was too far away, though, for anything except the faintest of cries to be heard.

"Should we go back," suggested Jules, "and see what's going on?"

Nathalie yawned. "I'd like to, but I am exhausted. As it is, we stayed out too late."

The others regretfully agreed with the sentiment. They watched the activity around the Exposition grounds until it was time to disembark. "Whatever it is," said Simone, "we probably can't get close enough to see, anyway."

They walked together for a while, then parted ways on weary feet.

Nathalie went to bed that night, full of affection for Jules, for her friends, for Paris, for France.

The effect did not last.

She woke up the next morning with a maddening headache and no appetite, and for a moment, she wasn't sure she was awake.

Because it couldn't be real, or at least she didn't want to believe it. The edition of *Le Petit Journal* in Papa's hand could have been a dream, or it could have been the delayed effects of the *vin de coca*.

But no, she was awake and sober, and this was the truth. The commotion they'd seen from the ferry, the activity they were too tired to return to and too far away to see.

Man's Body, Severed Head Found at Exposition:
Grisly Nighttime Discoveries at Uruguay,
Guatemala Pavilions;
Bloodied White Scarf Returns

18

Snippets of the article repeated themselves to Nathalie as she made her way to the morgue just over an hour later.

> The man's head donned a jester's cap. With hair cropped *à la Titus* like Enzo Farini of the Palais des Beaux-Arts, it was surrounded by a deck of cards.
>
> We received a tip that a female victim was discovered the same day as Farini, at the Fontaine de Coutain, depicted as a "queen." Several trustworthy sources have confirmed this, but the victim's identity is unknown.
>
> A king, a queen, and now a jester?
>
> Three balls, of the sort used for juggling, lay near the victim's hand.

To make sure everyone knew the head in the Guatemala Pavilion went with the body in the Uruguay Pavilion. As if there'd be any mistake along those lines.

She hadn't seen these pavilions yet, but the newspaper suggested they were an "ideal location for such diabolical stealth," being situated behind the vast Palais des Arts Libéraux with numerous trees surrounding each.

Yet for all that spectacle, the victim wasn't on display at the morgue. Had the decision from last time been repealed, despite the public nature of the discovery? Was it not there yet? Or was the man's body still in Autopsy?

She had her answers shortly after M. Cadoret opened the Medusa door for her. Before she could ask a single question, Gabrielle walked out of Autopsy, followed by Christophe.

I see she changed her mind about getting involved.

Christophe caught Nathalie's eye and motioned for her to follow them into his office. Gabrielle waved, a sheepish smile on her face. Nathalie walked down the hall, tempted to peek at what was behind the Autopsy door Christophe had just shut. She took a seat next to Gabrielle in the office—which now had, she was disappointed to note, *three* chairs instead of two—and told them she'd already read the newspaper.

"I sent for all three of you this morning. Jules is on his way. The courier left for you not long ago, so he's on an empty errand." Christophe rarely sent for Nathalie, given that she was at the morgue daily anyway for her column. Only if it was urgent and she had the day off or had otherwise communicated plans to be there late in the day, like the day Camille Bertrand's head was discovered in the Fontaine de Coutan. "Once again we'll be putting the body on display. Prefect of Police Lozé was adamant about that and doesn't want a controversy on his hands. As it is, news of Camille Bertrand got out, and we have all we can do to keep the details and her identity obscured."

Gabrielle stroked her amethyst ring. "Would there really be public outcry?"

"The police and some of the newspapers have one set of interests. The government and the organizers of the Exposition Universelle have another," Christophe said, opening an envelope and sorting through the contents. He took a pen and prepared to write on one of the documents. "To hide what was already on display, so to speak, is asking for trouble."

Before Christophe could proceed any further, Jules arrived. Nathalie had already told him about her initial encounter with Gabrielle, and she could see that it colored his impression of her. His greeting was stiff, more formal than usual. Even to Nathalie.

He stood behind her chair and rested his hands on it as Christophe described, for the benefit of Jules and Gabrielle, each of their abilities and how they could help.

"Three Insightfuls working on the case," remarked Christophe, smiling. "This is a police liaison's dream."

Nathalie glanced at Jules, who was fidgety, and at Gabrielle, who seemed both ill at ease and disinterested. Where Christophe saw a team, she saw herself alongside two people who did not want to be there.

"First," began Christophe, "I should note that the Guatemalan and Uruguayan representatives were interrogated and released. The police have no reason to think they were involved in the murder. Whoever is behind this knows Paris very well, which rules out any Exposition representatives here for the first time, really."

Nathalie and the others agreed.

Christophe continued, tugging the end of his sleeves. "Second, Gabrielle has decided that she would like to work with us in a limited, as-needed capacity for this case. She's already done her path tracing and was about to provide details."

Gabrielle's deep blue eyes landed on each of them, one at a time, like a quick drumbeat. The resentfulness she'd shown in their prior meeting had slipped away, only shy civility in its place. "This was in the same area as before, the seventh arrondissement, maybe the sixth. He exited a public place where people go in and leave at the same time—a concert hall, theater, church perhaps." She cast her gaze down, concentration pinching her face. "Then he moved on to a restaurant or bar just down the street, but it wasn't the same one the other victim had patronized. He left the establishment, footing unsteady, and paused to get his bearings. He went back the route he came and . . . and it went dark for me after that."

Christophe finished writing down what she said. "Thank you, Gabrielle. I recognize what an effort it was for you to make the decision to come here." He flashed Gabrielle a smile before turning to Nathalie and Jules. "Now, who'd like to go next?"

"I will," said Jules in an oddly discourteous manner. He cut in before Nathalie had a chance to open her mouth. She was going to suggest Jules go first anyway, and that she wait until the corpse was put in the display room, but even so. This wasn't the first time Christophe ever posed this question to them; however, it *was* the first time she could recall Jules not turning to her. What if she had somewhere to go and needed to provide her vision next?

Gabrielle leaned forward, placing her fingertips on Christophe's desk. "*Pardonnez-moi*, may I leave now? I'm due at the library soon. My feet aren't numb yet, and I'd like to walk there before that sets in." Gabrielle's voice was forlorn, so much so that Nathalie comprehended, more than she had the other day, how much this drained her. She reminded Nathalie of a schoolgirl asking the teacher's permission to get her coat because she was too cold.

"Certainly," said Christophe, his imperfect tooth showing with his smile. "I'll see you out."

Gabrielle said farewell, and Christophe escorted her out. As soon as they left the room, Nathalie turned to Jules and dropped her voice. "I told you she was peculiar."

"I don't know. I didn't get much of an impression either way. She wasn't rude. More like resigned. She isn't comfortable with her power, as you said." Jules sat in the chair beside Nathalie, pressing his palms into his eyes.

She watched him for a moment. "How are you feeling today? You seem—distraught, nervous. Not yourself. Did something happen at home? Was Faux Papa after you?"

"He was out gambling last night. He wasn't even awake when I left this morning. Not that."

Nathalie expected him to elaborate, to say why his behavior was so out of sorts. He remained there, palms still over his eyes, without saying a word. She moved her chair closer to him. "I feel some effects from that *vin de coca*, I think. I haven't eaten a thing, and I still have a headache."

"I'm not hungry, either. No headache. Just . . . extraordinarily agitated. I slept poorly. The *vin de coca*, I suppose. If I were inclined to bite my nails, I wouldn't have any left by now."

Christophe appeared in the doorway. "Now then. Shall we?"

Jules picked up his head and stood. His eyes looked bleary; it was clear his thoughts were elsewhere. He *was* prone to irritability when he didn't get much sleep.

They followed Christophe into Autopsy. The man's body was on the table, covered in a sheet from feet to neck. The decapitated head was placed several centimeters above the neck, as when Enzo Farini's body was on display. He was perhaps in his thirties, bearded with a square face and a thin, pointy nose. His clothes hung on the wall, nondescript evening clothes that were neither finely cut nor shabby. It was difficult to gauge stature when a body was in repose, but it seemed to Nathalie that he was on the shorter side. He looked like a man who should be gathering with his friends tonight after leaving the factory or who would be on a ship with Papa next month, not a decapitated murder victim.

But then, who did resemble what people envisioned when they conceived of a murder victim?

Everyone and no one, which was what Nathalie could never reconcile.

Dr. Nicot straightened out a pair of scissors. "We're about to move the body into the display room, unless you need a moment."

"We do," said Christophe. The medical examiner excused himself and stepped out.

Christophe pulled the sheet down to the man's stomach.

Beside the rib cage was a hole the diameter of a nail.

Nathalie made eye contact with Christophe, who gave her a knowing nod. "We know something else about this now. I'll explain later. Are you ready, Jules?"

He mumbled a "yes" without breaking his gaze from the corpse. Nathalie watched his Adam's apple ripple as he swallowed. He took slow, measured steps toward the head.

Nathalie had been discomfited when she first observed Jules

using his power. It was disturbing in its weirdness, and it made her uncomfortably cognizant of how she must have appeared. People in the display room who happened to notice her—as discreet as she aimed to be—seemed bothered afterward, having seen something that was as unnatural as it was natural, whether they guessed she was endowed with magic or not.

Jules's hands quivered as he placed them on the man's head, eyes shut, and exhaled. His eyelids fluttered, and he made a sound akin to stammering, trying to force out words that wouldn't go.

When he was done, he stepped back. The blood drained from his face and he was paler than the sheet. "His mother. The man was—was thinking about his mother." Jules kept his eyes on the corpse. "The smell of a laundry. He was fixated on that smell. Chess, he was forced to play chess. And his killer was boasting"—he paused, making eye contact with Christophe—"about being the descendant of an executioner."

Christophe slapped his hands together. "That's a tremendous lead!"

"Well done, *mon bonbon*," said Nathalie. Maybe this case would be solved sooner rather than later. Maybe it wasn't another Dark Artist or Jack the Ripper.

"Thank you," he said, mopping some sweat from his brow.

Nathalie took a step toward him. "Are you feeling worse than you've let on?"

"I—I think the *vin de coca* is still affecting me somehow."

Christophe looked from Jules to Nathalie. "*Vin de coca?*"

"Simone and Louis gave us some," said Nathalie, refusing to meet Christophe's stare of incredulity. "Something someone made at Le Chat Noir and it was, well, you know. Strong. With effects that were thrilling at the time but ultimately . . . disagreeable."

"I've not tried any, but from what I hear, it's not the mildest beverage to imbibe." Christophe spoke in a faltering voice. "Are you, uh, in the habit of drinking that? Either of you?"

Nathalie examined her fingernails. "No, we aren't. I didn't

want to, but I'd already had a glass of wine and . . . yielded. This was my first and last time. And I presume Jules's as well."

Jules murmured in absentminded agreement.

Christophe shook his head, muttering something about "risks" Nathalie tried not to hear, and covered the man's torso with the sheet once again. Tucking in the dead. "Let's allow Dr. Nicot to finish preparing the body for display. While he's doing that, I'll show you what was found with the body. Gabrielle asked not to be involved any more than she had to, but I suspect the two of you will find this most interesting—and familiar."

With the body? The newspaper account didn't mention anything of the sort, only that the head was found in the Guatemala Pavilion and the rest of the body in the Uruguay Pavilion.

When they returned to Christophe's office, he took an envelope and a pair of black gloves from a cabinet and sat in his chair. Nathalie and Jules remained standing. "This," he said, opening the folder, "was affixed to the victim's torso with a nail."

After putting on the gloves, Christophe removed a sheet of parchment paper, stained reddish-brown, from the envelope.

Parchment paper.

Nathalie peered at it from across the desk. "Is that blood?"

Christophe murmured a somber *yes* and slid the paper across the desk for them to read. The handwriting was immaculate, the ink heavy.

JESTER, *while juggling three balls: I went to the tavern last night.*

KING: *And this should surprise or entertain me? You go three nights a week.*

JESTER: *This time I had a glass of wine with Death, that cagey villain. He asked me to tell you that he plans to visit us all very, very soon.*

SUITOR: *Me as well?*

JESTER: *All of us.*

QUEEN: Are you speaking in earnest or in jest?

JESTER catches the three balls and grins.

KING: He's never to be taken seriously. He's a jester, not a fortune-teller.

JESTER: But also an excellent drinking companion. So said Death. He also said not to worry, it will be swift, as if we were going to Place de la Concorde for an evening with La Dame.

QUEEN, hand going to her neck with a nervous laugh: Then we'll station more guards. We aren't just going to walk to the guillotine.

KING: He's only telling a story, my queen. Do you think he'd be so cavalier if he thought his own life was in peril?

JESTER: On the contrary, I am in a state of utter despair. I'm drunk now, can't you tell?

SUITOR, sniffing the JESTER: He smells of drink.

JESTER: It will be painless, Death assured me. We won't know when to expect it.

QUEEN: But why, what have we done?

JESTER, pulling a flask from his belt: It's not what we have done, but what we will do. We have a part to play on the world's most magnificent stage.

19

Nathalie felt her jaw go slack. "A page from a play. On parchment." She pressed her finger over the word *Death*. "What we found in the sewer *did* mean something."

A soggy piece of paper with neat rows and unreadable text. A hole. Block lettering at the start of nearly every line.

Never had she thought it had been nailed to a corpse.

Jules looked up, blinking in apparent disbelief.

"I owe you an apology," Christophe said. "Looks like it wasn't some university student's glossary after all."

She blushed. "I wouldn't have taken it seriously, either."

"The one from the sewer was unreadable. I wouldn't have guessed it was a script," said Jules. He ran a finger under his collar, then spoke again. "Did the killer murder them to match the script or write a script to match the murders?"

Nathalie was pleased to see him draw from his well of natural curiosity for the first time today. It felt more like him, as if he was here and not just fulfilling an obligation the way Gabrielle seemed to be.

"We're still bending our minds around it, as you can imagine." Christophe took the sheet back and smoothed it out. "We don't know if this is something the killer himself wrote or if he transcribed some obscure text. Someone is running it over to scholars at the university as we speak."

"Place de la Concorde and La Dame, obviously a nod to the

Revolution of 1789," said Nathalie. At the Louvre end of Champs-Élysées, where an obelisk now stood, there was once a guillotine. It had been the site of thousands of executions almost a hundred years ago during the Revolution. She thought the attempt to mask the history of the space puzzling; an exotic, stark monument couldn't override its bloody history. "Consistent, too, with Jules's vision."

"You've provided us with an excellent clue, Jules. Thank you."

Nathalie was eager to have her own vision now. Diffident Gabrielle and slow-to-sober Jules had made valuable contributions, and she wanted to do the same. She was, after all, the original Insightful in this morgue.

Jules's fingers drummed the back of a chair. "Multiple references to a jester. Can this be taken seriously, or is the killer trying to make us the fools for believing this?"

Both Nathalie and Christophe remained silent. Anything was possible, wasn't it?

Jules, full of nervous energy, paced the room. Several times he came across as if he were on the cusp of speaking but refrained.

"Christophe?" said Dr. Nicot from the hall. He opened the door a crack. "The victim is in the display room."

"I want to elicit a vision." Nathalie took a step toward the door. It was her turn; she wanted to do this before they spoke any more about it. Christophe nodded, and Jules followed her. Reluctantly or distractedly, she couldn't tell.

Moments later, she was in the morgue viewing room. The queue had been long when she arrived; as news spread of the murder, it would only grow. Mme. Valois would certainly sell a lot of flowers today. Nathalie was glad not to have to stand outside the morgue these days, with the hot summer sun beating down on her for hours. There was no escaping the sweat stench of her fellow morgue-goers, Parisians and Exposition tourists alike, and the crowd in here today reminded her of that.

M. Cadoret stood beside the black velvet curtain in the display room, to the left of the viewing pane. Nathalie made her way to the far right of the glass for added privacy, Jules beside her. She gazed at the corpse she'd just seen in the Autopsy room and placed her hand on the glass.

The dead body that was once a man knelt before her, hands behind his back. His face was a mess of mucus and tears. She could see him sobbing but couldn't hear it.

A piece of paper with writing on it lay on the floor in front of him. Round, wet circles dotted it. Tears. Sweat. Maybe both.

A guillotine blade was poised for release, several meters above his head.

"Please. Please!" the man mouthed.

The killer crouched down. He slid the paper closer to the man and tapped it with a single finger. "Lines," he hissed.

The man picked up his head, sobbing, and choked his way through lines Nathalie could not hear. When he was done, the killer stuffed a rag in his mouth and kissed him on the cheek.

Nathalie stood in the morgue once again. As always, she felt here but not here. She drew a deep breath, relieved she didn't see the guillotine blade release.

"The victim appeared to cry 'please.' In French. Did I say anything?"

"Yes," Jules whispered, "but I couldn't make it out."

"'Lines.' That was all I heard. He wanted the victim to read from the script."

Disgust brushed across Jules's face. He shook his head. "My skin feels like it wants to raise up off me and walk away. Controlling others is obviously part of what drives him."

As Nathalie recounted it all a short while later, Christophe asked her if it was the same room as in the previous visions.

She frowned. "From what I wrote, I believe the answer is yes. I have no direct recollection of them, however."

Christophe looked as if she'd thrown water in his face. "I'm—

I'm sorry, Nathalie. I'm reading through the details I'd noted and I wasn't thinking."

Nathalie pressed her back against the chair. She studied the autopsy print, then the Switzerland one. Everything was off today. Gabrielle had been here, intruding on her realm. Jules had some lingering effects of *vin de coca* that had him out of sorts. And Christophe, ever mindful, had overlooked her memory loss. She wouldn't be so irritable about it if he hadn't had an oversight the other day as well. When she had a vision and gave a piece of her memory, for nothing. Not to mention he'd be disappearing to the Alps soon (Had he said when? Her notes on this were frustratingly vague) for a holiday with his betrothed.

"Did you see a chessboard this time?" Jules asked. "Or any chess pieces? Last time, the victim, Camille, used one to poke the killer in the eye."

"Nothing of that sort."

Christophe dipped his pen in the inkwell. "So this poor soul was the Jester in the 'play,' and Enzo and Camille were the King and Queen. Maybe it has nothing to do with chess."

Jules picked at a hole in a threadbare section of his sleeve. "My thought reading suggested otherwise," he said, not looking up. After a pause, he spoke again. "And the script. We found a piece of the first, no doubt the rest is long gone. What of the second?"

"Perhaps he changed his mind about attaching the second one. It was not in the valise holding the body," Christophe said, returning the pen to the inkwell. He shook his head. "That's not a phrase I have ever said."

Nathalie couldn't imagine opening up a valise and seeing a headless corpse. Who discovered it and how many nightmares had they had since? Her eyes fell on the parchment paper that had been nailed to the Jester.

"Four characters in the script, but three victims . . ." Nathalie didn't finish the thought out loud. It was obvious, and, given the expressions of Jules and Christophe, they all appeared to reach the same conclusion at once.

The next victim would be the Suitor.

If he hadn't already been killed.

Nathalie and Jules parted ways upon leaving the morgue, she for the newspaper and he for the chocolatier. They didn't have the opportunity to talk, both because his hearing was already starting to slip, even sooner than usual, and because he wanted to get there in time to assist with the first batch.

Or so he said.

Nathalie began writing her article on the omnibus (but stopped when a nosy passenger to her left continuously read over her shoulder) and finished at an unoccupied desk on the first floor of *Le Petit Journal*. When she ran it up to M. Patenaude, she shared the morning's news at the morgue. Including her opinion of Gabrielle.

"I don't know the family," he said, taking a seat behind his desk, "although I did hear that her father facilitated this, giving her little choice. If she's misanthropic, try to understand it through that lens. I've known self-loathing Insightfuls, and it's disconcerting to watch. Much like jealousy."

"I feel rather sorry for her, despite having an aversion toward her." Then she realized what M. Patenaude had just said. "Jealousy? You don't think I'm—"

He held up his ink-stained hands. "I'm not going to judge whether you are or aren't."

"In any event," she said, smoothing out a dress that didn't need smoothing, "Jules's vision was promising. It shouldn't take long to identify the descendants of executioners."

"If he wasn't lying."

"Who, Jules?"

"No." M. Patenaude dumped some ashes into a canister. "The killer. Could have been bravado or wishful thinking. After all, he's playing a part himself, isn't he?"

Nathalie considered that, then agreed. "Speaking of which, what if it *is* Jack the Ripper? I mean, what better ruse than to come to Paris and continue killing under a completely different guise? Going after men, too."

"It would be just like an Englishman to ruin the Exposition."

Nathalie laughed, and M. Patenaude shook his head.

"I wasn't joking," he said. "I doubt it's the Ripper, because the style is different—too different. With that in mind, they shouldn't rule out someone who has a grudge against France. It could be a French citizen."

"Which means, once more, that it could be almost anyone."

M. Patenaude took a cigarette out of his case and lit it. "It isn't hard to blend into the crowd in a city of two million with thousands more pouring in for the fair daily. And with all the exhibit and equipment transport, there's plenty of opportunity for moving a body around."

Nathalie hadn't thought of that. In the off-hours, men were always bringing things in and out, making deliveries, and so on.

M. Patenaude's gaze fell on his paperweight, a glass salamander, as he took a puff. "*Le Rasoir*," he said, exhaling a smoke plume. "That's what I'm going to call him in my editorial today."

The Razor. After *Le Rasoir National*, the nickname for the guillotine.

"It's frightful and completely disquieting."

M. Patenaude smirked. "Good."

Although Nathalie hadn't planned on going to the Exposition in the afternoon, she decided to after leaving *Le Petit Journal*.

M. Patenaude told her he was going to publish her piece on the horological exhibit at some point, and they'd talked some about the fair. When he referenced the intriguing beauty of the Aztec palace at the Mexican Pavilion, she decided she had to see it sooner rather than later.

High and steep, it was a structure unlike any of the other pavilions, with broad-faced statues along the exterior and geometric patterns in relief. Over the entrance was a round disc with symbols representing a calendar, if Nathalie remembered correctly. As she walked up the steps, she examined the figures more closely. They weren't all the same. Who did they represent?

She went inside and, having learned a few words of Spanish (which had many similarities to French, at least in spelling), approached one of the men talking to visitors. When he was free, she used a combination of hand gestures and "*Quién?*" to inquire about the statues.

The man responded with several sentences, most of which she did not understand. There were two words that were enough like French to convey what she aimed to learn: *emperadores* and *deidades*. Emperors and deities.

Nathalie thanked the man and walked around the interior, full of books, maps, and figures. Upon leaving, she contemplated visiting the nearby pavilions, but the crowd was thick in that section of the fair. Instead, she took the Decauville train to the Esplanade des Invalides, circling Mexico on her map and adding some notes on the short ride over.

She visited the pavilions of Tunisia and Algeria, both of which enticed her through scent above all else. At Tunisia she had some excellent, rich coffee that her palate welcomed like arms sliding through a favorite coat. In the Algeria Pavilion, a blend of deep, spicy perfumes beckoned to her; she found a musky oil with a touch of amber that appealed to her and bought a jar.

On her way out of the Exposition grounds, Nathalie stopped to survey her surroundings, deciding which route to take home. She took a step back to leave and bumped into someone. Turning to apologize, she found a white-haired woman who smelled of incense staring at her.

"Repent," the woman said. "Save yourself from the eternal flames."

"Sorry, I—"

The woman held a single finger up to her lips, indicating silence. Without a blink, she handed Nathalie a broadside, then turned on her heel and departed.

Nathalie looked at the broadside.

<u>Matthew 24: 24-28</u>

Should anyone say to you, 'Look, here is the Messiah!' or, 'There he is!' do not believe it. False messiahs and false prophets will arise; they will perform signs and wonders so great as to deceive, if that were possible, even the elect.

Behold, I have told it to you beforehand.

If they say to you, 'He is in the desert,' do not go out there; if they say, 'He is in the inner rooms,' believe it not. Just as lightning comes from the east and is seen as far as the west, so will the coming of the Son of Man be.

Wherever the corpse is, there the vultures will gather.

She didn't believe in omens or fate or divination of any sort. Nevertheless, the broadside unsettled her.

And ever so much more so when she turned it over.

The other side had a crudely drawn map of the Exposition grounds with some of the attractions marked, and crosses in three spots.

The Fontaine de Coutan.

The Palais des Beaux-Arts.

The Guatemala Pavilion.

A map, plotted with murders instead of wishes, being handed out like a souvenir.

The memory gap surfaced the next morning, as she was reviewing her journal entries from the past few days. She'd lost some time from the night at the Exposition, when she had ascended to the top platform of the Tour Eiffel with Jules, Simone, and Louis. Sadness washed over her that this memory of something so visual had been taken away. Her mind held on to a mere glimpse of the view, just enough to know she'd had it, just enough to lament that it was pushed into the chasm of wherever it was her memories went. Sometimes, she indulged in a daydream that one day she'd find all those stolen memories, almost like a magical land in an enchanted forest. Almost. A portal to truths she'd lived rather than longings she'd fancied.

She remembered the moment when they reached the summit, then time disappeared again until she was home with her night clothes on and Stanley on the bed (as she was telling him about Max and Lucy).

Her descriptions of Paris from that height, being that high above the city she adored, were as evocative and detailed and immersive as could be. Still, it wasn't the same as experiencing it.

Nonetheless, she knew she could go again—would go again. The Tour Eiffel wasn't going anywhere. It was magnificent and captivating and the epitome of tangible. There would be other visits.

What she was grateful for, however, was what hadn't been taken from her. Her map had been marked and her notes had been made, but it wasn't the same as retaining the feeling of *being at* the fair. Her most recent memories of it were intact. Her perspective had expanded some, enough to show her that there was so, so much more to learn, see, and do in the world. No wonder Papa loved the sea.

20

Beheaded Victim Was Parisian Actor

The third victim of Le Rasoir was Parisian actor Timothy St. Martin, age 34. St. Martin had been on hiatus from acting after recovering from an illness but most recently appeared as the Fool in *King Lear*. Police, for reasons they cannot yet reveal, believe St. Martin may have been chosen because of that role.

Le Petit Journal didn't elaborate, because the script was to be kept confidential. For now. The newspaper noted how the crowds hadn't deviated, despite three gruesome murders in the city:

> . . . one might even surmise that the Exposition Universelle has flourished because of this series of events, a grim rival to the Whitechapel murders in London last fall. France has put on such an admirable display of innovation and progress that not only are crowds undeterred in their quest to see it, they may even be enjoying the macabre excitement.
>
> Several international visitors spoke to us with the aid of an interpreter.
>
> "I came with a group and we travel together at all times. I feel safe," said a visitor from India. "We have even gone to the morgue."
>
> A tourist from Sweden considered it intriguing: "So much mystery! Each day, I look forward to the newspapers to see if anything else has happened."

Not everyone expresses such optimism or fascination with the dark events of the city.

"I've never been so ashamed of my country or my city. I myself am not unfamiliar with debauchery, but debauchery is not criminal," said a Parisian who wished to remain anonymous, save to note that he holds the title of duke. "That we can't solve this crime is an embarrassment."

Police are pursuing several leads, including the possibility that this murderer may be the descendant of an executioner.

A week passed without any more murders—and without much more information.

Mme. Valois had an abundance of flowers one day at the morgue, presumably to accommodate the tremendous crowds; her arms were so full of blooms, she could hardly carry them all. Nathalie bought two bouquets. One for Maman and one for Aunt Brigitte.

She stopped at home, then brought Aunt Brigitte some pink and orange flowers. The delight on Aunt Brigitte's face warmed Nathalie's heart. Her aunt was afforded so few pleasures in the dreary asylum that Nathalie was happy to bring some of the outside world to her.

"They smell like life. Like spring," Aunt Brigitte said. She peeked over Nathalie's shoulder at her slumbering roommate, and Nathalie's eyes followed. Véronique looked like a sad schoolteacher or someone's grandmother, not a woman who'd killed her neighbor.

"That one," Aunt Brigitte said, pointing to the woman for emphasis, "got in trouble for picking flowers in the courtyard."

The Saint-Mathurin Asylum courtyard, the only time outside patients had. A few hours a week of seeing the sun, clouds, and sky without barred windows to intersect the view. Véronique had been a gardener, as Nathalie recalled from the newspapers. She wanted to tell Aunt Brigitte that but refrained.

"My friend Simone and I once picked flowers from the window box of a neighbor across the street," whispered Nathalie. "We got in trouble, too."

Aunt Brigitte inspected the wooden vase. "Is this your mother's vase? I like the markings on it."

"Maman bought it at the Greece Pavilion at the Exposition. It's olive wood. She said you can have it; she'll buy another."

"Eh, the martinet denies us everything." Aunt Brigitte pointed to the corridor with disgust. "She's always confiscating something."

The "martinet" was Nurse Clement, the newly appointed head of the ward who maintained order with efficient pleasantness. Nathalie didn't bring glass or ceramic, because anything that could be used as a weapon or could cause injury was forbidden. A wooden one might not pass muster, either, but it was the only other thing she had at home.

"I'll ask her when I leave," said Nathalie, sitting in the uncomfortable chair near the bed. "If she doesn't approve, I'll ask if she can find something else for your flowers."

Satisfied, Aunt Brigitte set the vase on her nightstand and began to pet the flowers. "I had a dog once, a brown and white spotted boy. Not too big, not too small. He had long ears, soft as velvet. Did you ever meet him?"

"No, Tante. I didn't even know you had a dog." She learned about her aunt in pieces, here and there. Memories Papa shared, slivers of the past Aunt Brigitte revealed when she was lucid and in the mood. "Tell me about him."

But she didn't. She continued petting the flowers for some time, as though she'd forgotten Nathalie was there. And then, "I dream about him sometimes."

"Do you? Good dreams, I hope."

Aunt Brigitte turned to Nathalie with a grimace. "No. I haven't had a good dream since before you were born."

Nathalie smiled, the sort of smile you gave someone when you had no words yet wanted to convey empathy. No wonder madness had overtaken her aunt. Wouldn't nightmares every night for twenty years do that to anyone?

Taking a page from Maman's book of etiquette, she diverted the conversation back to where it had been. "What was your dog's name?"

"Choupinet." Aunt Brigitte sat up straight, crossing her legs in front of her like a little girl. Her shirt lifted up, showing her belly scarred with miniature crosses, so many of them it looked like one of Maman's patterns. It was something she'd done years ago, branding herself in a fit of religious fury just prior to going to the asylum, when she was living at Madame Plouffe's home. Nathalie remembered the day she had first seen those crosses as a child, how frightened she'd been.

"He was such a good dog. He loved to sit on my feet." Aunt Brigitte heaved a sigh. She clasped her fingers together and closed her eyes.

Nathalie let her be. Sometimes her aunt ceased to engage, like a door closing out the clamor of a room. After a few minutes, Aunt Brigitte would come back from whatever reverie she was taking.

The room was still, save for the tranquil breeze rippling the curtain. Nathalie shifted her position in the chair, causing a floorboard to creak. It echoed back in the otherwise silent room.

Even Véronique was quiet. No talking in her sleep, no snoring. Nathalie's eyes drifted to her bed. She was tucked under the sheet, sleeping on her side, face shrouded in a mass of blankets. It was a wonder she wasn't hot; Nathalie herself had broken a sweat despite the open window.

She kept her eyes on the woman. She stared for a few counts but didn't see the familiar rise and fall of a sleeping body in repose.

Nathalie stood, creaking the floorboard again. Véronique didn't stir. With gentle footfall, Nathalie stepped closer. She still couldn't see the woman's face.

Aunt Brigitte yawned. Nathalie glanced over; Tante's eyes remained closed.

Angling herself closer to the woman's bed, Nathalie leaned over until the sleeping face came into view. It was purple.

She lurched toward Véronique's neck to loosen the blankets, and in an instant the room fell away.

And yet it didn't. She was still in the room, crossing over to the bed, but the door was closed.

Véronique was snoring.

Nathalie approached the bed and, with hands that weren't her own, slipped the pillow out from under the woman's head without waking her.

In one swift motion, she put the pillow over Véronique's face.

After a few beats the woman startled awake and flailed. She clawed at the hands that pressed the pillow down, harder and harder, until her body went limp.

The murderer walked across the room, opening the door on her way past it, and got into her own bed.

When she returned to the present, her hands were still on Véronique's neck, loosening sheets that didn't matter anymore. One of the woman's eyes had opened. Flushed, Nathalie backed away from the bed and wiped perspiration off her forehead.

"He didn't bark much. Very even-tempered." Aunt Brigitte's brittle voice floated across the room, landing on Nathalie like a butterfly.

Nathalie peeled her sweat-dampened blouse away from her shoulder and faced her aunt, whose eyes were still closed.

Every question that passed through Nathalie's mind dissolved on her tongue.

Tante, how could you?

Tante, what were you thinking?

Tante, why?

A chill came into the room and wrapped itself around Nathalie. She closed the door, both to stave off the unusual draft and to have some privacy.

"Tante," she said, finally coaxing a word to emerge. "What ha—"

No. She didn't know how Aunt Brigitte would respond.

Nathalie cleared her throat and tried again. "It's good that he, uh, didn't bark much."

She sat in the uncomfortable chair again. The coldness followed, hugging her in an embrace she tried to reject. She took her journal out of her satchel and scribbled notes before it was too late.

"What are you writing?" Aunt Brigitte's eyes were open now. Focused on her.

"Just some . . . something I just remembered."

Nathalie's hand was so frigid, she couldn't write anymore; fortunately she'd gotten it all down. She tossed the journal back into her bag and stood. "I have to go talk to a nurse. I'll be right back."

Aunt Brigitte nodded and rolled away from her to face the wall.

Nathalie started walking toward the door. Before she got there, she forgot why.

She looked around the room. This was Aunt Brigitte's room.

When did I get here? What's going on?

Nathalie noticed the door was closed. Why? She reached to open it and noticed Aunt Brigitte's roommate, Véronique.

One eye open, staring at her.

The woman wasn't breathing.

Nathalie dashed into the hall to tell a nurse, but she didn't make it there.

Night descended on her spirit, right in the middle of the day at the asylum.

21

The first few days in the hospital (or was it hours?), Nathalie was so cold, she felt like she was trapped outside in winter, unable to find refuge. More and more wool blankets were piled on her by nurses scurrying in and out, until at last she felt comfortable. Day and night fell into one another, owing to the lack of windows. Time was everywhere and nowhere.

She had numerous visitors. Their presence faded in and out, sun playing hide-and-seek on a cloud. Streaky rays made it through.

Mostly Nathalie slept while they were there. When she was awake, her thoughts were in such disarray that conversation was exhausting. So she didn't speak much. Gestures, answers consisting of a word or two.

"Choupinet."

That she could say. Aunt Brigitte's dog's name.

She'd been doing something ordinary, sorting clothes, on some indistinct day. Then her next recollection was being in Aunt Brigitte's room, talking about the dog.

What followed was a patchwork of remembering and not remembering.

Véronique on the bed.

Touching her to wake her.

Holding a pillow, but not.

Talking to Aunt Brigitte and writing very quickly.

Then everything went black, and now nothing made sense and her mind didn't work right.

She'd had a memory gap. Then something happened. Something *else*.

Here and there someone held up a pencil and asked if she wanted to write anything down. No. Even a pencil was too heavy, not because of its weight but what it represented. Thinking and ideas and putting those together coherently.

It was a medical hospital, not an asylum. Else they wouldn't give her something sharp like a pencil. Whatever was going on, they didn't think she was mad.

No one told her why she was there or when she was going home. Either she couldn't articulate her questions well or they didn't answer. Or if they did, she couldn't remember next time she thought to ask. Maybe that was why. Until she remembered things, she wouldn't be able to go.

Being uncharacteristically quiet felt strange. As if she were not Nathalie but a mime portraying Nathalie. She missed her voice, and she missed being able to properly participate in conversation with . . . who was it who had come, anyway?

She had flowers and a card from someone (she'd read it several times—Jules, probably, but she kept forgetting) on her nightstand. The room was austere; the only ornamentation on the wall was a crucifix above her bed. She seemed to remember the other bed in the room being occupied by another patient, but it wasn't anymore. (Or was she merely thinking of Véronique?)

At one point, after awakening, she noticed a stack of two journals on a table beside her bed. The bottom one she recognized as her personal one. The one on top was not her newspaper one. (Where was that? Who was doing the morgue column in her absence? How long *was* her absence?) It was small, with a red cover, opened with a pencil down the center. She'd never seen it before.

She reached over and picked up both journals, looking at the red one first. Penmanship in several hands.

A guest register. Someone had thought to write down who came here and when.

Her parents four times. Jules once alone (he seemed to have trouble hearing her) and once with Simone and Louis, who'd also come by a second time. Christophe, twice. M. Patenaude and Roger, once.

Agnès visited her, too. It seemed impossible, and she hadn't signed the register, but Nathalie remembered somehow. Agnès had been there talking to her about taking the elevator up to the summit of the Tour Eiffel.

How long had she been here?

She ran her finger along the page. Four days.

Nathalie rolled onto her side, tossing off a blanket. She wasn't feeling nearly as cold anymore, and there were too many blankets. She wasn't hungry, either, so someone had been feeding her. She couldn't remember a single meal. She had a general achiness and restlessness. Had she been out of this bed? She must have. To use the chamber pot if nothing else.

She read through the register again. Pieces of those visits came back to her. Maman working her hands and tracing her scars, Papa telling her a story about Stanley. Simone and Louis doing some sort of play-acting from a performance Louis was in. Jules giving her flowers and talking about the play they had tickets for (which Nathalie insisted they go to, even if she was still in the hospital by then and didn't know how, precisely, that would work). Christophe in a gloomy, pensive mood. M. Patenaude pacing the room in thought as Roger talked about a talking doll at the phonograph exhibit at the Exposition.

Yet they were only fragments. A shattered plate rearranged, a fractured near-whole that barely resembled the original.

What kind of medicine had they given her?

She closed the register and opened her journal. As her eyes

ran over the text—"Tante suffocated her; pillow" and "thought she was asleep and being choked by her sheet" and "Tante sorry"—she had the impression she'd read all this before, but she wasn't sure.

Of anything.

Nathalie became drowsy as she read (truly, what *were* they giving her?) and she drifted off to sleep. She woke up minutes or hours later; she really did not know. Yet it was a refreshing sleep, somehow, and the viscosity of her thoughts was less thick. Thoughts were joining together the way they should, more or less.

She read her journal notes one more time.

Aunt Brigitte killed Véronique. Nathalie inadvertently touched her and the ensuing vision revealed everything. The effects of that were swift and intense, landing Nathalie here.

She read the pages before that and calculated the days. How long she'd been here, when the vision happened, and when her last memory had been sorting clothes.

No.

Six days?

Had she truly lost *six days*?

She wasn't clear as to why she was in a hospital and not at home. Papa could take care of her better than anyone, and Maman as well, if not with Insightful healing than with much love. Although Nathalie hadn't known about Papa's gift until a couple years ago, it explained a lot in hindsight. She'd been a relatively healthy child, with the occasional visit from Dr. Remy. Colds and fevers came and went, and hers were of shorter duration than those of her classmates, she'd often thought. At the time she'd believed, perhaps a bit too proudly, that it was because she was strong, of naturally excellent constitution, and diligent in following Dr. Remy's directives.

She remembered it differently now, the way you see the clues in a mystery when you read it the second time through. How

Papa was often beside Dr. Remy when he made a visit, for either Nathalie or Maman. How Papa often got sick after one of them did, which she'd attributed to close quarters, never realizing Papa took the sickness into himself as a quid pro quo for the healing.

One time she had more than a cold; she caught whooping cough. Horrible bouts of choking, so much so that her stomach hurt. Her parents stood over Dr. Remy's shoulder, Maman twisting her fingers together and Papa observing intently, giving Nathalie comforting pats as Dr. Remy examined her. The doctor had given her a tonic and some ointment, but Papa, who himself suffered from coughing fits days later, healed her. She was certain of it.

Why can't Papa heal me now?

"Because Insightful healers cannot mend matters of the mind and heart."

A man's voice. Friendly, neither very young nor very old, with a provincial French accent. Southern, perhaps. She opened her eyes and saw a gaunt figure silhouetted in the doorway. He stepped into the room wearing a black coat.

"Did I say that out loud?" Her voice sounded like she'd swallowed pebbles.

He came closer and offered her a mint, his fingers long and crooked. "This will soothe your throat." She thanked him and he continued. "I'm Dr. Delacroix. I understand you've suffered memory loss from an—an encounter."

She hadn't told anyone that she had a vision. Only that she didn't feel well and passed out.

Well. She didn't *remember* telling anyone.

Had she? Probably not. But maybe. Who knew what she did or didn't say in the past several days?

One thing was for certain. She wasn't going to admit to anything now. Not until she sorted out who knew what.

When she didn't reply, he bit his lip and tried again. "Gaps in memory are a consequence of your gift, I understand."

"They are." She paused. "You know that I'm an Insightful, then."

"I do." He smiled. "So am I."

Papa once told her there were fewer than a thousand Insightfuls, not counting those like herself to whom it was passed on. Her path crossed with only a few of them.

Still, she'd learned from M. Patenaude that impostors weren't uncommon. He'd had many people over the years introduce themselves as "a fellow Insightful" without knowing that his gift enabled him to hear the dishonesty in their words.

She arranged the pillows behind her so as to sit up better. "What ability do you have?"

He didn't respond. Instead, he pulled a notebook out of his pocket and took a seat. "Mademoiselle Baudin, can you tell me more about your memory loss? When it's happened, how long it lasts, and whether there are any accompanying symptoms?"

"Laudanum, that's it!" she exclaimed. "Dr. Lomme gave me laudanum. I made a joke about it at the time."

Dr. Delacroix smiled and hesitated, as if he expected her to say more. When she didn't, he repeated his initial question.

She wanted to challenge him and insist on an answer about his own ability. But not nearly as much as she wanted someone to listen, even if she wasn't as articulate as usual at the moment.

Nathalie spoke to him using her voice and her hands, shaping her story with both words and gestures. There was so, so much to tell about being an Insightful. And really, who wanted to hear it? Dr. Delacroix did; he asked and she was going to tell him, from the earliest days of the Dark Artist until the present. She left out, of course, the fact that Aunt Brigitte killed her roommate.

Why was she suddenly so inclined to talk? To a stranger, no less? It didn't matter, she decided.

Fatigue overtook her as she spoke, and she was vaguely cognizant that she may have repeated some details or left others out altogether, thinking she'd said them. She couldn't be sure, because the fog that had descended over her remained intermittent. Would this feeling ever leave?

"It will," said the doctor, thumbing a brass button on his coat. "I believe it will."

Nathalie propped herself onto her elbows and focused on the man. Papa's age, maybe older. Dark hair graying at the temples, good-looking in a professorial sort of way. "Why should you believe anything? If you're an Insightful, you know it's not a matter of faith. It's science. And did you tell me what your ability is?"

"I did," he said, smiling good-naturedly. "You asked a second time, while you were telling me about Jules."

Jules. Nathalie scratched her forehead. She'd talked about her envy for Jules's gift, so much more practical and helpful than her own. And she'd already forgotten what the doctor said about his own power. She was too embarrassed to ask him again.

"Nathalie," said Dr. Delacroix, "you're right. Dr. Henard's experiments were rooted in science. You also know—from your experiences and that of others—the unpredictability of the abilities and their consequences. That being said, your assumptions are correct. Direct touching prompts a much stronger response in you than indirect touching. As for this episode, it's very likely that your connection to Aunt Brigitte provoked a response in you, perhaps complicated by her own . . . problems."

Nathalie shook her head. "But all Insightfuls don't affect all other Insightfuls."

"Are you familiar with electromagnetism?"

"Jules is intrigued by it and has talked about it. I'm afraid I don't share his interest in the subject."

"It may clarify what transpired."

"What do you think transpired?" Nathalie sat up all the way.

He studied her before responding. "The events you've endured in recent weeks have had a cumulative effect, cresting sometime during your visit at Saint-Mathurin. Complicated by your connection to your aunt."

He didn't know she'd had a vision, then. Good. She must not have said anything.

"Insightful blood gives off a frequency of sorts. Some are more powerful than others—not necessarily the ability, but the potency, so to speak."

She reached for the journal and pencil and began to write; she didn't trust her mind yet, so it was important to record this. Her hand was stiff from lack of use and her handwriting, shaky. As long as she could read and understand it later.

"You and your aunt are attuned, perhaps even more so because of how you acquired your ability, by birth."

Had she told him that? She must have. Why did they medicate her so?

"That's my guess as to why you surface in her dreams—and not, say, your father." He stole a look over his shoulder, toward the doorway. "As unsettling as it is, your supposition about the Dark Artist was almost certainly accurate. You said your visions back then were in reverse, and then they weren't. It could have been the encounter with him, his power, that changed that."

Nathalie rested her fingertips on her temple. "Everything about this is outlandish. This laudanum makes me tired and forgetful, hardly conducive to aiding my condition and could be worsening it. Do tell Dr. Lomme when you have a chance."

"The laudanum would wake you up and then make you drowsy, but not forgetful, I'm afraid." He left the sentence suspended like that, and even in her diminished state, she concluded the rest. The medicine wasn't to blame.

"Is there anything I can take to get better? To hasten this . . . whatever it is my mind is enduring?"

Dr. Delacroix shook his head. "Time. It's the friend and the enemy of Insightfuls. Many have tried, and failed, to create a tincture or tonic to ameliorate the effects. It seems the good is destined to be forever linked with the bad. Don't ever despair too much. There's always, always hope."

"How so?"

The answer was lost to sleep or memory.

Nathalie didn't recall when she stopped taking notes, nor did she remember falling asleep or the departure of Dr. Delacroix, but she had to have fallen asleep, else a nurse wouldn't be rousing her to eat. She did (soup, and it was dreadfully in need of flavor. The bread wasn't bad).

As she handed the nurse her empty bowl, she strained to look at the makeshift guest register. "He didn't sign it."

The nurse glanced at the journal. "He who?"

"Dr. Delacroix. We had a nice discussion about Insightfuls."

"I don't know of any Dr. Delacroix," said the nurse, crinkling her brow. She was smooth-faced with wispy ringlets of hair. "But I only recently got transferred to this floor. It's possible I haven't met him yet."

Nathalie wanted to believe that explanation, but her curiosity couldn't be so lenient with uncertainties. When Dr. Lomme with his bushy eyebrows and clammy hands came in later that day, she asked him about Dr. Delacroix.

A slight frown preceded his response. "I'm afraid not, Nathalie."

She wanted to pursue it. To contest him, to show him the notes she'd taken. She knew how it looked, given the reason she was here. The futility was uncomfortably obvious.

And in truth, even she couldn't be sure that Dr. Delacroix and the conversation she had with him had been real.

22

Nathalie's ability to converse was nearly back to normal the next day. Although the sensation of coldness had mostly subsided, she still had the occasional hindrance in her thoughts and speech. Her memory had improved from shattered mirror to mostly repaired, passable from afar yet distorted upon closer examination.

Two thoughts dominated her mind, and when Simone arrived for a visit, Nathalie couldn't have been more relieved. Overnight she'd worked something out, something so obvious now, she didn't understand how she'd overlooked it yesterday, impaired thinking notwithstanding. She needed her confidante.

Simone came in with a newspaper under her arm. Once they discussed Nathalie's improvement and the rambunctiousness of Max and Lucy (Simone revealing kitten scratches on her arm to prove it), Simone sat in the visitor's chair.

"I don't know how much they tell you about the outside world, but I thought you'd be interested in seeing this." Simone held up *Le Petit Journal* tentatively, as if worried it would snap at Nathalie like an angry dog. "If it upsets you and you don't want to read about it, we can skip the topic entirely, and I can regale you with Le Chat Noir gossip."

Nathalie chuckled, then read the title.

Le Rasoir's Latest: Headless Body at
L'Histoire de l'Habitation Humaine,
Found in Pool Outside Persian Dwelling

"The Suitor." She clutched her own throat, a gesture her hand seemed to do of its own volition. Did others instinctively do this as well? "At the Human Habitation exhibit. Where I went with Christophe."

That made it even more real. Worse. She thought about their time together there, a stolen moment of friendship she hoped would never be taken from her.

Then another thought entered her mind. No, *invaded* it.

"Simone, do you think the killer is following me? Bodies turn up at the places I visited, then, obviously, they end up at the morgue . . ." The words came out too fast for her brain. She stopped and exhaled. "Is there a thread? Am I the thread?"

Simone shook her head firmly. "Absolutely not, Nathalie. A thousand other people who've visited the fair and the morgue could make the same claim. Do not allow yourself to think those thoughts."

Nathalie glanced at her, then away. Simone was right. Just because past events involved her directly, that didn't mean this series of murders did.

"You . . . all supposed correctly that the Suitor would be next." Simone had the careful voice of someone who wanted to change the subject but didn't know how well-received it would be.

"Yet we could do nothing to stop it." Nathalie had conveyed their working theory over lunch the day after their break-through. The theft of her memory had not, luckily, reached far enough back to eliminate that. Despite feeling like it happened *months* ago, she was able to remember everything about the case that hadn't already been taken from her. "No, I didn't know Le Rasoir took another life. Thank you for telling me. I don't like being treated as though I'm suddenly too delicate to cope with reality."

"That's my Nathalie," Simone said with a grin. She adjusted the corset on her peach-and-white checked dress. "You must truly be feeling better."

"Not completely better. I read my journal this morning and

had to reread several sentences in order to understand them. But . . . I'm greatly improved." Nathalie reached for the paper, smoothed it out on her lap, and read.

Le Rasoir cuts down another at the Exposition Universelle.

A man's headless body was found in a small, decorative pool outside the Persian dwelling early this morning at the L'Histoire de l'Habitation Humaine. He was well-dressed, with an evening suit and silk tie. His age is presumed to be between twenty-five and thirty-five.

Speculation abounds as to the whereabouts of the head, including from international visitors in Paris for the Exposition who spoke to us through a translator.

"Maybe it will show up in another exhibit," said a young female tourist from Russia.

"What," asked a Moroccan visitor, "if it never appears?"

"Jack the Ripper might be taking heads now," said a Scottish tourist.

A traveler from Japan shared these thoughts. "I think the river should be watched closely," he said. "Or the fountain with the lights."

"The fountain. If he only knew," said Nathalie.

"I wonder if that's deliberate," said Simone. "If someone knows or suspects something and attributing a quote to a tourist is a way of getting it out there."

Nathalie's mind turned that over a few times. She wished she'd deduced that herself. "The newspapers have gone from trying to brush aside these murders for the sake of the Exposition to embracing it, more with every issue. Even *Le Petit Journal*."

"They didn't say anything about a nail and a script page."

"So either there wasn't one," Nathalie said, handing the paper back to Simone, "or they withheld it again."

Simone agreed. She reviewed the newspaper before folding it

and placing it beside her on the chair. "Jules won't have a thought reading from this, but maybe your favorite Insightful did."

"No, I'm certain Papa didn't have a vision."

Simone smiled. "Céleste said to tell him hello. She's very fond of him."

Papa had healed Simone's younger sister a couple of years ago. Although Céleste wasn't aware of what he'd done (only Simone did, not even her parents), she'd taken a liking to him and his storytelling. "I certainly will."

"You do know I meant Gabrielle, *oui?*"

"I don't know what to think of her. She's polite at times and clearly shy, but her condescension toward Henard's magic? It's hard not to take that personally." Nathalie got out of bed and stretched. She didn't like it that Gabrielle was able to help right now while she herself was bedridden. "On the topic of Insightfuls . . . I have something to share with you. Two somethings, in fact."

Simone studied Nathalie before replying. "Your face is telling me they aren't good somethings."

Nathalie crossed to the door and closed it.

"They aren't." She stepped closer and put her hands square on Simone's shoulders. "Why do the doctors and my parents say I'm here?"

"Memory loss," Simone answered without hesitation. She placed her hand on top of one of Nathalie's. "You're not nearly as cold as before. That's good."

"Better every hour, I think. Finally. So . . . what else, besides memory loss? That's happened before. This"—she said, gesturing around the drab, windowless room—"has not."

Simone's deep amber eyes fell on her, unblinking. "You weren't able to remember anything from one moment to the next. Complications from visions around Le Rasoir's murders, too close to one another. Maybe discovering that Aunt Brigitte's roommate died brought on some sort of hysteria. That's what your mother told me, anyway. They don't know for sure."

And yet Dr. Delacroix knew. Nathalie looked away and began to pace the room. It felt good to stand, to walk. To pace. "Has anyone read my journal?"

"I wouldn't know." Simone crossed her legs at the ankles. "Why?"

Nathalie stopped pacing and faced her friend. She mustered the strength to say the sentence, an uncomplicated one in and of itself, that she'd been formulating since Simone had arrived. "Because I didn't know that the woman—Véronique was her name—was dead. I assumed she was sleeping. I put my hand on her to help untangle her from her sheets and . . ."

The realization spread across Simone's face. "You had a *vision*? I thought that only happened when someone died at the hands of anoth—" Simone clapped her hand to her mouth. "No, don't tell me your aunt . . ."

Nathalie bit her lip so hard she briefly thought she'd pierced the skin. After a deep exhale, at some point, "yes" emerged from her mouth.

She had difficulty believing these facts, this story, this uncomfortable truth about herself. It was real and it wasn't.

"Simone, you don't know how badly I need to tell someone." She sat on the edge of the mattress. "Not tell someone. Tell *you*. Who else could I possibly confide in?"

Simone took her by the hand. "Nathalie, *ma soeur*."

That was all Simone had to say and do for Nathalie's emotions, barely buried under broken earth, in an unmarked oh-so-shallow grave, to surface. She told Simone who Véronique was, guessing (correctly) that she'd recognize the case as soon as Nathalie mentioned it. Then she described what happened at the asylum, nomadic words alternately coming to her and drifting away as what she remembered intertwined with what she'd written down.

The empty bed made for an unexpected, ironic accessory, allowing her to pantomime parts of her story.

"Do you—do you think anyone suspects anything?" asked Simone.

Nathalie gently pulled her hand away and pressed her fingers into the mattress. "As lamentable as it is to say, I don't think they investigate the deaths of patients at Saint-Mathurin closely unless it's obviously violent. There have been some horrific episodes in that regard." Several months ago, a fight had broken out on the men's ward below, with one patient killing another with a blow to the head. Although the asylum kept such matters from the public, Nathalie and her parents happened to be there shortly after the commotion. Nathalie had seen drops of blood in the stairwell where it had taken place. "It doesn't matter, though. I know what happened."

Simone nodded, her face full of questions she was reluctant to ask.

Nathalie stood and walked over to the wall, placing her hand where a window should be. "If they find out Tante did this, they'll isolate her. Patients who kill other patients are essentially prisoners within the asylum—no daylight, visitors only on the first Sunday of the month, no outside time, not much of anything besides meals."

"Are you . . . thinking of not saying anything?"

"I don't know." Nathalie's shoulders slumped. "If I do, she suffers that fate. If I don't, I'm protecting a . . ." She swallowed. Thinking the word was one thing. Saying it out loud, the heft of the syllables in the air, was another. "Murderer. One that I love and pity, but a woman who took the life of another all the same. What if someone did that to her? I don't know what brought her to this. What if she kills her next roommate?"

"I'd be consumed by the same questions," Simone said. "She's never shown any signs of violence, has she?"

"Not toward another patient." She'd harmed others before

coming into the asylum. To prevent them from killing a child, or so her dreams had told her. But there were no children in the asylum.

Simone clasped her hands over her knees, tension turning her fingers white. "Perhaps she'll confess."

Nathalie waved off the suggestion. "I doubt it."

"Perhaps she can be . . . convinced to confess." Simone's voice was rife with foreboding. "Then the dilemma isn't yours to bear."

Nathalie hadn't thought of that. She'd been so focused on the burden of secrecy and its various iterations that she hadn't considered Aunt Brigitte's own volition. It was, unfortunately, a pattern of thinking she and everyone else were prone to when it came to her aunt. "I suppose that's where I should start. When I feel better. And when I discern whether or not anything's transpired."

Simone rose from the chair and, without a word, embraced her.

"Thank you," said Nathalie, stepping back after a moment. "As if that weren't enough, there's something else I—"

The door opened and a nurse poked her head in. "Nathalie! Good that you're up and about. Unfortunately," she said, opening the door wider, "this needs to stay open."

With a nod, she left them. Nathalie stared at the open door before speaking. "I can't wait to go home." She got back into bed. With a dramatic billow that made Simone laugh, she pulled the sheet over her head.

"I'm sure they'll let you go any day now." Simone lightly tugged the sheet. "So, what was it you were going to tell me?"

Nathalie uncovered her face and sat up. "I know this is going to sound strange, but I had a visit yesterday from a doctor no one else seems to know."

Simone sat back. "How can that be?"

"I don't know. He said he was an Insightful. He seemed to know . . . a lot."

"I mean the part about no one else knowing."

Nathalie ran her fingers along the edge of the sheet. "I asked the staff about him. Dr. Delacroix. They claim there's no such doctor."

"It's been a troubling few days. Are you sure you weren't dreaming?"

Nathalie opened her mouth to say no, then stopped. *Am I sure?* "I don't think I was . . ." Her voice faded. "I thought Agnès paid me a visit, too. This was different."

"You thought you saw Agnès?"

"I just said that. And I also said it was *different* from seeing this Dr. Delacroix."

It was too late. Simone's features floated in a sea of incredulity. "Perhaps. When in relation to the—to when you thought Agnès appeared, did this doctor stop in?"

"Not at the same time. Listen, Agnès seemed real at the time, but I know now it had to be a ghost or a dream—a dream, because I don't believe in ghosts. The doctor came here after all of that. It doesn't matter. You don't believe me."

"No, no!" Simone put up her hands. "I'm not saying it *didn't* happen. Only that you should *consider* the possibility that it didn't. The duress you've been under, the confusion you've felt, the paths your thinking has taken . . ."

Nathalie folded her arms. She wanted Simone to tell her she hadn't hallucinated the visit. It was one thing for her mind to conjure up Agnès, but how could it invent a person she'd never met? "I already considered that. What I'm wondering is if Delacroix is . . . I don't know. There's supposedly an Insightful who helps other Insightfuls with how to be an Insightful."

Simone repeated the sentence to herself, then studied Nathalie with a raised brow. "'Supposedly'?"

"Well, I don't know if he exists. I do think he was here, though." Nathalie cringed. "That's not what I meant."

Simone hesitated, as if calculating how to respond, then broke into an appeasing smile. "It could be him. It could also be that, as with Agnès, you were thinking about him. Or who he might be, if he were to show up."

Sometimes Nathalie appreciated Simone's ability to reason. Sometimes, like now, she was mildly irritated with it. Especially when what Simone posited was undeniable.

Before they could say another word, a welcome face peeked into the room.

"Hello, Christophe!" said Nathalie with a grin. Maybe she grinned *too* much; she didn't care. "I'm more talkative today. I think we might be able to hold a conversation."

The three of them exchanged a few pleasantries before Simone, in charming Simone fashion, held up the newspaper. "I brought this for Nathalie. Is there anything else you're able to share?"

Christophe's eyes danced between them. "I wasn't going to mention it because I thought—"

"That I'd be mumbling nonsense and too incoherent to discuss it?"

"No," said Christophe, blushing. "Well, somewhat. More so to see if you were . . . agreeable to discussing it."

"I'm still me. Impaired, albeit it much less so now, but not fragile. Never fragile." If she reiterated that aloud frequently and to enough people, it must be true, right?

Christophe shook his head in exaggerated fashion. "I would never call you, Nathalie the Brave, anything but."

Nathalie smiled. She was proud of *Baudin* because it meant exactly that. Brave.

"Christophe the Police Liaison," cut in Simone, wearing a conspiratorial expression she'd picked up from Louis, "*can* you tell us anything more?"

"I'm afraid not."

Simone, who looked as if someone had just stolen Max and Lucy from her, took a step toward the door. "Ah well. I tried! I must be going now anyway. Take care, both of you." She gave Nathalie a hug. "With any luck, my next visit to you will be at home."

She blew a kiss at Christophe as she said goodbye. As soon as he turned his back, she held up the newspaper, pointed to it, and threw Nathalie a "you'd-better-tell-me-everything" look.

Christophe, blushing from Simone's gesture, waited a few beats and settled into the chair. "Thank goodness you're feeling better. I was—we were all wondering if you'd improve. *When* you'd improve."

Or if I'd end up like Aunt Brigitte.

"You know how sometimes you're sleeping and get ensnared in this bizarre in-between? You're not awake, nor are you in much of a slumber." Nathalie closed her eyes then opened them. "Sort of a half dream, where things make sense but they don't? That's what it's been like."

"It wasn't pleasant to observe, I can assure you," he said, pulling at his cuffs.

"I hope I can leave soon. I miss Stanley."

"Not your parents?"

"Of course! But Stanley can't visit me." Not that she could remember much from her parents' visits, other than their worry. Or Christophe's last.

Oh goodness. What had she said? What must she look like, after being in the hospital so many days?

Suddenly her consolation about feeling better was overshadowed by her self-consciousness. She smoothed back her hair and sat up taller.

Christophe reached into his coat pocket. "I've been carrying this to show you for when you were feeling up to it. It ran in *Le Petit Journal* the other day."

He handed her a newspaper page folded to display a single article.

Her piece on the horological exhibit. She grinned. "That was a lovely way to pass the time, wasn't it?"

He smiled in return. "Was that a joke?"

Her mind caught up: time, horological exhibit. Nathalie laughed out loud. "No, actually. I guess I'm not *quite* myself yet."

She read the article. Descriptive and factual with an undertone of muted but genuine zeal. Had Christophe perceived that as well? She thanked him for bringing it and put it inside her journal. After a several quiet moments that were neither comfortable nor awkward, Christophe looked over his shoulder. "So . . . I couldn't share this with Simone, but there is something else to report about the murder."

"A script page, written on parchment paper. Yes?"

"Indeed." He wiped his knuckle over his mouth. "Not on the body, though."

Nathalie pressed her palms into the sheet as she leaned forward.

"It was delivered to the morgue this morning," he said in a whisper. "Along with the Suitor's head."

23

Nathalie envisioned that moment, more vividly than she wanted to. Untying a bundle, just another administrative task, expecting it was documents or supplies. Peeling back the wrappings to see a gaping mouth and human hair and blood.

She was certain she'd just grown five or six shades paler.

Or maybe her mind was deceiving her again and Christophe hadn't said any of that.

"A head arrived in a box. Who . . ." She gasped. "I hope you weren't the one who discovered it."

"No. Dr. Nicot retrieved it and opened it, thinking it was some equipment he'd been expecting. It was addressed to 'The Paris Morgue.' I wasn't there when he opened it, but when he ran in to tell me . . ." Christophe shook his head. "I've never seen the man so flustered. I've never seen him flustered at all, in fact."

Her skin prickled. If a physician was unsettled, it had to be even more grisly than what she'd imagined.

"The package was about this size," said Christophe, indicating a rectangle with his hands taller than she'd have guessed. "Five kilograms or so. The man had *la coiffure à la Titus* and a silk top hat, and the white scarf at the base of the neck. The script was folded up in a leather pouch. All of this was cushioned and covered by dozens of white bow ties."

Nathalie sketched that in her mind, each word a line, a curve, a shadow enhancing the image. "What did the script say?"

Christophe took a step closer. "I brought a transcription of it, in case you asked." He reached into his coat, producing a black-and-beige marbled notebook. "Here, from my own notes."

Christophe opened his notebook to the right page and handed it to her. His handwriting was elegant except at the end of the words, where his final stroke was abrupt, as if he were in a hurry to get to the next word. She quickly curbed her curiosity about what else these pages might contain (Notes about her? Not just her visions, but her?), slid her finger down the center, and read.

SUITOR, *wearing a top hat and formal dress, enters throne room and halts. He cries out, then catches himself.*

KING, QUEEN, *and* JESTER *have been beheaded.* KING *and* QUEEN *are on the throne, heads in laps.* JESTER *is on the floor in front of them.*

KING, *killed while eating grapes.*

QUEEN, *while holding a bird in a cage.*

JESTER, *while playing solitaire.*

SUITOR *(whispers): Jester spoke the truth.*

PRINCESS *(off stage): What's that, love? My darling brother thought it would be funny to put chrysanthemums instead of roses in my hair.*

YOUNG PRINCE *(off stage): They suit you better!*

The bird in the cage chirps.

SUITOR *(in a daze): But who would do this? Who could do this?*

To the side, the edge of a cloak appears from behind a curtain, then disappears.

SUITOR *looks around, as if he's heard something.*

PRINCESS *runs into the room holding flowers, and screams.*

Nathalie read it through a second time. Her mouth had caught up to her brain today, but reading wasn't yet seamless.

"Repulsive and repugnant, just for the sake of being so. This is all a tease. It doesn't tell us anything."

"Except who his next prey is likely to be," Christophe murmured.

She thumbed the edge of the notebook. "A Princess we can't help any more than we could help the Suitor."

"We hope to get to him before that." Christophe took in a deep breath and let it out. "We're surveying buildings above and near laundries, and we have four or five leads about 'suspicious men' carrying valises, though given the number of visitors in the city right now, there's not much weight to assign that. An anonymous source cited a 'volatile' actor—aren't many of them so?—who should be investigated. Both university scholars and theater professionals say they've never seen or heard of this script, so we believe it's the creative, unpublished work of the killer. Oh, and as a result of Jules's vision, we've been interviewing descendants of the Sanson family."

Nathalie always thought it strange that one family would have generations of executioners spanning decades, from the Revolution of 1789 until the 1840s. What must those holiday gatherings and dinner conversations have been like? "I'm assuming nothing came of it, or we wouldn't be reading about another murder."

"They're a proud family and were insulted, as one might expect," Christophe said, shrugging. "Somewhat understanding once we presented, insofar as we were able, the reasons for the inquiry. There's nothing to suggest any of them are involved. Monsieur Patenaude was able to assist us for several of the interviews and confirmed it."

Nathalie's heart warmed at the sound of M. Patenaude's name. All she recalled of his visit was that his glasses had been very thick. She was pleased to hear that his gift had been there when he reached for it during those interviews.

"The Deiblers also spoke to us and, in fact, offered to consult. Monsieur Patenaude engaged with them as well."

The heirs to the Sanson throne enjoyed their own renown for being at the helm of *Le Rasoir National* in recent decades. Was that who had pulled the rope on the guillotine when she'd watched the murderer Pranzini's execution two years ago? "It's not every day a father-and-son execution team can share their intimate knowledge of the guillotine with a murder investigation." She closed the notebook. "Then what about Jules's vision?"

"It's *possible* that Monsieur Patenaude was mistaken. After all, he . . . as you know, things have changed for him."

Nathalie frowned. The glee she'd felt on M. Patenaude's behalf was punctured with disappointment.

"However," Christophe said, his tone optimistic, "we, too, came away from the interviews secure in the conclusion that none of them are suspects. We're pursuing three other theories at the moment: One is that Le Rasoir was making a false claim and isn't really the descendant of an executioner. The second is that he's a distant branch on the Sanson family tree, say the grandson of a third cousin or some such. Or an illegitimate one, which would be even harder to unearth. Third, he may be talking about some other executioner, in France or elsewhere."

"It's wide open, then. We're not much further along." Nathalie handed the notebook back to him, her arms feeling weak. The rest of her felt weak as well. Catching Le Rasoir seemed to be an impossible task, and she had done so little to help. "What will make it into the newspaper?"

"Everything except the details of the investigation—we're not going to mention the Sansons or Deiblers, needless to say. The body will go on display in the morgue. Both . . . sections." He tucked the notebook into his jacket. "Gabrielle traced his path to a theater, seemingly in the fifteenth arrondissement—this time inside, possibly with a companion. The walking pattern suggests someone alongside him. Until after the theater, whereupon they parted ways. The man went into an establishment of some sort, seemingly alone."

"That would be some coincidence, for both victims to be milling about a theater in the vicinity of the Exposition."

"Correct. So, we've positioned some officers in that area and the investigation team will be asking questions there, making lists of all actors, playwrights—everyone involved in theater," said Christophe.

"All over Paris? That must amount to hundreds of people."

"Better than thousands, *non*?" Christophe's gaze drifted to the flowers. "Jules was called in but hasn't yet arrived."

He knew the flowers were from Jules without looking at the card. Was that a guess or did he know from a previous visit?

She pressed her lips together. Gabrielle had helped, Jules would be helping. "Do you need me?"

"No," he said abruptly. Too abruptly.

A lump swelled in Nathalie's throat. She swallowed it down immediately.

"I didn't mean it that way. We always need you," he said, his voice much softer. "But we need you to be well. Healthy. Of sound mind and body. Take care of yourself for a while longer. Please?"

His words warmed her heart, a daisy smiling at the sun. She couldn't say no to that. "I will."

Christophe stood, announcing he had to go soon. As the conversation finished up, he pointed to the nightstand. "Ah, I suppose I don't have to sign your guest register today."

"Not unless you want to practice your signature." Her eyes darted to the register. Too bad the doctor hadn't signed it.

A thought inserted itself into her mind. Simone didn't believe her because she'd discredited herself by mentioning Agnès. Perhaps Christophe would, if she framed it differently.

"You've interacted with a multitude of Insightfuls. A far greater number than I have. Do you know of one directly connected to Dr. Henard? An apprentice who might have had more intimate knowledge of his work than anyone else? Or a mind reader or thief who stole his secrets?" Yet as she said it, the latter suppositions felt false. Dr. Delacroix didn't seem insidious. But what did she know?

Christophe's eyes creased in thought. "I'm afraid not. Why?"

A flutter went through her chest. He'd either doubt her or believe her. Smile with distant politeness or knit his brows in concern. "I had a . . . strange conversation the other day with a doctor no one here has ever heard of. I'm starting to think he wasn't a doctor at all, but rather this mysterious Insightful I once heard about who helps other Insightfuls. I'm not sure how he helps them—I mean us—specifically." She waited for his reaction. Inscrutable thus far, so skilled was he at listening with a passive face. "I can't say if he's real or some sort of Insightful legend. I just . . . I don't know how else to explain it."

Christophe's expression changed at last. He didn't look at her as though she were mad, he didn't dismiss her idea or tell her she had to be mistaken. His eyes glistened with compassion, and kindness tugged at the corners of his mouth. "I don't have the answers for you. I wish I did. I think you should ask as many questions as you have to in order to gain peace of mind."

She grinned at him. How was it that he almost always knew what to say and how to say it?

24

Nathalie was released from the hospital the following day. The chill had abandoned her completely. Her thoughts and speech, now that they were properly assembled, hadn't stepped out of line. Her memory sharpened once again, and last of all, her ability to read returned to normal. The doctor strongly encouraged her not to put herself in a "precarious situation" by using her Insightful power. When she scoffed at this, he urged her to rest as long as she was "reasonably able" with a meaningful look at Maman and Papa.

As she gathered her journal, guest register, and flowers, she noticed something on the floor near the wall. She stooped to pick it up.

A brass button.

She was almost certain Dr. Delacroix had been wearing one. Almost.

Or was that Christophe? Or Jules or Louis?

Her memory wasn't that gracious to her, such that she knew for sure, but she took the button anyway.

While leaving the hospital with her parents, flowers from Jules in hand, Nathalie asked the question she'd been formulating all morning. She wanted to have this conversation before they boarded a steam tram. "How is Aunt Brigitte?"

Maybe *now* someone would answer.

Maman threw her a sideways glance. "She was very upset that you'd collapsed; she cried a lot, more than I've seen her cry in some time. We assured her that you'd be well, even—even when we didn't know if that was true."

Nathalie squeezed her eyes shut and opened them again. Aunt Brigitte knew of Nathalie's memory gaps, but she didn't know they intensified if Nathalie touched the victim's body. "Does she know why I collapsed?"

"We told her you were under a lot of strain lately," Papa said. "Without details."

If Aunt Brigitte had been under suspicion for murder, they'd tell her. Wouldn't they? Or would they keep *details* from her like they did from Tante? They'd kept plenty of secrets from Nathalie in the past. "How is she, uh, coping with the death of her roommate?"

"She wavers between indifference and being overwrought," Maman said. "Which I suppose is often true of her responses anyway, so it's hard to determine. We don't talk about it unless she does, and even then, well . . . you know how it is. Best to steer away from such things."

Nathalie's stomach clenched as they boarded the steam tram. She was convinced: Her parents didn't know it was a murder. What now?

Maman and Papa made a fuss over her at home, and Stanley wouldn't leave her side. Papa had made bread, and Maman had made pistou soup and a chocolate soufflé, some of her favorites. Jules had left a note saying he was looking forward to seeing her. Simone was visiting her parents and Céleste and stopped by for a while. Among other things, they made plans to go to the Buffalo Bill–Annie Oakley show in a few days.

Her heart was filled with gratitude; it was good to be home.

Over piquet that evening, during which she took turns playing against Maman and Papa, Nathalie told them about her mysterious visit. She presented the button as well, and asked Papa if it was his. It wasn't.

She hadn't wanted to tell them until she knew, and they knew, that she truly had her faculties about her once again.

"He said his name was Dr. Delacroix," she said. Neither of them reacted as if the name meant anything to them.

"It was probably a doctor from another floor," offered Maman, "or another section of the hospital."

Papa put down a card. "Could it be that you're mistaken about his name?"

Nathalie hadn't considered the latter. She wasn't in a reliable state at that time. But no. Even if she'd gotten the name wrong, it couldn't be so far off that it didn't even *sound* like someone else.

"It could be," said Nathalie, laying down a card. "It could also be that he gave me a pseudonym."

Maman rearranged her cards. "Why should he do that?"

"Because he might have a reason for anonymity," she said. Stanley jumped onto her lap. "I've heard that there . . . might be an Insightful out there who helps other Insightfuls. Jules told me once. Someone with mind-reading power or someone who helped Dr. Henard or maybe even stole from him."

Her parents fell silent, and for a moment the only sound was Stanley purring. Papa put some tobacco in his pipe and lit it.

Maman knotted her fingers. "There *was* supposedly a young assistant who disappeared—left or sent away, who knows—when things started to go badly with the experiments. His last name was . . . oh, something with an S."

"Suchet," said Papa without missing a beat. "I remember because I knew a sailor with that name."

"Yes, that's it," Maman said. "I never saw him."

Papa took a puff of his pipe. "Neither did I."

"He's *real*," Nathalie said. Her eyes went to the flowers from Jules, now starting to wilt. They had another day, maybe two. "That in itself is reassuring."

Maman shrugged. "Is he? Even if he is . . . real is one thing. That this is the same individual who showed up in your hospital room is another."

"I forgot about his existence until you asked about it." Papa collected a trick and tossed it to the side. "It's all rumor. Some say he moved to another part of France, to America, to Morocco. I've heard he assumed a new identity, that he died, that he didn't, that he was a city official in Paris under a different guise, that he was a priest. He's no one and everyone."

Nathalie wondered if Madame la Tuerie had known of him or the rumors. Had she ever tried to contact him—or worse, attempt to have him killed, like she did Henard? Between that and angry, frustrated Insightfuls, it's no wonder he vanished. "Why so much mystery? Dr. Henard had an apprentice. So what?"

"There are stories about what happened to him as well as about who he is, what he does or can do. Some said he was purely an academic who could answer obscure questions about Insightful power," Papa said. "Others said he was a paternal figure of sorts. Still others said he was working on something to reverse Insightful power."

"A . . . cure?" Nathalie frowned. "We aren't diseased."

Maman placed a gentle, scarred hand on the table. "You have to understand, *ma bichette*, this is from a time when many people regretted having gotten the transfusions. When Insightfuls were mocked and those who suffered like Tante weren't pitied but rather 'got what they deserved.' So this man was whatever people needed him to be—as you can tell by the stories of what might have become of him. He was only a university student at the time. Who can say what was real and what was delusion?"

Nathalie added that to the list of other claims she'd heard. Helping Insightfuls get new identities, making something to change the effects of using a power. "Past tense. Was, were. You don't believe it?"

"I haven't heard the same story twice." Papa rested his pipe on its leather holder. "What's more, I haven't heard any in years and years. I don't know."

Maman agreed. After a pause, she spoke. "If this mysterious doctor is one and the same, how would he have known who you were?"

Nathalie had been trying to work that out for days. "Maybe someone at the hospital told him. That's all I can conclude."

Papa put his hand on hers. "I don't know if there's any way to know for sure who this man was. I don't think there's anything to indicate that he's this 'secret' apprentice who has become an Insightful legend of sorts. Does it matter? You had a conversation with him that left you feeling better. That's what's important."

Nathalie focused on her cards. "It is."

Yet, it did matter. Maybe she, too, wanted a man, or myth, to help her make sense of life as an Insightful. After all, she'd conjured Agnès in the midst of this mess in the hospital.

Strange, how time and grief worked together, and yet they didn't. At the time of Agnès's death, Nathalie had told herself time would heal her. She'd heard people say it to Agnès's parents during the wake, too. But the passage of days then weeks then months and finally years didn't heal the wound. Parts of it thickened up with scar tissue, maybe. Other parts festered. Her grief didn't go away over time. It simply changed forms.

She couldn't bring herself to think of Agnès for some time after the murder. Then she realized she was actively putting Agnès out of her head, which was an abysmal and inauthentic feeling. Perhaps this specter of Agnès during Nathalie's convalescence was punishment for that.

Or maybe she just missed her friend, and being in the hospital surfaced those emotions, maybe rooted in her fear that she'd lose her memories of Agnès and everyone else who meant something to her.

"That reminds me," Papa said as he shuffled the cards. "I spoke to Monsieur Patenaude yesterday. He invited you to return to work whenever you're ready."

"He did?" This brightened her thoughts. She stroked Stanley's back. "Good. I'm ready now. Well—not tomorrow. The day after. I have some affairs to tend to tomorrow."

"Such as?" Maman asked.

Nathalie swallowed. "A visit to Aunt Brigitte, for one."

25

A visit to her aunt, yes.

But first, a trip to the morgue.

She didn't know whether she'd touch the glass when she got there. She didn't tell her parents she was going. Couldn't tell them. They were already worried about her health, and Maman was reluctant to even let her visit Aunt Brigitte alone. Adding the morgue and the idea of pursuing another vision to their concerns wouldn't do any of them any good.

The queue was so long, it stretched almost to the front of Notre-Dame. She made her way to the entrance with more than a few grumpy complaints trailing her.

M. Arnaud smiled when he saw her. "I'm so very happy to see you're back. How are you, my dear?"

"Better, much better." She didn't want to say much more, especially in front of strangers. She wanted to ask M. Arnaud about the bruise on his cheek but didn't for the same reason. "Ready for my routines and to go back to normal."

M. Arnaud shushed a few complainers and let her inside. The stuffiness of the viewing room struck her almost as much as the noise. People were chatting and pointing, strangers talking to one another in various tongues. The room was full of tourists, some of whom were asking M. Soucy questions. M. Cadoret stood in the display room rocking back and forth on his heels, watching them all as if he were at a menagerie.

When at last she glimpsed the Suitor, a feeling of genuine uncertainty overtook her.

He had a trim beard and wavy, light brown hair. The rest of his body, pale and freckled, was separated from it by a few centimeters. *Why at all? Couldn't they put it as close to the head as possible?* His hanging bloodstained suit was fashionable and black with a subtle pattern. The top hat, white scarf, and bowties, all of them, lay on a small table nearby. He looked like a man who'd gone out for an evening stroll. Which he had.

What should I do?

No Christophe or Jules or Simone to help her make this decision.

Prompt a vision and it could result in nothing out of the ordinary. Or it could lead to a significant memory loss and another setback. Or something she didn't even anticipate yet.

She regarded the corpse, and it reminded her of the last time she was indecisive about touching the glass. Except that it had been Agnès on the concrete slab.

And so she made the same decision now as she did then.

Nathalie moved as far to the right as she could, turning her back to the other visitors. She placed her hand on the glass.

The touch carried her to a room, the same as in the previous visions, with the Suitor's beheaded corpse. The blood dripped up from the floor and seeped back into the neck, crimson streaks crawling into the flesh like a vampire crawling back into a coffin. The disembodied head rose from a bucket of sawdust and attached itself to the neck as if by some invisible hand.

Everything happened in reverse.

The guillotine blade went up. Then—blackness so absolute it almost looked solid. The darkness flickered away. After a beat, she was walking backward in the killer's room, this stark, windowless room she couldn't identify as a parlor or bedroom or anything else other than space itself.

She walked *away* from the man kneeling with his hands

behind his back, past a table with a candelabra, a chessboard, and what looked like costume pieces.

In a breath, she returned to the viewing room.

Backward. Why?

Her earliest visions had been in reverse. It was only with Agnès's death that they proceeded along a normal means of chronology.

Because of what happened with Aunt Brigitte and what it did to me?

It had to be. She couldn't think of any other explanation.

Good. That meant it wasn't a problem, even if it happened again. It was the *opposite* of a problem, because there was a reasonable correlation. As reasonable as Insightful powers could be.

Nevertheless, she was worried about the effects. If the vision took on a new form, then perhaps the consequences could, too.

Don't think like that.

She sensed a few people much closer to her than before; almost certainly she'd said something and they'd come to investigate. As if she were part of the Exposition, the morgue, the show.

She excused her way past them all and knocked at the Medusa door.

M. Cadoret answered. He asked her how she was feeling and warmly welcomed her back. When she started to walk down the corridor, M. Cadoret called after her.

"I'm afraid Monsieur Gagnon isn't here today. He's had a headache and took the rest of the day off. I can take your statement, if you don't mind."

Nathalie acquiesced with a courtesy that she hoped hid her disappointment. *Of all days.*

They went into the office. Although she'd given her statement to M. Cadoret several times before when Christophe had been out or otherwise unavailable, it felt different this time. Different because she wanted to talk to Christophe. When he left for Switzerland in a few days, it would be like this for weeks.

She didn't *need* him, obviously. But it was . . . very nice to have him around. And to be around him. And to talk from time to time.

Nathalie didn't tell M. Cadoret the vision was in reverse; it had no bearing on the information conveyed. He wasn't involved in the investigation anyway. He was a morgue worker who occasionally performed administrative duties on Christophe's behalf (he even hummed as he did it, such that she wondered if he even really heard her as he transcribed), but he wasn't privy to the details in connection with the police.

She presented it matter-of-factly, like someone who'd done this so very many times before. Which was true, of course. Except that maybe she was a bit more broken now, imbued with knowledge that served more to antagonize her than help her.

Who am I fooling?

She wasn't the same. Or feared she wasn't the same, and that was almost the same thing.

Wasn't it?

She watched M. Cadoret, with his small, precise penmanship, write down every word crisply, as if he didn't want to make a mistake. He read what he penned, appearing pleased with himself for capturing it so well.

"Do you have access to the statements from Jules or Gabrielle?" she asked, snapping him out of his self-congratulatory reverie.

"Yes, as a matter of fact, I took down Jules's statement from the other day. He happened to come in when Monsieur Gagnon was gone for several hours." M. Cadoret creased his browless forehead in thought. "Actually, I believe it was while he was visiting you."

Nathalie remained passive but sensed the blush betraying her. "How's Dr. Nicot?"

"He's well, I presume. Why?"

She touched the edge of the desk. "After the delivery of . . . of the Suitor's head."

M. Cadoret seemed to go a shade paler. "Oh, that." He closed his eyes and shook his head. "Horrible, horrible fright. You know how stern his demeanor is, how steady? He was trembling for an hour after that."

Nathalie shuddered. She was glad she wasn't here when it happened. And that it hadn't happened to Christophe.

M. Cadoret leaned forward and lowered his voice. "Did you happen to notice the gathering outside the exit? Not the one from the viewing room. The one we use."

"No, I came from the other direction. What gathering?"

"Ever since news of the Suitor's, uh, 'delivery' was reported, people stand under the tree across from the door. They have coffee or lunch or smoke . . . and watch. Monsieur Soucy noticed it and asked them why." M. Cadoret leaned even farther forward. "To see if anything else resembling a head gets delivered."

Nathalie winced.

"Paris craves spectacle, it seems." He pursed his lips in apparent displeasure.

Nathalie's eyes went to the volumes of photographs dedicated to documenting the dead. "The city of lights, the city of sensationalism."

M. Cadoret shuffled the papers and inspected them. "Here we are," he said, presenting them.

She read through Gabrielle's, despite knowing from Christophe what it would say. The path ended after the theater, at a restaurant or tavern.

Jules's vision focused on something else entirely.

The victim's thoughts were murky, as with the others. His mind was on his fear, visceral and to the bone, and on his family. His mother and father, his sister, his betrothed, his favorite cousin.

Other thoughts involved confusion as to his killer, who boasted of familial lines as an executioner, and chess. He didn't know how to play chess, but the killer made him anyway.

A victim who'd been to the theater, a killer who was the descendant of an executioner and enjoyed chess, a table of costume pieces. Pages of a script nailed to the victims.

Again with the thoughts being unclear. Sleepy? Drugged? Drunk?

The police would continue their pursuit of the theater route, but the executioner detail remained elusive.

She slapped her hand on the table. "I have it!"

M. Cadoret started. "What?"

She blushed. "Sorry. I—I think I have an idea for Monsieur Gagnon. May I write it down and leave it for him?"

M. Cadoret paused, scratching where his eyebrow would be. He searched her face, as if he were about to say something, then shook his head. He dipped the pen in ink and handed it to her along with a sheet of paper.

> *What if Le Rasoir is an actor playing a part, as his "play" suggests? And what if he isn't the descendant of an executioner, but of Guillotin himself?*

26

Angst seized Nathalie and imprisoned her, dangling the key with a taunt. Only when this was over might the key enter the lock.

Often when she'd come to Saint-Mathurin, she'd felt uneasy, fascinated, and replete with pity. At times she'd been apprehensive, because the patients—Aunt Brigitte included—often displayed behavior that was sad or uncomfortable to witness. Barking instead of talking. Weeping in a corner. Squatting in a corridor as if over a chamber pot, urinating with nothing underneath. On this visit, she was laden with fear and dread, not because of what she might see but because of what she had to do.

Aunt Brigitte was alone in her room, and the bed opposite was unmade.

A new roommate? Or had the one from the infirmary returned?

"It's been some time since I've seen you," Aunt Brigitte said, apprehension walking along the perimeter of her voice. "Your parents said you'd taken ill for a few days. Are you better now?"

Was she? Would she ever be?

"I—I suppose everything passes eventually."

"Does it?"

Aunt Brigitte's eyes were on her, vacant yet penetrating.

"Most things. Some things never leave us."

"The forbidden Greek vase did." Aunt Brigitte pointed to the hall. "The martinet has it. I forgot to tell your mother."

Nathalie peeked up and down the corridor before shutting the door. "I'll get it before I go."

"Why did you close the door?"

"So that we can talk without being overheard." She balled up her fists.

Aunt Brigitte stared at her a moment. She tossed her blankets to the side and swung her legs over, putting one petite foot at a time onto the floor.

Nathalie instinctively stepped back, then was embarrassed by her reaction. *As if she's going to attack me.*

Aunt Brigitte went over to the sliver of a window that overlooked the courtyard. "Why should we need to talk without being overheard?"

Nathalie balled her fists up again. "I saw something, Tante. Something you should know about."

"I know."

"You do?"

Aunt Brigitte continued looking out the window. "I saw your trance. Heard your trance, then saw it. My eyes were closed, thinking of Choupinet. You mumbled. I opened my eyes and . . ." Her voice wavered. "I know what I saw."

One of Aunt Brigitte's preferred phrases and one she often used to defend her dreams. A phrase that had landed her in the asylum in the first place. She knew the priest and nun were going to kill their illegitimate child, knew the man was going to throw the baby in the river. Because she knew what she saw. And that's what she'd told the police when she tried drowning the man in the Seine.

Aunt Brigitte turned to Nathalie. "I know what *you* saw."

It was distressing to hear that. Yet also comforting.

Nathalie's throat went dry. "Then you know why we have to have a conversation about it."

"I feel guilty about it sometimes, and my nightmares are dark, dark, dark. Worse than ever." Aunt Brigitte crinkled her brow. "Isn't that enough?"

"No, Tante. It isn't."

Had her aunt truly lost her sense of right and wrong? And if she had, when?

"She was going to kill me," Aunt Brigitte said in a tone of rigid certainty. "She was going to suffocate *me* with a pillow. I saw it in a dream. She said she poisoned her neighbor."

"You said you didn't believe her, remember?" Nathalie shifted her weight. She couldn't tell Aunt Brigitte that she knew the truth about Véronique. What would that accomplish? "If you thought you were in danger . . ."

"I did it in my sleep." Aunt Brigitte stepped toward her. "Sleep but also not sleep. I was confused."

Nathalie studied her aunt, this fierce-yet-fragile woman, wispy as a bird. "And so now what?"

"I have a new one," Aunt Brigitte said, gesturing to the opposite bed. "I forgot her name, but she does not snore. I haven't had any dreams about her."

"Tante, you—"

"Don't tell on me."

Nathalie didn't answer. She couldn't answer.

Aunt Brigitte got back into bed and tucked the sheets under her chin. She resembled a little girl, all bundled up and waiting for her bedtime story. "I feel guilty more than sometimes. Most times."

And just like that, Nathalie's frustration dissolved into a dull ache for an aunt whose Insightful power had forsaken her. Ruined her years ago, then failed her. "It's very sad, Tante. For her and her loved ones. And also for you."

Aunt Brigitte's fingers moved along the edge of the sheet like spiders. "I should be punished. I know that." She dropped her voice. "Arsenic would do it. Slowly toward forever."

"Don't be foolish."

"Not foolish." Aunt Brigitte sat up and leaned forward. "Bring me some. I'd rather die than be locked in a room. A broken doll stuffed into a box."

A flush crawled up to Nathalie's face. This wasn't how she'd envisioned the conversation. "Absolutely not, Tante. I—I won't be complicit in your death."

"Or my life." Aunt Brigitte closed her eyes and murmured something indecipherable to herself, going to whatever place it was she went from time to time.

Several minutes passed. The conversation was over, it seemed.

While Aunt Brigitte was quietly talking to herself, Nathalie opened the door. She went to the nurse's station and asked someone to fetch the vase. When she returned to the room with it, Aunt Brigitte had her eyes open and hands folded as if in prayer.

"I had a dream about you the other night. When you were in the hospital, I think." She put her hands to her heart. "You were strolling along a path through the woods. You didn't see me because I watched from behind a tree. After you passed me, two shadows joined you, one on either side."

Nathalie wanted to tell Tante to stop, that she didn't want to hear it, that she wasn't in the mood to hear about foreboding dreams.

She did want to hear it, though. At least part of her did.

"The three of you walked into the darkness together," Aunt Brigitte continued, "and then all three of you became shadows. Then one of the shadows evaporated, just ceased to be."

Acid crept up Nathalie's throat and she swallowed it back. What did the dream mean?

Death. Someone was going to die. Again.

What else could it be?

One of them was in danger. Maybe even herself.

"I fear my dreams don't mean anything anymore." Aunt Brigitte put her head on her pillow and stared up at the ceiling. A tear trickled down the side of her cheek. "Maybe they never really did."

27

The nightmare was rich in color and sensation, hardly distinguishable from reality, in the strange way dreams could be. While experiencing them everything seemed so authentic; only upon waking did a dream's logic give way to nonsense.

Aunt Brigitte stood in a room. Le Rasoir's room, that dimly lit place with a high ceiling and nothing distinct save for its penetrating darkness, a firmament absent of light and hope. Nathalie stood there, too, an immobile observer with muscles made of marble.

Two guillotines were in place.

Simone was bound and gagged, on her knees with her head placed on one of the guillotine blocks. Louis was in the other. Both wept.

Aunt Brigitte released the blade, first severing Simone's head, then Louis's.

Nathalie couldn't move her head so she closed her eyes. She heard the shuffle of the sawdust buckets. When she opened her eyes again, Aunt Brigitte stood before her, holding a pair of heads.

Not those of Simone and Louis.

Jules and Gabrielle.

"Which one, Nathalie?"

Somehow, somehow Nathalie found her voice. "Which one what?"

Aunt Brigitte smiled without answering.

And then Nathalie woke up.

When she went to the morgue for her report, she noticed the crowd of sandwich-eaters and coffee-drinkers lingering under the tree, watching the door. How vulgar.

Inside, the black velvet curtain was drawn. Impatient visitors speculated in breathless wonder which corpse might be pulled. Perhaps it was the so-called "Suitor" (parlance available to all, now that the newspapers had released details about the script pages). Or maybe the old woman with the paisley dress? Or the scrawny young man with the beard? It could be that none were being removed but rather added.

Oh, and what if *that* was another murder victim?

The collective curiosity was satisfied soon enough. M. Cadoret drew the curtain back and the horde groaned. (She could swear she'd heard M. Soucy wheezily chuckle at them.) The Suitor was gone.

Amid the whispers and hushed conjecture, Nathalie made her way to the Medusa door. Christophe opened it before she got there.

In his office moments later, he told her that twenty-six-year-old William Fitzgerald of Dublin had been the Suitor. He was a university student who'd aspired to teach music; he'd gone to the theater in the 7th arrondissement with a young woman he'd met earlier that week. The young woman said when she'd parted ways with him that night, he'd been in good, if heavily intoxicated, spirits.

Nathalie considered telling Christophe how her vision had felt different, with a pause in the middle and in reverse like her visions had been years ago. And how contrary to what she feared, the resulting memory loss wasn't worse (maybe even better—she lost about a quarter of an hour after she'd gotten home from visiting Aunt Brigitte, nothing significant). Yet she refrained from saying anything. For now, this secret would stay with her, lest anyone deem her weak or her visions unreliable.

"Well done on your Guillotin supposition," he said with a nod of approval. "Are you certain you'd rather write for the newspaper than become a detective?"

"If only a woman were admitted to the profession. Or do all the men consult their wives this way?" Heat reached her cheeks instantly. "Oh goodness. I didn't mean—that's not—"

Christophe pinched the edge of the desk, gaze focused on his inkwell. His lips curled upward, a grin just barely suppressed. "I know what you meant. I wouldn't be surprised if there were some conversations along those lines, to say the least." He looked up at her again. "Also, this reminds me. Would you be able to come by tomorrow morning at eight?"

"Yes," she said, relieved by the subject change. "I'm going to the theater tonight—of all places—but we shouldn't be out too late."

"As you know, I'm leaving for Switzerland in two days. Tomorrow is my last day here for almost three weeks, so I wanted to make sure . . . everything is in order."

Her face was placid, but she beamed on the inside. *He wants to say a proper goodbye.*

That thought carried her for the rest of the morning. She didn't want to dwell on the fact that he'd be gone and that it was to be with his fiancée. Instead, she held on to the idea that he cared enough to bid her a temporary farewell.

After dropping off her article with Arianne, Nathalie made her way to Parc de Neuilly to meet Simone.

They'd been looking forward to the Wild West show ever since the *Je viens* posters with Buffalo Bill's face had appeared all over the city. (Nathalie thought it should have said "We're coming," given that Annie Oakley and others were in the show.) They didn't know much about it but had heard of a young woman who could shoot anything with incredible precision.

They were not disappointed. The first part of the show had a lot of men in various kinds of dress, some with paint on their faces, running and galloping and play-acting fights. There were horses, the reenactment of a horse thief being hanged, and *real buffalo*, the latter of which Nathalie never thought she'd see. Buffalo Bill himself was handsome, if rather showy for Nathalie's liking. But it was steady Annie Oakley, with her unusual dress ("Is that leather?" asked Simone) and hat (someone called it a "cowboy" hat), who seized their attention completely. She was short—shorter than Maman, even—and took guns of various sizes to shoot glasses and flat clay objects, one after another, without missing. While riding a galloping horse besides, which was the most astonishing feat either of them had ever seen.

Nathalie and Simone were speechless. They enjoyed her so much, they promised each other before so much as rising from their seats that they'd come again.

"I have to say," Simone said as they exited the performance, "I've never held a gun and I have no desire to live in the United States, but I think I want to be Annie Oakley when I grow up."

"No more cabaret?"

"Eh, maybe on Fridays and Saturdays." Simone winked. "Have to do something after dark."

"Hmmm . . . so would that make Louis Wild Bill?"

Simone pretended to think about it. "*Non. Jamais!*"

"It must be nice to be that good at something," said Nathalie. They followed the vast crowd out to a street full of carriages-for-hire. "Among the best in the world."

"You mean like being an eighteen-year-old girl with Insightful powers who helps the Paris police solve crimes?" Simone elbowed her in the ribs.

"Actually, yes," Nathalie said, concealing her mirth. "I wouldn't mind that pursuit."

A man handing out pamphlets walked between them, followed by a vendor selling Buffalo Bill posters. After waving them off, Simone turned to Nathalie. "I know this isn't a pleasant topic. I'd be a shoddy friend if I didn't ask. Have you . . . heard anything more about your aunt?"

Nathalie had been waiting for the right moment to bring up Aunt Brigitte. Before the show, Simone had practically tackled her with inquiries about the Le Rasoir case. Since the conclusion of the show, their shared mood had been so buoyant, she didn't want to say anything to alter it.

She was nevertheless relieved Simone had asked.

They took a carriage (Simone's treat) and resumed their conversation. Nathalie described the visit she'd had with Aunt Brigitte, in all its circuitous dissonance, minus the dream. And without Nathalie's own disturbing nightmare.

Simone twirled an errant blond tress around her finger. "What are you going to do, then? Keep her secret?"

"I'm going to visit her again," said Nathalie. "Ask . . . ask her to confess, I suppose. I didn't mention that yesterday."

"That's the right thing to do. It is."

"It doesn't feel like it."

"Then what would?"

Nathalie didn't have an answer for that. She didn't have an answer for anything concerning Aunt Brigitte. "I recognize that it's the best option. Not a comfortable one, that's all."

Simone placed her hand on Nathalie's. "If she takes responsibility for this, it saves you from feeling responsible. Because you *aren't*." Simone paused. "What if Aunt Brigitte was right and Véronique was going to kill her . . . what if that happens next time?"

Nathalie gave her a pointed look. "The chances for that are

minimal. It's a lunatic asylum, not an institution for the *criminally* insane."

"Even so. You need to protect Aunt Brigitte."

Nathalie listened to the slow *clop clop* of the horse and continued. "And others from Aunt Brigitte."

"Yes," Simone said, not unkindly. "You do."

She didn't find fault in Simone's argument, not at all. She just didn't want to have to *think* about any of this.

Simone tugged at a thread on her skirt. "I wish I'd met her. I regret never going with you—I suppose I was afraid I'd be too uncomfortable. Perhaps I'll come with you some time, depending on . . . what happens."

Nathalie didn't expect that. Even if it never came to pass, she appreciated the sentiment. "Thank you."

"I believe your once-monthly Sunday visits to her—I think that's what you said?—would become the most important thing to her. Even more than now." Simone nudged Nathalie's shoulder with her own. "Maybe solitary quarters aren't as bad as you think. It's not like you know someone who's gone through it."

"No, but Tante did." Aunt Brigitte had once talked about a patient who'd been released from isolation because she'd taken ill; she died within several weeks. Nathalie had overhead Papa talk to the nurses about the nature of solitary punishments after that, and what she'd caught supported Aunt Brigitte's claims. Despite being prone to exaggeration and fiction at times, her aunt had been right. (Why had Papa asked, anyway? Was he worried his sister might someday do something deemed unacceptable within the walls of an asylum?)

Simone made a soft "hmm" sound before continuing. "Well . . . your aunt might even like being alone. It doesn't sound like she likes being around the other patients."

Perhaps. Nathalie had nothing to base that on, but it was a kinder truth to tell herself than that Aunt Brigitte would suffer.

What did right and wrong mean at Saint-Mathurin? Did the

same societal rules apply in an asylum? Many patients seemed governed by their own sense of ethics, and sometimes those clashed with the ones to which most people adhered.

Don't make excuses for her. Or yourself.

Simone stopped the carriage a few minutes later, so they could each take an omnibus for their separate routes home.

"Busy day for you, is it not?" Simone gave her a hug. "Your best friend during the day and your second-best friend this evening?"

Nathalie smiled. "Yes, I bought Jules tickets to see *Around the World in 80 Days* for his birthday. I didn't come home from the hospital a day too soon."

"We enjoyed it," said Simone. She leaned in close. "That was before the murders, I should note."

Nathalie rolled her eyes. "So dramatic. Louis truly is affecting you."

And yet, she'd been concerned herself about going to the theater, of all places, tonight.

28

The lobby of Théâtre du Châtelet bustled with eager theatergoers pushing to get to their seats. Nathalie and Jules, who was uncharacteristically impatient with the crowd (that was usually Nathalie's attitude—was she influencing him?), stood off to the side for a few minutes to let the crowd thin out.

"Everyone wants to arrive in their row, their seat at once," said Jules. "No matter how mathematically impossible it is."

"Strange to be in a theater of all places, isn't it? Given what Gabrielle has seen."

Jules waved his hand. "I don't know. I get the impression she's uncertain or that her ability isn't all that precise. Or helpful."

"She doesn't like doing it. It's probably that. And lack of confidence." Despite being hasty to criticize Gabrielle herself, she felt oddly compelled to defend her. Because any flaw in Gabrielle's power might admit to a weakening of her own, somehow.

"That could be. Either way, it is . . . an unusually unusual place to be right now. You're right." He looked over his shoulder before ascending the staircase. Their seats were on the second balcony. "Let's not think about that. We'll have a splendid evening; I'm sure of it."

He touched the small of her back and escorted her to the second balcony. Before entering their row, he stopped. "All that time downstairs and I forgot to check my coat." He eyed the row and sighed. "I'll run down to the cloakroom."

He squeezed her hand with affection before leaving. She made her way to the seat, but no sooner had she begun to read the program than she realized she'd left her shawl on a column in the lobby. It was still there, she hoped. She'd taken it off to adjust the bottom of her bodice (subtly) and neglected to put it back on.

She turned to see if Jules was still in earshot, but he'd already disappeared from sight.

With a series of "*Pardonnez-moi*" apologies to the very same patrons she'd crossed moments ago, Nathalie exited the row. She trotted down the sweeping, polished wood staircase and over to the ledge, grateful to see her shawl where she'd left it. Just as she turned to go back up the stairs, her eyes fell on Jules.

Walking out the door.

With his coat on.

Nathalie followed, of course.

The doors were always open at the theater, owing to the gas fixtures for lighting and the need for air to circulate. She made herself as narrow as possible as she slipped through people shuffling in the other direction.

When at last she went outside, she stood in the shadow of a column and looked out. Jules had on a nondescript brown coat like most other men and boys on the boulevard, and the fading sun wasn't enough to illuminate faces. Her eyes trained on the *vespasienne* across the way, its modesty screens surrounded by hedges, as Jules walked under the gaslamp in front of it.

Why wouldn't he use the water closet in the theater?

He didn't use the *vespasienne*, either.

Jules went to a bush beside it, inspected the greenery, and reached his hand into it. He pulled something out. A slip of paper small enough to fit in his palm. He read it and shoved the paper into his coat pocket.

Turning on his heel, he crossed the boulevard again toward the theater.

Nathalie slipped back inside and hoped he didn't see her.

What was that?

She hurried back upstairs, glancing once to make sure he wasn't directly behind her. He was not.

Nathalie inundated her fellow theatergoers with another round of apologies and returned to her seat, mildly short of breath, and opened up the program. Her eyes moved across the text, but she read the same opening sentence again and again. Her mind was too full of questions about what she'd witnessed to absorb any of the words.

That discovery wasn't random. Jules had arranged something that she was not to be privy to, for some reason. The *why* was so pervasive it rang in her ears like a railway bell.

"Is the Passepartout understudy performing tonight?" Jules said, taking the seat to her left. She hadn't even heard him approach. "I thought I overheard someone say that."

"Huh? Oh, uh . . . I don't know. Let me look." Nathalie turned the program over. Was he going to mention that he'd taken a note out of a bush just now?

Or why he still had on his coat?

She gave him a moment, to see if an excuse or explanation was pending.

Instead, he grinned. "I'm delighted that we're here. I really am. I've longed to see this for a year already. Thank you, *ma colombe*." He punctuated the sentiment with a kiss on her cheek.

Her smile in return was weak, but Jules didn't notice. His eyes were traveling the walls and the ceiling, taking in the ornate reds and golds.

"You decided against the cloakroom?"

Jules's face turned as crimson as the drapery. "Yes, the, uh, queue was rather long and the attendant looked harried. I didn't want to wait."

Nathalie shifted in the seat, pinching the program as if it were alive and trying to escape. "Oh."

He faced her, a brow lifted. "Why? Was I gone long?" he asked, sounding as though he was trying to keep his tone light.

She clutched her shawl and forced a smile. "Perhaps I'm just impatient for the show to begin."

"What about that understudy?"

"Oh, no. Not that I could see," said Nathalie, though she couldn't be sure what she had and hadn't read in the last several minutes.

Jules was about to continue when the lights dimmed. After a brief pulse of darkness, the plush red curtain, reminding Nathalie so much of the black one at the morgue, lifted.

She couldn't concentrate. All she could think about was that slip of paper in Jules's pocket, the curiosity burning a hole through her like a flame through papyrus.

That mysterious slip of paper was in Jules's right pocket.

Just centimeters from her left hand.

If only she could grab it, read it, and return it without him knowing.

As soon as the thought hit her, she flushed. *What's wrong with me?* Jules was entitled to his private business. He needn't tell her everything. Maybe he saw a slip of paper in the bushes and grabbed it because he wondered what it was. Maybe he didn't mention it because it was nothing worth mentioning. For all she knew, he'd already discarded the paper.

That was where her mind rested, more or less, until intermission. She enjoyed the show (it was not, in fact, the understudy playing Passepartout), taking in the colorful set and ambitious staging, with its hot air balloon, trains, and ships. The performances were confident and the script closely followed the novel.

When the lights came up for intermission, Jules took his coat off and stood to stretch.

Before she could think twice about it, as if her hand had decided all its own, Nathalie reached into his right pocket. She took the paper out, then let it fall on the floor. In the next moment she herself stood to stretch and dropped her program. She stooped to pick it up, nimbly sliding the paper underneath and picking up both.

She took her seat again. Jules stood next to her, hands on hips and looking more like a fussy professor than a boy of eighteen. She placed the paper inside the folded program. Discreetly, she opened it just enough to read.

Continue. Proper path has been set.
Fifty francs, to be delivered as before.

What was he involved in?

Something unseemly. Almost certainly so.

She closed the program and cast her gaze on the bracelet he'd gifted her with last month. A family heirloom that had belonged to his mother's aunt. Now it felt as if it were wrapped around her wrist like a serpent, constricting more and more. Surely her hand would turn blue.

Nathalie put her finger between her wrist and the bracelet.

"You look perturbed," Jules said, peering over his shoulder. "Are you feeling unwell? I hope it wasn't the terrine."

"No, dinner was excellent. I—" She struggled for an excuse. They'd spent a lot of time at the restaurant talking about the Dr. Delacroix visit; pretending that was still on her mind or troubling her somehow wouldn't be convincing. As they left, they'd passed M. Soucy sitting with friends outside a tavern, giddy and slightly drunk on wine. That was entertaining, not upsetting. And the rest of the evening had been normal and enjoyable, other than the occasional frustration that came with crowds. Nothing else from tonight would suffice.

So, she reached for something she hadn't shared, and wouldn't (couldn't) except vaguely, that genuinely did bother her. "My aunt has been on my mind a lot. I had a conversation with her yesterday that's still nibbling at me."

Jules leaned in close. "I'm sorry to hear that. Is there anything you'd like to discuss?"

Nathalie shook her head, eyes on the stage. She didn't even want to look at him right now.

"You've been through a lot and so has she in the past few weeks," said Jules in a low voice. "You're so very good to her."

He kissed her on the cheek and sat back.

The kiss of Judas.

Nathalie wished she could throw up. She wasn't actually nauseated, didn't actually have the feeling that she could or might. But she *wanted* to. Wanted to purge this feeling and everything else inside her, spew until there was nothing left inside of her and she was an empty vessel, waiting to be filled up again with a feeling that was anything other than . . . this.

29

Nathalie wanted to tear the paper to shreds. And she wanted to keep it. *Let him think a pickpocket took it.*

No. That wasn't the approach to take.

She waited for the lights to go down and dropped the paper on the floor beside Jules's coat.

The disquiet she'd felt over coming to the theater tonight had been nearly irrational. Of all the wild, dramatic, and mostly improbable scenarios she had envisioned (watching a man abduct someone, having the curtain go up and a severed head be on center stage, coming across some overwhelming evidence pointing to the killer's identity *in this show*), she never guessed a scrap of paper would be of concern.

When the show was over, they stood to applaud. As they turned to exit the row, Nathalie pointed to the note.

"Did you drop something?"

She hoped Jules didn't notice how shaky her voice was for that simple question.

His eyes searched the floor, freezing on the paper. "Oh, this." The utterance came out with effort. A recitation, nearly.

He stooped slowly to pick up the note, much to the agitation of the gentleman behind him who was eager to get out.

Nathalie moved in beside him to see. Surely he'd understand her inquisitive spirit, given that it matched his own?

"This is for Faux Papa," Jules said, looking her in the eye.

Oh.

The gentleman behind Jules tapped him on the shoulder. "Could you continue moving, *s'il vous plaît?*"

Nathalie proceeded out of the row. She turned around. "Well?"

"Not here. Let's wait until we get outside."

They continued along with the crowd until it poured onto the boulevard like stones from a burst bag. Nathalie couldn't get out of the fray quickly enough and moved to the doorstep of a dress shop.

Jules came up behind her. "Faux Papa's doing . . . something to pay for his gambling debts. Some series of 'favors' for someone connected to his job at the railroad." He looked down at his scuffed-up shoes. "I don't know what, but I doubt it's honest and in keeping with the law."

She hadn't thought of that. Faux Papa was the one with the unsavory character. Not Jules.

Even so. "If it's for him, then why are you picking up the note?"

Jules kept his eyes downward and put his hands in his pockets. "They don't want to be seen together. Faux Papa made me the messenger. I pass the communications and collect the money, sometimes at a designated place and sometimes at the hat shop. I'm disgusted by it."

Nathalie studied him. He suddenly seemed very boyish. And embarrassed. She felt guilty for having thought he was involved in something—much more than being a messenger—and for forcing him to confess. If she hadn't been so suspicious, Jules could have quietly done his wretched duties without having to explain himself.

She wanted to apologize, but to do so would mean telling him what she'd witnessed. That she'd hidden behind a column, that she'd taken the note from his pocket, and that she'd deliberately put it on the floor so as to ask him about it. She opted for an apology that didn't require admitting any of that.

"I'm sorry you're in the middle of it," she said, imbuing far more meaning into that "sorry" than he knew. "You're trapped in a web of other people's bad choices. I hope it's over soon."

"Me too."

She put out her elbow for him, and he took it. Together they walked down the boulevard. After a brief silence, they talked about the play. Nathalie still watched every man who passed with a skeptical eye.

None of them looked as if they could be Le Rasoir, yet all of them did.

Nathalie didn't get much sleep that night. Her thoughts bounced between Jules, whose life at home was more troubling than she knew, and Christophe, who would be saying goodbye tomorrow for the longest three weeks she'd had in some time.

After a while she went up to the Rooftop Salon with Stanley. It was a clear night despite the humidity, and she fell asleep watching the stars.

A paw pad on her lips awakened her. Stanley ogled her, then meowed. Azure streaked across the sky into orange, with the sun winking from the horizon. She lay there a moment, listening as the faintest sounds of horse clops and rickety wheels heralded deliveries and early morning workers streets away.

Another meow from Stanley roused her from the momentary peace. She went downstairs to feed him and get ready for the day. Because she dawdled too long as she scrutinized her wardrobe, finally selecting a yellow-and-white linen dress with a floral pattern, she ended up having to rush.

Maman was up as well and gave her some blueberries and cheese when she went into the living room to gather her things.

"Nathalie," Maman said, handing her a cloth napkin, "could we speak for a moment?"

"I'm supposed to be at the morgue at eight o'clock, Maman. Can it wait?"

The pleading in her mother's eyes said no. Maman glanced back at the closed bedroom door behind which Papa was sleeping. "Now would be better."

Nathalie's shoulders slumped. A delay now, of all times?

Maman took a step toward her. "Before your father wakes up."

Nathalie flopped onto the sofa with a sigh. Christophe would wait for her, right?

Maman sat next to her, putting her hand on Nathalie's knee. "This requires a lot of discussion so I'll get to it straight away."

Whatever could Maman want to address with such gravity? Nathalie stretched the napkin, loosened it, and stretched it again. "Is something wrong?"

Maman met Nathalie's eyes then looked away. "I—I know what happened with Tante."

"What?"

"I know what you saw." Maman removed her hand and rested it on her own knee. "I understand why you had an . . . especially significant episode."

Nathalie's lungs shriveled. "She *told* you?"

"No," Maman said, gazing at a dress bust in the corner as she spoke. "I read your journal. Not all of it. Just the most recent entries, after your collapse. Enough to see what happened."

Nathalie wrapped the napkin around her hand. She didn't want to disclose anything—to admit too much without knowing for sure what Maman knew, or thought she knew. It was possible this was a bluff. Her mother was good, too good, at gathering information subtly at times. *What does she know?*

"Which was what?"

Maman hesitated. She rearranged a small pile of fabric on the table before continuing. "That Tante took her roommate's life. With a pillow."

Nathalie actually felt her eyes widen as she focused on Maman. "So you *did* read my journal."

"Why wouldn't I? My daughter, who suffers from devastating memory loss, collapsed with a display of the same symptoms."

Both too many words and none at all came to Nathalie's mind. She studied her mother and, after a lengthy pause, spoke. "I understand, Maman. I'd have done the same. Not only do I understand, but I'm grateful." Then she gave voice to the very concern she'd shared with Simone. "I was perplexed as to why no one had thought to read my journal."

"Someone had," said Maman. "I told your father and everyone else there was nothing there. Who doubts a mother? Everyone took my word for it."

"Why didn't you say anything?"

"For the same reason you haven't, I assume."

Often Nathalie thought about how much she was like Papa. Clearly she had plenty of Maman in her, too. "To protect Aunt Brigitte."

Maman gestured toward the bedroom. "And your father."

Nathalie contemplated the weight of all this; she had a hundred other things to share, to ask. She began with the question that was simultaneously the simplest and the most complicated. "What should we do?"

Maman didn't answer. Nathalie was about to repeat the question, though it was impossible her mother didn't hear. Before she could, Maman said one word.

"Nothing."

What? Nathalie tossed the napkin to the side. "How can we do *nothing*?"

"It would damage Brigitte and your father. We've all suffered enough as Insightfuls, and your father worries enough about his sister. Besides . . ." She traced her scars from the Opéra Comique fire two years ago, the same scars that led to Nathalie's job at *Le Petit Journal*. Papa had healed the pain in Maman's hands and helped them move nimbly again, but he could not remove scars, on Maman or anyone else. "I think Papa knows anyway. Or guessed. He didn't seem to find the explanation surrounding your incapacitation entirely plausible."

Nathalie couldn't believe what her mother had just uttered. Maman, who attended vespers and made clothes for the poor every Christmas and had a beautiful soul . . . *she* would cover this up?

When it came to Aunt Brigitte, the rules *were* different. The very question she thought of yesterday after speaking to Simone echoed here in another way.

Somehow Maman, and possibly Papa as well, found it acceptable to cover up a murder.

She was nonplussed at her mother's willingness to do this. Then again, not really. They had kept Aunt Brigitte's power and the whole Insightful family history from her for many years, after all. Her loving, caring parents could keep secrets when they thought they needed to do so.

Nathalie found it reprehensible.

"This is wrong," she said, poking the sofa cushion with each word.

Maman put up her hands. "I didn't say it would be forever. For now, today, we do nothing. We need to—to think this through."

"What's to think about?"

Nathalie knew the answer as soon as she asked the question: wait to see if Véronique's family came forward, if the personnel at Saint-Mathurin suspected anything, if another patient happened to see something, if Aunt Brigitte herself confessed.

"Your father and I have been worried about you. That was our primary concern, as I'm sure you can guess. Now that you're well again, we can think about what to do."

Nathalie stood. "Which 'we' do you mean? You said you think Papa guessed, but you can't confirm it. And clearly you don't want him to know about this conversation."

"We," Maman whispered, "is you and me."

30

Nathalie didn't have time to go to the viewing room before meeting with Christophe—she had all day to do that—and went through the side door instead. Upon knocking on the door to his office and announcing herself, someone opened the door for her. Christophe sat behind his desk, and Jules was seated across from him. Gabrielle, too. That didn't surprise her.

But M. Patenaude opening the door certainly did.

"What's all this?" asked Nathalie. Ostensibly to everyone, although she made eye contact with only Christophe.

"Monsieur Patenaude would like to do a feature on the three of you," Christophe said, his voice courteous but absent the tranquility to which she was accustomed. There was an effort to his affect. "Without saying who you are or where you work. To accompany a piece on Le Rasoir."

She didn't believe for a moment that M. Patenaude was here for that reason. Christophe would have mentioned that yesterday, or M. Patenaude would have told her. An omission from one, perhaps. But both?

Nathalie felt like she'd entered a room where the mood hadn't yet settled, like walking into a surprise party a minute too soon. This setting wasn't what it seemed.

She took the empty seat between Jules and Gabrielle, acknowledging each. Did they suspect, like she did, that something was amiss?

Christophe relinquished his chair at the desk and busied

himself at the cabinet. M. Patenaude took the seat, opened a leather-bound journal, and took the pen from the inkwell. After fidgeting in his chair some, he smiled at the three of them. "Shall we?"

They nodded in unison, and one by one, he asked all three of them questions about their Insightful powers. Read aloud the descriptions of their contributions related to the Le Rasoir case. Nodded in understanding. Adjusted his glasses. Asked questions to clarify responses. Wrote everything down that they said, and based on the extensiveness of his writing, much more.

Nathalie spoke to him with more formality than she usually did, in keeping with the pretense that filled the air. Jules's tone was respectful, and his bearing was that of a deferential young man tending to a customer in a hat shop. Gabrielle was visibly uncomfortable, spinning her crucifix ring around incessantly, as well as earnest. Jules had only met M. Patenaude once or twice, and Gabrielle not at all, as far as Nathalie knew.

When they were finished, Christophe turned his attention to them once again. He thanked them for coming and went over a few procedural matters relative to his absence. "There are no new cases yet today, so we aren't in need of your services." He smiled like a man about to embark on travel, the first time he'd seemed like himself since she walked into the room. "I'll see you all in three weeks."

Gabrielle and Jules wished him well; Nathalie said she'd be back to talk as soon as she made her reporting observation. The three of them bid farewell to M. Patenaude and got up to leave.

"Oh, Jules," said M. Patenaude, rising from the chair, "would you mind staying for a moment?"

Jules halted. Nathalie was behind him and thus unable to see his expression. When he did turn around, his face was impassive. Slowly he took his seat again.

M. Patenaude crossed the room and opened the door for Nathalie and Gabrielle. He shut it behind them as they left.

"What do you suppose that was all about?" whispered Gabrielle, eyes locked on the door.

"The interview?" *Or keeping Jules behind?*

"Yes, the interview," Gabrielle said, furrowing her brow. "People don't know the extent of our involvement with the morgue or the police. There are dozens of other anonymous Insightfuls who vaguely assist, somehow. Why would he feature us?"

Gabrielle didn't know M. Patenaude was an Insightful, much less that he could perceive dishonesty.

Nor did Jules.

But Nathalie knew.

"To provide a story the competitors cannot, I suspect." Nathalie's eyes went to the office door.

"Why not assign a reporter? Or have you do it?"

She could feel the pressure of Gabrielle's scrutiny, that deep blue-eyed gaze seeping into her.

"I don't know. He and Monsieur Gagnon have a friendly relationship, maybe that's why."

"I suppose." Gabrielle shrugged. "Why do you think they've kept Jules behind?"

For someone who was apathetic much of the time, Gabrielle had no small amount of interest today.

Nathalie didn't want to raise Gabrielle's suspicions. What if her own conclusions were wrong, and this *was* for a newspaper feature? What if the conversation with Jules had to do with the trouble Faux Papa was mixed up in?

"I'm not sure," Nathalie said, feigning nonchalance. "Seems like a private matter. I have something to speak to Monsieur Gagnon about so I'm going to wait."

Gabrielle wrung her hands together. "How are you feeling?"

"Much better," Nathalie said, standing up tall. She didn't know how well-informed Gabrielle was about the matter, and now wasn't the time to find out. She had some eavesdropping to do, and she couldn't do it if this discussion continued. Yet she also wanted to make it clear she wasn't feeble in any way. "Back to normal. As normal as can be for an Insightful, I suppose. An inconvenient episode and thankfully over. How has your, uh, consequence been? The numbness in your feet?"

"Uncomfortable. Most of the time it passes in less than a day, which seems both long when I'm enduring it and short when it's over."

"Duration is a strange concept to Insightfuls, I think."

Gabrielle agreed and fell silent.

The two of them stood outside the door, tethered to the moment in awkwardness. Several times Gabrielle appeared to be on the brink of saying something, finally abandoning the attempts with the excuse that the library beckoned.

"Have a good day, and I hope your recovery continues to go well." Gabrielle took a breath. "If you'd ever like to converse about it, I'm happy to—to do that."

Nathalie was taken aback by the glint of empathy. She'd taken the question about her well-being to be mere collegiality, perhaps even with gossipy intentions. That Gabrielle, whose favor she did so little to curry (to put it mildly), endeavored to convey such an offer impressed her. Perhaps the hostility toward Insightfuls had lessened, now that she was among them, working alongside them, using her ability for good in conjunction with them?

"Thank you, Gabrielle. I appreciate that."

And she did. Nevertheless, she still needed her to leave. Now.

Gabrielle said goodbye and made her exit. As soon as the door shut, Nathalie's ear was on the office door. She faced away from the exit and placed her hand on the door casually, lest someone enter the hall.

"—still don't understand why, Jules. For fifty francs?" Christophe's words were laced with agitation.

"I needed the money and was too scared to call his bluff. I—I didn't think I had a choice." Jules sounded as if he was struggling not to cry. "Am I in trouble?"

The note from last night.

But that's not what he just said.

I needed the money. Not my mother's husband. Or even, as much as it would have pained him to say it, *my father.*

Was Jules protecting him?

A pause, followed by Christophe's voice. "His intention was to compromise the investigation, and it worked."

His who? Was he speaking to M. Patenaude about Jules, or to both of them about someone else?

And . . . which investigation was compromised?

She pressed her ear to the door harder; maybe she wasn't hearing this properly.

"Just because you're anonymous," M. Patenaude added, "doesn't mean rumors wouldn't get out that there was an Insightful lying at the morgue on purpose."

Jules lied?

Her instinct last night had been correct. The note involved him. *He* was the one doing "something." Lying. For who? About what?

His thought readings. What else?

And for the killer, or someone working for him.

Everything inside of her tightened, rope knots drawn taut, one after another after another. It couldn't be. Not Jules. Not her *bonbon.*

A drawer slammed shut and Christophe spoke again. "We hope to avoid a scandal here. You're dismissed effective immediately, and you won't receive wages for your work the past week." She'd never heard him this upset.

"I understand."

Obviously the interview had been a ruse. M. Patenaude was there to see if one of them was lying. She suspected it immediately; he *knew* she suspected it.

"The official version I'll tell everyone privy to such things will cite the 'declining, unreliable abilities of an Insightful who assists the police,'" Christophe said. Some papers rustled. "The staff here will be told the same, and I'll say you confessed this only to me in order to save face. Monsieur Patenaude will make certain that some appropriate version of the rumor finds its way into *Le Petit Journal*."

Nathalie flinched at the notion of M. Patenaude having to issue that particular story.

"Fodder for the killer," M. Patenaude added, his tone even. Unearthing lies must have given him exceptional calm in the face of them. "And you will play along—for your sake and for ours. With any luck, Le Rasoir will discover this, somehow, and accept it as truth. It's the best we can do. Other than the Prefect of Police himself, no one outside this room will know the real reason for the cessation of your duties."

I do.

"I'm still astounded by the poor choices you made, Jules. I took you for far more sensible than this." Christophe's indignation remained, and she thought she heard him pacing. "I knew something was amiss, something was different. I'd hoped it *was* a declining ability, not lying."

"I recognize that what I did was wrong," said Jules. "I'm deeply, deeply sorry."

Silence. Three people on the other side of the door, and she couldn't hear a thing.

What was Jules's expression like right now? How were they positioned? What was M. Patenaude doing as Christophe spoke so firmly?

M. Patenaude coughed. Nathalie pictured him repositioning his glasses. "Monsieur Gagnon, before Jules leaves, I want to confirm that we've made a comprehensive assessment. I've identified the laundry and executioner ancestry as falsehoods, but I realize there are other cases and other opportunities to prevaricate."

He misled them about the very avenues they explored most.

"I didn't lie about anything else." Jules sounded hurt.

How dare he sound hurt?

M. Patenaude continued. "Is there any other line of questioning you'd like to pursue?"

No answer came. Did Christophe nod? Shake his head? Write something down? She wanted to burst open the door and confront all of them. Why had she been sent out of the room? Jules was her beau. And morgue work was hers before it had been anyone else's.

The anger bubbled up in her like stew in a cauldron as she waited.

He'd helped the killer.

Jules, her *bonbon*, her friend, and the source of so much warmth in her heart, had aided Le Rasoir. A man who beheaded people and played a revolting game with Paris, the Exposition, and everyone in the city.

Jules *assisted* this man by misdirecting the police? For money?

The door opened.

Jules was startled at the sight of her.

Good.

As he walked across the threshold, she slapped him with as much force as her hand could unleash.

"Liar!" She flounced into the room, forcing him to back up. Christophe and M. Patenaude were on either side of him.

"Nathalie, please, it's not that simple—"

"Did you *help* the killer?"

The four of them stood there a meter apart, tension ricocheting like a bullet in a barrel.

Jules was sweating. "I didn't help, I—"

"But you *did*! I heard it. How about that note? Did you lie to me about that?"

Jules heaved a sigh, refusing to make eye contact. She brought herself up to her full height.

"You haven't heard the whole story, Nathalie." Jules's voice was much too composed for her liking.

"What's there to tell? And how could I believe you if you did?"

Jules heaved another sigh. "You're in no state to listen."

"I'm in *no state* to listen?" She raised her hand to slap him again, but M. Patenaude caught it.

"Please don't, Nathalie."

She darted her eyes toward him. He released his grip as she lowered her hand.

"Why? He deserves it."

M. Patenaude pointed to the exit. "Jules. Let's go." He took him by the elbow and escorted him out.

She followed them into the hall. "Don't dismiss me as if I'm beneath you," she said, voice cracking.

Nathalie felt a hand on her shoulder and shrugged it off. She followed Jules and M. Patenaude as they walked toward the exit. "This isn't about me. This is about you!"

The hand reappeared on her shoulder, more resolute this time.

It was Christophe, of course.

She turned to him with a scowl. "And you? You bring me here under a ruse? I—" Nathalie caught herself. She was *not* going to cry in front of him. "I was a pawn in a game, like the stupid chess game the killer plays. Or is that a lie, too, Jules?" Nathalie called over her shoulder.

Jules didn't answer. The door opened, then closed with a click.

She turned to Christophe again, glowering. "I thought you wanted to say goodbye. How foolish. What was I thinking?"

"I did want to say goodbye."

Nathalie backed up. "Goodbye, then." Her voice was as icy as she could make it. "Enjoy Switzerland. Give your betrothed my kindest regards."

She stormed out, ignoring Christophe as he called after her. She marched over to Notre-Dame, not to pray but to be subsumed by the Gothic dimness and serenity. For almost an hour she sat in the darkest corner she could find, wishing she could vanish into the shadows and not come back.

31

The letter was propped against the apartment door when she returned from *Le Petit Journal* that afternoon, accompanied by a chocolate wrapped in red tulle.

Minutes later, after greeting Maman and giving her the chocolate, Nathalie sat on the bed. Stanley rubbed his chin on her shoulder as she read.

> *My Dearest Nathalie,*
>
> *I'm sorry for what happened this morning at the morgue.*
>
> *I should very much like to speak to you in person. Although it can't undo what's been done, I would like to explain what happened and why.*
>
> *If you wish to meet, I will be at Jardin des Tuileries at six o'clock tomorrow evening. I do hope to see you then.*
>
> *Warm regards,*
> *Your Bonbon*

Jardin des Tuileries. Naturally he would ask to meet there, to appeal to her sentimentality. They'd strolled it together many times, often following an afternoon at the Louvre. It was a place they shared. A public space, yet somehow *their* space.

The day of their first outing together in February stood out among their visits to the garden. She'd thought of it many times since.

"There's not much to see in the winter," Nathalie had said.

"The greens are browns and the leaves are sticks. Why would we want to come out here now? Besides to make footprints in this snow, which I love."

Jules wrapped his arm around her. "May I be romantic?"

"Refined romantic or mawkish romantic?"

"Mawkish."

She'd liked seeing this side of him—and hadn't known it existed until recently. "Proceed."

"I wanted to come out here so we can appreciate the cycle of life," he said, gesturing to the open space before them. "Every time we come here, it will be greener and more lush, and we'll think about today. In the autumn when things start to change, we'll be reminded again of today. And on and on as the seasons progress."

"Absolutely mawkish." Nathalie had smiled and leaned into him, feeling the warmth between them despite the cold air.

But now there was no warmth anymore. Not after what he'd done.

Yes, she'd meet with him. If only to hear how, precisely, he would try to exonerate himself.

He would try to appeal to her emotions, of that she was certain.

Tuileries or not, she was determined to remain steadfast. He'd broken the link between them. When she met him, she'd have to remind herself that a garden was just a garden.

Nathalie left early, so much so that she scarcely got irritated by the tourists on the omnibus who were sluggish to disembark. She was convinced she'd arrive early. Yet there stood Jules, punctual as usual, inspecting the shrubbery in the garden. He was facing the opposite direction, but she nevertheless stepped behind a bush to observe him. She wanted to ascertain his temperament. His arms were crossed, fingers gripping his elbows. He kept his gaze on the ground. He suddenly seemed so young and small to her, despite being a month older and just as tall.

For the duration of the omnibus ride she'd seethed, nails digging into her palms as she went over what she would say. Now that she was here, now that he was in sight, twenty paces away, sustaining the fury she'd worked herself into proved taxing. It was easier to be angry with intangible Jules than with the one who stood before her looking distraught.

They'd never had an argument. Few cross words, really. Theirs had been an uncomplicated relationship. Not passionate or thrilling, but sweet and comfortable and satisfying because they could and did speak of so many subjects. Yet here she was, prepared to end everything between them, like snuffing out a flame.

As well I should. His choices are unforgivable.

Then why did it feel so unwieldy?

Nathalie set and reset her posture several times before stepping into the garden. She tipped the brim of her hat up and approached him wearing what she hoped was an aloof expression.

"You look contemplative," she said, startling him.

"I am," he said, more composed than she expected. "More than ever."

"Why did you want to meet here?"

He opened up his arms to their surroundings. "Why wouldn't I?"

She stared at him. He met her eyes for a moment, then turned away.

"I think it's quieter off to the side here." He took several steps to the right. "Shall we?"

She shrugged and followed him to some benches near a pool of water, passing an enamored couple sitting on one of them. Nathalie made a sniff of contempt she hadn't intended to be audible and cleared her throat to cover it up. *Don't begrudge others their moment.*

She tried to hold on to that thought, but it slipped away like a river fish through the hands.

The next bench, beside a rhododendron bush full of purple blooms, was unoccupied. Jules sat on it and Nathalie joined him, putting as much space between them as the seat allowed. Jules glanced at the exaggerated distance and up at her. He opened his mouth to say something, then stopped.

Nathalie sat up straight. "Let's discuss whatever it is you wished to discuss."

"I think you know what I'd like to discuss. I said as much in my note." His tone was cool but not cold, shrouded ever so slightly with regret.

"Go on, then." She folded her arms.

"Do you recall the morning after the four of us went to the Exposition?"

"The Jester's body was found in two pavilions, yes. And you were still in quite a state from the *vin de coca*, as I recall."

Jules shook his head. "That's not why I was so shaken up, or why I was so standoffish toward Gabrielle during our first encounter, or why I had difficulty doing my thought reading. I felt tired and had no appetite, but that wasn't the whole story." He curled his fingers into fists. "When I removed my coat at the end of our evening at the Exposition, I discovered a note. Le Rasoir—I assume, unless he had an agent working on his behalf—slipped it into my pocket."

"What?" Nathalie was incredulous. This didn't seem plausible. "How? When?"

"On the tram, on foot, on the ferry . . . who can say where or how?" Jules clenched his jaw and released it. "The note demanded that I lie about my next vision regarding the guillotine killings or my mother and sister would be next. By name, Nathalie: 'your mother, Clotilde, and your sister, Suzanne.'"

Nathalie kept her face stoic in spite of the emotions that

bounced around inside her. She wasn't sure which one would emerge. Dubious frustration clawed its way out first. "If so, then why didn't you go to the police with it? Or show Christophe that morning instead of give a false reading?"

"The note wasn't the only thing I found in my pocket. There was also a considerable sum of money," he added, rolling his shoulders. "Much more than my wages."

She couldn't tell if he was weaving a tale or not. He seemed to be speaking in earnest; then again, the same had been true for his claim at the theater when he "found" the note and she confronted him about it. Presumably Monsieur Patenaude had made similar inquiries—there was plenty she hadn't overheard yesterday—but she still wanted Jules to be answerable. To her. She *witnessed* him do that reading, tell the first in a series of lies. "And where is this note and this money?"

"I destroyed the note immediately."

"Convenient," Nathalie scoffed. Yet she herself had once poured blood and a note into the Seine, so fatigued had she been by the Dark Artist's games.

That was different.

"And the money I kept because I—"

"Did as Le Rasoir asked," she sneered, "without even going to the police or Christophe or me or *any other option* that wouldn't have involved abetting a murderer."

Jules looked up at the sky, a gray blanket of clouds, then at her. "*Ma colombe*, I—"

"Do not call me that."

He put his hands in his lap. "Nathalie, I owe you and all of Paris an apology. I was wrong to take the money. I was wrong to throw off the case. I should have gone to the police without hesitation. I don't know what I was thinking." He paused and knotted up his fingers. "That's not true. I do know what I was thinking. About my mother and Suzanne. Is that not reason enough?"

It was. Yes. If other lives weren't at stake. She threw up her hands. "That's what the police are for!"

Jules put his hands on the bench, knees bouncing. "My mother is prone to drink and can't keep a job. Faux Papa has gambled away what little money we have. I believe the weight of the family and the betterment of Suzanne's life to be on my shoulders. Who else will do anything? The temptation was too great. How much do you think I make in a hat shop, or as a chocolatier's apprentice?"

Nathalie regarded him. A kiss of pity touched her heart. She didn't know things were that dire for his family; he complained about his mother's husband, and he said his mother often changed jobs. He'd never said why.

Perhaps they didn't talk and share as much as she'd assumed.

But then she thought about the victims, and how as much as Suzanne deserved saving, so did Le Rasoir's victims. How much further would Jules have led the police astray? What if their wasted efforts had been focused on something else, a path that could have led to the killer? "It isn't your right to determine who gets saved and who doesn't."

"Nor is it yours to decide how I respond to a threat from what I assume is the killer." His tone was stiffer than it had been. "I was desperate, and I made a devastating mistake. And I was terrified. It's not an excuse, but it's the truth. You yourself have refrained from using your ability at times."

"That's because I didn't understand it. I didn't know any better. And if I could revisit that choice and change the past, believe me, I would." *Because I might have been able to save Agnès.*

Nathalie paused, the moment plummeting her into water, like getting pushed off a boat in the dark.

She'd been robbed of Agnès. Their friendship had been immediate and meaningful, but it had also been of too short a duration. It wasn't only that she longed for one more lunch, one more letter, or one more shared joke. Nathalie also wanted a greater repository from which to draw her memories and a deeper history to stay connected. Part of what tore at her was the loss of Agnès, and part was the loss of what might have been, a friendship cut down just as it was flourishing into new branches to explore. Nathalie had never traveled outside of Paris, save for the outskirts. What might that summer have been like?

Agnès's murder would forever be an anchor around her soul. The one and only time Nathalie underwent hypnosis, or tried to, it ended with her being dragged away into the frothy depths of the sea. Agnès was still alive at that time, but the episode was embedded in her deepest self. For now, in her darkest dreams, a nightmare that had haunted her for two years, Nathalie was stuck in the shallow waters of the ocean where Agnès spent her final summer. A Tantalus of Normandy, never able to swim or return to shore.

"Yes," she said again, her voice as far away as that shore. "I would change the past."

Jules hung his head and spoke in a quiet voice. "So would I."

Her own guilt about Agnès, unfounded or not, channeled into annoyance. "But you can't take it back, Jules. It doesn't matter how sorry you are or how well you justify your motives. People may have died or might still die because of you. Your lies and inaction may have perpetuated this terror upon the city."

Jules turned his head and rested his gaze upon her. Frustration, anger, and sadness teemed, a storm behind his gray eyes. "What would you have me do? I can't reverse my mistakes, and every day I walk around with invisible chains of guilt weighing me down." He lifted his wrists with effort, as if wearing manacles. "I don't sleep at night because I'm so full of shame. Your judgment doesn't help."

"What did you expect?"

"At least this much understanding, perhaps?" He pinched his fingers together to indicate a minute amount. "From the young woman I cherish, with whom I've shared more of myself than anyone?"

And yet still left so much unsaid.

Nathalie turned away. "Well, you—you've lost that."

Jules was soundless for so long, she turned around again to see if he'd left. He was there, as motionless as one of the garden's statues, eyes forward and unblinking.

Ever since the incident at the morgue, she'd been angry at him. Another feeling gnawed at her, too, one she'd ignored until now: worry. Something about the way he sat there brought it forward. "Are you . . . still worried for your safety? For your family's?"

His focus remained in front of him. "My mother and Suzanne are with some family in Chartres. Faux Papa, as you might guess, isn't afraid of anything. He carries a pistol everywhere. Always has." He shrugged. "He gave me a knife to carry and said as a 'man,' I should be able to use that and my fists to defend myself."

Nathalie swallowed. How different from the police protection she'd once received.

Then another thought occurred to her, one that would render all of this—the anger, the worry, the betrayal—irrelevant. "What if—what if it's a joke? And not Le Rasoir at all, but someone pretending to be him?"

"If only," he said with a resigned snort. "I don't have any enemies I'm aware of. To what end would someone craft a trick like this? I'm certain it's not that."

"Are you? It would be a prank of pure wickedness, but not impossible."

He shrugged with indifference. She had to admit, the possibility that someone would torment Jules this way for no obvious reason weakened the theory.

Maybe there was hope yet for his redemption. If this was, in fact, Le Rasoir, perhaps he could lead them to him. "Who else knows you're an Insightful?"

Jules swung his eyes toward her. "Family, friends, classmates, teachers . . . and anyone they might have told, and so on. I've had my power for years, and while I didn't tout it, I also didn't hide it." He clasped and unclasped his hands. "Are you looking for clues about Le Rasoir? Because Monsieur Gagnon asked me this same question yesterday."

Nathalie was proud to have thought like Christophe, but also embarrassed to be proud of such a thing in this moment. "People might know of your ability, but you're still an 'anonymous Insightful' as far as the city is concerned, so the circle might be smaller than you think."

"I'm inclined to believe the opposite. How anonymous do you think we are? All it takes is someone knowing what my gift is and then seeing me go to the side entrance of the morgue every day to associate the two." His voice was one of disenchantment and defeat. "You'd be amazed how many secrets Paris can't keep."

He was correct. But Nathalie didn't want him to be correct. She wanted his mistake, this lapse in judgment and ethics, to be fixable. Explainable. She wanted a glorious conclusion to an inglorious choice.

Jules really had ruined everything, hadn't he?

She gazed at him, worry and pity washing away as a wave of deeply felt disappointment crashed over her once again. "Well then, we're back to where we were. You've made a mess of things and I—I can't comprehend it. I'm trying to, I think I do, but the sense of understanding doesn't persist."

Jules looked at her, the ground, his hands, and her again. Finally he spoke, his tone steely. "Nathalie, not everyone has it as easy as you."

"Easy?"

"You wear dresses above your class because your mother is a seamstress. Your father is a sailor and the République will take care of your family. Those are blessings."

She remained silent. Her family had neither money nor money troubles. Her jobs as morgue reporter and Insightful adviser had helped considerably. Her parents were responsible and lived within their means.

The amorous pair from the bench strolled past them, oblivious. Blissfully oblivious.

"It's more than that," Jules continued. "Not everyone has parents who love them, much less parents who comprehend what it's like to be an Insightful. How nice it must be simply to *have* a father, and not be a bastard or a daily reminder to my mother of all that she's suffered." He broke free of the statue pose and turned to her with blazing eyes. "Do you even know what pain is, Nathalie?"

If she'd been standing, the question would have knocked her back on her heels. She leaned toward him, gripping the edge of the bench. "No, not at all, dear Jules. You're the only one who's ever experienced it. Tell me, what's it like to have one of your dearest friends murdered in your stead? Then to witness it? What's it like to carry that burden day and night?" She clasped her hands to her heart. "Oh, I remember now. You're not the one who went through that. I did. I *am*. It's not pain. It's a soothing balm of good feelings. I'm surprised they don't sell it outside the morgue or in a stall at the Exposition."

Nathalie stood, hands on hips. Jules stood as well, waves of hair falling across his forehead. He took a deep breath. "I'm sorry. That was inappropriate and callous on my part. I know you've endured pain."

"Yes, I have, and—"

"It—it comes in many guises, does it not?" He brushed his hair back.

She was ready to fire more words at him and halted abruptly. There was no one way to define pain or to quantify it. He didn't walk in her shoes, but he wasn't wrong—she didn't step into his, either, day in and day out.

She reached into her pocket and presented him with the silver-and-red bracelet. "Here. Give this to Suzanne."

He waved her off. "Keep it. It was a gift."

Jules started to walk away, shoulders slumped.

Let him go.

Nathalie wound the bracelet around her fingers, then put it back in her pocket. She took several steps in the opposite direction.

No. Don't leave.

She kept walking, another few steps, until she got to the topiary they'd stood under that first time together in the garden. He'd held her hand and told her all about topiaries.

After a few more hesitant steps, she glanced over her shoulder. Jules was shuffling away, downtrodden. Did she want to end things this way?

Nathalie followed him on quiet feet and grazed his shoulder with her fingertips. "I'm sorry, too. For being so harsh just now."

He nodded, venturing a small smile. "Do you forgive me?"

She put her hands to her temples with a sigh. "I don't know how to answer that. I'm not sure if what I'm feeling toward you is forgiveness or understanding or sentimentality for affections past."

Jules cocked an eyebrow.

"I can't be with you, Jules," she continued. "Not right now. I can't hook my arm around your elbow and go to cafés and concerts and have chocolate and pretend this didn't happen. I—I don't feel that way about you anymore. Maybe I will in time. Or maybe I won't ever again."

Jules swallowed. "I expected that."

"I don't hate you. And I think we can be friends of a sort. Don't you?"

He took her hand and she let him. Tenderly he lifted it to his lips, then kissed her knuckles. "No."

Nathalie withdrew her hand. "You came here hoping to keep me, but you're rejecting my offer of friendship?"

"I care for you too much to be your friend, Nathalie." He

moved away, just out of reach. "I've long suspected that you mean more to me than I to you. I allowed myself to accept that feeling because I figured that in time, your heart would change. And it has, but not for the better. Even though that's my fault, I don't think I could bear the distance."

Nathalie's throat swelled, suddenly and against her will. "And so, what?"

He took one more step backward. "I think for now, it's best if we don't see each other at all. Should I see you on the street or should our paths otherwise cross, I'll smile warmly. I don't know that we should pursue much more than that."

Regret drifted around her, a mist on an English moor, dissipating as she admitted to herself that he was probably right. It would ultimately be best, and eventually less painful, this way. The mist left behind the damp, uncomfortable feeling of sadness.

"Well, then," she said, giving him a soft kiss on the cheek. "I—I will be on my way. I wish you the best, Jules Lachance."

"I will read your column every day," he said with a bittersweet grin. "And be grateful for the memories, brief as they were."

With that, he walked away, and she turned on her heel and strolled in the other direction. She felt a lot of things, none of them familiar, all of them complicated.

32

For two days, her heart swelled and shrank and maneuvered itself into shapes a heart couldn't possibly be, rendering pain a heart couldn't possibly hold. For Jules. For the way she'd parted ways with Christophe. For Aunt Brigitte. For Agnès, yet again and always. And even for her own memories. That which she'd endured and that which haunted her congealed into one ugly morass of emotions.

When Maman announced that something had come in the mail for her, she thought—hoped—that it was from Christophe. Not that she'd expected to hear from him, because it would be scandalous if he was on vacation with his betrothed and her family and writing to Nathalie. She'd mentioned a postcard, yes, but it was a begrudging acknowledgment of his departure, not a sincere request. Similar to, as she'd heard at the wake for Agnès, people telling a grieving family to call on them should they need anything. Much was needed, and none of it was what a well-intentioned neighbor or doting family member could provide. Such gestures were heartfelt assurances that one's emotions mattered, and while appreciated, rarely carried the weight of expectation.

Not that she deserved correspondence from Christophe after how she'd left things, anyway. Or that it made any sense or was good for her spirit to indulge in such reveries.

It had nevertheless been nice to contemplate. More pleasant than reflecting on the end of her courtship with Jules.

Maman handed her the letter then sat at the table, humming to herself as she measured fabric. Nathalie settled onto the sofa.

The letter wasn't from Christophe or Jules or anyone else whose hand she recognized. The return address was merely Toulouse. No name, no street.

Dear Nathalie,

I am hopeful this letter finds you well—much more so than our last meeting. My understanding is that you've made a remarkable and complete recovery. That both pleases and relieves me greatly.

I apologize that I couldn't be entirely forthcoming during my visit. You might have deduced I am not a medical doctor of the sort affiliated with the hospital. My research is theoretical and dwells in the shadows of a judgmental public (none more judgmental than my fellow scientists). Given our conversation, I suspect you know well the realm within which I work and under whose tutelage I learned.

Your case has been on my mind since our encounter. Dr. Henard's blood transfusions left us with many unknowns; however, my observational and qualitative analyses in the ensuing years have provided me with a comprehensive body of research. My conclusion is that the consequences of your power were indeed magnified because a relation by blood (i.e., your aunt) provoked the immediate manifestation of your gift. Although rare, several examples exist in which the intersection of Insightful gifts among close relatives has also led to a recalibration of powers for one or both Insightfuls. This is all highly variable, due to the individual nature of abilities, and I suspect even more so given your aunt's condition and the unfortunate amplification of your consequences with direct contact.

The impermanent effect was your extended memory loss. As to whether there will be effects of lasting duration,

I am afraid I do not know. For all the research I have done,
this remains a singularity.

Nathalie, I am a recluse by necessity. Although there
are many who wish me ill, I communicate with those who
would benefit from my knowledge or assistance. While I
do not hold a profession situated at the University of Tou-
louse, should you wish to write to me, address your letter
to: General Inquiries, Muséum de Toulouse. I assure you I
will receive it.

Sincerely,
Delacroix

Nathalie read the letter a second time, uncertain where to put her feelings about it. First and foremost, Dr. Delacroix—she would still think of him as a doctor—was real. Not a fantasy her then-unreliable mind had fabricated. He wasn't a mind reader or a thief. He *had* learned from Dr. Henard. That made her feel better. Most everything else he said did not. He confirmed what she had already supposed, but that wasn't what bothered her.

"Maman," she said, waiting until she looked up before continuing. "I have something to show you. That mysterious visitor I had in the hospital wasn't so mysterious after all. He was exactly who I'd guessed he might be."

Maman arched her brow. "Is that from him?"

"Yes. Don't tell Papa—you'll see why. The part about Aunt Brigitte." She handed her the letter.

"I can't believe it," said Maman. "What is it that brought him to you in that hospital?"

Nathalie lifted her shoulders. "I couldn't begin to guess."

When she asked Maman what her interpretation of calibration meant, she didn't like the answer. Even though it coincided with her own.

Her visions, or the consequences of them, might change.

Or they might not.

The idea of Dr. Delacroix, of this man whose breadth of Insightful knowledge could answer at least *some* questions, appealed to her. Even if she didn't truly want to know the answers.

Nathalie felt very out of sorts in the days that followed. The perpetual rain didn't help.

So much was out of her control now. Nothing seemed right, or like it could be made right. Or like it could ever be right.

Le Rasoir's blade had fallen silent. Long enough, Nathalie thought, to lull Paris and its plethora of tourists into the belief that he'd stopped. ("After all," she'd heard someone say in the morgue viewing room, "Jack the Ripper ceased to be.")

This killer wasn't Jack the Ripper, pulsing through the streets of Whitechapel with salacious rage. He was deceptive. He'd gotten to Jules and used newspaper accounts, the police maintained, to validate that the lies were told.

Yet Jules didn't know him, couldn't identify him. Someone knew he was an Insightful helping the police, worked two jobs, and was in a state of financial hardship.

M. Patenaude told her this had all been done through typewritten correspondence that arrived at the hat shop. The shop owner, M. Lyons, had been interrogated at length, as had his son, Jacques, other shop personnel, vendors, and frequent customers. Everyone at Rue du Chocolat was interviewed as well.

Jules's family and neighbors were interrogated. The police themselves were interviewed by their colleagues. Morgue personnel were interviewed, Nathalie included. Christophe, M. Patenaude said, would be spoken to upon his return. Other anonymous Insightfuls helping the police were also questioned.

The volume of interviews was too much for M. Patenaude, between his wavering ability and the number of people involved, so he was only called in for the ones deemed most in need of closer inspection, for one reason or another. Compounding this was the ongoing investigation into people involved in theater throughout Paris.

Too many people, too many interviews, no promising leads, and a killer who, if he hadn't disappeared, was almost certainly choosing a young woman to be his Princess.

When Nathalie next went to see Aunt Brigitte at Saint-Mathurin, her aunt was sitting in the courtyard, a quaint space far more serene than any ward of the interior. On the days when Aunt Brigitte went out, it was typically early and long before visiting hours commenced. To be out there together in the sun, especially in the aftermath of so many rainy days, was an inviting rarity.

Nathalie found her aunt caressing the leaves of a flowering bush. "Cornflowers," Aunt Brigitte said. "Not much scent, but beautiful."

"Gorgeously blue."

They had a corner of the courtyard to themselves. Another patient sat with his visitors and moved his hands about in animated fashion. On the opposite side of the courtyard, three women and a man sat at a table, playing cards with an invisible deck. Estelle wandered around, repeating "What's trump?" and "Who led?"—both of which must have come from the card game. A nurse supervised from a window.

Nathalie carried over a nearby chair. Following some pleasantries, she clasped her hands together and rested them on her lap. "I've been thinking of you a lot, Tante. And the . . . problem you have."

Aunt Brigitte held a cornflower by the stem. "The one that made my dreams worse?"

"Yes," Nathalie began, then slowed down to choose her words. "I thought of something, a means of proceeding, that might ultimately bring you peace. A way to approach the . . . problem."

"God is mad at me."

"He forgives."

"I don't know if I forgive myself. I feel very guilty, but sometimes I don't at all." Aunt Brigitte let go of the stem. "I need to arrange the words properly."

Nathalie leaned forward. Aunt Brigitte's speech was stilted today, the conversation disjointed. "Which words?"

"For my confession."

It was as if the weight of Saint-Mathurin Asylum itself had been lifted off her back. She had thought for sure she'd have to convince her aunt, to point out to her all the reasons she might wish to confess, either of her own accord or if they questioned her. "I think that's an admirable choice, Tante. Confessing might be painful, but it's the right thing do. You are a good person who made a mistake."

"I did. I am responsible. I have to tell someone. I don't want God to be mad at me anymore."

"He isn't," said Nathalie. She couldn't know that. But she could hope it to be true and pray for it.

Aunt Brigitte sank into the chair with a deep sigh and crossed her ankles. Resignation floated about her like the scent of the nearby rosebush. Nathalie felt foolish for wondering if the ethics of right and wrong governed the asylum. Why wouldn't they? People were people, whether they were having a sandwich at a café or confined to a dingy room with bars over the windows.

"Consequences," said Aunt Brigitte in a harsh voice. She reached for the cornflower, looking for a moment as if she was going to snap off the bloom, then paused. She plucked a single petal and let it go, watching it as it glided to the ground.

Nathalie surveyed the courtyard. "What made you decide?"

"Her sisters," Aunt Brigitte whispered. "I saw their sadness and tried to forget it. But my dreams never permit that."

Nathalie didn't know what to say. She put a tender hand on top of Aunt Brigitte's bony knuckles. They sat quietly like that for a few moments. What would the consequences be—better or worse than Aunt Brigitte feared? Than what Nathalie and

Maman feared? Nathalie didn't want to speculate aloud. She hoped Aunt Brigitte would still be able to have visitors. Surely they wouldn't deprive her of that? Perhaps her otherwise good behavior toward other patients over the years would mitigate her punishment.

Aunt Brigitte slid her hand away. She picked up the scentless flower petal, resting it on her palm.

A soft, simple gesture from hands that had killed.

Maman always tried to keep Aunt Brigitte's mood from darkening, if only for a while. As Nathalie observed her aunt, it occurred to her how she could do that, too, right now.

"Tante, I have something nice to share with you," she said, picking up her satchel. "Close your eyes."

"Oh?" Aunt Brigitte studied her for a few moments, then snapped her eyes shut.

Nathalie took the jar of musk-and-amber oil out of her bag and unscrewed the lid.

Aunt Brigitte sniffed, then grinned, eyes still closed.

A bee buzzed between them. Nathalie waved it away and tipped the jar until a few drops fell on her fingers. She dabbed the oil on the thin skin of Aunt Brigitte's slender, once-graceful neck, feeling the delicate bones underneath.

"Can I open my eyes now?"

"Yes," said Nathalie. "Isn't that a magnificent scent? I bought it at the Algeria Pavilion at the Exposition. It reminds me of . . . I don't know. Elsewhere."

"I've never smelled this kind of perfume. I think I like it." Aunt Brigitte's hand went to her throat. She smeared some oil on the back of her wrist, inhaling deeply. "Elsewhere. I've never been elsewhere. I've never left Paris."

"Me either," said Nathalie. "Except through the Exposition. I hope to travel someday."

"You should." Aunt Brigitte's grin diminished. "Before it's too late."

Nathalie almost replied that it was never too late. Except that it was, for everyone else in the courtyard. Especially her aunt.

Aunt Brigitte inhaled the scent again and closed her eyes. "Do you have a beau?"

She asked that every now and then. Once, it was when Nathalie and Jules were several weeks into their courtship. She'd been coy in answering, because the idea of having a beau was fresh and exciting and a little fanciful. *I might,* she'd said with a wink. *We'll see if he behaves well enough for the title to be bestowed for the duration.* They laughed, she and Aunt Brigitte and Maman.

Nathalie wasn't coquettish this time. "Not anymore." Her tone chiseled the syllables like a pickaxe.

"Oh, I remember now," said Aunt Brigitte, her brow crinkling in recollection. "He'd gotten you a scent with bergamot."

Yes, he had. And she'd worn it every day since, until the incident at the morgue. Now she wore only the Algerian oil.

"I knew love. Several times. None of them mattered in the end except one." Aunt Brigitte's hand went to her midsection. The dressing gown covered that belly scarred with tiny crosses, a womb that once held the promise of a baby. The child was a stillborn. "It was extraordinary for a time."

Nathalie studied her aunt. She couldn't reconcile the two images that came to mind: this scrawny, birdlike woman whose appearance was that of someone two decades older than her years and a youthful, vivacious girl who sought to spend her days at a perfumery.

"Love. It's here and then it isn't." Aunt Brigitte stood and turned away from Nathalie to face the sun. She swayed her hands lightly. "Here and gone. Gone and here."

Aunt Brigitte's voice softened, and she repeated it again. *Here and gone. Gone and here.* Again she said it, and again, quieter each time, until Nathalie couldn't tell whether she was hearing it in the asylum courtyard or in her own mind.

33

If Nathalie took a certain route home from the asylum, she could pass by the tailor shop where Maman worked. She debated what to do until her legs decided for her, and she walked into Hardy Brothers Tailor Shop.

"Caroline, your daughter is here to see you," called one of the Messieurs Hardy.

The tin-ceilinged shop was cramped with clothes, material, and extensive displays that mirrored Maman's sartorial works in progress at home. Silks, cottons, wools of every color and quality lined the walls, with bins of buttons, ribbons, lace, and every other accoutrement imaginable. Maman came out from the back room with swift movements. Her eyes darted to the clock as she greeted Nathalie with a taut smile.

Nathalie considered stepping outside but concluded that Maman's gossipy coworkers would have more to talk about if they sought privacy. She chose to speak in vague terms instead, knowing that Maman (who had taught her this tactic) would understand.

"I'm on my way home from a visit. The matter we discussed . . . there's going to be an admission. I went intending to suggest it, but she, uh, came to that decision on her own."

Maman watched Nathalie intently as she took in the words; after a few moments, her face registered the meaning. "Are you certain? And do you know why?"

"As certain as one can be," said Nathalie, peering over Maman's shoulder at a coworker who busied himself taking inventory while pretending not to listen. "The why had to do with the family. I can explain more later. Will you . . ."

"Tell Papa?"

Nathalie nodded. How did Maman guess?

"He already knows. Concluded it on his own, as I thought he might. We discussed it several days ago. Not a lot. Just enough to . . . admit to mutual understanding. I also told him about Dr. Delacroix's letter, now that there's nothing to hide. One less secret to keep." Maman's gaze lingered on her. She lowered her voice. "I'll tell him about Tante's decision today."

Would she?

Or was this part of some larger fiction?

Nathalie didn't know. She wasn't even sure if she could believe Maman would tell him, or that, as she'd inferred, he'd guessed that his sister had killed someone. Her parents weren't necessarily forthcoming about secrets involving Aunt Brigitte. The fact that she'd talked to Papa days ago about these things and hadn't said anything until now was proof.

"I suppose this is the best course for all of us," Nathalie said, staving off the misgivings that nagged at her before the sentence even left her tongue.

The queue at the morgue the next morning was long, even without a murder victim on display. Based on the conversations she overheard, people were hoping to see Le Rasoir's latest victim before the newspapers had a chance to report it. The killer's Princess had yet to be harmed, so it was just another day at the morgue with the same display as the previous. Her column would be brief.

As she left, she passed by a woman distributing broadsides. At first she barely noticed—there was always someone handing out papers, selling wares, announcing a lunch special—until a waft of incense tickled her nose.

"I'll take one," she said.

The white-haired woman, eyes boring into Nathalie like a drill, handed her a sheet of paper. "Repent."

Nathalie read it as she walked away. The biblical quote was on one side; she recognized it from last time because of the final line. *Wherever the corpse is, there the vultures will gather.*

Last time, Nathalie had seen the woman at the Exposition, after getting off the Decauville train that brought people from one part of the fair to another.

Lurid but fitting to be outside the morgue. Was she here every day now, like the people who took their lunches in sight of the door in case another head showed up?

Nathalie turned over the broadside. A cursory map of the Exposition with crosses where heads had been found, now with the addition of the morgue.

"That's popular now, it would seem," said a familiar female voice.

She turned to see Gabrielle, who was wearing such a sizeable hat, Nathalie's own felt small.

"Death maps," Gabrielle continued. "That's the third person I've seen handing them out. One showed several prominent murder locations, including those of the Dark Artist. The other had an advertisement for the services of a medium on the reverse."

"Murder tourism," Nathalie said. She didn't want to admit it to Gabrielle, but had she not been directly involved in the morgue, visiting murder sites was the sort of thing she'd explore with Simone, Louis, and Ju—

With Simone and Louis. Not Jules.

She folded the broadside and put it in her bag. Gabrielle stood there, not saying anything yet making no move to leave, either.

Nathalie spoke, if only to free them of this awkwardness. "Are you doing, uh, something at the morgue or only passing through?"

"The Prefect of Police asked if I wouldn't mind helping with other cases." She toyed with a pearl button on her beige frock.

"Ah, I see." Both Gabrielle and Jules had powers independent of murder, which made them more useful than her. It was an uncomfortable thought she'd entertained for some time. Jules had offered assistance on other cases at times, so she shouldn't have been surprised that Gabrielle had been invited to do the same.

Still, she didn't like it. It was one thing to work together. It was another when they—or rather, only Gabrielle now—might be perceived as more valuable.

But she had to get over that, didn't she? She didn't own the morgue, didn't own what Insightfuls did with their powers. Jules had been right about that.

"Part of me almost likes being an Insightful now," added Gabrielle. "Yet part of me still feels like it's penance."

"I'm glad you're making peace with it. Or that part of you is." Nathalie tilted the brim of her hat. "I'm sure I'll see you here, then. Have a good—"

"Are you free for a few minutes of conversation?" interrupted Gabrielle, an air of subdued gravity about her.

34

This was the second offer she'd made to talk, this one more direct than the last. What was so pressing that Gabrielle wished to speak with her? Evidently she wanted to go beyond pleasantries. Nathalie had been focused on getting her article done, seeing as it was late in the day. Her manners and curiosity colluded, and rather than making an excuse, she found herself saying yes.

"You mean here? Or . . . ?" Nathalie purposely didn't suggest a café. She wanted the opportunity to leave gracefully, and a café would come with certain social trappings.

"There's a spot along the river that I like. Perhaps that?"

Nathalie acquiesced, following her a short way to a staircase beside the bridge (the one Nathalie resented). Gabrielle, her limp nearly imperceptible, wound her way through excitable families and jaunty tourists to a spot alongside the Seine. Bathers were along the edge of the river, clear of the small boats and sightseeing ferries. Gabrielle sat on the wall, feet dangling over the edge. Nathalie sat a meter or so away and watched the other people as she waited for Gabrielle to begin.

It wasn't immediate. Gabrielle was silent, then remarked on the whimsical red-and-white paint scheme of a passing boat, her thumb spinning the crucifix ring the whole time.

"That ring means something to you, doesn't it?" Nathalie said, eyeing it.

Gabrielle looked at her hands and held them up. "Both of them do. A tale of two grandmothers."

Nathalie raised a brow.

"The amethyst one is from my grandmother Marguerite, a widow whose husband, long gone from cholera, gave her this after a year of marriage."

"Striking."

"The other is a confirmation gift from my grandmother Jeanne. A ring she herself wore for many years. She was most religious." Gabrielle touched the crucifix ring with her other hand. "I find a lot of solace in prayer myself."

Nathalie hadn't anticipated such openness. She was drawn to it and put off by it at the same time. Gabrielle was a puzzle, and she still didn't know what to think of her. "I have, too, at times. I'm not as consistent about attending Mass as I'd like, but I find serenity at Notre-Dame."

"Conversations with God have helped me accept myself as an Insightful." Gabrielle tucked a braid under her hat. "I never thought I'd use my power this frequently. I have a long way to go to make peace with it, but my contempt turned to resignation. Prayer has helped, the experience has helped. Some other . . . relationships I've cultivated. And you."

Nathalie turned to her. "*Me?*"

Gabrielle stared at the river and swung her heels, kicking them against the bank. "I've observed you, how you approach it all. Confident and with a sense of duty, even a speck of conceit."

Nathalie went to argue the point, then realized that perhaps Gabrielle was somewhat right. "Conceit is a strong word."

"That's why I said a speck. The smallest dash is acceptable, I think." Gabrielle smiled in such a way that Nathalie couldn't help but return it.

Yet even as Nathalie warmed up to Gabrielle's overtures, the *why* gnawed at her. Was she building up to ask about Jules's absence? Because Nathalie wasn't about to answer that. Not in a straightforward manner, anyway.

"I haven't been in the company of many Insightfuls unafraid

to use their powers," Gabrielle said. "Even after spending time in the hospital, you're so filled with dedication, you returned almost right away."

Nathalie's stomach twisted like a tree in a fairy tale. Gabrielle held an exaggerated view of her, her ability, her sensibility in grappling with it. "It's, uh, not that effortless for me. Especially after this last episode of memory loss."

"It was heartbreaking to see you that way."

Nathalie blushed. Was that what Christophe had told her? Jules wouldn't have told her anything so personal. Besides, she was much better by the time Gabrielle had seen her. "If you thought I looked unwell when I came home, you should have seen me at the hospital."

"I did."

"Oh?" Nathalie looked at her askance. "There was a guest register. Your name wasn't in it."

"Purposely."

"Why?" Nathalie narrowed her gaze.

"To be discreet." Gabrielle paused before continuing. "We talked about going to the top platform of the Tour Eiffel."

Nathalie's bones disappeared, every one of them, and she feared she'd slide right off the bank into the Seine.

Agnès hadn't visited her in the hospital.

Gabrielle had.

How distorted was my mind?

"I can't believe it. I remember but I don't. You . . . didn't resemble you." She turned away, unwilling to let Gabrielle study her visage. "In my bizarre convalescence, I mistook you for someone else."

Gabrielle seemed both unbothered and unsurprised. "You were asleep when I arrived. I shouldn't have done it without asking first but I—I touched your feet to discern your path."

Nathalie recoiled. "What? I would have preferred to give you permission, yes."

Yet she couldn't blame Gabrielle. Might not she have done the same?

"I don't know what happened in specific terms, but I saw that you were in a space with a lot of rooms and beds. I knew from Christophe that it was Saint-Mathurin Asylum because you were visiting your aunt when this happened." Gabrielle hesitated, as if she were waiting for Nathalie to interrupt. "There was a great swell of energy from you and you . . . almost seemed to disappear with lightness. You returned and lingered in the room, then walked into a hall and collapsed."

Energy followed by disappearing.

Gabrielle knew she had a vision, and she knew visions only came when someone died at the hands of another.

Surely she'd deduced the truth. After all, Dr. Delacroix had cited "an encounter" when he spoke to her in the hospital.

Which meant he knew the truth as well, yet never pried. His focus was helping Nathalie, not making Aunt Brigitte accountable.

As with Gabrielle, Nathalie presumed.

"Your power is remarkably impressive," said Nathalie, attempting a lighthearted tone. "That is, uh, what happened."

She decided not to elaborate. What were Gabrielle's motives? To seek justice for the woman Aunt Brigitte killed? To scold Nathalie for holding on to the secret? Or something far more benign?

"I can see the distrust on your face," said Gabrielle. "Maybe my approach was wrong. I won't interfere—I trust that your family and the asylum will take care of the matter."

Nathalie considered both not responding and explaining everything. Each had appeal. Ultimately she settled on a single word. "Yes."

She still didn't understand the point of this conversation, unless Gabrielle was exercising subtle power and sought to make her squirm. Which was why the next questions were not at all what Nathalie was expecting.

"Did you have anyone to discuss it with? That is . . . someone who understood? Besides your parents or your friends."

The words came to Nathalie's ears slowly, as if entering her mind patiently and single file.

What were the chances those questions were random, coincidental?

Rather slim.

Nathalie responded using a phrase Maman had taught her for whenever someone's questions were too pointed. "Why do you ask?"

Gabrielle watched a pair of bathers swimming on the other side of the river. "I think you know."

"Do I?"

"I sent him to you," said Gabrielle, her voice faint. "I correspond with him regularly."

Was she talking about . . . ? No, that was so unlikely. Nathalie pressed her palms into the wall. "Him who?"

"Delacroix."

Some other . . . relationships.

Could it be?

It was balmy and they were in the sun, but a chill nevertheless tickled up Nathalie's arms. The first time she'd met Gabrielle, they'd gone to Café Maxime's with Christophe. Gabrielle had expressed how disgruntled she was over her Insightful identity, and Nathalie remembered thinking about the mysterious Insightful who supposedly helped other Insightfuls. And how, if she'd known him to be real, she'd have suggested Gabrielle seek him out.

Gabrielle watched her expectantly.

"*You* sent him to me? I—when I tried to think of—I never considered that it might have been you."

"Why not?"

Because I didn't think we liked each other.

Or was it only Nathalie who hadn't liked Gabrielle?

Nathalie flicked a pebble into the Seine. "I didn't know you . . . were inclined to demonstrate such a courtesy toward me."

"We all need help sometimes. If you didn't want it or seek it, no harm would have been done."

"I wasn't sure he was real. I don't remember all of our conversation, but I think I told him the entirety of my story as an Insightful. He's since sent me a lovely letter, maybe not revealing everything about who he is but . . . enough. He invited me to correspond with him if I felt like I needed to or had questions." Nathalie lowered her voice. "So you told him how . . . I ended up in the hospital?"

Gabrielle gave a timid nod.

He did seem to know, Delacroix. She'd thought so at the time but neither trusted her mind nor understood how he could have. She wasn't sure at the time what she'd said out loud and what she hadn't.

"His gift is one of profound empathy," said Gabrielle, a note of admiration in her voice. "He can feel the pain of others—pain of the heart and mind. He perceives it in a pure way, and the toll it takes on him is an immediate manifestation of physical discomfort. An ache."

"No wonder he's a recluse." Nathalie thought about what that would be like. Every loved one, every social exchange of any significance bringing pain because everyone carried something. How could you possibly shun the pain of others unless you removed yourself from the world most of the time? It didn't sound like something he could choose the way that Nathalie or Gabrielle could. She either touched the dead through glass or she didn't. Gabrielle either sought a path tracing or refrained.

What barriers could one put up so that the hurt of another didn't seep through?

"That sounds like a most unfortunate ability to have," Nathalie said, her voice soft.

Gabrielle crossed her feet at the ankles. "He considers it the price of having worked so closely with Dr. Henard. He uses it for benevolence, to support and try to understand the troubles of Insightfuls. He listens, he explains. He cares."

"What of his name? Or names?"

"From what I've heard," said Gabrielle, "he used several early on. In recent years his choice of name became more deliberate."

Delacroix. Cross. But also near a crossroads.

Gabrielle swallowed and continued. "That, combined with his ongoing research, makes him . . . very important to someone like me."

"I'm glad he's been able to help you. You've undoubtedly learned from him."

Gabrielle blushed.

Nathalie's heart was filled with gratitude in that moment. While she didn't reach out to place a hand on Gabrielle, part of her wanted to. "I don't know that there's a greater display of empathy than what *you* did, both in seeing the situation with my aunt for what it is and in sending Dr. Delacroix to me. Thank you for that."

"You're welcome. Some good soul sent him to me; I never found out who. I've been grateful ever since." Gabrielle stood and dusted off her dress. "He gives sound advice and is knowledge-able. He can't solve every problem or use his gift to eliminate your worries, but he's a good person to have supporting you."

He wasn't a rumor, wasn't a legend. He was someone who might be able to help from time to time with perspective the other Insightfuls in her life might not have. "I've not yet written to him, but I certainly will. Thank you again."

Nathalie was about to get up as well when she noticed some-one crossing the bridge who looked like—no, it couldn't be him.

Yet it was.

Christophe.

35

Why wasn't he in Switzerland? He wasn't due home for weeks.

She wanted to wave but didn't, not in front of Gabrielle. They might have taken a step toward friendship, but Nathalie still didn't care for the way Gabrielle beamed at him and sought his attention (or had she been mistaken about that? Well, now wasn't the time to evaluate it). Keeping her eye on him, she almost lost him in the crowd while saying goodbye to Gabrielle. She increased her pace and reached him before he got to the steps of the morgue.

"Christophe," she called out.

He turned and waved at her, squinting into the sun.

"What are you doing back so soon?" she asked as she closed the gap between them.

He exhaled. "I spent a lot of time thinking and arrived at a decision on the train to Switzerland. Before that, really. I needed a few days there to confirm that my thoughts were in order, and indeed they were." He wrung his hands together and lowered his voice. "I called off the engagement."

Shock, curiosity, elation, even a touch of pity—all tackled one another in her head at full force, like boys wrestling in a schoolyard.

She wanted to ask why. He read the question on her face; he had to have, like he'd read so many before. Yet as inquisitive as she was, she didn't want to intrude on his privacy. She wanted to know but also didn't. She'd never asked about his fiancée before, never spoke a word about his prolonged engagement more than necessary. Other than the young woman's name, which she herself never used, Nathalie knew nothing of her. To ask now about her, about them, would be disingenuous.

Someday maybe she'd ask. Or someday maybe he'd share.

For now, she chose words of respect and comfort. "I'm sure that was a taxing decision to make, and I'm sure you're both experiencing a flood of feelings right now. May your heart heal soon."

Because in truth, as satisfied as she was to learn of this news, her own heart had yet to mend from Jules's betrayal and the end of their relationship. Christophe didn't know any of that, but again, this wasn't the occasion to discuss it.

"It's difficult, but I know it's for my best interest as well as hers. Better to recognize that now than after marriage."

Finally he met her gaze. When he did, it was she who looked away first. She spoke without making eye contact. "I, um, also wanted to apologize for how we, that is, how I left things. Before your departure. I was incensed that day. Not at you, though I . . . certainly made it seem so."

She felt heat rushing through her, head to toe, and not because of the sun.

"That's very considerate of you, Nathalie." His tone was even, hard to interpret. "Thank you for being so forthright."

She faced him and was relieved to see geniality on his face. Not a smile exactly, but something approaching tranquility.

"I—I didn't begrudge you your anger that day," he added. "Although I can't say I *enjoyed* being on the receiving end of it." The faintest of smirks teased the corners of his mouth.

"Well," Nathalie said, relaxing into a humble smile as she took a step back. "I am grateful for your understanding. It's good to see you again so soon, despite the circumstances. We'll speak at length before long, I'm sure."

Christophe agreed, and they parted ways. As Nathalie strolled away, her insides became engulfed in a waterfall of emotions old and new.

After turning in her article, she went to Montmartre to Simone's apartment. The two of them and Louis had plans to attend the Telephone Pavilion and perhaps try a "long-distance call" (Nathalie was skeptical; it had to be a trick), have dinner at a nearby restaurant beside the Finland Pavilion, and take in a fireworks display to end the evening. Tomorrow morning, they were going to explore a small, abandoned theater Simone had heard about at Le Chat Noir.

She arrived just prior to the agreed-upon time of four o'clock and knocked on the door. No answer. She waited a moment and tried again.

"Simone?"

Nathalie more than half expected her friend to answer the door with a yawn. Simone's vampire hours (as she called them) from working at the club often had her on an unusual sleep schedule.

Another soft knock.

Nothing.

She tried the doorknob. Locked.

Odd. She put her ear against the rough-hewn, overly varnished door. Other than a distant "mew" from one of the kittens, not a sound carried through.

Nathalie went to the end of the hall and peered out a mildly dirty window that overlooked the boulevard. Louis should be here any moment, too. Perhaps Simone was out running an errand.

When the clock on a building across the way struck half past, she gave up.

Did I make a mistake? She'd written it down and hadn't had any memory gaps of late, not that she was aware of, anyway. Were they supposed to meet somewhere else?

Or maybe it was Simone who'd misunderstood. She and Louis might be at the Telephone Pavilion waiting for her.

She made her way to the Exposition as swiftly as her feet and public transportation would take her. The exhibit was at the front of the Tour Eiffel and to the left, so she didn't have much ground to cover. Even if she was late, she could catch up to them quickly.

She slipped inside, oblivious to the people around her as she searched for Louis's red locks and Simone's blond curls.

Nathalie wrapped her long arms around herself. Where were they? Had she gotten the *day* wrong?

One last effort. She made her way to the restaurant where they were going to have dinner. Again the search ended in futility. Both disappointed and annoyed, she traipsed the grounds for a while, smelling a variety of sweet and savory foods and watching *Guide Bleu*–bearing visitors pass by. After one last return to the pavilion, she went home. Simone would be at her parents' apartment in the morning to spend time with Céleste, so she'd stop by then.

She truly hoped the mistake was on Simone's end. Not because she needed to be right or even cared all that much about the time spent chasing apparitions at the Exposition. She was worried that somehow, despite her certainty as to the time and place, she'd gotten it wrong. No, that her mind had gotten it wrong. That her sense of chronology had become erroneous and wasn't to be trusted.

After dinner, she sat at her desk and took out a sheet of stationery. Her pen hovered over the inkwell as she composed her thoughts, then she began to write.

Dear Dr. Delacroix,
  Thank you for your kindness, both in visiting me and in your gracious offer. You'll be pleased to know that I'm doing very well, surprisingly so, following my convalescence.

My mind was hazy when you came by, so forgive me if this letter repeats something I've already shared or if I'm speaking to something you don't know. I'm left with the feeling that we discussed much, so I'll proceed on that assumption.

Gabrielle Thayer and I had an enlightening conversation. It was incredibly thoughtful of her to establish this connection, and I'm grateful for her intervention. I respect and admire the work she says you are doing.

Some Insightful questions have long resided in my mind, yes. I recognize that you may not have the answer to all of them, but any insight (I jest) you might provide would be of value.

As I believe you know, I discovered my ability in the morgue. Did I always have it, or did it merely emerge when I matured to a certain age? Did something bring it on? Would I have found out some other way, or would it have remained latent? Are there other "natural" Insightfuls who never see a manifestation of their power?

I did notice one strange difference in a recent vision. (It was perhaps premature to use my gift, I admit. I am pleased to share the subsequent memory loss was minimal.) I might have told you that when I first discovered my Insightful ability, my visions were in reverse. That changed when I witnessed the murder of my friend Agnès. It has remained that way ever since, except for the other day. Although I know one incident doesn't constitute a pattern, I'm interested to see if it continues. Might it signify anything?

One other anomaly remains to be seen. Today I was to go out with two friends. I'm certain I had the day and time correct, but they were nowhere to be found. While I don't know the source of the misunderstanding, there's a small part of me that's wondering if my memory is flawed. I'll have this sorted out by the time you receive this, and I'm *sure it's nothing of concern. I am mentioning it here in the unlikely event that it is.*

I have taken up enough of your time, I'm sure. Much appreciation, again, for welcoming this correspondence.

With kind regards, I remain sincerely yours,

Nathalie Baudin

Nathalie slept later than usual the next morning. Following a leisurely breakfast with Papa, she stopped at the Marchands'. Céleste, who was a nine-year-old Simone in appearance and in vigor, answered the door. She had a book of fairy tales in her hands.

"Oh! Your sister isn't here?"

"She was supposed to be here an hour ago," said Céleste with a shrug. "She probably forgot."

Nathalie chewed the inside of her cheek. That wasn't like Simone.

"Well, if she comes by, uh . . . you know what? Let me write her a note." Nathalie retrieved her journal and tore out a page.

I went to your apartment yesterday as planned . . . or maybe didn't plan? I had it written down, but I doubt that's foolproof. Much to share. Come visit! If I'm not there, leave a note with Papa.

However, even as she wrote, it felt false. Her gut was telling her there was no misunderstanding. Still, she didn't want to alarm the Marchands, so it was best to keep the tone blithe.

Where are you, Simone?

Céleste took the note from her and, as Nathalie expected, read it immediately. "I haven't been to Simone's apartment in a long time. We're supposed to go next week to see Max and Lucy. Have you met them?"

"I have," said Nathalie, grateful for the subject change. Her palms were sweating. "Soft, sweet, and full of tiny *mews*. You'll love them."

Céleste beamed. "I love kitties. My parents said maybe for my tenth birthday I can get one. Give Stanley a hug for me, will you?"

"I most certainly will."

"And say hello to your papa."

"I'll do that, too." Nathalie's voice was much more cheerful than she felt. She attempted to tuck away her journal but dropped it instead. After kneeling to pick it up, she made a joke about her clumsiness, put the journal in her satchel on the second try, and said goodbye to Céleste.

Nathalie planned a route for the rest of the day. She'd post her letter to Dr. Delacroix and go to The Quill where Louis worked, as well as his apartment, before the morgue. She could stop at Le Chat Noir after going to *Le Petit Journal*. Then she'd go to Simone's apartment again.

Her stop at The Quill was unsatisfying. Louis had been at work two days ago; he had yesterday off and wasn't scheduled to work again until the afternoon.

She went to his apartment next, knocking so many times, her knuckles hurt. It was then that her heart began to thump with ominous, brooding weight.

Because once the thought entered her mind—the whisper of a thought, really—it was too late. There was no unthinking it.

Like the first raindrop in a storm, where at first you think it's your imagination or dew from a tree. As soon as you question it, another falls, then another, then more in rapid succession until it's obvious that it's raining and you're soaking wet and now you're utterly consumed by the rain and focused solely on getting out of it.

What if something . . . happened to them?

She scolded herself for thinking this way. *Too much time at the morgue.*

But the rainstorm in her mind had already commenced.

36

At the morgue, there were two new bodies, an older man with dropsy and a woman around Maman's age who was missing several toes. Nathalie touched the glass to confirm that neither were murder victims, then knocked on the Medusa door.

"Nathalie," whispered M. Soucy. He came up behind her, last night's alcohol on his breath. "You seem very upset. Has something happened?"

She was taken aback, both that he noticed and that he cared. He'd always been pleasant enough, but rarely did he call out to her after the initial hello, much less remark upon her mood. "I—I am concerned about something. I'm sure it will be resolved well enough. Thank you, Monsieur Soucy."

He gave her a polite bow just as the door opened behind her.

M. Cadoret let her in. "Looking for Monsieur Gagnon?"

Wasn't she always? "Yes. No murder victims. Something else."

"He's rather busy with documents. I'm sure he has a few minutes for you."

Just then she heard Dr. Nicot shouting from the Autopsy room. Nathalie couldn't believe it—mild-mannered Dr. Nicot, yelling?

She pointed to the closed door. "Whatever could he be so upset about?"

"His new assistant, the young Monsieur Olivier." M. Cadoret closed his eyes and shook his head dramatically. "He only started this morning, and it's not going well."

"I hear that."

M. Cadoret adjusted his glasses. "I didn't know Nicot had a temper. Monsieur Soucy, who can usually never hear anything taking place in the back of the morgue, indicated twice already today that he's heard Nicot yelling. Which means the visitors can, too."

Who was this assistant, and why was he here? More important, why was Nicot so impatient with him?

M. Cadoret indicated that she could go down the corridor to the office and stepped away with a polite nod.

The door was partly open. "Christophe?"

"Come in."

She opened the door to see him perusing some papers.

"A few days away and the folders double, eh?" She crossed over to the chair, resting her hands on the back of it.

"Truly."

He had yet to look up. Maybe he was upset with her, despite their reunion having gone smoothly.

She tapped her fingernails idly on the back of the chair. He lifted his eyes from the document and looked at her expectantly. Had he been sleeping well? He looked fatigued.

"At what point do we consider a person missing?" she blurted.

"What do you mean?" He stood from the desk. "Nathalie, why are you asking me that? Who's missing?"

"Simone," Nathalie said, scratching an itch under her collar that wasn't really there. "Only I don't know if she's *missing*. She wasn't home yesterday afternoon when we had plans, and she didn't come to her parents' this morning. At least she hadn't when I left."

Christophe put his fingertips on the desk and pressed his weight on them. "Your concern is understandable, because that's unlike her." He paused, pressing harder into the desk. "Nevertheless, I don't think we have reason to worry at this point. It's only been what, eighteen hours?"

"About that."

"Perhaps Simone is at her apartment by now? Or at Louis's?"

"I stopped by there. He wasn't home, either. Or at the bookshop."

She swallowed despite a dry mouth and continued, speaking much more rapidly than usual. "After I submit my article, I'll go to Le Chat Noir, then to her apartment again."

"I'm sure you'll find her, or learn about her whereabouts. Likely those of Louis as well." His blue eyes shone with reassurance. "Please don't derive grim conclusions. I wouldn't want you to turn your stomach inside out when it's much too soon to think that way."

Nathalie knew, though. She could tell from the look on his face that he was concerned and didn't want to say so.

She turned to go, then paused. "Who's this . . . assistant I heard Dr. Nicot shouting at? Olivier?"

Christophe clasped his hands together. "A young man from the university, not yet a doctor, who would like to be a medical examiner. Dr. Nicot has decided to be his mentor, but . . . it's been an arduous beginning, let's put it that way. I'm not sure if Nicot resents sharing his position or if Monsieur Olivier is making errors or both."

Had Christophe ever wondered about her resentment of Gabrielle? She wanted him to know that it had dissolved, mostly if not altogether. Gabrielle had an awkward affect at times but wasn't such a terrible addition after all. And all those smiles she'd directed his way didn't seem to be returned by anything other than cordiality, so that had helped, too. But today wasn't the day for that conversation. "Well, I hope the second day is better."

"I think it will be. Again, please don't wrap yourself in worry too much." The reassurance came back to his eyes. "The chances are slim that anything is truly amiss."

With a half-hearted thank-you, Nathalie departed. Weaving through the crowd, she made her way to the front of Notre-Dame to write her article there, while sitting atop a low wall. She penned it in haste and dropped it off at the newspaper, then hurried over to Le Chat Noir.

The only employees at the club this early in the day were a bartender and the stalwart man with the unkempt beard who'd greeted them at the door the night she and Jules came to the show. His clothes weren't ill-fitting this time, but he still leered at her; if she could have avoided speaking to him, she would have. Casting her distaste aside, with a passing wonder at how Simone could work in an environment with such people, she asked after Simone. Unfortunately, neither he nor the bartender could attest to Simone's whereabouts. They suggested she come back after three o'clock when the owner, M. Salis, would be there.

When she left, she practically ran to Simone's apartment two blocks away.

Nathalie bolted up the worn, creaky stairs to the apartment. After twice knocking and calling Simone's name, she leaned against the door in frustration. Mews and kitten-scratches came from the other side of the door.

Simone had told her once where the key was hidden. Not above the door ("too obvious," Simone had said), but rather above the window frame at the end of the hall, the same window she'd stared out of yesterday.

Nathalie regarded the window casing. *I have no choice.*

She walked over to it and stretched, her fingertips dancing across the top until she found the key. Hurrying back with tremulous hands, she put the key in the lock. The soft click made her flinch. Her stomach seized up so badly, she was afraid she'd throw up as she crossed the threshold.

Max and Lucy, noticeably bigger since the first time she'd seen them, mewed incessantly. She scooped them up and dashed through the two-room apartment. Somewhat messy, as always, with clothes strewn about. Nothing out of place any more than usual. The kittens had food and water. A good sign.

Wasn't it?

She kissed the kittens on their heads and put them down. Frantically she paced around the apartment one more time, as if Simone would suddenly appear. With shaky hands, she took her journal out of her satchel. For the second time today, she left Simone a note.

> I've been looking all over for you and Louis. We were
> supposed to go to the Exposition yesterday, unless I am
> mistaken. I thought I was in error. The club, home,
> your parents—no one's seen you for the last day.
>
> Yes, I let myself in. I am worried.
>
> I need to know as soon as possible that you are safe.
> Until then, I will fret.

Nathalie positioned the note on the floor near the entrance so Simone couldn't miss it. She locked up after herself, returned the key to its spot, and ran down the well-worn stairs.

She leaned against the outside of the apartment building, watching the noisy activity of the street, life happening all around her. What now? If she went to Christophe, he'd still tell her not to worry; it had only been a couple hours since their last meeting. She didn't know what to do with herself.

The rainstorm in her mind was raging with thunder and lightning, because no matter how much she tried to convince herself otherwise, she couldn't shake the possibility that maybe Simone was Le Rasoir's Princess, and Louis his Young Prince.

Blood coursed through Nathalie's veins like a train hurtling along a track. People everywhere but not the ones she needed to encounter in order to calm down.

It was too early to go back to The Quill to see if Louis had showed up. Besides, she didn't want to go in circles again, checking on apartments and workplaces, trapped on a carousel of frustration and angst. Not for another few hours.

Although she doubted anything could hold her attention at

the Exposition, she decided to go there anyway. If nothing else, there would be people and noise and sights to see, or tell herself to see, to pass the time.

On the omnibus to Trocadéro, she thought about Agnès. Things could have gone differently. In fact, the odds were that they should have. If one or more variables had played out another way, her sweet friend might still be here.

Wouldn't she?

Yes, because Nathalie didn't give much credence to fate.

The source of her anxious conclusions about Simone was guilt over Agnès; she was aware of that, even as she tried to reject it. Being taunted by the past didn't erase the concerns of the present. It didn't make the rain stop.

She wandered the grounds of the Exposition for some time. She'd been to the Rue du Caire, brimming with Egyptian wares, several times already, even taking a donkey ride on a previous visit. (When she'd circled Egypt on her map, she also drew a camel next to it. Some day she hoped to ride one.) The Cairo bazaar had façades on either side representing various kinds of architecture—a part of a mosque, stores, a structure for public water, and a café.

The Turkish coffee from the café smelled delectable. Despite not having the time or inclination to idle at a café and think any more than she had to, she couldn't resist buying one to enjoy as she walked (really, the Exposition was a delightful place to try new kinds of coffee).

"Mademoiselle?"

One of the merchants called to her, holding up a display of silver rings. She approached him and examined his offerings.

He pointed out several. "*Hieroglyphs.*"

Nathalie tried on one, then another, then a third. She liked the second one best and asked how much. Jules had told her last time to ask for the price and then propose something lower, then reach a bargain.

Jules, where are you today? Would you be worried for Simone with me, or would you be convinced all was well?

She and the merchant agreed upon a price, and Nathalie slipped the ring on her fourth finger.

Her feet were tired. She'd been wanting to take something called a "rickshaw" ride, where men with broad hats that came to a small point in the center pulled a sort of one-wheeled wagon. Someone hurried in front of her just as she was about to signal one, so that would have to wait until another day. With a sigh, she turned away. Her ability to stay distracted was waning; she was ready to go home anyway.

Nathalie was accustomed to crowds. The collective sight, sound, smell, mood, feeling. She'd seen them shrink and swell, ecstatic and fuming, and pulsating with anticipation. And so it was that, when she observed a shift, subtle at first and then brazenly frenetic, she followed. Dread was close behind, fastened to her with a leash around her throat.

Hundreds of people gathered toward the front of the Tour Eiffel, near the Mexican Aztec palace and some of the South American pavilions. She couldn't get anywhere near whatever it was they were seeing, but the Venezuela Pavilion seemed to be the focal point. The gasps and susurration of voices traveled back to her, a rustling of leaves before a storm. When she heard someone cry out, she was certain she knew.

She'd heard a cry like that before.

Nathalie nudged her way through the crowd and got a few rows closer, but the phalanx of onlookers was too dense to penetrate. Even with her height, she couldn't see anything but people.

"What's there?" she asked a woman beside her.

"*Nie rozumiem.*"

Russian, Polish, Czech. Something she didn't speak.

"Does anyone know what's there?" she asked aloud.

No one replied. They either didn't understand her or didn't know. Or they were too appalled to say.

Just then, the crowd moved forward, as if heaving a sigh, and back again. Long enough for her to get a glimpse of a shallow staircase—eight or nine steps. At the top of the bannister and to the left, in a birdcage, was a young woman's decapitated head.

37

It was not Simone.

"*Grâce à Dieu*," Nathalie uttered, putting her fingers to her lips.

Before that moment, she'd felt as if a leg of the Tour Eiffel had been crushing her chest. Now, she felt mollified while also being unspeakably perturbed. And guilty—she shouldn't have thanked God, she decided a moment after doing so. A life had still been taken.

The young woman, neck swathed in a white scarf, had *la coiffure à la Titus*, and it was the most jarring display of the style yet. Never before had the cut hair appeared with the head. This time the long, dark blond locks were draped beside it, like the shawl Nathalie had left on the bannister at the theater. On *that* night, the one that had since symbolized Jules's betrayal.

Red, white, and blue flowers encircled the birdcage; some had fallen to the ground. Nathalie wasn't close enough to see but knew those petals had to be soaked in blood.

She stood there, fixated on the scene until the police arrived and compelled the crowd to disperse. They surrounded the head of the presumed Princess, shielding the public's view.

There was nothing else to see, and she couldn't use her gift. Not here, not yet.

She trekked home. She'd sweated through her dress and wanted to change before going back to the morgue. Simone's whereabouts were still a mystery, and until Nathalie could verify her friend's safety, she wasn't going to stop searching. She knew it was possible she was wrong; in fact, she wanted nothing more than to be mistaken, to have assumed something far afield from the truth. Her conscience wouldn't allow for that possibility, even if her rational self did.

The Marchands' apartment was on the second floor. She was going to stop there first, though she wasn't sure what she was going to say; it depended on who answered the door. Best to be casual until she could talk to Christophe about what, if anything, to do next.

Outside the apartment door, she stood straight. Being tall always felt like an advantage when she was uncomfortable. Raising herself to her full height made her calmer and more confident, even when she was anything but.

Nathalie knocked; the doorknob turned before she withdrew her hand. When the door opened, she jumped.

"Simone!" She threw herself across the threshold to embrace her friend. "I've been so worried about you. What happened? Where have you been? Did you get my note?"

"I don't think you've ever given me so enthusiastic a reception. Maybe you should worry about me more often," Simone said in a scratchy voice, giving her a kiss. "I received the note you left with Céleste, yes. And I left one with your father. You didn't see it?"

Nathalie peered over Simone's shoulder to see Céleste waving from the sofa. Now wasn't the time to say why she'd been so concerned. "I haven't been home in a while. I, uh, decided to stop by here on my way up, and . . ." Her voice fell away as she studied Simone's face. Dark undereye circles, bloodshot eyes, an overall appearance of fatigue. Even her usual rosewater scent was absent. This wasn't the Simone she was accustomed to seeing. "What happened to you?"

"Happened?"

"You don't seem . . . yourself. Are you sick?"

Simone snorted. "Not in the traditional sense. I'll come up and tell you what happened. Let me finish up my backgammon game with Céleste. Shouldn't be long because *someone* is about to win," she said over her shoulder to the little girl, who giggled and pointed to herself for Nathalie's benefit.

Nathalie winked at Céleste and said goodbye to Simone, giving her one more embrace before turning to the stairs.

Maman and Papa weren't home. Only ever-faithful Stanley, who sniffed the hem of her dress excessively as soon as she entered. "Yes, you smell kittens. You have nothing to worry about; they're Simone's. Speaking of which, where did Papa put her note?"

She saw the folded paper on the dining room table.

Apologies, N. You were correct about our meeting time and place. L. and I were able neither to go to the Exposition nor to communicate that to you. All is well now. I hope you are not angry with me. I am sorry and will explain.

Nathalie read the note again, trying to decipher if there were any clues in there. Presumably Simone didn't want to risk Papa or anyone else reading it and gleaning details.

Before she had time to reflect further, there was a tap on the door.

"It's unlocked," said Nathalie, putting the note down again.

Simone came in, closing the door behind her. She leaned her back against it with a theatrical exhale. She took a fan out of her pocket and fanned herself.

"Your note was vague." Nathalie motioned for Simone to join her on the sofa. "Deliberately so, I presume. Why so mysterious?"

Simone half strolled, half waltzed toward her. "You know that *vin de coca* we had at my place?"

"Yes," said Nathalie. Moving a pillow to the side, she sat on the sofa. "Even I couldn't forget that, no matter how many visions I have."

"Louis and I went to a party the night before last, some of his acting troupe friends, and had . . . a lot of *vin de coca*." Simone joined Nathalie on the sofa and whispered in her ear. "A *lot* a lot."

"So? You had too much to drink. I'm sure that's not the first time."

Simone shook her head lazily and fanned herself some more. "I have never, ever been in a state like that. Nathalie, it was both glorious and miserable. Louis was *hilarious*. We danced and laughed and slept and woke up again and ate and drank some more. Ten of us."

"How long did this go on?" Nathalie's mouth was pinched so tight, she could barely get out the question.

"We completely lost all sense of time," Simone said, throwing up her hands with a giggle. "The party was Thursday night, and nobody truly roused until this morning. I came straight here a couple of hours ago."

Nathalie clenched her jaw. This wasn't funny at all. She'd been on the verge of paranoia, letting herself think a murderer might have targeted her best friend (again), meanwhile Simone and Louis spent a day and then some drunk on *vin de coca*?

Suddenly the joy and relief she'd felt upon seeing Simone dissolved into simmering resentment. "What is the matter with you, Simone? It's all well and good to have fun and partake in indulgences here and there. But this?"

"We didn't plan it that way."

"That, I know. The plans you did make you broke."

Simone snapped her fan shut and folded her arms. "Remind me again. Is your name Nathalie Baudin or Irene Marchand?"

"It's not about missing our evening out or going to some abandoned theater." Nathalie's brows knit together. "It's about prudence."

"Ah," said Simone, putting up her hand. "Your name *is* Irene Marchand. I'm glad you clarified that, Maman."

Nathalie stood. "Take your mother out of it. And your father. And me as well. Even your kittens, who are fine by the way, as I let myself in and left you a note."

"I always leave plenty of food and water for them. I don't mind that you let yourself in, but that was an unnecessary panic." Simone rolled her eyes.

"Like I said," said Nathalie, rolling her eyes in return, "take almost everyone else out of it if that makes you feel better. You do have a younger sister. Did you ever think of that? How devastated Céleste would be if anything ever happened to you?"

Roger came to mind as soon as the words left her. The bothersome little brother who played pranks on Agnès and irked her as younger siblings do. The boy who lost a part of himself when she died, a hole in his heart a lifetime wouldn't fix.

"You're making too much of this, Nathalie. I indulged in narcotic wine for a day." Simone folded her arms again. "If we didn't make plans to see each other, you wouldn't have even known."

Nathalie threw up her hands. "There's a murderer on the streets beheading people. We had reason to think he'd be choosing a Princess next. A Young Prince, too. Can you blame me for deriving a hasty conclusion?"

"Millions of people live in this city," Simone said, her gaze hard. "And there are millions more visiting this summer. If you truly thought Le Rasoir came after me . . ." She closed her eyes and opened them again. "I'll present it this way. Your guilt about Agnès is coloring your viewpoint."

Nathalie gave her an unflinching look in return. "Yes, it is. It unquestionably is."

Simone softened at this, and for the first time in this tense conversation, she seemed to have heard what Nathalie said.

"Don't be reckless," Nathalie said, "that's all I'm asking. Keep your risks in check."

As soon as she said it, she understood something else. Christophe. All those times he'd come just short of scolding her about putting herself in potentially perilous situations. How he'd asked her to be careful more than once, and while she always promised to, caution didn't always lead the way. She'd been flattered and amused by it, but she hadn't taken him seriously enough.

Simone put her hand on Nathalie's forearm. "I'm sorry to have worried you so. And I'm sorry to bring up Agnès. That was unkind."

Although Simone never said it, Nathalie often wondered if she was envious of Agnès. Or rather, the memory of Agnès. How could one live up to the idealized spirit of a friend, preserved in time with the benevolent lens through which we sometimes see the deceased?

"Thank you," said Nathalie. She didn't want to prolong this; they had too much to discuss. "Now, I have a lot to tell you. Including what I just saw at the Exposition. How long can you stay?"

38

Obtaining a vision in the refrigeration room might have felt eerily familiar to Nathalie, had that memory not been taken from her.

Several hours after talking to Simone, she found herself recreating a scenario she knew only through her own written description of it. She'd recorded her experience with Enzo Farini, the first of Le Rasoir's victims to come into the morgue. Of all memories to have to reconstruct.

She stood with Christophe and Dr. Nicot, ready to invoke a vision. With a forced swallow in a dry throat, she observed the face before her.

The Princess was older than Nathalie, closer to Gabrielle's age. The beauty of her face was striking, even in this state. Nathalie was so unsettled by this up-close view, she wasn't certain she could go through with it.

The victim had beautifully angled cheekbones and long lashes. Nathalie imagined captivating eyes under those forever-shut lids. They'd placed her silky, pin-straight hair alongside her on the slab.

There was something about the victim's face, too. As if she were on the cusp of telling a story when she was killed.

Nathalie wasn't sure she could do this.

You have to.

Why?

Because this is what you do, it's who you are.

Was it?

"Do you need some time?" asked Christophe.

She shook her head.

Christophe held the decapitated head of the Princess on a cloth for Nathalie, like before. She could tell he was eager to put it down.

This time, rather than Jules positioning the glass, it was Dr. Nicot. "Like so?"

"Yes, that'll do."

She hesitated, making eye contact with Christophe.

He nodded in encouragement.

Her right hand hovered over the pane of glass, as if she were afraid touching it would burn her. She lowered her hand until her fingertips grazed the glass.

Again the vision was in reverse. The guillotine was about to touch the young woman's neck. It shot up to the top of the structure. The hand holding the release rope let go and stepped backward.

Blackness dropped, then disappeared, and she saw the victim. The Princess bowed over a script. Her tears trickled.

Up her cheeks instead of down.

Blackness again. The murderer walked backward past a table with a playbill on it, a palette of stage makeup, a white scarf, and a basket of red, white, and blue flowers.

When she came to, both Christophe and Dr. Nicot looked as though they wanted to speak. They remained silent.

A knock at the door seemed to startle them. It was M. Soucy.

"Yes?" Christophe called.

"An American came into the display room with an interpreter asking for help. He wants to see if the body—I mean, the head—is that of his wife."

Her body hadn't yet been found.

Nathalie cringed. "There's no preparing him for this."

Dr. Nicot rested the pane of glass against the wall and put on a pair of gloves. "Let's do this in the Autopsy room. I don't want the poor man to see a disembodied head, and I certainly don't trust Olivier to tend to them alone. I can arrange the sheets in a way that will look . . . less jarring, at least."

He asked if they needed him for anything else. Christophe said no, gingerly passing him the woman's head. Dr. Nicot wrapped it with a cloth he took from the drawer and followed M. Soucy out.

The door had barely shut when Nathalie spoke. "Did I say anything?"

"Not this time. What did you see?"

She relayed the details, then hesitated a beat. "Something was different this time. Last time as well."

"About the scene?"

"About how I witnessed it. In reverse. It wasn't continuous. The vision . . . skipped."

Christophe collected the glass as he crossed the room. "Does that concern you?"

"I don't know," she said, trailing him. "It could just be that I'm mostly well but not entirely, not yet."

She knew it might be more than that.

Christophe paused in the hall. "Your demeanor was different this time." He bit his lip, his imperfect tooth showing. "I wasn't going to say anything, but . . . your face contorted as if you were in pain."

Her eyes widened. "It did?" This had never happened, not to her knowledge. Her face was "ghostly and impassive" during a vision, according to Simone. Now her face was almost certainly red, as a result of his comment.

He swallowed. "Discomfort is perhaps a better word."

"I wasn't in any pain," she added, suddenly sorry she brought it up. Why did she tell him, anyway? She could write to Dr. Delacroix about this sort of thing.

Christophe studied her for a moment, his own countenance unreadable, before he resumed walking. "Good."

She watched his gait, how well his trousers were cut, the tidiness of his hair. Even when walking behind him, she could find something to admire. "I don't think I mentioned this before, but I ended my courtship with Jules while you were away."

"Did you?" he called over his shoulder.

Nathalie frowned at his apathy. He didn't even care to face her with such news? How was she to read him if he didn't turn around? Maybe he thought it inappropriate.

"How could I choose otherwise, after what he did?"

"Understandable."

Something about the way he said it, that one word, was awkward. He didn't want to talk about this, she could tell.

Perhaps he was worried it would lead to questions about his own ill-fated courtship.

They passed M. Soucy, an official in a suit, and a slender man in the hall who was stupefied and distraught, the look of someone unable to believe in his own reality. A look Nathalie had seen so many times before at the morgue.

Christophe handed M. Soucy the glass pane. When the door opened to Autopsy, she caught a glimpse of this M. Olivier, source of Dr. Nicot's frustration (the shouting phase had ended, Christophe noted). The young man was around Christophe's age. Tall with a flat nose, he looked more like a soldier than someone who would perform autopsies. His hair was so blond, it was nearly white.

She knew him from somewhere.

But where?

Here.

Outside here, actually. The young man beside her on the bench under the linden tree, reading the Revolution of 1789 book. The one who'd turned his pages loudly, then stood in the morgue queue. She'd included him in her journal entry that day, inclined as she was to capture minutiae sometimes.

How interesting that he should end up at the morgue in a different capacity.

The Princess was Ida Blackwell, she found out a few minutes later. She and her husband were American tourists, here for the summer. She was an aspiring actress and he, a painter. In addition to the Exposition, they'd frequented salons and the theater. They'd gone to a show and then a restaurant but, having gotten into a quarrel after no small amount of wine consumption, left separately.

Nathalie followed Christophe into his office, noticing the Switzerland print had been taken down. "As you know," he began, "the body hasn't turned up yet. Based on what we found on the victim's tongue, we think that might be intentional."

She sat in the chair—there were only two now—and gripped the arms in anticipation.

Christophe took an envelope from the cabinet and presented it to her. Its contents consisted of two pieces of paper with crease marks from having been folded.

A chill rippled across her skin, lingering on the back of her neck. She slapped her hand there to stop it.

The first item was a "death map," as Gabrielle had called it. The one handed out by the woman who smelled of incense, but with a cross on the Venezuela Pavilion penned by another hand.

"These . . . these are everywhere. I saw the woman handing them out at the fair and so did Gabrielle. She's been distributing them outside the morgue, too," said Nathalie, gesturing in the direction of where she'd seen the woman.

"He's enjoying the attention."

She pushed the map away slowly and reached for the second item, the one she'd expected. Parchment paper.

> YOUNG PRINCE, *seated and wrapped in a French flag, is surrounded by the beheaded bodies of SUITOR and PRINCESS on the palace steps. An empty birdcage is beside him.*

He unfolds a map.

*I tried running but all the gates are locked. I tried screaming
    but no one can hear me. Can I not just disappear, go
    somewhere else, become someone else?*

*YOUNG PRINCE sobs as he traces a route along the map
    with his finger.*

A man comes out from behind a curtain wielding a sword.

"Cruel and dastardly and disgustingly vain. Le Rasoir cast
people as parts in his play," Nathalie said, sliding the script even
farther away than the map. "He made Timothy St. Martin read
from the script, but that might be because he was French. And
an actor. I didn't see any other victims reading. Maybe he placed
it in front of Ida Blackwell, or maybe he forced her to read it,
whether she knew French or not."

"I don't think it mattered to him," said Christophe.

Nathalie agreed. "It was all for his own sick pleasure—no one
else would ever know they were forced to read lines or had a
script before them. But still, he makes the murders theatrical for
the public. Why? What does that achieve?"

"Is there any bigger stage in the world right now than Paris?"
Christophe returned the papers to the envelope. "No bigger pool
of empty leads, of that I can assure you. Not one thread we've
pursued remains promising or realistic to pursue. One theory
is that perhaps he follows his victims from the theater to a restaurant or tavern and goes after those who were especially intoxicated. Under the guise of helping them or otherwise gaining
their trust. Unfortunately it's not the same theater or establishment each time, and it's impossible to watch every theatergoer
and every inebriated patron in the city."

The Dark Artist case had seemed impossible, something
never to be solved. Ultimately it was. Not so for Jack the Ripper, which reminded her, and no doubt Christophe as well, that
sometimes the killer wins.

It was a thought too heavy to bear, too leaden to utter out loud.

"We're looking for patterns," she said. "Maybe there isn't one."

"Or maybe he's breaking them on purpose," Christophe replied. "Which, again, leads us nowhere."

She left Christophe to his work and exited the morgue a few minutes later. The pack of observers near the door was almost double what it usually was.

Waiting for the body to be found and delivered.

She'd just swept her eyes from them when she thought she saw Jules coming around Notre-Dame. She moved to the other side of some pedestrians twenty or so meters away, hoping he wouldn't see her. Then he called out to her.

Nathalie pretended she didn't hear him.

When she was confident the distance between them was such that he'd kept walking, she turned around.

Just in time to see him lift the knocker at the side door of the morgue.

Nathalie's memory loss was minor—later that night, while getting ready for bed, she lost the several minutes leading up to that. All of a sudden, she had on her nightclothes and her hair was brushed, and she didn't recall doing either. Considering all that had happened lately, she was relieved it was something insignificant, especially given Dr. Delacroix's letter. Her power still wasn't back to normal but at least the penalty hadn't been too harsh.

Her dreams, however, were tauntingly realistic that night. Among the worst she'd ever had.

She was in the morgue. Every corpse on the concrete slab was someone she loved or who'd touched her life. Her parents. Agnès. Simone and Louis. Christophe. Aunt Brigitte. Jules. Gabrielle. M. Patenaude. The head of Ida Blackwell.

Mme. Jalbert was next to her, weeping. Nathalie touched

the viewing pane and heard a crack, then another and another. Hundreds of cracks streaked across the glass. As she pulled her hand away, the glass shattered. The entire viewing pane fell at once like a sheet of ice.

Agnès's mother cried even louder, and that's when Nathalie woke up. But the sobbing followed her.

Maman.

Her mother was crying in the parlor.

Nathalie moved around Stanley and got out of bed. Her door was closed, so she placed her hand on the doorknob and turned it cautiously. She opened it several centimeters. Maman and Papa were on the sofa together, she weeping into her handkerchief, he rubbing her back.

"What's happened?" she asked, opening the door wider.

"*Ma bichette*," Papa said. "Come."

Nathalie took a seat in Papa's burgundy leather chair and gripped the arms. Her parents shared a look, and Maman nodded.

Papa placed his hand over one of hers. "Aunt Brigitte has died. She—she took her own life."

39

Nathalie's hand lost its flesh and was stripped of all but bone. The rest of her peeled away until the only thing that remained was her bony hand, like Aunt Brigitte's hand, under Papa's.

Or so it felt, there on the sofa, as her body felt the words that Papa uttered.

She cried after that. Tears of sadness and guilt and anger and regret, all draining into a pool of intense and unexpected grief.

Tante, did you do this because of me? Because you were afraid I'd tell?

Finally the question that had been trapped, a bird in a flue, made its way out of her mouth. "How?"

She didn't ask why. She knew.

Papa patted her hand and stood. "She sliced her throat with a shard from a ceramic pitcher."

Her throat, where Nathalie had applied the musk-and-amber oil from the Algeria Pavilion. How Aunt Brigitte had indulged in that simple pleasure.

Elsewhere.

"It's from a pitcher that broke several days ago," Papa continued. "One of the nurses was removing it from a patient's room and bumped into Tante."

"Brigitte bumped into her," said Maman, her voice faint.

"Yes," Papa continued. "And in the confusion, she picked up a piece. The nurse didn't see her do it, so they think she may have kicked it away and gathered it later."

"A vase. I brought her the wooden vase."

"You brought it back, Nathalie. And it was wood, not anything that could shatter," said Maman. "This was a—a ceramic pitcher."

"What if I gave her the idea, though? She knew the vase would be confiscated, but she also said it happens often. Vase, pitcher. Wood, ceramic. Not breakable, breakable. It's not such a leap . . ."

"Stop blaming yourself, Nathalie. You didn't give her the idea," Papa said with a firm furrow of his brow. "I'm sure of that. You're trying hard to make a connection that isn't there. You know, Maman knows, I know: Brigitte's soul was an anxious one, especially after the incident with her roommate."

Nathalie crossed her legs and leaned forward. After a pause, she spoke. "There is one connection I don't have to try hard to make. Because there *is* something to it. My dream. I—I had a dream that was . . ." Her voice trailed off. Too many thoughts, too many conclusions rushed toward her at once.

Shattered glass, shattered pitcher.

Mme. Jalbert's tears, Maman's tears.

Aunt Brigitte dead on a slab.

She covered her head with her hands.

"What is it, *ma bichette?*" Maman's voice, delicate as lace.

Nathalie sank back into the chair and described the nightmare to her parents.

"It's as if your gifts . . . crossed," Papa said, moving his hands past one another.

Again.

They lapsed into silence, broken after a few moments by Maman's sigh. "I suppose we should go. The asylum would like to meet with us, and the courier didn't elaborate."

Nathalie's stomach lurched. *What did they know?*

A short while later, Nathalie and her parents found out.

Nurse Clement sat with them in a spare, unadorned room. Her demeanor was even graver than usual. After issuing condolences, she presented a folder. Nathalie's pulse quickened.

"This is unusual to say the least, but Brigitte . . . left something behind, I suppose you'd put it."

Something? It couldn't be a note. Patients didn't have writing instruments or paper.

The nurse put her hand on the folder. "You're familiar with Estelle? She came to us about two years ago, and she's often in the hall talking to herself or repeating something she's heard. Often docile, occasionally . . . less so."

"Yes," Maman said. "Her room is near Brigitte's."

"Yes, that's correct. Estelle was especially restive and distressed, both last night and this morning," Nurse Clement said, as if she were dispensing a secret. "We think Brigitte spoke to Estelle. Possibly on purpose, to convey a message. Or that Estelle overheard her talking to the chaplain."

Papa gripped his knees. "What did Brigitte say to the chaplain?"

"I don't know; I was too far away to hear. She accosted him on his way out. And I do mean accosted—she took him by the hand and wouldn't let him go, hanging on his hand as she spoke. She was . . . desperate, it seemed." She gave them a sympathetic look. "He was kind to her and gave her a blessing."

Nathalie's throat swelled. A confession. She confessed like she said she would. Only to a priest, not the doctors and nurses at Saint-Mathurin, as Nathalie had assumed.

"Estelle was in her own room at the time. I saw Brigitte look in there," Nurse Clement added. "Estelle must have heard the exchange."

Aunt Brigitte hoped Estelle would relay this, took a chance that she might.

"Do you write down everything Estelle says?" asked Maman, skeptical.

"When Estelle is particularly upset, we record her words in case she's trying to tell us something or needs help. Something she said was very specific." She pursed her lips. "You'll forgive me,

Monsieur and Madame Baudin, if this is upsetting? Perhaps your daughter shouldn't hear this?"

"*Au contraire*," Papa said, "she can."

Nurse Clement opened the folder and read. "'Brigitte sorry for death.'" She gauged their reactions. "I think she was apologizing for her death in advance."

No, that's not what it meant. Not at all. But it was good that Nurse Clement made that observation.

"Did Estelle say anything else?" Maman asked, her tone particularly sweet. "I'd be curious. Even if it seems irrelevant. If you're able to disclose that."

Comprehension registered on Nurse Clement's face. "Normally we wouldn't, but given the circumstances, I don't see the harm." She pointed to something on the page. "Other phrases include 'Who knows?', 'Guilty guilty,' 'Time for breakfast'—for that one, Estelle was repeating 'me'—and 'Divine punishment.' And counting. She did a lot of counting."

Nathalie tried to make eye contact with her parents to no avail.

Of those, "Guilty guilty" and "Divine punishment" *had* to be messages from Aunt Brigitte. Intentional? Yes, Nathalie decided. Brigitte would want them to know why she took her life. Whether she said these things directly to Estelle or knowing—or hoping—she'd repeat them didn't matter.

Aunt Brigitte had known it during Nathalie's last visit, didn't she? Consequences. She meant afterlife consequences. Facing God. She knew she was going to take her life.

Is this my fault?

Did I drive her to a choice she didn't want to make?

Nathalie told herself no, even though she knew those questions would always live inside her.

She thought about her last conversation with Aunt Brigitte. It had been about love, a topic about which they'd spoken so little.

Here and gone. Gone and here.

40

Nathalie went to the morgue that afternoon as if in a trance. Maybe she *was* in a trance. She felt as if she were trapped in that state between dreaming and wakefulness. As if she'd never leave it.

Even getting elbowed on the omnibus didn't faze her. She was marching through the city like a marionette, going from place to place as if someone else were moving her body there.

There were three new bodies on display, all of them men. One of the concrete slabs was empty. Ida Blackwell was not there, as expected. Had they found the rest of the body yet?

She touched the glass. No vision, nothing new. Two of the men were exceedingly thin and dirty, likely men who lived on the streets. A third was a suicide, the purple-black rope marks prominent on his neck.

Nathalie covered her mouth with the back of her hand. A suicide.

Aunt Brigitte's reflection appeared in the viewing pane; Nathalie blinked and it disappeared. A lump swelled in her throat, and despite trying very hard not to cry, a few tears trickled out. M. Soucy approached and asked after her. She considered telling him the reason for her reaction. The words didn't surface.

"A difficult day, is all," she said, feeling and sounding forlorn. As she started shuffling toward the Medusa door, M. Soucy spoke again.

"Monsieur Gagnon is running an errand, I believe."

"Oh." M. Cadoret wasn't standing in the display room, but she didn't want to talk to him, either. She had much to share and wanted to know why Jules had come here yesterday, and these were conversations to have with Christophe. Not M. Cadoret, not Dr. Nicot. And certainly not with Dr. Nicot's new assistant.

Nathalie left through the viewing room with the rest of the crowd. She went to Maxime's and wrote her article over coffee that she didn't remember drinking. And wrote words she didn't remember writing. Only this time, it wasn't due to memory loss but rather the opaque haze of raw, unaddressed sadness.

When she went to *Le Petit Journal*, she was glad to see that M. Patenaude was available. She wanted to tell him about Aunt Brigitte. She wanted to tell *someone*. Tante didn't have anyone to mourn her except Nathalie and her parents. She had nevertheless mattered. Locking her in an asylum didn't erase her from the world.

Which was perhaps part of what drove Aunt Brigitte to suicide, Nathalie believed: her realization that Véronique, too, had mattered. She was important to someone, loved by someone. Taking her life left a tear in the fabric of someone else's.

Both women were troubled; both had committed murder. Each had been wrong to do so. Nathalie had never known or thought through such moral dissonance before and was ashamed she hadn't. Her time at the morgue should have shown her that taking a life was more than killer and victim, guilty and innocent.

M. Patenaude understood her melancholy about Aunt Brigitte's death—of course he didn't know why she'd committed suicide—and the nightmare that preceded it. He offered condolences and thoughtful words. Nathalie found comfort in their conversation, even as she noticed a pensiveness in him that spoke of something else on his mind. A pile of discarded cigarette butts lay in his ashtray; his glasses were thinner than usual.

Heaving a deep exhale, he drummed his fingertips on his desk. "When's the last time you spoke to Monsieur Gagnon?"

"Yesterday. He was away when I went earlier. I'd like to talk to him, so I'll stop by on the way home."

The cadence of M. Patenaude's drumming slowed to thumps. "Jules went to the morgue yesterday."

"I saw him go there," she said, shifting her weight. She'd already told him the courtship had ended; it was Christophe she'd held off on telling for so long. "What did he want?"

"News of Le Rasoir's victim spread quickly. He went there to provide assistance."

"A thought reading?" Nathalie was exasperated. "He wasn't permitted to, was he?"

M. Patenaude folded his arms, and his hesitation told her everything she needed to know.

"Why would Christophe permit that?"

"Because it does no harm to see if he's being honest. And he could help."

Nathalie flushed. "Then why disallow him in the first place?"

"I didn't make the decision," he said, putting his hand up. "I was called in to see if he was being truthful."

"Oh." She swallowed. "And?"

"We couldn't coordinate it until this morning, so he had to come back. They didn't put the head on display, but they left it in refrigeration so we could tend to this. Christophe, Jules, and I met at ten o'clock this morning."

While she was at the asylum.

"He did the thought reading in front of me," M. Patenaude added.

Oh.

"What was it? Was he lying?"

M. Patenaude opened his cigarette case, studied its contents, and snapped it shut. He tossed it on a stack of newspapers. "I couldn't tell. My gift . . . wasn't there."

Her heart sank for him. "I'm so sorry."

Did those three words convey it?

No. She needed to say more. "Remember I once asked you about a rumored Insightful who helps other Insightfuls?"

"Vaguely . . ."

"He's real. He goes by several names. Suchet. Delacroix. Maybe some others. I know him as Dr. Delacroix"

"I read a written account once of an Insightful who communicated with him—Suchet, at that time," said M. Patenaude. "I don't recall the details, but I know the account was true."

"Then you know maybe Dr. Delacroix can help you make sense of it."

"It's too late for me, Nathalie." He let the words sit there, like the plumes of smoke he so often exhaled.

"If you change your mind, I can tell you how to reach him."

"Thank you." He uncrossed his arms and stood. "As you know, it's happening more and more lately. I wasn't able to help. Jules offered to come by again today, so he should be here any time now."

"He will?" Her cheeks reddened.

M. Patenaude nodded. "Christophe is proceeding anyway on instinct and the hope that Jules's repentance was genuine. It seems so, else Jules wouldn't have agreed to be interviewed again. Even if I can't read him, the intent may signal his honesty."

The cover on the box she'd put her feelings for Jules in loosened, jostled by a carriage bump. If he truly sought to redeem himself, then maybe she could find it in herself to be a bit kinder toward him and not ignore him on the street.

"What did he see?"

M. Patenaude put his hands in his pockets. "He claims the victim's final thoughts were that the killer looked familiar. She'd seen him the previous day but didn't know where."

"Tens of thousands of people go to the Exposition daily," she said, studying the framed issues of *Le Petit Journal* on the wall. The one announcing the opening of the fair had been added since she last noticed. "Who knows how many faces anyone sees in a given day? Impossible lead to pursue, I should think."

"The police had already spoken to the husband concerning her disappearance," M. Patenaude said, and "Monsieur Gagnon proposed that the police speak to her husband concerning their whereabouts the previous day, if they hadn't already. In fact, that's probably where he was—paying a visit to the Prefect of Police."

Someone knocked. Arianne's voice carried through the door. "Monsieur Patenaude, a Jules Lachance is here to speak to you."

Apprehension passed through Nathalie like a ghost. "I'd best be going. Thank you for speaking with me."

She stepped out to meet the gaze she hadn't expected to meet again, not in such proximity.

"Hello, Nathalie." Jules's voice was tinged with caution. "Or are you going to pretend you didn't hear me again?"

"I would not pretend that, because you're here for somewhat noble reasons," she said, chin up. "I think."

He tapped the toe of his boot on the wood planks. "Indeed, I am. I've been filled with regret every hour since that first lie at the morgue, and it's only gotten worse." He shrugged. "I thought if maybe—maybe I could help, it might make matters right. Or start to."

"It's an admirable start, yes. Good luck."

He replied with a smile, winsome as ever. That cover on the box of Jules feelings slipped out of place some more. Far from open, but at least she might be tempted to look inside at the contents before snapping it shut again.

"How did you talk your way back in?" asked Nathalie. She eyed Arianne, who was listening despite trying very hard to look like she wasn't.

"I nearly didn't," Jules said, tapping his fingertips together. "Monsieur Cadoret wasn't going to allow me in at all. Monsieur Gagnon overheard us talking and permitted me to come inside."

"Jules?" said M. Patenaude, standing in the doorway. "Are you ready for our discussion?"

She took this as her cue to leave and said goodbye.

"We can keep talking," said Jules, "if you'd like. Later."

When later?

Nathalie opened her mouth to say something before deciding what that something should be. At some point "yes" tumbled out.

"Half past seven at the Tour Eiffel? Outside the office of *Le*—" He peeked over his shoulder at M. Patenaude. "The other newspaper?"

"Half past seven it is," she said, her voice friendly but not too friendly.

Was Jules to be trusted? His bearing was authentic, as was his affection for her. Nevertheless, she'd been fooled in the past. They all had. And he may well have been gambling on the idea that M. Patenaude's power had faded so much as to be ineffective.

What would he have to gain by lying again?

She wanted to believe him, and she did.

Mostly.

41

Nathalie hurried back to the morgue, so much so that she was out of breath when she arrived at the door. She had no need to go through the display room and knocked on the side door instead. Dr. Nicot answered; he told her Christophe was still away and might not return for several hours.

Her shoulders sagged. It would have to be tomorrow.

As she left, she started to take her normal route home before stopping in the shadow of Notre-Dame. Last time she'd gone in, she was angry and craved darkness. Today, she sought it for a different reason. She needed a sanctuary of solitude and contemplation.

She walked around the front of the cathedral, taking in its staggering beauty. Centuries in the making, a realm of magnificence that only time or misfortune could undo. Notre-Dame was a tangible embodiment of forever, a sight to behold by her and countless others who had and would traverse this square. She greeted her favorite gargoyles on the façade (she'd named them Abelard, Tristan, and Bruno), and went inside.

It was full of tourists, so she went toward the front of the church. She knelt, let the chatter of the crowd fade away in her mind, and prayed for the repose of Aunt Brigitte's soul, for God to show her mercy. She prayed for Jules, too. Then she sat in the pew and contemplated the exquisiteness of the structure. Every time she came in, she lost herself in one facet of it; she could live inside it decades and never truly contemplate it all. Her eyes glided to the circular Rose Sud, the intricate stained-glass window from the Middle Ages that was, to her, the epitome of sublime.

The smarmy organist sauntered past her. Moments later she heard Mozart's *Requiem*, precisely the kind of music one expected to hear in a centuries-old Gothic cathedral.

She asked for guidance on the dream, what it did and didn't mean. Would God deign to help with that? She didn't imagine He was pleased with the Henard experiments and all they entailed, trying to make humans something more than what He'd made them. That hadn't stopped her from praying about it from time to time, and Gabrielle had cited prayer as a facet of her Insightful journey as well. Surely He listened, man-made magic aside.

From there, she went home, where she saw Simone leaving her parents' apartment. Nathalie greeted her, happy to see that she looked more like herself now, and asked if she had a few minutes to talk on the Rooftop Salon.

Simone responded by hooking her elbow. "Let's go. I'm off to watch one of Louis's rehearsals later—he's playing Puck, suitably enough, in a café performance of *A Midsummer Night's Dream* that begins next month—but I have some time. I can tell something is on your mind."

"Everything is on my mind. Several big things, anyway."

They made their way to the roof and settled into the late-day shadows along the outer wall. Simone stretched out on her back as Nathalie bunched her legs up.

Nathalie hugged her knees. "We received bad news this morning. Aunt Brigitte, she took her own—she killed herself. A pitcher shattered the other day. She took a piece as they were cleaning and . . . that's what she used."

"Oh, *mon Dieu!*" Simone sat upright, wide-eyed.

Twice already Nathalie had shared that news, and still the words felt like another language coming out of her mouth.

Simone crawled over and put her head on Nathalie's shoulder. "*Ma soeur.* I'm so very, very sorry. You must be devastatingly stunned. I know she said she was going to confess and you thought the matter was finished, or going to be."

"She confessed in a different way, I think," Nathalie said, her voice quiet. She ran her fingers along the hem of her dress, and after a breath, told Simone everything they'd learned at the asylum.

"What did your parents say? I know they've been strange about this whole affair."

"Right now, they're focused on her death, not what sent her to it," Nathalie said. In front of her, anyway. They might have spent all day discussing it when she was gone. "Frankly I don't know if they're ever going to address her crime again. I wasn't there when Maman told Papa, and you know how it is. If they want to be silent on something, they will, and that's the end of it."

Simone stood and leaned against the wall. "I suppose it doesn't matter anymore. What else is there to be done?"

It was a rhetorical question. Nathalie assumed it was, anyway, and left it there to drift off the roof to join all the other unanswerable questions that rose above the city at that particular moment.

"Last night I had a morgue dream." She wanted to fill the silence, and she wanted to share this with Simone to see what her interpretation might be. "Everyone on the slab was someone in my life—including you and Louis—and I shattered the glass."

"*Shattered?*"

Nathalie elaborated on the nightmare, her muscles tensing with each word. She stood when she finished and paced the roof.

"That's some coincidence, Nathalie."

"Isn't it, though?"

"It's almost as if . . ." Simone paused. Her eyes darted to the sky and then to Nathalie. "I wonder if, when your aunt . . .

crossed over, her gift passed to you. Based on everything you've told me, that dream sounds like the sort she has. Had."

Nathalie was relieved Simone said that, because it reflected Papa's theory as well as her own. Yet she was also disappointed for the same reason. She didn't want that to even *be* an option. Was it possible for an Insightful to pass a gift to another?

"I'll ask Dr. Delacroix, but I hope it's nothing like that. I don't want her ability. Or the consequences."

Simone shook her head. "I wasn't thinking forever. I was thinking perhaps . . . a goodbye."

That was a much less worrisome, much more heartwarming interpretation. "Why is it that I need you to point out these possibilities? My mind goes straight to the unlit path through the bleakest of alleys."

"You haven't closed your eyes except to blink since then. Don't think that way until you have reason to, yes?" Simone waited for her to respond in the affirmative. "Now. You said *several* big things. I can't conceive of what else you've got to share."

Nathalie stopped pacing. "Jules."

"Oh," said Simone, visibly surprised.

Those two words initiated a ten-minute discussion on that subject and concluded with two more that culminated in another seemingly unanswerable question from Simone. "What now?"

"I meet with him and see where the conversation takes us," Nathalie said, shrugging. "We won't be resuming a courtship. I—I can't do that."

"He's a clever conundrum, that one."

That he was.

For all the questions on the roof, Nathalie had several answers, and more questions to contend with, when she and Simone parted ways a short while later.

A letter from Dr. Delacroix, which came in during her absence, answered some of them.

42

The mood in the apartment was understandably somber. Papa sat at the desk and pored over documents from Saint-Mathurin; Maman worked on a chartreuse brocade dress, giving the color of grief on her face a pale, greenish-yellow tint. Nathalie sat on the sofa, Stanley pressing his paws against her hip, and read.

> *Dear Nathalie,*
>
> *I appreciate your thoughtful response. Thank you for your candor in describing your experiences and the questions that have surfaced for you.*
>
> *Please know that my responses aren't infallible but rather based on the research behind them and other cases as I have studied them. My understanding of naturals (such is the parlance, as you know) is less than that of those who received transfusions directly, but I'll nevertheless aim to help.*
>
> *My contention is that there are indeed naturals—and even those who had the transfusions and consider themselves "failures" in the experiment—who never discover their ability, just as I believe there are people with musical talent or proficiency in mathematics who don't find themselves in circumstances to uncover that truth in themselves. It's possible you'd have been among them were it not for your initial, accidental incident in the morgue (fortunately most people don't often have direct or indirect physical contact with the deceased). Although I don't believe anything*

elicited your power per se, I do theorize that Insightful gifts can present at an early age as well as later in maturity. Our gifts arise from the essence of who we are, and as I'm sure you know from your own life, there are parts of ourselves we've always known and others we don't perceive until we age. And some, life and reveries suggest, we never come to know at all but forever wonder about.

As well, many Insightful gifts are capricious and develop new traits (or lose them) as time goes on. The power itself is, if not a sort of life, than akin to the cycle of it. That your visions are in reverse again could signify one of two possibilities, both of which are elaborations of ideas I put forth in my previous letter. One is that the overwhelming response your mind and body had to the situation with your aunt caused a deviation—a recalibration, as I termed it last time—that may be temporary or permanent (as you noted, with only one instance, a conclusion cannot be derived).

The other potentiality, and I regret to mention this, should it upset you, is that your power may have weakened. Reverting to the nascent stage of an ability is often a symptom of waning magic. Again, this may be temporary or permanent.

You mentioned keeping an appointment with friends. If that was connected to erroneous memory, then it's consistent with the first of the two options mentioned above. A shift in ability can also result in the shift of the power's consequences.

I hope these responses have been satisfactory, and I hope this finds you feeling even better than before. Do understand, dear Nathalie, that the state of your gift notwithstanding, you are whole. No matter how much our gifts consume us, it's important to remember that we are always us, always complete, with or without them.

Sincerely,
Delacroix

Her muscles felt like boulders, weighing her down. *My power might change or weaken?*

Papa's didn't. Aunt Brigitte's changed, but so did Aunt Brigitte; who could say what had begotten what? M. Patenaude's was unreliable now, yet only after decades. She'd heard of Insightfuls whose gift disappeared abruptly, too. Long ago, in the early days. At least, that had been her perception.

Might she lose it entirely?

No, that wasn't a possibility she was willing to accept. A shift, perhaps, though even that was unconvincing. There hadn't been any memory loss relative to Simone and Louis, so the example she'd provided Dr. Delacroix wasn't relevant after all. Her memory loss had been brief following the last two visions, and one could argue that represented a deviation.

It had also been very soon after her hospital stay, and she *had* gone against the medical doctor's recommendation. Not to mention, well, as unsettling as it was to admit . . . maybe the vision was different because the body was different and not a body at all but a head. The other visions might have been influenced by it in a way she hadn't perceived.

Had Dr. Delacroix accounted for that?

Nathalie put the letter back in the envelope and tossed it on the table. Neither of her parents looked up. Her eyes lingered on Maman, who'd had Henard's blood transfusions but never manifested a gift. Was she truly deprived of one, or was it an obscure power like Nathalie's that required an unusual set of circumstances to discover?

Maman had suffered because of that, or so she'd thought years ago. Did she now? Or was she glad not to have the blessing and curse that was being an Insightful?

After petting Stanley for a while, Nathalie went into her bedroom to pick out a dress for her *rendezvous* with Jules, pausing by her collection of important-to-her objects. The brass button had been Dr. Delacroix's. All of her other visitors denied it was theirs, and it didn't look like it went on anything the hospital staff wore. Sure, she could ask him in a letter. It was nicer this way, she decided. A memento of their conversation, of his thoughtfulness. And of Gabrielle's.

She picked out a navy-blue-and-white linen dress. Briefly she contemplated wearing the bracelet from Jules, but she opted not to, lest she convey ideas she didn't intend to suggest.

A clever conundrum indeed.

Mon bonbon.

He knew how to appeal to her, didn't he? She wanted not to care. She *didn't* care, not in the way she had during their courtship.

Yet he still meant something to her. A hint of that had stirred within her at *Le Petit Journal* today. It must have stirred Jules, too.

She missed him. Talking to him, laughing with him. She couldn't give him her heart again. Maybe he would accept her friendship after all?

Nathalie laid out her clothes and returned to the living room. Papa sighed over his paperwork, rubbing his eyes.

Maman's eyes went to him. "What did you find out?"

"Nothing."

"How can that be?" Maman tilted her head.

"There's no mention," he said, scratching his chin, "of anything untoward or criminal. As far as Saint-Mathurin Asylum is concerned, Brigitte Baudin never harmed a soul and died in her sleep."

Nothing criminal. Her parents, the asylum . . . everyone was going to pretend this never happened?

No further anguish for Véronique's family.

Or for Tante's.

Another realization descended on her, dew glistening on a grass blade. "They're not classifying her as a suicide. Is that so she can have a proper funeral Mass and burial?"

"Yes," said Maman, returning to the lace she was sewing. "Perhaps her troubled soul will . . . be less troubled."

"Or even find some peace," added Papa, dragging his thumb across his mustache. "After many years without."

Nathalie wanted to ask more questions. A hundred of them. About Aunt Brigitte. About what kind of sister she was to Papa. About her disappointment in love. About her stillborn child. About her dog, Choupinet. About those early days after the transfusion.

Not now. Not today. Someday she would, because that was one way to keep Tante alive. Ask questions about her. Get to know her in death maybe more than in life. It didn't have to all be on the day they learned of her death.

Today she had other questions to ask. Of Jules, in several hours.

A light rain tickled Nathalie's skin as soon as she left the apartment building, and she considered making that her reason not to go.

The sun nestled behind buildings to the west. Clouds prowled overhead like a pack of restless wolves.

Would this deter Jules?

No, it wouldn't. He was as stubborn as she, if not more. If he was determined to meet her, he'd be there no matter what.

She quickly ran back to the apartment for her umbrella and resumed her trek.

The wolves unleashed their attack just as she arrived at the base of the Tour Eiffel.

He had better be here.

Nathalie took a seat on the elevator for the slow, grinding ride up to the second landing. Although it had room for dozens of people, the elevator only had ten or so people in it. Some curious stragglers were ever-present. As with the morgue. One could always count on some people forging on in inclement weather to see whatever it was they wanted to see.

The elevator thudded to a dull halt. A slew of tourists huddled in a group, eager to take the ride back down. The wind on the second landing was gustier than on the ground, so much so, she was afraid she'd lose her umbrella. Most of the souvenir carts and snack stalls were closed, and one lone woman selling cigarettes was packing up.

The rain pounded with such intensity she couldn't see the temporary *Le Figaro* office clearly. Was Jules there?

Someone brushed against her shoulder, and she slipped, regaining her footing just before a tumble. She reprimanded the clumsy party and got a response in a language she couldn't identify. She wished she knew how to reprimand in every language.

Jules came into sight. He was standing under a crossbeam near *Le Figaro*'s office, closed with curtains drawn.

Nathalie called to him, but he didn't hear her. Of course, she realized; he'd done a thought reading yesterday. She waved, and when he finally caught sight of her, he waved in return. His face was in silhouette. Between that and the rain, she couldn't make out his expression until she came up to him.

Nervousness.

Or discomfort.

Was he that concerned about a conversation with her? She hadn't wounded him that badly last time.

Had she?

The rain intensified even more as she drew closer. It was a mistake to come here under these conditions, but at least she'd found him. They could retreat to Café Brebant on the first platform and talk there, regardless of weather.

"Where's your umbrella?" she said, holding hers over both of them.

"When I left, it was clear. I didn't expect . . . this. I'm so glad you came," he said, his voice suggesting otherwise.

Someone tapped her on the shoulder.

She turned around. It took her a moment to realize who it was—somehow he looked unlike his usual self. Maybe it was the wide-brimmed hat?

Ah, he wasn't wearing his glasses, either.

"Monsieur Cadoret, you're out in this rain as well? If we aren't all so very dedicated to the République, no one is. How are you?"

"I'm very well, Nathalie," he said, smiling. In a way that didn't at all seem familiar. And this was a man she saw nearly every day.

Nathalie glanced at Jules, and only then did she truly understand what his face had shown, what his tone had conveyed.

Profound, soul-clenching fear.

43

Nathalie tried to garner more from Jules's face, but his eyes wouldn't meet hers.

They were riveted on M. Cadoret.

She followed his glare. The man's bland, nondescript face betrayed nothing.

"This all worked out splendidly, despite the weather. Thank you for joining us," said M. Cadoret, his voice deeper, with a different timbre than usual. He presented her a folded sheet of paper with two hands, as if it were a gift. "I didn't want to have to reconceive the ending again today."

The ending to what?

Jules tucked a wind-blown tress behind her ear, his fingertips brushing her head and pressing lightly. "To the play," he said, voice low and strained.

Notes of comprehension played in Nathalie's head. A broken melody in the wrong key, familiar and foreign all at once.

"You're Le R—" The word caught in her throat, able neither to stay there nor to emerge. She swallowed hard. "Le Rasoir."

She unfolded the paper. A biblical quote on one side.

A death map of the Exposition on the other, with the cross over the Venezuela Pavilion as found with the Princess.

And a giant cross in red ink over the Tour Eiffel.

He smirked as he adjusted his coat, deftly moving a pistol into his outside pocket. She thought she saw the glint of a knife as well. "I recognize the look on your face. *Him?*" M. Cadoret's lips twisted in mockery. His voice *was* different. Had he been altering his voice all this time? "'I walked by him daily, hardly took notice beyond mere courtesy.' Yes, you and everyone else."

Nathalie was too stunned to reply. She shoved the map inside her skirt pocket.

"I was thrilled to get that gruesome map from that religious lunatic outside the morgue. What a keepsake." He put his hand over his heart. "It was so unintentionally appropriate, I couldn't help but use it the last time. And now."

Nathalie swung her umbrella at him. The wind slowed the momentum and he deflected it with ease.

"You won't need that, just like Jules didn't need his knife." M. Cadoret swiped it out of her hand. He held it out to a woman who was rushing by, shielding herself from the rain. The woman took the umbrella, thanked him in what sounded like Dutch, and hurried off to take cover.

M. Cadoret turned back to them just as Jules threw a punch, glancing the killer's jaw and knocking off his hat. Jules tried again but M. Cadoret, taller and stronger, caught his fist, shoved him away, and aimed the pocketed pistol at him.

"Help!" Nathalie's cry died in the wind and came right back to her. No one heard her. No one saw her. Everyone was either looking out at the city or taking cover. All were too far away.

"Don't try that again, *Young Prince*."

"You wouldn't." Tiny icicles moved through Nathalie's veins, rendering her cold and still, and slowing down her thoughts. The only thing she could do was extend her hand to help Jules as he regained his footing.

"You don't know me at all, Mademoiselle Baudin. You don't even know my name. Samuel Pelerine, as it were." He stooped to retrieve his hat, eyes on both of them. The wind flapped open his coat, just long enough for Nathalie to get a glimpse of something in his inside pocket, bulky with candle-like strings.

"Now, every show needs an audience, particularly for the last act. That's what this is all about, after all. The finale. The *denoue-ment.*" He made a dramatic, sweeping gesture. "My initial ending was going to be uncharacteristically subtle. A knife to the back for Jules and disappear, like Jack from across the Channel. Now that he has an understudy—it's not the first time you've played the part of a boy, Nathalie, from what I hear—I have to improvise."

"You're bluffing," sneered Jules. "I don't suppose you smuggled a guillotine up here?"

"Obviously not. But did you know one of the designs proposed for the tower at the Exposition Universelle was a titanic guillotine?"

Nathalie *had* heard that.

Pelerine pointed to the elevator. "Worry none; you won't be donning a white scarf, and you get to keep your hair *and* your head. In a manner of speaking." He stared at each of them, not caring about the rain, the wind, anything. His eyes were filled with manic purpose, drowning out the humanity she'd thought she'd seen in him, day in and day out. "No need to read from the script, either. Most of my victims couldn't read French anyway. It was enough to see them weep over it; gave some flair to the humiliation, you know? Come now, let's promenade up to the third platform."

Nathalie didn't budge. "Absolutely not."

"Absolutely yes. Did you not see the bomb I'm carrying? A pistol, a knife, a bomb. I'm prepared! I've been wearing this bomb here and there for ages. *Finally* I get to do something with it," he said, patting his coat. "Potentially, that is. I'll throw it into a few gawkers trying to get a scenic view, if you resist. Same is true if you alert anyone."

"A bomb won't work in the rain," snapped Jules.

Pelerine leaned in between them. "Are you so sure?"

No. Nathalie wasn't so sure. Jules's grimace suggested he wasn't, either.

"Not another sound," said Pelerine, his voice slithering around them. "I do the talking now. I do everything now."

The rain and wind let up as they crossed the platform and up a few stairs to the elevator. A couple walked by, huddling under an umbrella. Oblivious to the fact that they were brushing coats with a killer and two hostages.

Disbelief emitted from her like sweat. M. *Cadoret is Le Rasoir. How?*

The thought played in her head again and again. Her stomach roiled as she thought about how he'd observed her having visions, watched her touch the pane from the other side of the glass. How he'd taken her *statement* down for the Suitor, William Fitzgerald. Saw her distress about the murders. Spoke of Dr. Nicot being upset at the delivery of a human head.

She shivered, and she couldn't stop shivering. It could be noon in July and she'd still be shivering.

They reached the elevator in silence, squeezing in with a handful of people speaking various languages. As the doors narrowed, Nathalie saw a familiar gait across the platform. The head was down in the wind, but she'd know that walk anywhere.

Had he seen? Did he know?

It couldn't be a coincidence.

How?

The elevator doors closed. Nathalie held her breath, debating whether or not to scream.

No. Think. Be deliberate.

Shoulder-to-shoulder with Jules, she briefly squeezed his quivering hand.

Or was it hers that was trembling?

She knew he was thinking of an escape, too. What to do, when to do it. She'd been robbed of the memory of this top platform, but he wasn't. He'd take action.

Wouldn't he?

The *chug, chug, chug* to the top viewing platform was a chime on a clock, dooming them.

A man next to her hummed, and a boy on the other side

sucked on a lollipop. A pair of French girls behind them talked about the landmarks they hoped to see, wondering just how far the view would extend.

When the doors opened, Pelerine held them by the shoulders and let everyone else exit. "Time for the conclusion," he said with a wink, nudging them forward onto the platform. The rain intensified again. "Where the Young Prince, distraught by everything, jumps off the castle. As does his understudy. Then, after pretending I was only a bystander to this *Romeo and Juliet* tragedy and feigning shock, I'll move on to the next of my plays."

Nathalie's muscles tensed.

"If we're lucky," Pelerine snickered, "Monsieur Gustave Eiffel is in his apartment and will see the whole thing."

Fury raged through Nathalie like a greedy fire. "Jules, go!"

He glanced at her and ran. She thrust her elbow into Pelerine's side, almost knocking him into a group rushing onto the elevator. Nathalie dashed after Jules, passed him, and rounded a corner.

The bomb.

"Wait, Jules! His bomb!"

A guard straight ahead put up his hand. "*Arrêtez!*"

"That man has a bomb!" Nathalie yelled, pointing. She came to a halt, Jules right behind her.

"*I'll* get him." Jules took off in the direction they came from before her outstretched hand could stop him.

Nathalie raced after Jules; the guard followed. She crashed into Jules as she turned the corner. Pelerine marched toward them, pistol aimed at Jules. Nathalie and Jules backed up.

"*Arrêtez!*" shouted the guard from behind her, weaker this time. She could tell he was scared.

Weren't they all?

Pelerine fired the gun.

She flinched at the sound, her heart thumping ever louder.

The guard howled in pain. Where was he shot? She was afraid to look but ventured a peek. He gripped his shoulder.

Not fatal.

He'll live.

Jules lunged at Pelerine. He swiped at the gun and missed. The two grappled until Pelerine grabbed Jules's arm, twisting it behind his back.

Then he pressed the barrel of the gun against Jules's temple.

Nathalie froze, just for an instant. Unable to swallow, to breathe, to do anything other than see what was in front of her.

"Let's try this again." Pelerine gritted his teeth and dragged Jules over to the railing. "Get up there."

Jules ceased to struggle, making himself dead weight, purposely clumsy to push. Nathalie lurched toward them, but Pelerine trained the gun on her.

"I said, I need an audience," Pelerine hissed. "But I'll shoot you if I have to."

Nathalie's eyes picked up movement near the elevator as a lone figure emerged.

It *was* him she'd seen.

"Christophe!"

He ran toward them.

Pelerine spun around, dropping Jules.

"A *deus ex machina?* Don't you get yourself killed, too, Gagnon," taunted Pelerine. He pointed the gun at Christophe. "He isn't worth it. He lied to you for me, remember? For money."

Christophe angled himself low and charged him. Pelerine fired a shot. The clang of a bullet striking iron reverberated across the platform as Christophe threw himself at Pelerine's knees. The killer sidestepped the move and ran. A powerful gust of wind burst through the tower as he turned the corner.

Pelerine slipped on the wet surface and slammed into the railing.

Right over the edge of the platform.

The lower two-thirds of his body hung off the railing in between the steel girders. Nathalie hurried over to him and looked him in the eyes. Eyes that she'd seen almost daily for the last few months on a cordial, smiling face, that had greeted her with convincing friendliness.

Eyes she had looked through while he was killing his victims.

Eyes that now looked hollow to her, filled with nothing but what was before them. A reflection. No better than a mirror. Just another disguise in this man's show.

What do I do?

Time stopped.

The rain stopped.

The wind continued.

Pelerine stared back at her. He swung his legs and tried to hoist himself up, unable to find any purchase.

"Take my hand," she said, offering it to him. Not because she wanted to see him live, but because she wanted him to withstand the humiliation of a trial. To pay for what he'd done and tried to do. To get the guillotine he'd given others.

He laughed.

Laughed?

"It wasn't even a real bomb," he whispered. "Made for an entertaining threat, didn't it?"

Nathalie fought the urge to strike his hands. She was better than that.

Yet she couldn't look him in the eye anymore.

"Come on," she said, peeking over her shoulder. Christophe and Jules were coming her way. "We'll help you up."

Pelerine shook his head. "Last bow."

He let go.

44

Pelerine's body hitting the surface below made a sound Nathalie hoped she'd be able to forget someday.

Thank goodness she'd looked away.

Christophe and Jules came up behind her, as did the rest of the crowd that had taken to hiding.

People pressed forward in a counterpoint to that day at Palais des Beaux-Arts, which saw everyone scatter.

"Are you all unharmed?"

"Who was that?"

"Why didn't you help him up?"

"How's the guard?"

And so on and so on. Even people speaking other languages approached them, voices trailing up in the manner of queries. It wasn't the first time Nathalie heard a swarm of questions that both did and didn't need to be answered. Nor was it likely to be the last. Not in Paris, not among the crowd that wanted to be a part of everything.

The guard was gone. A trail of blood dotted the platform like bread crumbs in a fairy tale, leading to the elevator.

The poor man. Is someone helping him?

Three other guards stormed across the platform, and Christophe hastened through an explanation of what happened. With a combination of words and gestures, Nathalie and Jules politely assured the small gathering of concerned visitors that they were not hurt.

"I'm afraid we can't say anything else at this time," said Christophe, raising his voice so all could hear. "Thank you all for your concern. At this point, the matter is delegated to the police."

Rather than silencing the crowd, Christophe's remarks reinvigorated the clamor. He held his hand up, leading Nathalie and Jules toward the elevator without a word. They were careful not to step in the blood.

"Monsieur Gagnon, how is it that you're here?" asked Jules in a faraway voice. He still hadn't regained his color, Nathalie noticed. Even in the dusk, he looked extremely pale.

"Cadoret's own path led me here," Christophe said. "I had someone follow him when he left work yesterday. He didn't come in today, but I kept a man on him."

Nathalie wrinkled her brow. "Why?"

"He adamantly refused to let Jules into the morgue yesterday."

"I don't understand," said Jules. "I didn't think anything of it."

The elevator opened. Christophe turned to the onlookers seeking to embark. "Would you mind permitting us to take the car alone?"

An assortment of apologies filtered through the five or six people standing there as they moved out of the way.

Christophe gestured for Nathalie and Jules to enter the elevator, then got in behind them. "I never discussed the details of your departure with him. As far as everyone else at the morgue knew, Jules's power had begun to fade. Dr. Nicot relayed that to Gabrielle in my absence. I even asked him to tell her Patenaude's newspaper article might not run as a result, to protect the ruse. Did either of you tell her more?"

They shook their heads. Nathalie silently thanked Gabrielle for never having pried when she so easily could have.

Christophe steadied his posture for the descent. "No one

besides the three of us, Monsieur Patenaude, and the Prefect of Police knew the truth. Not even the men I had following you," he said. "All three of you, actually. Beginning that very day."

Nathalie gaped at Christophe. "You—you had people protecting us?" She stole a glance at Jules, who looked equally dumbfounded.

How had she not noticed anyone following her?

Following *them*, in fact. At Tuileries, a conversation that felt so intimate, so discreet, even in a public setting.

"The Prefect of Police authorized it for five days," Christophe continued. "One, to make sure the two of you and Gabrielle were safe. Two, in the event Le Rasoir betrayed himself by approaching you."

Jules tapped his fingers on the side of the elevator, chewing the inside of his cheek. Was he embarrassed? "He approached us *every* day, except with a cordial greeting and a smile. He'd have recognized some or all of the police officers protecting us. No wonder he stayed away."

"Yes," Christophe began, "which ultimately proved beneficial. As it were, Monsieur Cadoret wasn't *in* the morning of Monsieur Patenaude's discovery—I remember this well because it was my last day before going to Switzerland. Monsieur Soucy stood in the display room and Cadoret came during the afternoon. I never saw him, only left instructions for the news to be conveyed to him."

"We might have been overheard in your office, and someone might have passed it on to him," said Nathalie. "I was—not subtle, if you will."

Christophe waited as the noisy hydraulic brakes slowed them down. "You weren't as loud as you think. Dr. Nicot cannot hear much if the door is closed, nor can Monsieur Soucy. It's very unlikely anyone else heard us."

"So you didn't leave instructions that I wasn't allowed into the morgue?" asked Jules. "Other than with, uh, the rest of the public?"

"Not at all. I told the staff the 'official version,' as I said. Never that you should be refused entry."

Nathalie thought this strange. She still wasn't clear how Christophe put all of this together, knowing the facts available at the time. "That seems to be a minor infraction at worst."

They paused the conversation as they proceeded from one elevator to the next, Christophe again asking for privacy from the nosy crowd that had seen or heard enough to know some drama had taken place. Nathalie's eyes fastened on the corner of the platform where, not twenty minutes before, M. Cadoret became Le Rasoir who became Samuel Pelerine.

When the door to the car was closed, she shut her eyes then opened them. The image remained even when she could no longer see the platform.

"I agree with Nathalie. Why should refusal to let me enter the morgue warrant suspicion?" asked Jules.

"It wasn't so much the refusal as his *behavior*." Christophe put his palms together. "He was extraordinarily—and atypically—agitated about it for someone who was, supposedly, merely turning away an Insightful whose power had become unreliable. Why was Cadoret so upset?"

"Because he knew, somehow." Nathalie thought about it. "Did you write down the real reason for Jules's dismissal anywhere?"

"I did. Not in the case documents, and not even in Jules's file. A separate file I keep under an obscure title, precisely to protect such secrets. I even gave Jules a pseudonym in the documentation."

Jules squeezed some water out of his shirt. "So he either found out by some other means . . . or searched the paperwork. He must have followed me at some point during those five days." He shook his head vigorously. "He trailed me so well without my notice. The man was like an apparition, it seems. And he might have followed Nathalie or Gabrielle. Seeing police near any one of us on multiple occasions would have made him not only stay away but become suspicious. I don't think he believed the 'lost ability' excuse. Or if he did, he wished to ascertain it and found it to be untrue."

"Exactly," said Christophe, exhaling deeply. "This *also* illustrates how, prior to that, he'd know whether or not you were honoring your . . . arrangement. We assumed 'the killer' knew from what the newspapers reported. There was a more direct method, wasn't there? To look in the case files in my office. He'd been studying everything all along."

"How better to stay a step ahead, to evade capture," said Nathalie.

Christophe glanced back and forth between them. "We can't know for sure, but I suspect that's why he broke his pattern at times, with the bodies, the scripts, the way the murders were similar but not too rigidly the same. To keep from being too predictable."

Nathalie rubbed her temples. None of this seemed real.

"The man knew everything, then. Even took our statements at times." Jules spoke in a hushed voice. "He was obviously a masterful liar. He was interviewed, not by M. Patenaude I'm sure, and weaved whatever falsehoods he needed to."

M. Patenaude did some, not all, of the many interviews. Jules was right; he probably hadn't spoken to Pelerine.

"He certainly did, and for the most part, he succeeded. But his missteps began to add up." Christophe pulled on the end of his sleeves. "Claiming illness and leaving precisely when Jules came inside yesterday, then not coming in today—and this is a man who never missed a day since he started months ago—seemed to be . . . something else."

Nathalie shifted her weight. Something else indeed. She was impressed with how perceptive Christophe was. Had always been, really.

"Even so," Christophe continued, "it was unusual, but I didn't know what to make of it. A conversation with Ida Blackwell's husband proved to be most . . . insightful, if you'll pardon my use of the word."

They reached the ground. It was no longer raining, and the wind was much less intense than it had been at the top of the Tour Eiffel. Scores of people and police were gathered around where Pelerine had fallen.

Christophe began walking toward the crowd. "We knew from Jules's thought reading that Ida had seen her killer before. She and her husband had been at the morgue hours before her death. A 'nice man with very small glasses and no'—here the man pointed to his eyebrows to demonstrate—'came running out of the morgue to return a dropped scarf.'"

A scarf.

The irony.

"They—they asked him for a restaurant recommendation, using a guidebook and whatever French they could manage," Christophe added. "They took his suggestion. We don't know whether he followed them, showed up at the restaurant later, or waited near the restaurant and happened to see them again . . . we can only guess it was one of those three. At some point, Monsieur and Madame Blackwell quarreled after having had too much to drink, then, well. The rest."

What if the Blackwells had simply gone back to their hotel together, or never gone to the restaurant at all? Or hadn't had too much to drink, or hadn't argued? Any number of scenarios could have happened to prevent Ida's death.

And yet Nathalie was all too keenly aware of another truth. If it hadn't been Ida, someone else would have been cast as the Princess.

Nathalie put her hand to her throat. "All of this pointed you to Monsieur Cadoret. I mean, Pelerine. He said his real name was Pelerine."

"Ah," said Christophe, holding up a finger. "*That* brings me to the final element. I've been perusing the interviews with the theater professionals. Several actors and a director mentioned

Samuel Pelerine, a costumier no longer employed there. He fit Cado—uh, Pelerine's physical characteristics: forties, brawny, and absent of all hair."

A policeman caught sight of Christophe and called out to him. "*Un moment!*"

Christophe turned back to Nathalie and Jules. "I thought of him when I read the description, because it reminded me of him. I didn't suspect him, not at all. When applying for the morgue position, he'd furnished the Prefect of Police and me paperwork 'proving' his identity as a civil servant from Fontainebleau; I had no reason to think he wasn't the man he said he was."

His shoulders dropped, and a flash of disappointment crossed his face. Nathalie knew him well enough to know that this oversight, this inability to make the connection sooner and to see through Pelerine, would follow Christophe around.

"Anyway," he said, "I added this Pelerine to a list of thirty or so people to be interviewed again or investigated."

"And so somehow it all came together," Jules concluded, his voice weak.

"Enough for me to be interested in Monsieur Ca—Pelerine's whereabouts," said Christophe. "I gave it a low probability of manifesting anything but left instructions that I was to be contacted immediately if he was seen with either of you or Gabrielle. She's safe—she was at the morgue when I heard from the man I sent to follow him earlier. So here we are."

Here they were, at the base of the mighty Tour Eiffel. With Le Rasoir's body, or whatever was left of it, thirty meters away. Nathalie gave in to the temptation to look and (for once) was grateful the crowd blocked most of it.

Christophe was called upon again and excused himself to talk to the police. One of the officers stayed behind to take statements from Nathalie and Jules.

When the policeman walked away, Nathalie studied Jules, still ghostly white, and took him by the hand. "*Mon bonbon*, it's over."

"Le Rasoir or us?"

Perhaps she shouldn't have used a term of endearment.

Our courtship has been over for a while, she wanted to say. Why hurt him? He knew.

She hoped.

They moved away from the crowd. Nathalie had no wish to hear people discussing Pelerine's remains (as it was, she thought she heard someone throw up), and Jules was in no state to be further upset. They crossed the Seine and walked across the Pont d'Iena. They walked to the Palais du Trocadéro, a relic from a fair decades ago that Nathalie thought looked like a church and a coliseum put together. They sat on a wall beside the fountain in between a pair of puddles on the steps, so soaked they were indifferent to the dampness of the stone.

"He must have followed me all day," Jules said, shaking his head. "I went to the morgue after I left *Le Petit Journal.* By then, Christophe was back. I had the day off, so from there I went home, dressed, read, and made my way here."

Nathalie thought of the other ways Pelerine could have ended his play. Would he really have stabbed Jules on the Tour Eiffel, or was that part of his performance tonight? Would she have been next, or was it happenstance that she had a "role"?

The answer died with him. And it was probably better that way.

"You know me, always early for an appointment." Jules ran his fingers through his hair. "I was milling about on the second platform, and he presented himself. Collegial, ordinary Monsieur Cadoret striking up a conversation. He asked what I was doing there, then remarked how this was the second time we'd met at the Exposition."

"Second?" Nathalie raised a brow.

"He reminded me. I met him the night all four of us were here, the night we had the *vin de coca,* then went up the Tour Eiffel." He stared at the structure across the Seine as he said it.

"The three of you were ahead of me at the Galerie des Machines. Don't you—"

Remember? No. She didn't.

Jules shook his head. "Sorry. I don't remember, either—it was just a quick exchange and so much of that night was imprecise. Anyway, that's when he slipped the note and money into my pocket. I'm sure of it now. The next morning was when the head and body were found in the Guatemala and Uruguay Pavilions."

Oh goodness. Jules saw him right before . . . or after . . .

"I was surprised he remembered a chance encounter but didn't think anything of it," Jules said. "I told him I was waiting for you."

What if I'd changed my mind and didn't come?

Would he have stabbed Jules, as he claimed?

Jules ran his fingers through his hair. "I didn't suspect a thing until he asked me if I knew he used to be an actor. No, I said. He said, 'How am I acting now? Could I pass for an executioner?'"

"Oh, Jules." Nathalie felt a chill despite the humidity.

"I was frozen, absolutely frozen with worry. For myself, for you." He rested his head in his hands. "He flashed his coat so I'd see the gun and demanded that I keep up the ruse when you arrived and more orders would follow. I pulled the knife on him, but he dispensed of it swiftly, kicking it to the corner of the platform."

She couldn't imagine the strain Jules had been under, waiting for her to show up. Seconds must have felt like minutes, and minutes like hours.

"He rambled. My hearing still isn't completely back yet, so with the rain . . . I missed some of what he said." Jules bit the inside of his cheek. "This I heard: he'd been planning to seek a job on the Exposition grounds, so as to make 'everything less complicated,' but considered it a stroke of good fortune when a position at the morgue opened up."

Nathalie frowned. M. Robert, the droopy older gentleman who'd often stood inside the display room before, had left for health reasons several months ago.

"When he found himself in the company of not one but two Insightfuls, then recently a third, he was delighted." Jules paused. He was silent for so long, Nathalie thought he was done. When he resumed, his voice was quiet. "Then he said, 'You'd be astonished how quickly someone's strengths and weaknesses are revealed through observation and polite banter.'"

Nathalie put her finger in the surface of a puddle, watching the ripples of the shallow water. Pelerine had chosen Jules, not her. Her insides turned to liquid, then rock, then liquid again as she thought of the conversations he must have overheard, the observations in and out of the viewing room, the conclusions he must have derived from the contrast in their clothes.

"It doesn't matter what he said up there," Nathalie said. "He wanted you to feel inferior and helpless. Just another game."

His head was still buried; she couldn't gauge his reaction. She said it to make him feel better. Did it?

Jules tugged at his chestnut waves. He lifted his head with a sigh. "I can't describe the state of disbelief I was in, Nathalie. I was still piecing it together when you came several minutes later. I'm still piecing it together *now*."

She put her hand over his. "It will be a while before it feels like the killer is gone," she said. How dreadful to speak from direct knowledge. From memory. "And it will never leave you. Only grow quieter in your mind."

He took her hand and kissed it gently before letting it go. "Thank you."

People walked around them, talking about the mess of human remains at the Tour Eiffel. She heard other languages, too, and wondered if they were discussing the same rumors. A suicide, a lover's quarrel, a worker climbing the exterior falling to his death by accident.

None guessed that the swamp of blood and flesh was once Le Rasoir.

"I've had enough of these wet clothes," Nathalie said, getting up slowly. She put her hand to her pocket and felt the outline of the map.

Jules saw the gesture. "You should give the map to Louis."

"Yes. For his collection of 'morbidities and oddities.'"

Although she wanted to rip it to shreds, she recognized that Louis *would* appreciate it.

"I'm going to hire a carriage and go home," she said. "If you'd like, I'll give him enough money to bring you home as well."

Jules straightened out his collar as he stood. "That's kind of you, but I think I'm going to wander the grounds awhile. Clear my mind." He hesitated, then took a step closer to her. "When will I see you again?"

Nathalie gave him a demure smile. "At the morgue here and there, I suppose."

"I've left the hat shop, you know," he said. "I'm now at Rue du Chocolat six days a week. My future as a chocolatier is promising. I hope to own my own shop someday."

"If your early creations are any indication, you'll succeed marvelously."

He beamed. "I'll still be going to the morgue. For now, anyway. It's not something I want to do forever."

"Me neither," she said, giving voice to the sentiment for the first time. "At this point, I'm glad our paths will cross there, anyway. We're—we're friends again, as far as I can see."

But nothing more.

"Friends," Jules repeated, his tone, his eyes, his expression all the epitome of bittersweet. "I said before that was too much, that I couldn't be your friend because I'd want to be more. That was a foolish sentiment, the words of a broken heart. It would be an honor to be your friend."

He smiled a sad smile, kissed her on the cheek, and walked away.

45

Le Rasoir Plummets From Tour Eiffel

The words were on the lips of hundreds of thousands by the next morning, and gauging from the foreign newspapers she spied on the omnibus, the news went far beyond Paris. En route to the morgue she read and reread anonymous accounts provided by Jules and herself, Pelerine's fellow morgue workers, and former theater colleagues. Together they crafted the story of "a bitter soul exacting revenge on a city that rejected him."

Samuel Pelerine was a gifted actor—of that there is no doubt. He was frequently overlooked for roles earlier in his career, though, and believed it to be because of his condition.

"Not true at all," said one theater source. "He was insecure and sought to attribute his failure to others. Personally I think he felt inferior because he'd inherited a modest fortune and didn't think he deserved it. Can you imagine? Nevertheless, I don't think it had anything to do with his appearance."

Another source contradicted this contention. "Unfortunately, that's why he was relegated to small roles and eventually gave that up, in recent years, for creating stage dress and scenery."

Pelerine mastered that as well, skills that would explain his ability to craft a working guillotine (how he secured a blade remains unknown) and, police say, his knack for disguises. Investigators posit that he had several "versions" of himself that he'd "wear" in public.

"This is a man whose attention to detail was unparalleled," said an actor who'd worn several of Pelerine's costumes. "As was his propensity for the dramatic."

Pelerine's discontent with the theater scene heightened over time, reaching its peak almost a year ago. He and an actor— the rumored lover of the "Jester" victim, Timothy St. Martin— got into a physical altercation, and Pelerine stormed out of the theater for good.

Police propose several theories as to why he sought a job at the morgue: to be in proximity to corpses so as to understand them better, to learn about body disposal in the public domain (i.e., where bodies were found such that they ended up at the morgue), to feed his desire for an audience, to see alleged morgue Insightfuls at work. One or more of these suppositions could be true.

At the time of press, police were investigating the basement of an abandoned theater they suspect may have been where Pelerine committed his crimes. The body of Ida Blackwell has also yet to be found. It may well be in the murderer's den, according to a member of the police.

Here Nathalie's breath caught.

Could it have been?

Her body tingled with fear, discomfort, and realization.

An abandoned theater. Was it the one she was supposed to explore with Simone and Louis? Their *vin de coca* episode had gotten in the way of that, and they hadn't chosen another time to do it.

What would they have walked in on?

Nathalie shuddered and continued reading.

An initial search of Pelerine's apartment revealed newspapers with coverage of the crimes, some of them framed and placed on the wall; guillotine sketches; illustrations depicting *la coiffure à la Titus*; several theater manuscripts on parchment paper listing himself as playwright; and of particular interest, the remaining pages of the "play" he attached to some of his victims. This is the preface, published today exclusively by *Le Petit Journal*:

Title: SENSATIONAL
Playwright's Note: This is my work in honor of the 100th anniversary of Guillotin's proposal and the storming of the Bastille. I aim to have it performed in front of the grandest stage Paris has ever known, the Exposition Universelle.

She crossed paths with Gabrielle, whose limp was the most prominent she'd seen yet, outside the morgue. They conversed at length about Pelerine ("I always found him a little *too* well-mannered," Gabrielle claimed) and all that had happened. Nathalie thanked her, again, for the connection with Dr. Delacroix.

"I'm going to write to him today or tomorrow, in fact." Nathalie left out her concerns and her reasons for writing, and Gabrielle didn't pry.

"You're most welcome," said Gabrielle. "As to your gift, there is a murder today. A man was shot. I provided my reading and am curious what you'll see."

A vendor thrust a trinket between them. "Tour Eiffel necklace, ladies?"

They declined, Nathalie less politely than Gabrielle. As they were about to part ways, Gabrielle seized her in an embrace.

Nathalie hardly had time to respond in kind when Gabrielle stepped back and waved, retreating without a word.

She's still strange.

But now I like her.

Nathalie realized that maybe her possessiveness relative to the morgue wasn't the most appropriate response to change. Sharing responsibilities, making new friends (for what was Gabrielle to her if not that?), learning new perspectives both at the morgue and elsewhere—these were important, too.

M. Arnaud, busy giving directions to someone, acknowledged Nathalie with a nod as she slipped into the morgue. (To the annoyance of others, as usual.) M. Soucy, who appeared to be the most distraught of all the morgue personnel by Pelerine's horrifying truth, gave her a subtle wave.

Several Americans and a pair of French soldiers were in the viewing area. Nathalie stood before the pane, noticing not only what was in the display room but what wasn't. *Who* wasn't.

The space where M. Cadoret once stood was empty. Nathalie stared at it. He was there, his placid face and friendly smile. Then the grin slipped into something more sinister and he became Samuel Pelerine.

She blinked. Of course he wasn't there. And yet he always would be, no matter who took his place.

As M. Soucy prodded the group along, Nathalie stayed behind. She studied the corpses, her eyes falling on the one with a gunshot wound in his chest. She rested her fingers on the glass.

The victim's face wrenched in pain, hands over his heart. He let go and held his hands up as the bullet left his chest and returned to the gun.

Then she came to the present.

That was it.

A gunshot in reverse.

It lasted mere seconds.

A vision that told her nothing but what she already saw. What anyone walking into the morgue could see.

An utterly inconsequential, unhelpful vision.

Nathalie told no one.

She didn't even go see Christophe. She exited the morgue like all the other onlookers and went straight to a shop selling post-cards, figurines, and other tourist wares. She bought a postcard; as soon as she left the shop, she filled it out, leaning against a wall to scratch out the words.

> *Dear Dr. Delacroix,*
>   *My visions are still in reverse. They continue to diminish in length and significance, as does my memory loss.*
>   *Am I losing my ability?*
>   *If so, will it return?*
>   *I know you've explained this. I know you don't know.*
>   *I still feel compelled to ask.*
>

Warmly,

N. B.

46

Two days later, Paris was still talking about Le Rasoir. Several unknowns had become known after a more extensive search of the apartment and Pelerine's background.

The newspapers reported on his meticulous attention to detail; the search in his apartment revealed that he'd had the guillotine blade made in a village in eastern France. He paid a blacksmith a substantial sum not only to forge the blade but to keep quiet about it. He must have had it shipped home via train, although this couldn't be ascertained.

Pelerine had an older brother who'd moved to America and lived in Chicago. He was helping the police paint a picture of Pelerine's early life, if for no other reason than to establish something in his background prior to theater life in Paris. He was raised in Neuilly-sur-Seine, not Fontainbleau as he'd claimed. Of note was a wealthy, abusive father who was a chess enthusiast and member of several high-profile chess societies. Among his aims was to have his sons show a similar penchant and gift, which they did not. The brother noted that when their father was drunk, he'd often force them to play chess against him, then beat them if they lost.

Chess.

Seeking out intoxicated victims.

A perverse inversion of how his father treated him.

Mad at the world, thought Nathalie. At his father, at the theater, at himself.

Lastly, the basement of the abandoned theater had indeed served as Pelerine's subterranean chamber of death. Police found the guillotine, the chessboard, and trunks and valises in various sizes.

One of the trunks contained the body of the Princess, Ida Blackwell. Nathalie was sickened reading that but hoped the return of her body for a proper burial provided more closure for her loved ones than never finding it at all. Police speculated that Pelerine was in a rush—perhaps he heard someone, perhaps he was eager to execute his elaborate display of the head—and hadn't had time to dispose of the body.

Paris was still talking about Le Rasoir and Nathalie was still thinking about him. Having nightmares because of him.

She hadn't had any more dreams in the vein of Aunt Brigitte, even last night, the night before her funeral.

As for Aunt Brigitte's last dream to involve her, Nathalie expected she'd always wonder. The three shadows in the woods, one disappearing. Nathalie's own dream after that, Aunt Brigitte beheading Simone and Louis, then holding up the heads of Jules and Gabrielle instead. The disappearance represented loss, of that she was certain, and she understood it to be Jules. Her own dream had asked: *Which one?*

Which one was the next victim of Le Rasoir?

Jules. She'd worried about Simone, but it had been Jules. He'd come away with his life. He'd lost so much else.

Aunt Brigitte's funeral was a small affair at Saint-Ambrose. The Baudins and the Marchands, Christophe, Louis, and Jules. She thought she saw Gabrielle in a veil slink into a back pew, but if so, she left before the recessional. Several staff members from Saint-Mathurin were in attendance, even though Nathalie was almost certain they'd been paid to go.

The priest spoke of the Beatitudes.

Blessed are the poor in spirit, for theirs is the Kingdom of God.

Blessed are the meek and humble, for they shall inherit the Earth.

Blessed are they who mourn, for they shall be comforted.

There were other beatitudes, other words. Nathalie didn't remember many of them. Not because of a vision or memory loss, but because they'd been consumed by the sadness that had overtaken her.

Aunt Brigitte had always been there. "There" was Mme. Plouffe's, then the asylum. Smiling Tante who spoke of bizarre nightmares, something Nathalie took for an odd trait and symbol of madness until she'd fully understood.

No, not fully. No one could fully understand what Aunt Brigitte had endured for having gotten one of Dr. Henard's blood transfusions for the sake of magic.

Later that week, a letter arrived for her, inviting Nathalie to a different kind of grief.

She knew what it was going to say before she opened it. She'd had no memory loss at all following the brief vision of the gunshot victim. Not so much as an unaccounted-for blink of the eye.

And the day after Aunt Brigitte's funeral, there had been another murder at the morgue. Or so she'd heard from Christophe, Jules, and Gabrielle, for despite placing her hands on the glass, she'd had no vision at all.

So when she did read Dr. Delacroix's words, they didn't fill her with dread. She'd been full of dread for a week already. Instead, the words made their way into her heart, the part reserved for sorrow.

> *Dear Nathalie,*
>
> *Nothing is certain in the world of Insightfuls, of that I can assure you. The nature of our gifts continues to amaze me.*
>
> *I am sorry to have to share this opinion with you, and I wish we could talk in person rather than through pen. I regret to inform you that given what you've told me, yes, I*

believe it's highly probable that your gift is dissipating or will leave altogether.

I do not know of a case in which an Insightful ability, once completely gone, has returned.

Perhaps you will have an extraordinary turnaround, or perhaps what you've shared with me is incomplete. You might be writing me at this very moment to say all is well. We can never dismiss the possibilities magic might render. We Insightfuls are something of a miracle, are we not? You especially, as a natural.

Again, my dear Nathalie, I am very sorry not to have better news, yet I ask you not to despair. Please do keep up your correspondence with me should it be in your interest to do so.

With warm regards, I remain,

Delacroix

She wasn't in the mood to talk to her parents about the letter. Not now. With all that had been going on, she hadn't told them of her dwindling ability. They had other concerns, and so did she.

Mostly it was denial. Not speaking of it made it easier to ignore.

There was no pretending anymore. It was time to be pragmatic and let her mind explore this new reality, how it might look, feel, smell, taste. Touch.

Explore. Wasn't that who she was, too? Someone who wanted to explore life? Her power and her work at the morgue had given her plenty of adventures. Some she'd sought, others she'd run from, figuratively and literally.

Still. She wanted to control it. She wanted to be the one to say when her time was done at the morgue. Not the magic.

Since when have you been able to dictate how it works?

This was what it meant to be an Insightful. And she'd still be one, even if her visions did fade entirely.

She put Dr. Delacroix's letter away in her room, under the watchful eye of Stanley, and sat on the bed.

There was only so long she could keep this to herself.

In a few hours, she'd be joining Simone and Louis on a cruise along the Seine. There was to be a band on board and a stellar view of fireworks, or so Simone said. If she had the opportunity, she'd discuss it. *If she could do it without sounding like a killjoy.*

Nathalie wasn't on board the boat a quarter of an hour before she regretted it. It was crowded, for one, but more important, she felt exceedingly out of place. Some of Louis's acting friends were on the other side of the deck, but she didn't know them beyond a passing greeting. Simone and Louis were in an amorous mood, and she wanted neither to interrupt nor to witness it too closely.

Moroccan musicians played melodies unlike any she'd ever heard. It was alluring with a mystical quality; it stirred something in her, a longing.

Or maybe you're just feeling sorry for yourself.

She rested her hip against the railing, watching the musicians and those who ventured to dance, like Simone and Louis. Although the formal European style of dance didn't fit, people did their best to make the steps work with a different beat.

"Bewitching tunes, aren't they?"

A voice that was so unexpected, she almost thought she'd heard wrong. But there was no mistaking that woodsy, orange blossom cologne.

Nathalie turned to see Christophe beside her, smiling broadly enough to show his charmingly crooked tooth. "What are you doing here?"

Christophe threw his hands up playfully. "Even serious police liaisons at the morgue are allowed an evening of good cheer. Occasionally."

She laughed. There was no one she'd rather see today.

Wait. Is he alone?

Nathalie peeked around him. No one who looked like a fiancée, no mysterious woman standing too close to him.

"Louis asked me to come," he continued, tracking her gaze and glancing behind him, "but I'm not allowed to say why."

"That only makes me all the more curious."

"Is there anything that doesn't make you curious?"

She blushed. He knew her too well.

They spoke for a while about music and riverboats and then music again, when Simone rushed over to Nathalie, sparkling with joy.

"Nathalie, I have the most glorious news. Louis has asked for my hand in marriage!" Simone threw herself into Nathalie's arms before she even finished the sentence.

"He has?" Nathalie caught Christophe's eye, and he gave her a knowing smile. *That* was why he was here. "*Felicitations*, my wonderful friend! I am so happy for you both!"

"Now," said Simone, stepping back, "don't think this changes anything between us. We still have adventures to embark on. Only I'll be doing it as Madame Louis Carre."

Louis came up behind her just then, and Nathalie and Christophe shook his hand. They spoke until the band played a song at a slower tempo. Louis held his hand out for Simone, and together they moved onto the makeshift dance area.

Nathalie gazed at them a moment, then Christophe came into her view.

"Mademoiselle Baudin, shall we dance?"

She melted, then and there, onto the top deck of the riverboat. As if made of wax and warmth and everything that could rob her of the ability to move.

"Of course," she said, taking his hand. "You do realize, I don't know how."

Christophe chuckled as he escorted her a few steps to the dance area. He leaned in with a grin. "Neither do I. Let's be terrible dancers together."

EPILOGUE

"You're being silly," said Simone, kicking sand at Louis.

"And you'd be disappointed if I were otherwise," he said.

Nathalie rearranged her sun hat. "You've been engaged a month already, and she still loves you dearly. There's no risk. Throw her in the water already, Louis."

Simone stuck her tongue out and ran toward the ocean with Louis in pursuit. Nathalie watched her friends with a sense of contentment, despite the occasion. They were at a beach in Normandy, and the last few days had been solemn.

Summer 1888 was the "next year" of which Nathalie and Agnès had spoken in their letters. They'd hoped to pass the days in charming Bayeux and occasionally at the ocean. Nathalie didn't know at the time if she'd ever have been able to take such a holiday the following year; it had nevertheless been an indulgent reverie.

Needless to say, there had been no such leisure. A year after the Dark Artist and his mad accomplice shattered both her world and worldview, Nathalie had continued to work as both morgue reporter and an Insightful assistant to the police. Last summer was a depressing one, where it seemed to rain every day even though it almost certainly didn't. Those were the days she remembered most—long, dreary days absent of color.

Today wasn't at all absent of color. The orange and yellow of bright sun, the ominous dark blue of the ocean, and the earthy beige of the sand, they all instilled in her a sense of vitality. Of now.

"Are you ready?" asked Christophe from behind.

"I think so." Nathalie took the glass jar from her bag. Agnès had given it to her during their last day together, sand taken from the Deauville beach resort farther up the coast.

You have to give it back next year, Agnès had said. *Not to me. To the beach itself. I want you to bring it when we go next summer. Pour it out on the beach and get some of your own!*

"I feel badly pouring out any at all," Nathalie said, turning to Christophe. "Although I can hear Agnès chiding me if I don't."

"You've waited a long time to do this. Your heart knows what to do."

Her plan wasn't to dispose of all of it, but rather pour out half and take half. She had a glass jar to fill with sand, too.

She drank in the vista before her. The ocean smelled saltier and more complex than she'd expected, and the roar was as fierce and encompassing as she'd imagined. The waves were hypnotic, each beckoning her senses more than the last.

"I'll remember this," she said. "I mean, truly remember this. I don't have to fear anything being taken away ever again."

Christophe put his hand on her shoulder. They'd had numerous conversations about this in the past month, beginning with that evening on the riverboat.

"Except when I get very old, I guess," Nathalie added. "Did I ever tell you that as a young child I thought having wrinkles made people forgetful, because my grandmother had wrinkles and forgot things?"

He laughed and shook his head.

How much her perspective had changed. Since childhood. In the past two years. Over the course of the past few months.

The power of Insightfuls was something that grew and flourished and withered and died. Nathalie thought this so strange and imprecise at first, for magic administered by scientific means. Then she realized—and recalled quite clearly when it happened, because watching a leaf fall from a tree in Bois de Boulogne had inspired the thought—that Dr. Henard's experiments challenged the rules of nature while also being subjected to them. Blood was physiological and the powers were rooted in one's own personality traits. Life changed, and so Insightfuls sometimes changed.

She struggled with it daily, this shift in her identity. Sometimes she only saw the worst of it, like not being able to help at the morgue anymore. At other times she saw the favorable element, the idea that she'd never again lose a memory to anything but time.

She was still Nathalie. She just had to find a new means of being Nathalie, at least in some ways.

Her parents loved her. Jules had been right about that; not everyone was so fortunate. They cared for her, understood her. So did her friends. And so did Christophe. He was proving to be everything she'd hoped he'd be in a suitor, even taking a separate train with Louis to Rouen so the girls' parents wouldn't object to the holiday. Nathalie felt a touch guilty about the deception, but only a touch. All the proprieties remained in place, yet she needed him at her side right now.

And maybe, if she was lucky, forever.

She wouldn't always see him at the morgue. Because did she want to be the morgue reporter indefinitely, despite losing her gift?

No, she wasn't ready to give it up. Not at all. But she could see herself, someday, doing something else. M. Patenaude understood. Better than anyone, perhaps. He also encouraged her to write more Exposition columns. So when she'd asked if she could do a series of travel articles about her journey to the coast, he agreed.

That felt true to her soul. She wanted to go places, write about her experiences. Not just write everything down for fear of forgetting and needing a record; no, she wanted to write about the wondrous marvels of the world, great and small, because they touched her, changed her, made her think and feel. She wanted to absorb everything she could at the Exposition about other countries and the people and cultures that called them home. While the fair still had several months to go, she knew deep inside that somehow her journey would extend beyond it.

Elsewhere.

Nathalie found a clean, dry patch of ground. She unfastened the bluish-green jar and carefully poured out half the sand, tracing a heart around it with her finger. Moving a few paces to the right, she stooped down and filled up the empty part of the bottle. Then she filled the glass jar.

When the four of them got back to Bayeux later that day, they passed a café. Simone excused herself and went inside. She came out a minute or so later, hands behind her back.

"For you," she said, presenting Nathalie with a *pain au chocolat*.

Nathalie smiled and hoped the tears that welled up in her eyes wouldn't fall. By the time they did, she didn't care. "It's messy to split four ways," she said. "But I think we should."

After a stop at their hotel to change out of beach attire, they walked several blocks to the home of Agnès's grandmother. Nathalie had written to her in advance, and the idea had been received well.

Although the property wasn't large, it had been in the family for some time. The elder Jalbert regarded them through eyes that reminded Nathalie so much of Agnès, expressing gratitude before escorting them through a gate into the backyard. The grass was verdant, and the yard smelled of dirt and vegetables, scents that were new and not unpleasant to Nathalie's nose. Hydrangea bushes lined their path; a bee darted out from one, spooking her before it flew away.

"Here." Agnès's grandmother had the hands of someone who worked the earth and the face of someone who did so with pride.

Agnès's grave was marked by an oblong outline of rocks with daisies at the head. So simple yet so powerful.

Nathalie wept. She hadn't expected to, and she hadn't wanted to, not in front of everyone. Someone put a hand on her back. Christophe, Simone, and Louis all stood behind her, so she didn't know whose touch it was. It didn't matter.

Wiping her eyes, she knelt at the grave. Agnès's grandmother gave her a hand-sized trowel.

She dug twenty or so centimeters deep and spread out the soil with her fingers. Christophe handed her the glass jar. She buried it with care, as if it had been a living being.

When she was done, she stood, brushing the dirt off her knees.

It had taken two years, but finally she had paid her friend homage. A swell of emotions flowed through her. Nathalie stood there a moment, contemplating all that had happened in the last two months. The last two years.

She glanced at Christophe, Simone, and Louis, grateful to be here, to live this moment.

One thing she knew for certain.

She'd remember it.

ACKNOWLEDGMENTS

I knew upon finishing *Spectacle* that Nathalie's story would extend to a second and final book, so the end felt more like "see you soon" than "goodbye." But *Sensational* is farewell to Nathalie, these characters, this world, and this two-book experience that has represented a chapter in my own life. I look forward to the rest of my journey as an author, deadline-driven junk-food cravings (I'm looking at you, Mini Eggs) notwithstanding.

I didn't know what I was looking for in an agent several years ago, but it turns out I found it in Ginger Clark of Curtis Brown, Ltd. She's a wealth of industry knowledge and expertise, a fierce advocate, exceptionally organized, and yes, hilarious. I'll follow you into battle anytime, Ginger, as long as there's an elephant somewhere on the sigil and adequate snacks (including fine cheese). Thank you as well to Nicole Eisenbraun, who stepped into a new role as agent assistant seamlessly.

I took a few plot and character chances while drafting this book, and I wasn't sure how my editor at Tor Teen, Melissa Frain, would receive them. It turns out that we were yet again very much in sync, with similar inklings as to what was working and what wasn't. There's nothing quite like the feeling of a great collaboration, and I'm lucky enough to have felt that throughout this project. To my publicist, Saraciea Fennell, thank you for showing such savvy and professionalism in all that you do to bring visibility to these books. I'd also like to thank editorial assistant Elizabeth Vaziri for being so prompt and courteous on administrative matters.

The behind-the-scenes elements of publishing are many; there are always people working on your behalf that you haven't met, a team behind the team. At Curtis Brown, that team consists of foreign rights agents Jonathan Lyons and Sarah Perillo as well as film rights agents Holly Frederick and Madeline Tavis.

My gratitude to Tor Teen for giving me the opportunity to share this story and put "twice-published author" beside my name: publishers Fritz Foy and Devi Pillai, production editor Melanie Sanders, production manager Jim Kapp, and copy editor Christa Desir. And to art director Peter Lutjen and jacket designer Lesley Worrell, thank you for the gorgeous jacket for *Sensational*. I'm honored to have my name on a book that looks this good. To everyone on the Macmillan and Tor Teen teams in sales, marketing, and production, thank you.

Once again, Scott Erb and Donna Dufault of Erb Photography bring out the best in me. Thank you for the author photo and the support.

Thank you to my band of "whodunit" helpers, who read an early draft and answered a single specific question to help me further refine the story: Maria McDaniel, Shahnaz Radjy, Danielle Tedrowe, and Anna Wetherholt.

One of the highlights of being an author is becoming friends with other authors. Addie Thorley and Gita Trelease were indispensable in that debut year buildup as well as for "draft support," and I have easily a dozen other Novel 19s to thank and another dozen after that whom I'd forget to mention, so I won't name names—but you know who you are. (The Oscar panic of forgetting names is real, people.) Another author perk: engaging with readers. Thank you to those who've reached out to me on social media, sent me an email, or came up to me at a book event. I'm thrilled that you enjoy my work (and maybe my tweets).

Thank you to some people I know outside of publishing: to

my "Facebook family and friends," for lack of a better short-hand: I appreciate those of you who enthusiastically cheered me on. A special shout-out goes to my Vero Beach contingent; you all couldn't possibly be more excited for me or more thoughtful in your support. And my Portal Crew in Raleigh—Vicki, Alisha, No-H Natalie, Kathy, Stacie, and the rest of the team—thank you for reading and listening to me chatter about book stuff.

I'm blessed to have good friends who have hopped on this train with me. You show remarkable patience when I wander off at a depot and don't come back for a few weeks (aka "on dead-line"). Your friendship goes far beyond my writing life, though, and for that I am grateful: Libby, for taking time to talk to me daily in this oh-so-busy world and for getting it (all of it), and also for cat pictures; Rachel, for such meaningful conversations and such depth in understanding and always so much support; DK, for correspondence ranging from the everyday to the literary, and for being endlessly interesting; Bobby, for decades of conversa-tion, your heartfelt pride in me, and being so true for so long, as ever; Jessica, for being my Lucky Charm, "oldest" friend, and as genuine a friend as can be; and Johnny B, for going on so many travel and food adventures with me and for the wealth of happy memories.

I dedicated this book to my brothers in a magnanimous act of overlooking all the big-brother teasing from my youth. To Kenny, brainstormer extraordinaire, who suggested the 1889 Exposition Universelle as the setting for my sequel (ta-da!) and who is as excited about this stuff as me, and to David (GWS), even though he thought Stanley was the culprit in *Spectacle*, for shouting his IMS pride from the rooftops. You are both 100 percent behind me 100 percent of the time in this endeavor, and I am most grateful.

To my parents, whom I love so much it was hard not to dedi-cate a novel to them again. What more could I ask for, not only for support in my author life, but for everything, always? I'm proud to be a Zdrok and equal parts "Ma and Dad" in terms of who I am and how I see the world. You showed me how to live a life well-lived. (And have we had some fun together or what?)

If cats were mentioned in acknowledgments, I'd thank Minnie for serving as consultant on the Stanley, Max, and Lucy sections as well as for social-media assistance.

Lastly, my forever gratitude to Steve, who somehow manages to write these novels with me without penning a word. Everyone should be so lucky to have such love and support. You've deepened my creativity and my heart, and here I am, soaring and roaring.

*   *   *

For nonfiction works on the cultural history of France in the late nineteenth century, consider the following resources:

The Fin de Siècle: A Reader in Cultural History c. 1880–1900
    edited by Sally Ledger and Roger Luckhurst
Eiffel's Tower by Jill Jonnes
France, Fin de Siècle by Eugen Weber